DAKWÄKÂDA WARRIORS

COLE PAULS

CONUNDRUM PRESS

DAKWÄKÃDA WARRIORS © COLE PAULS, 2019
FIRST EDITION
PRINTED AT GAUVIN, GATINEAU, QUEBEC

LIBRARY AND ARCHIVES CANADA CATALOGUING IN PUBLICATION

TITLE: DAKWÄKÃDA WARRIORS / COLE PAULS
NAMES: PAULS, COLE, AUTHOR, ARTIST
DESCRIPTION: INCLUDES TEXT IN ENGLISH AND SOUTHERN TUTCHONE.
IDENTIFIERS: CANADIANA 20190165650 | ISBN: 9781772620412 (SOFTCOVER
SUBJECTS: LCGFT: GRAPHIC NOVELS.
CLASSIFICATION: LCC PN6733.P38 D35 2019 | DDC 741.5/971—dc23

CONUNDRUM PRESS
WOLFVILLE, NS, CANADA
WWW.CONUNDRUMPRESS.COM

CONUNDRUM PRESS WISHES TO ACKNOWLEDGE THE FINANCIAL CONTRIBUTION OF TH
CANADA COUNCIL FOR THE ARTS, THE GOVERNMENT OF CANADA, AND THE GOVERNMEN
OF NOVA SCOTIA TOWARD THEIR PUBLISHING PROGRAM

DAKWÄKÃDA WARRIORS

TABLE OF CONTENTS

DEDICATED TO ANDREW MARTIN PAULS

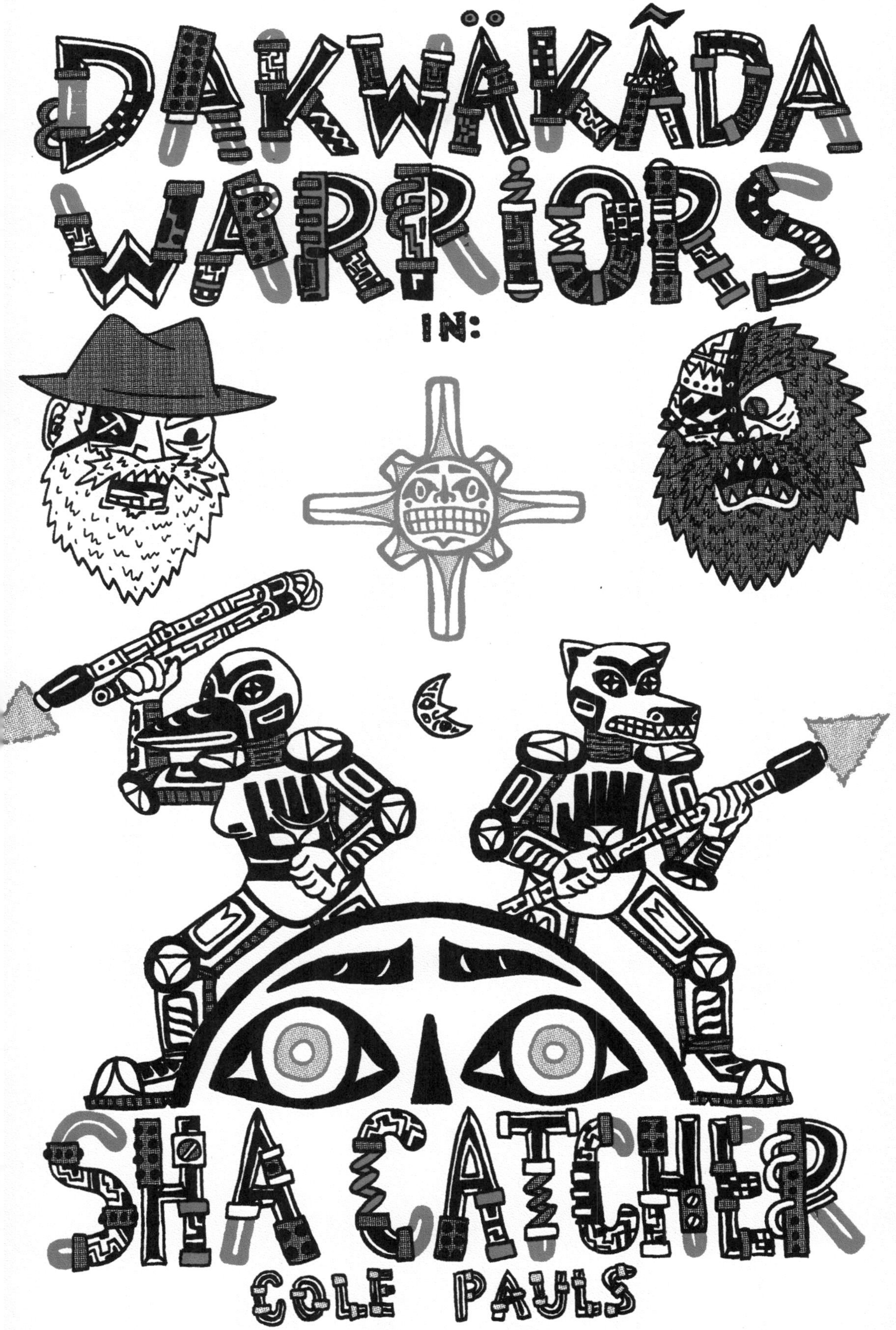
DAKWÄKÃDA
WARRIORS
IN:
SHA CATCHER
COLE PAULS

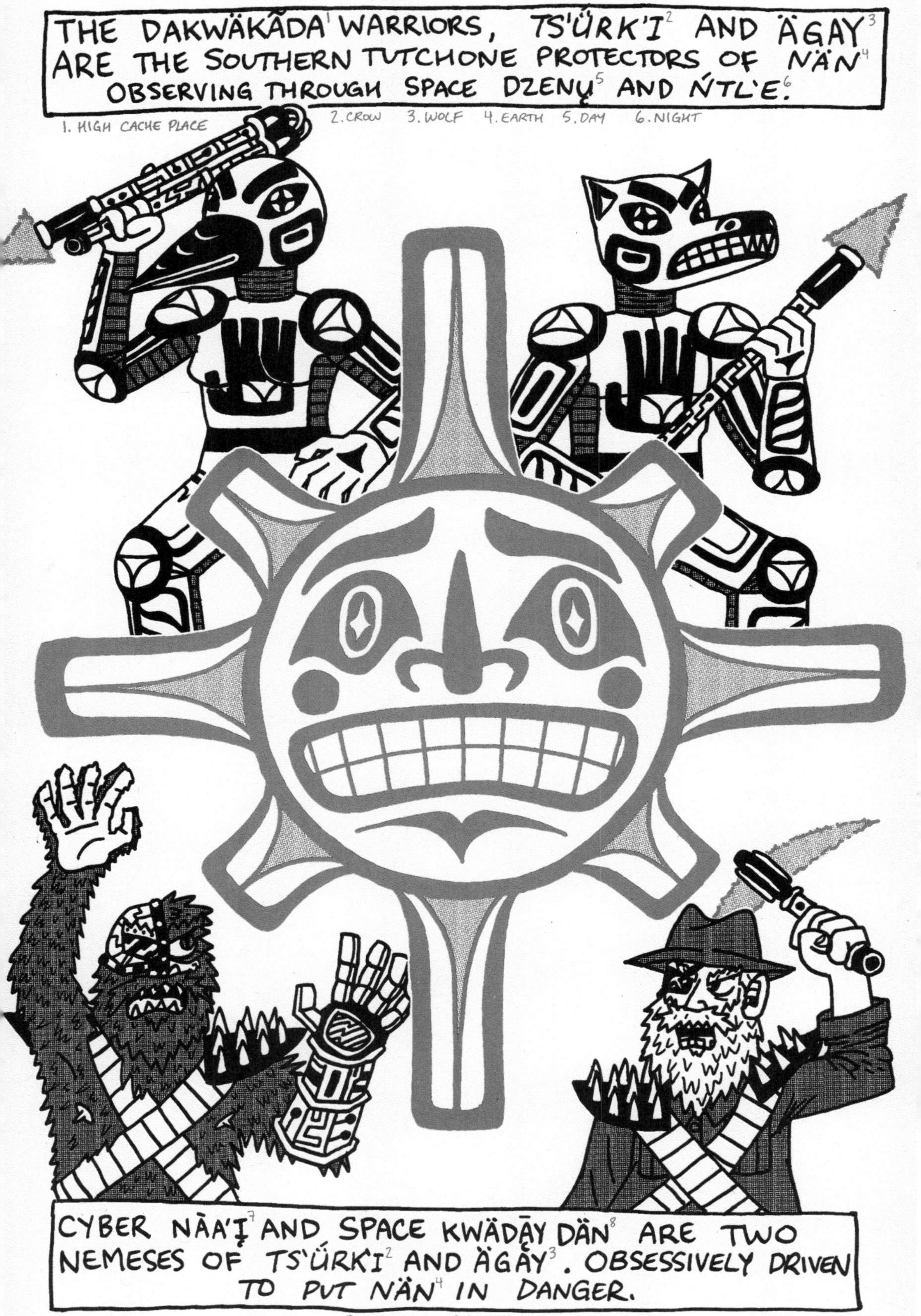
THE DAKWÄKĀDA[1] WARRIORS, TS'ÜRK'I[2] AND ÄGAY[3] ARE THE SOUTHERN TUTCHONE PROTECTORS OF NÄN[4] OBSERVING THROUGH SPACE DZENŲ[5] AND ŃTL'E.[6]
1. HIGH CACHE PLACE 2. CROW 3. WOLF 4. EARTH 5. DAY 6. NIGHT
CYBER NÄA'Į[7] AND SPACE KWÄDĀY DÄN[8] ARE TWO NEMESES OF TS'ÜRK'I[2] AND ÄGĀY[3]. OBSESSIVELY DRIVEN TO PUT NÄN[4] IN DANGER.
7. BUSHMAN 8. LONG AGO PEOPLE

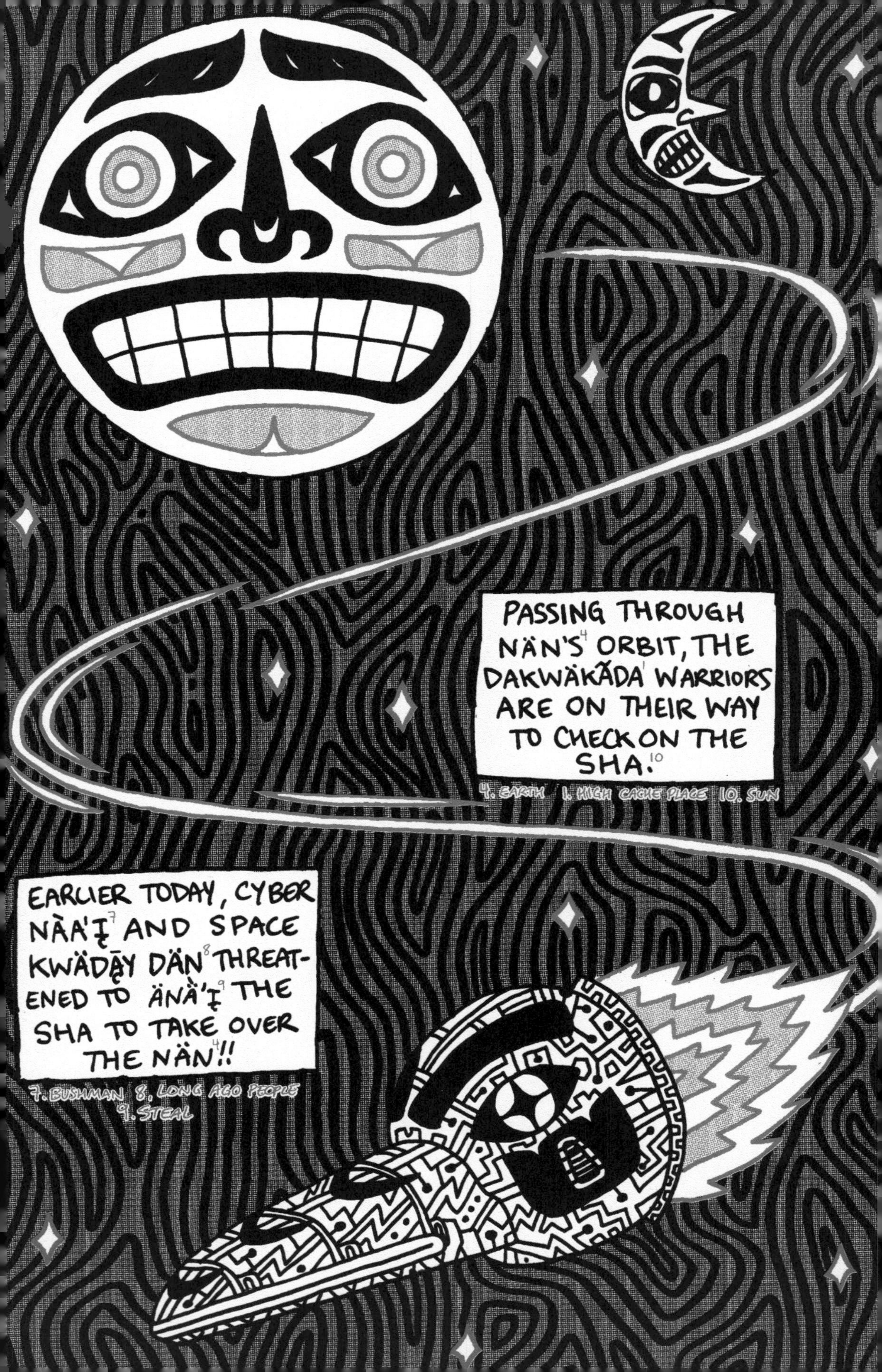
PASSING THROUGH NÄN'S[4] ORBIT, THE DAKWÄKÄDA[1] WARRIORS ARE ON THEIR WAY TO CHECK ON THE SHA.[10]
4. EARTH 1. HIGH CACHE PLACE 10. SUN
EARLIER TODAY, CYBER NÀA'Į[7] AND SPACE KWÄDĄ̄Y DÄN[8] THREATENED TO ÄNÄ̀'Į[9] THE SHA TO TAKE OVER THE NÄN[4]!!
7. BUSHMAN 8. LONG AGO PEOPLE 9. STEAL

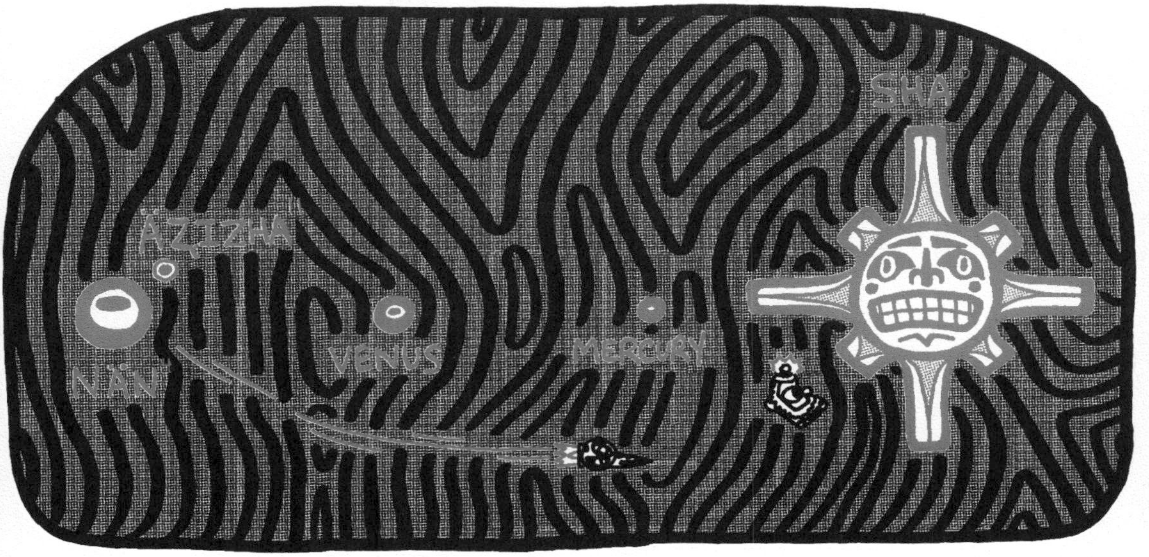
ĀZIZHĀ[11]
NĀN[4]
VENUS
MERCURY
SHA[10]

4. EARTH 10. SUN 11. MOON 12. STOP

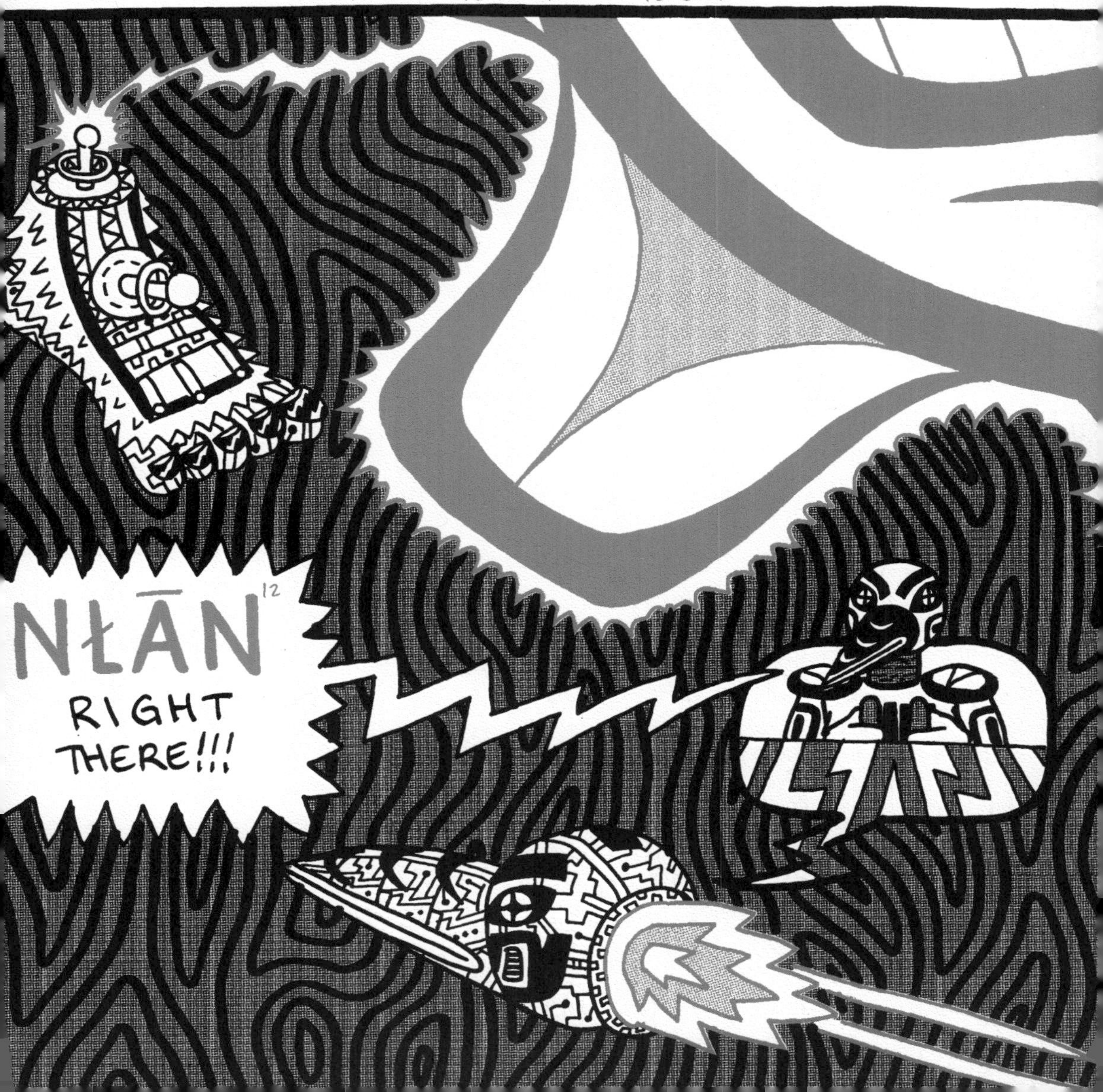
NŁĀN[12]
RIGHT THERE!!!

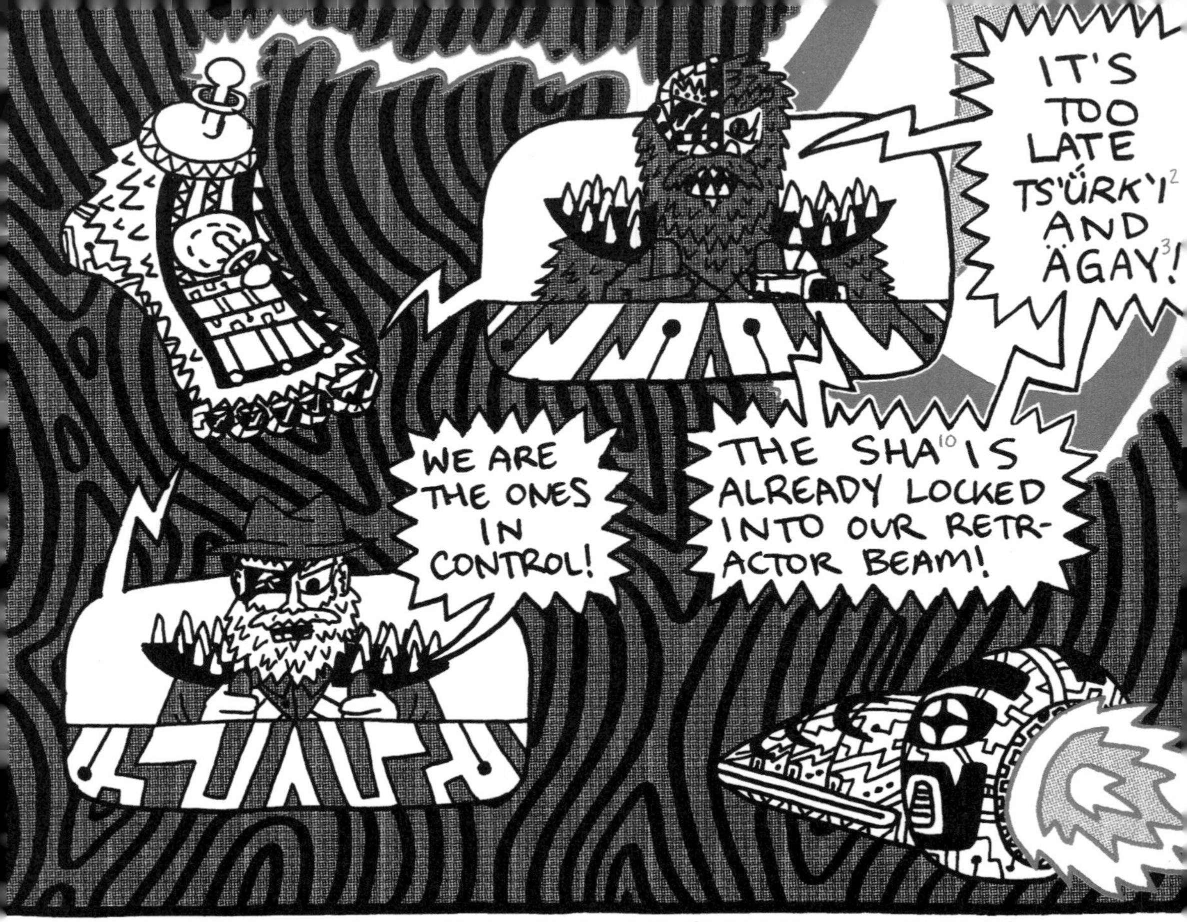
IT'S TOO LATE TS'ǗRK`I[2] AND ÄGAY[3]!
WE ARE THE ONES IN CONTROL!
THE SHA[10] IS ALREADY LOCKED INTO OUR RETR-ACTOR BEAM!

2. CROW 3. WOLF 4. EARTH 10. SUN 11. MOON 13. FROZEN MAMMOTH 14. PEOPLE

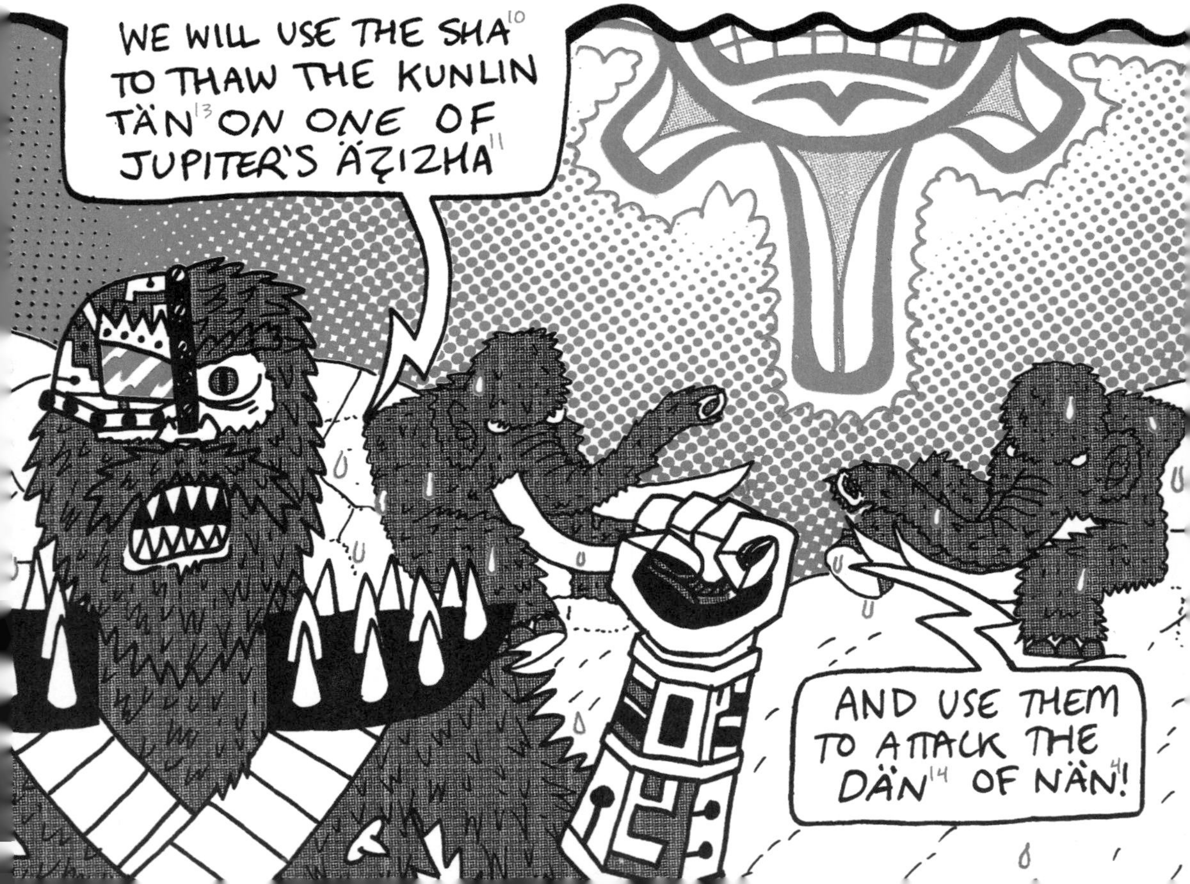
WE WILL USE THE SHA[10] TO THAW THE KUNLIN TÄN[13] ON ONE OF JUPITER'S ÄZ̨IZHA[11]
AND USE THEM TO ATTACK THE DÄN[14] OF NÄN[4]!

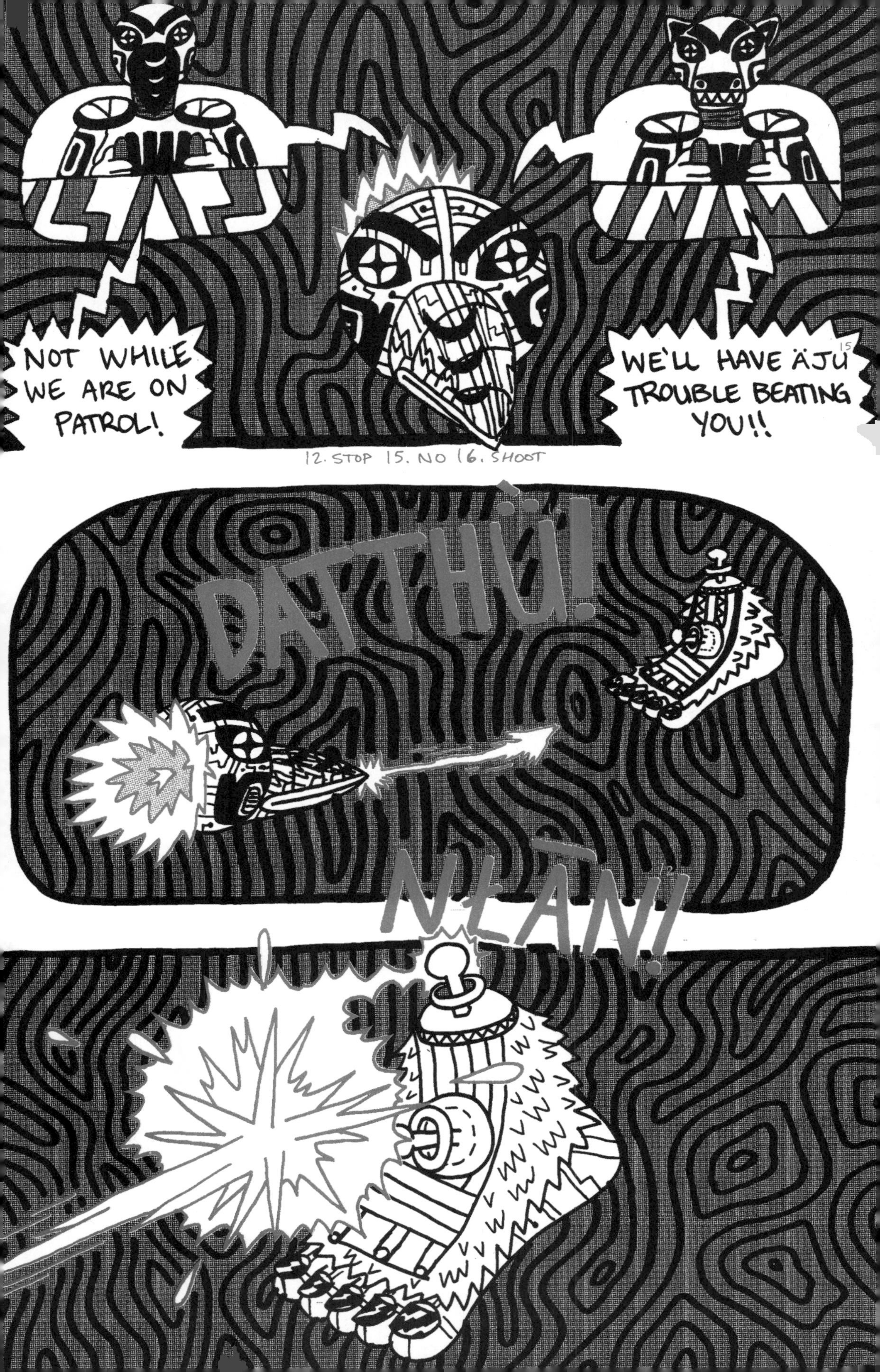
NOT WHILE WE ARE ON PATROL!
WE'LL HAVE ÄJU[15] TROUBLE BEATING YOU!!
12. STOP 15. NO 16. SHOOT
DATTHÜ!
NŁĀN!

NJÈDÀO[17]
NÄYÄNIYÜ[18]
NÄNÄNTÄN[19]
SHAADÄTRU[20]

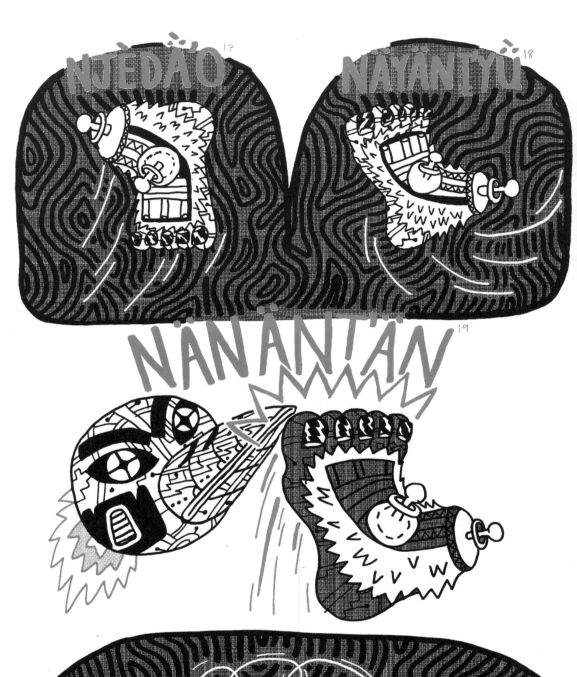

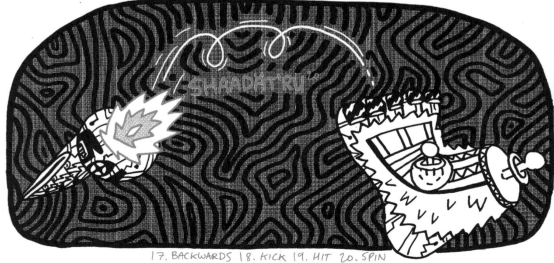

17. BACKWARDS 18. KICK 19. HIT 20. SPIN

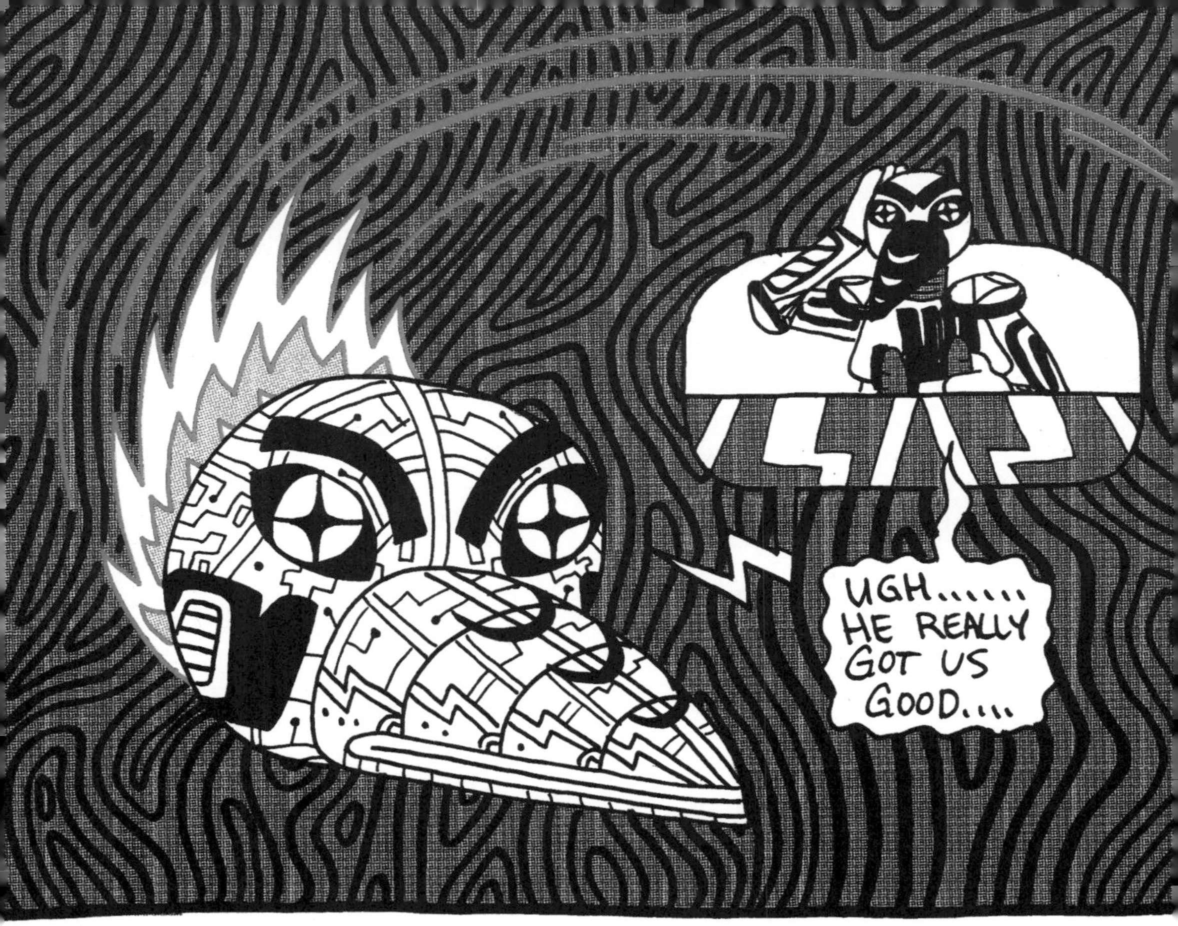
UGH...... HE REALLY GOT US GOOD....

21. TALK

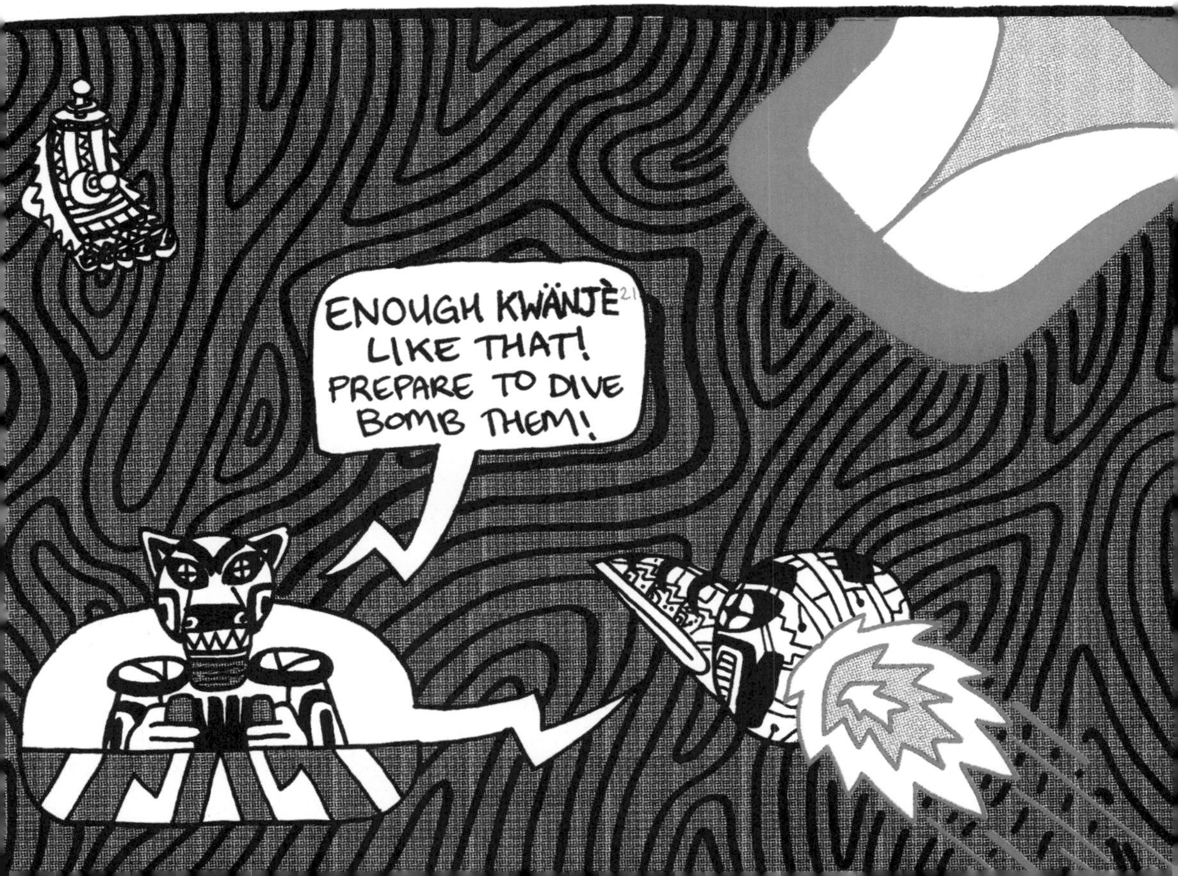
ENOUGH KWÄNJÈ[21] LIKE THAT! PREPARE TO DIVE BOMB THEM!

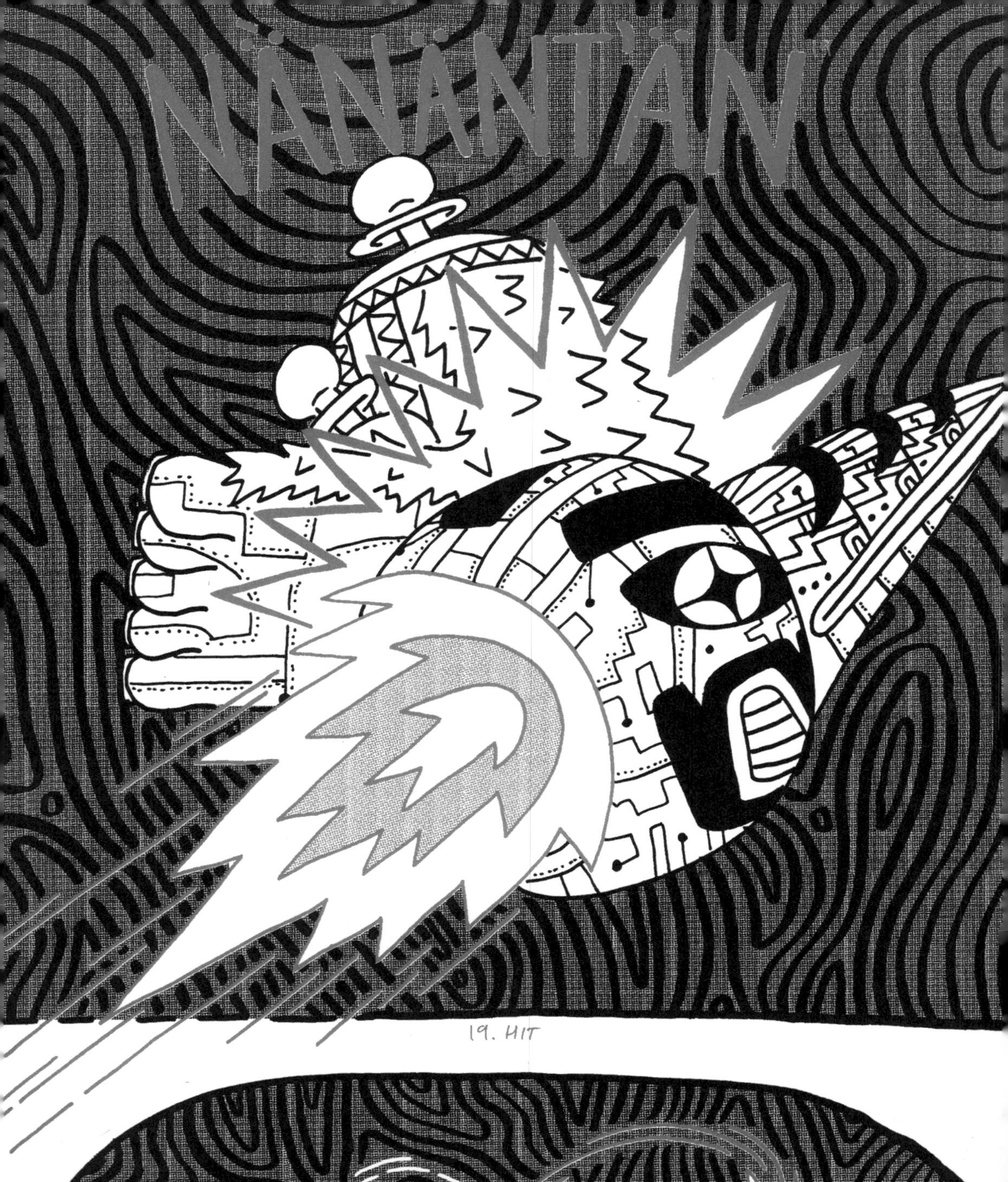
NÄNÄNTÄN

19. HIT

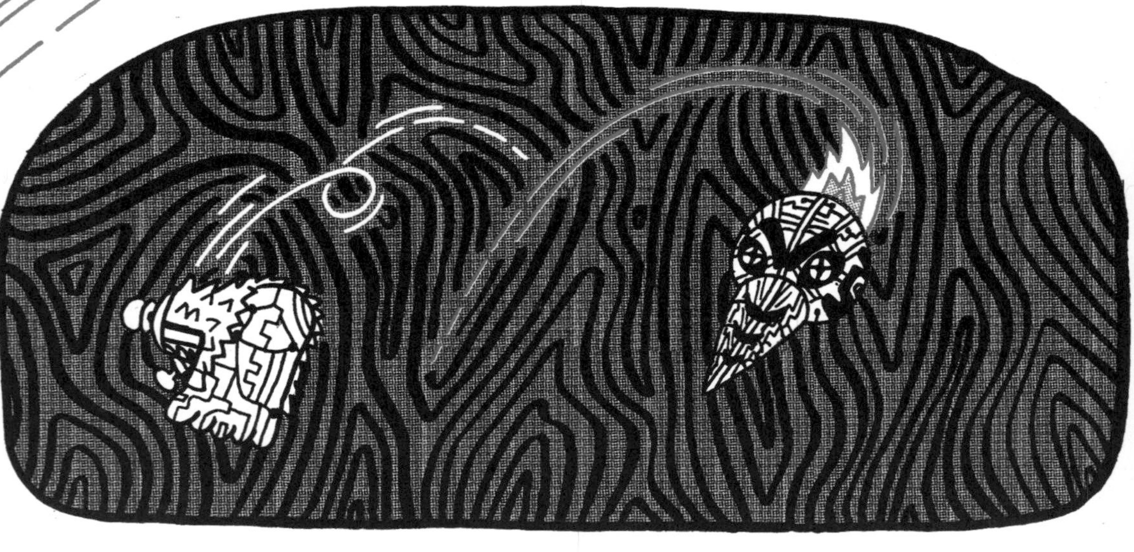

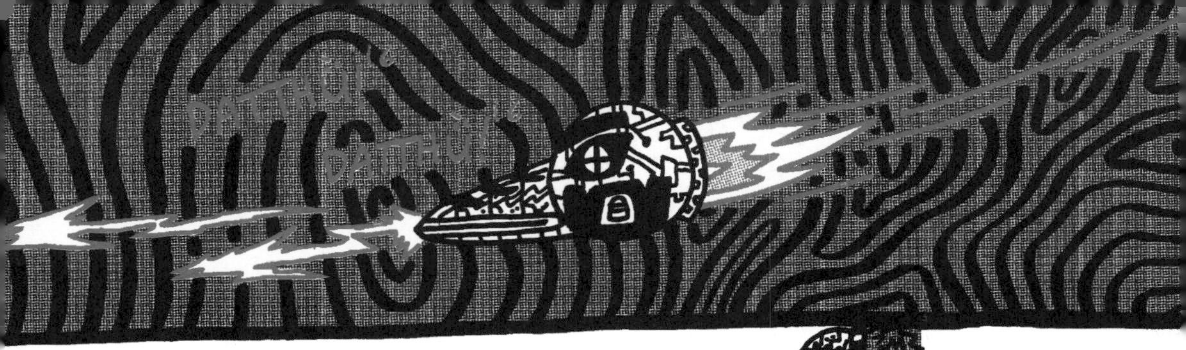
DATTHŪ![6]
DATTHŪ![16]

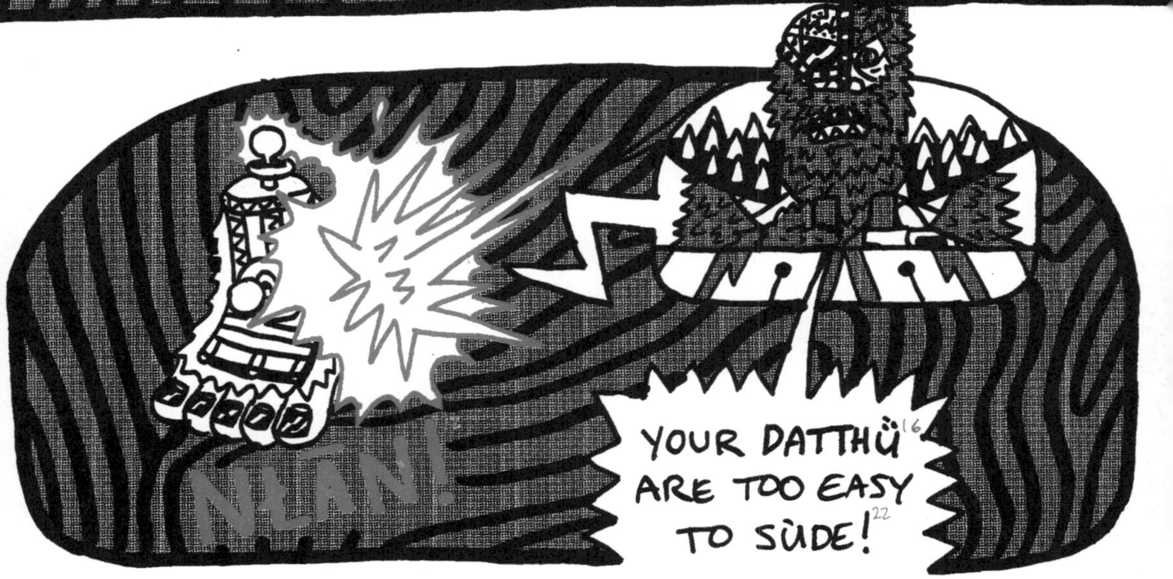
NŁĀN![12]
YOUR DATTHŪ[16] ARE TOO EASY TO SÙDE![22]

12. STOP 16. SHOOT 22. BEAT

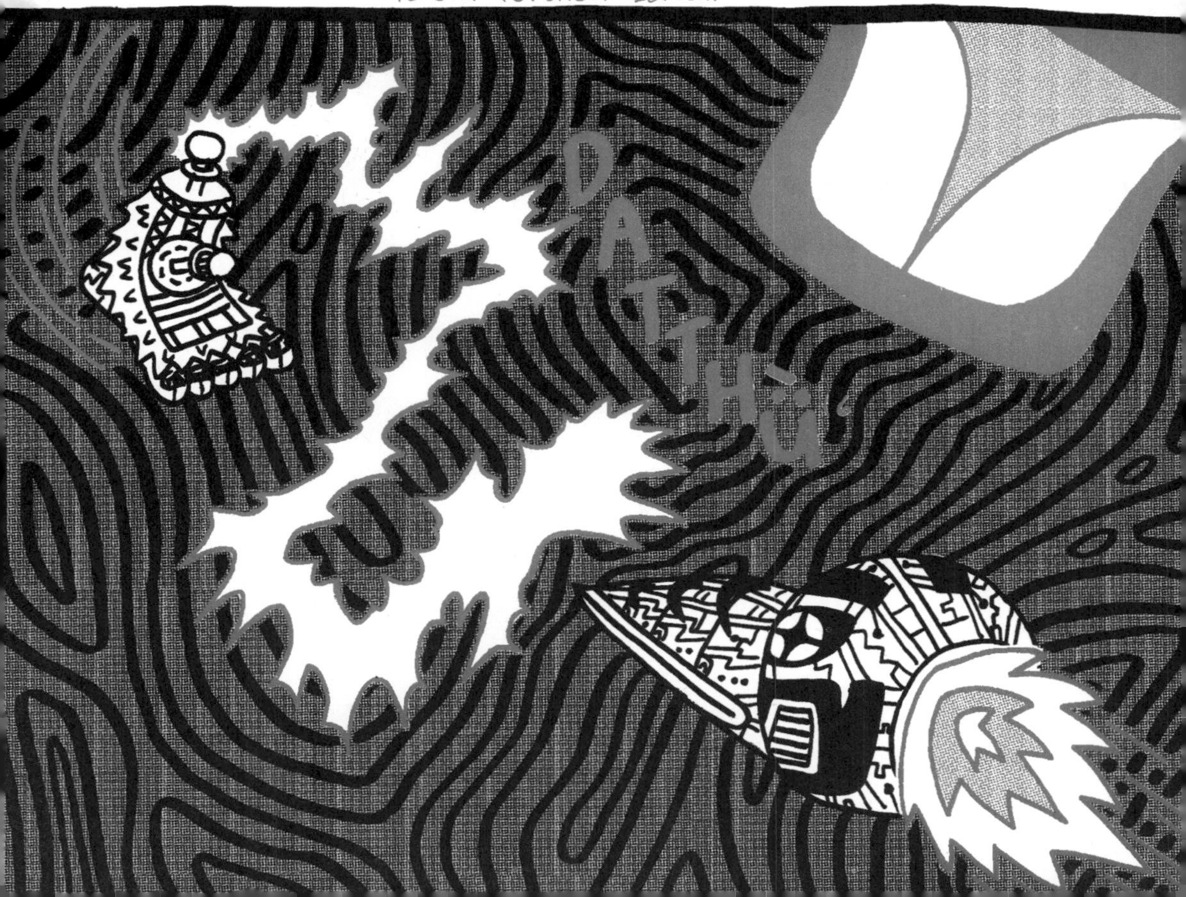
DATTHŪ[6]

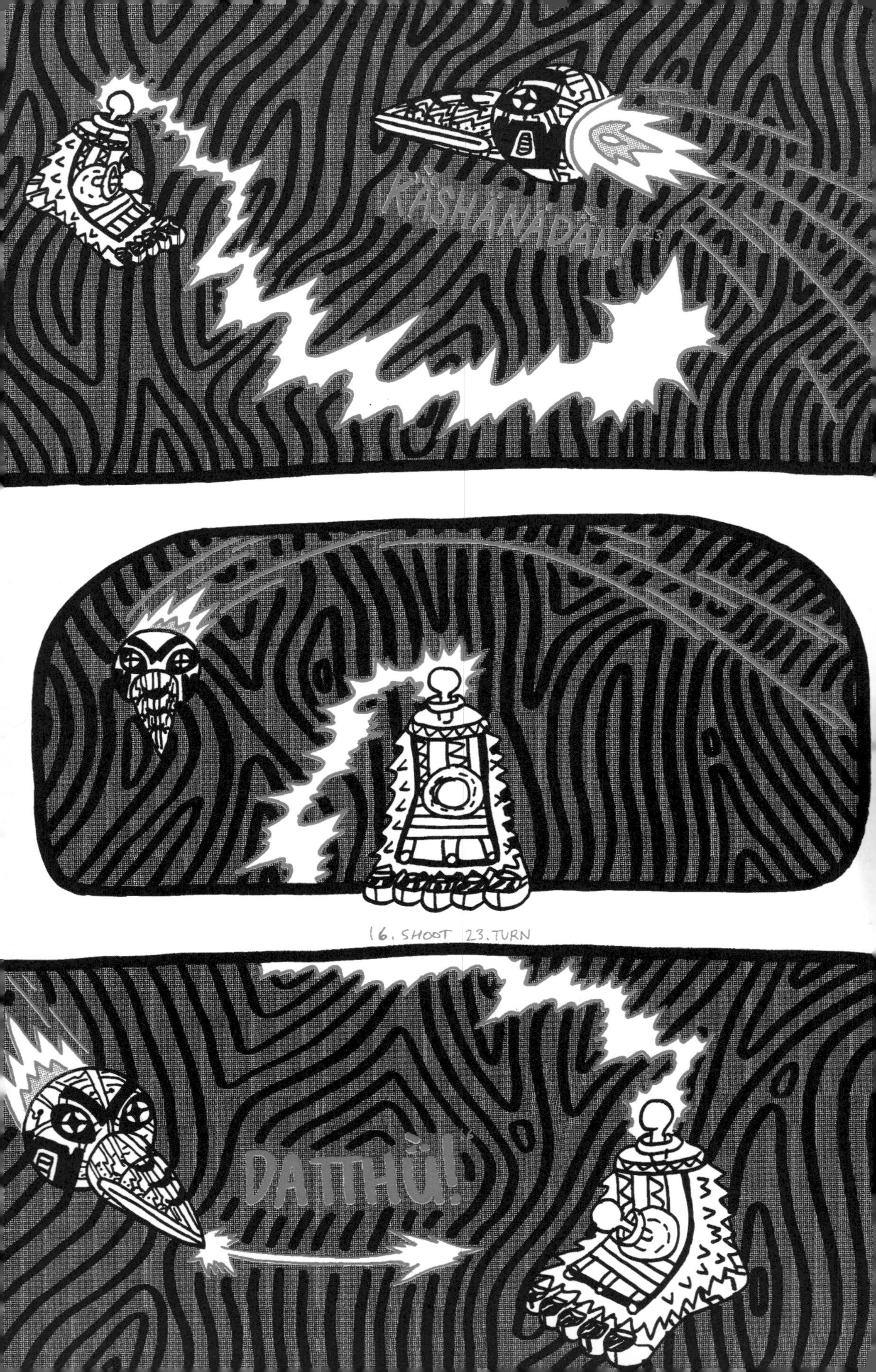
KÄSHÄNÄDÄL!
16. SHOOT 23. TURN
DATTHÜ!

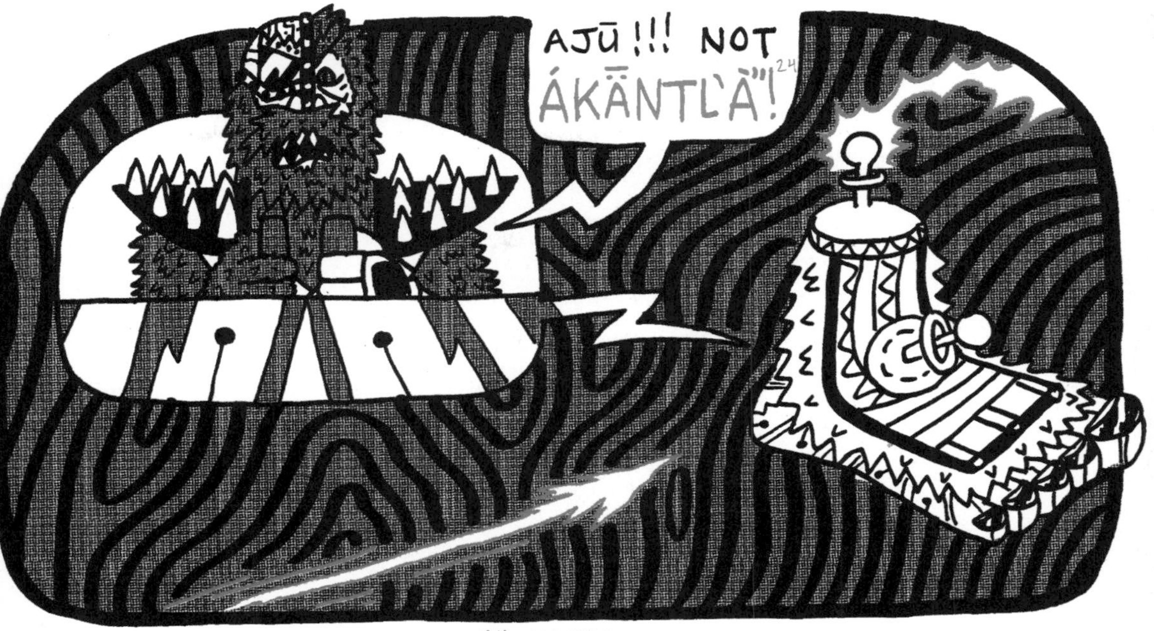
AJŪ!!! NOT ÁKǞNTL`Ā̀"![24]

24. MY HEEL

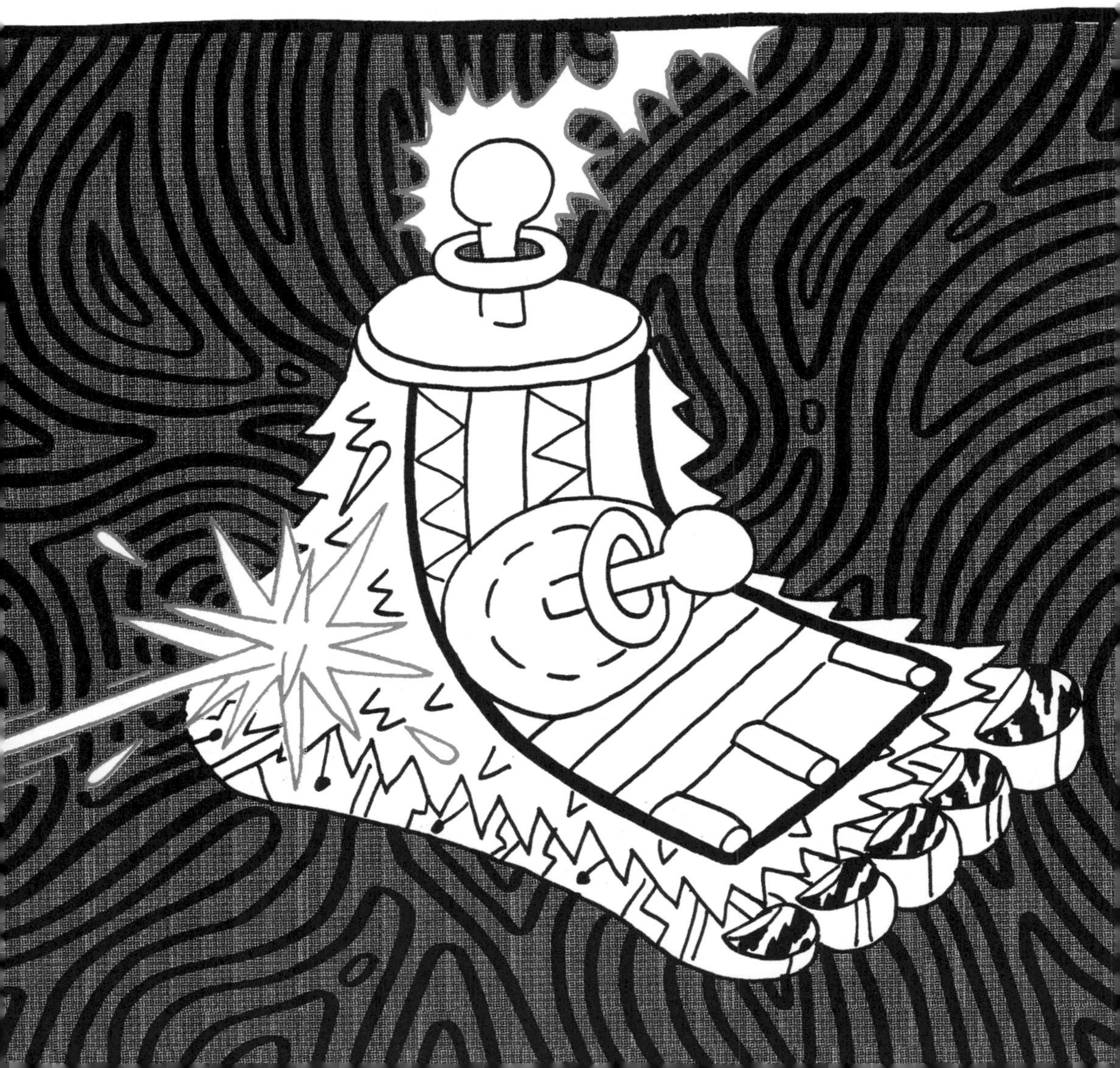

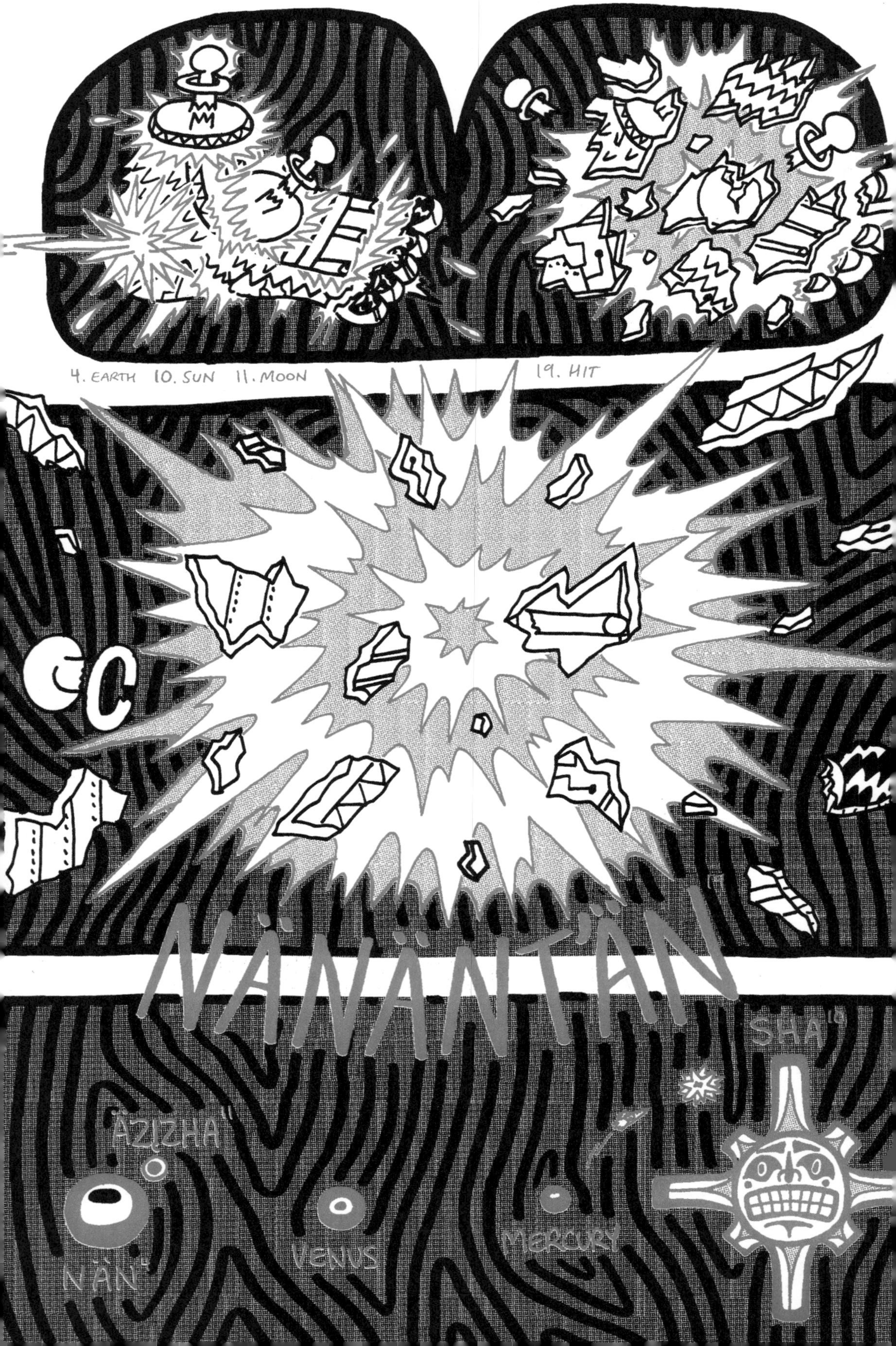

4. EARTH 10. SUN 11. MOON
19. HIT
NÄNÄNT'ÄN[19]
SHA[10]
ÄZĮZHA[11]
NÄN[4]
VENUS
MERCURY

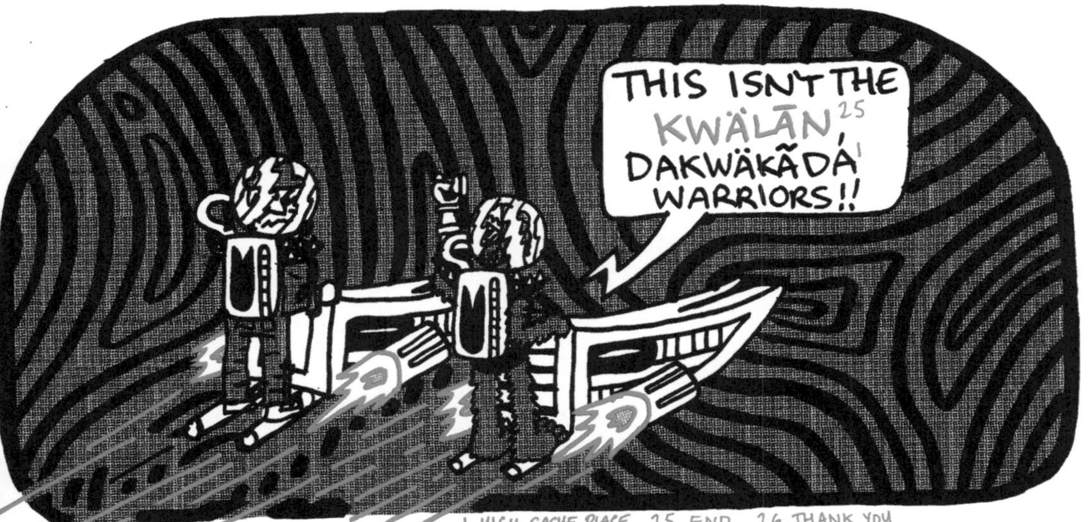
THIS ISN'T THE KWÄLĀN,[25] DAKWÄKÃDÁ[1] WARRIORS!!

1. HIGH CACHE PLACE 25. END 26. THANK YOU

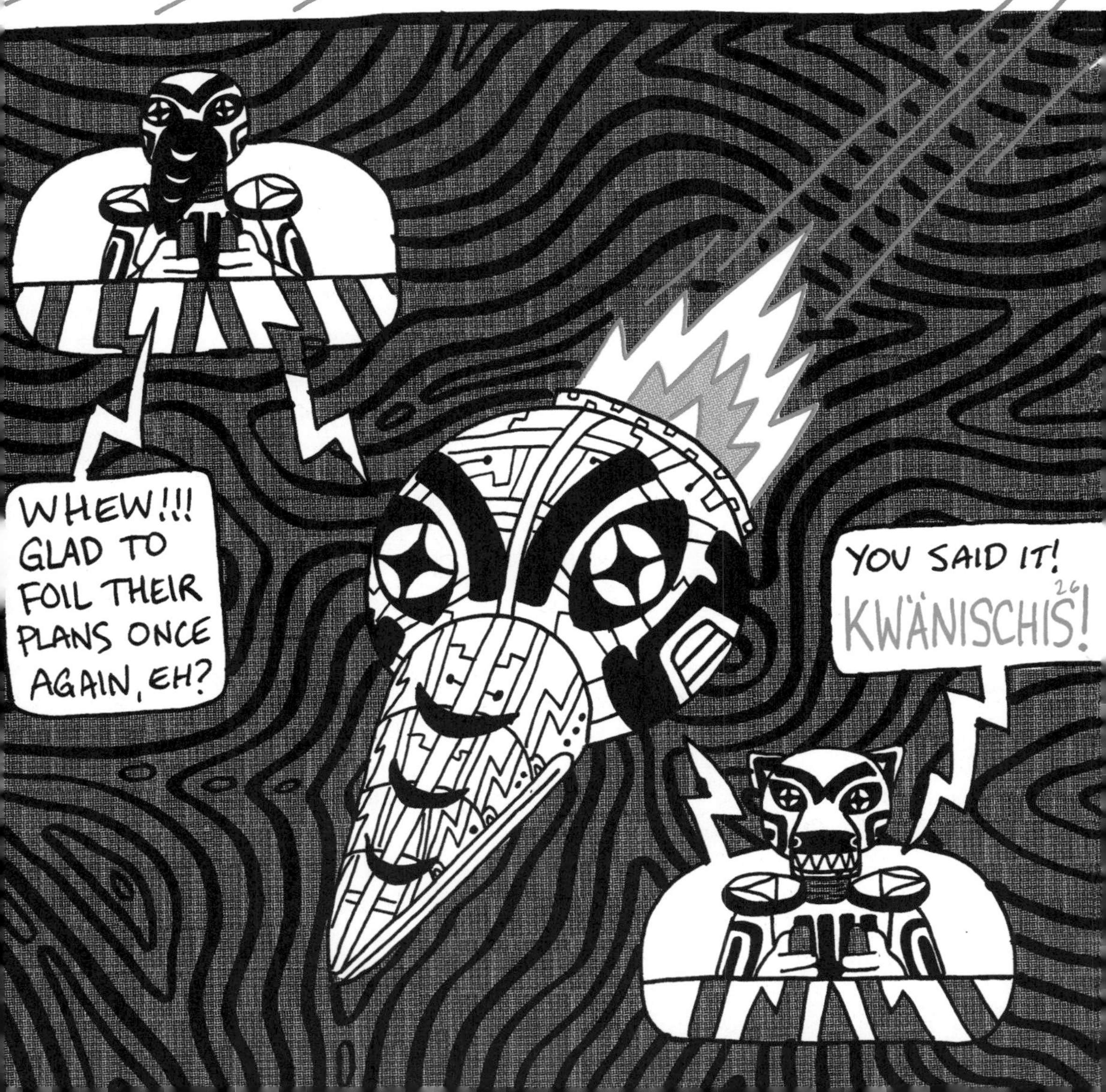
WHEW!!! GLAD TO FOIL THEIR PLANS ONCE AGAIN, EH?
YOU SAID IT! KWÄNISCHIS[26]!

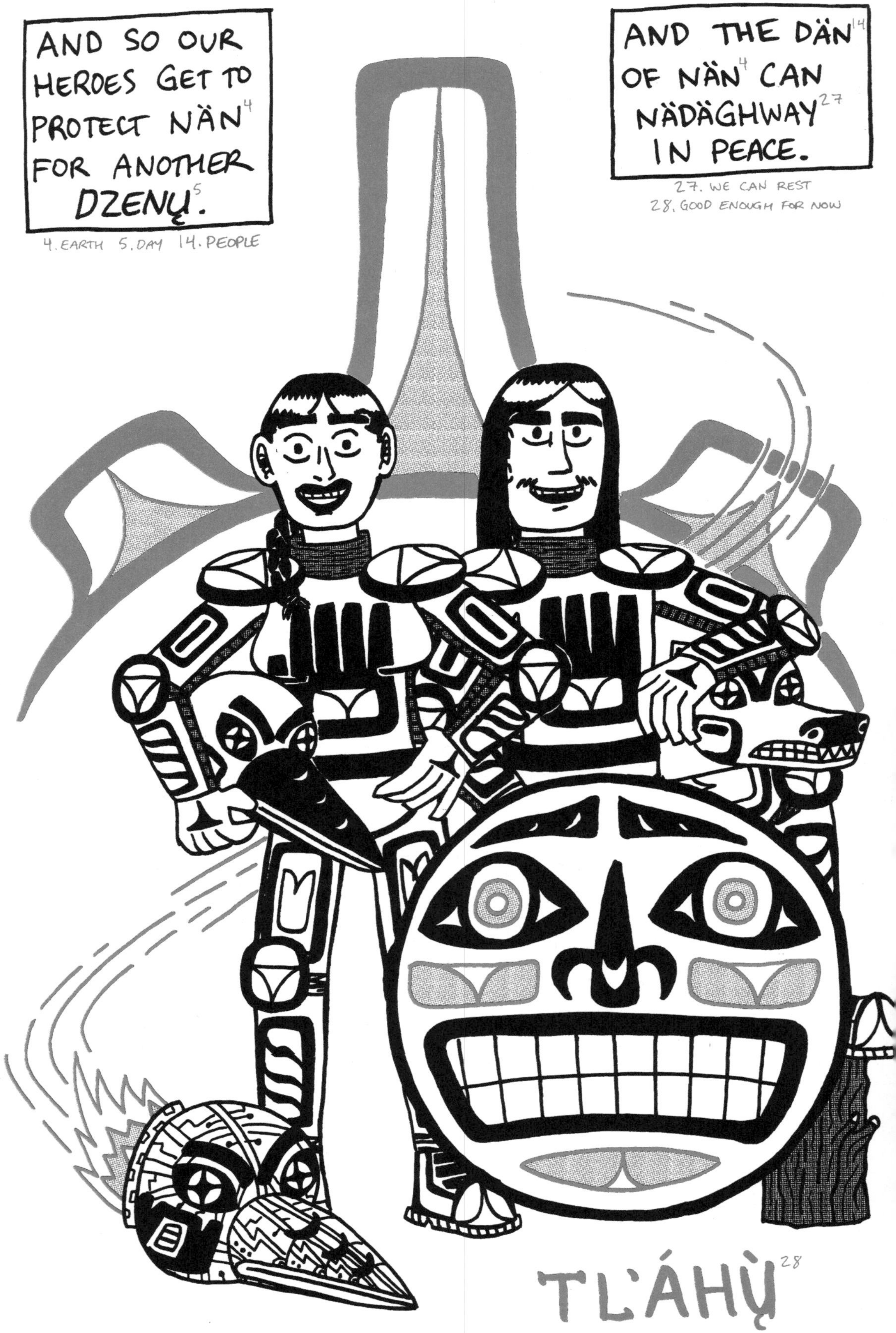
AND SO OUR HEROES GET TO PROTECT NÄN[4] FOR ANOTHER DZENỤ[5].
4. EARTH 5. DAY 14. PEOPLE
AND THE DÄN[14] OF NÄN[4] CAN NÄDÄGHWAY[27] IN PEACE.
27. WE CAN REST
28. GOOD ENOUGH FOR NOW
TL'ÁHỤ̀[28]

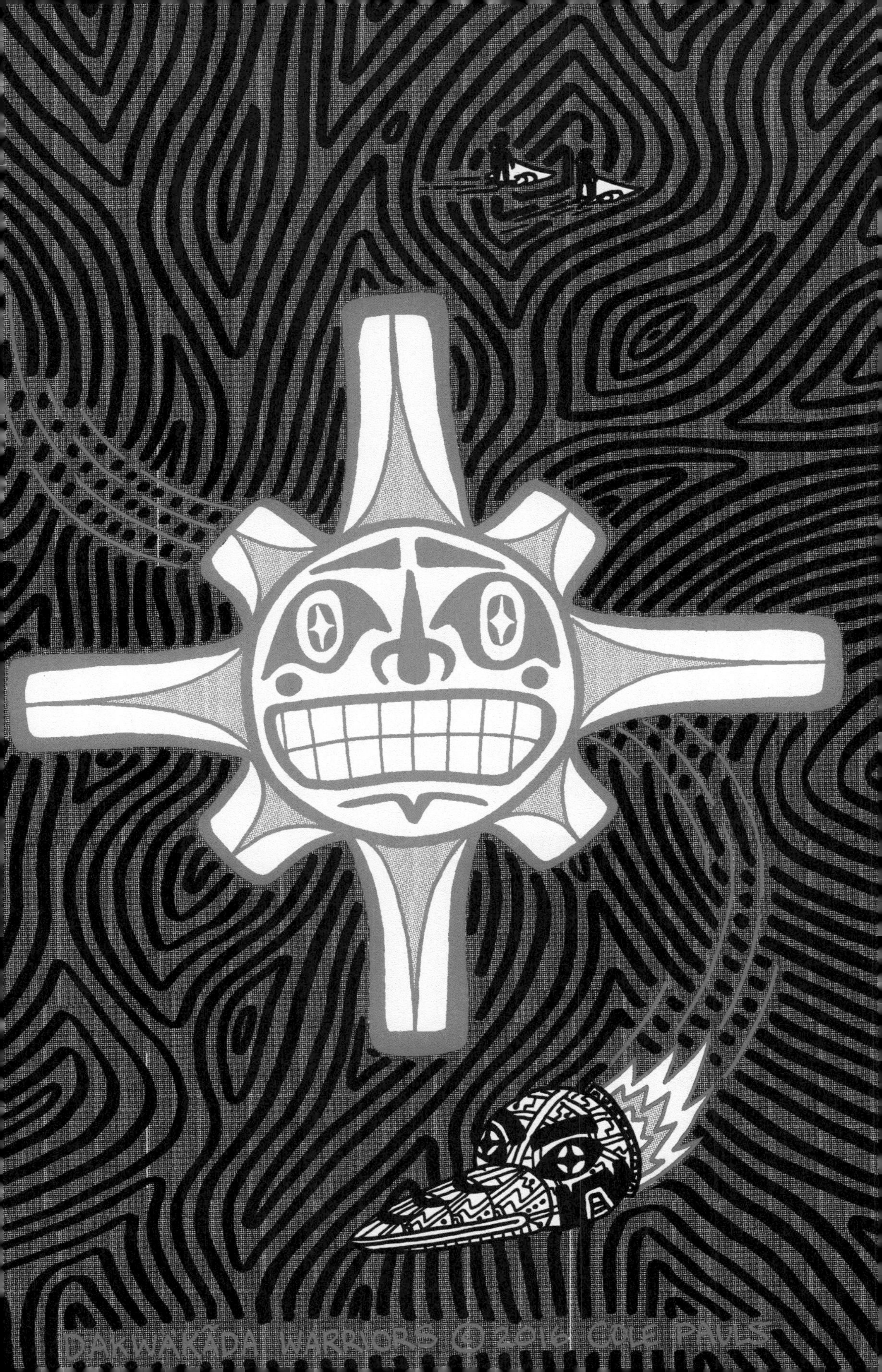
DAKWAKĀDA WARRIORS © 2016 COLE PAULS

DAKWÄKÃDA WARRIORS II

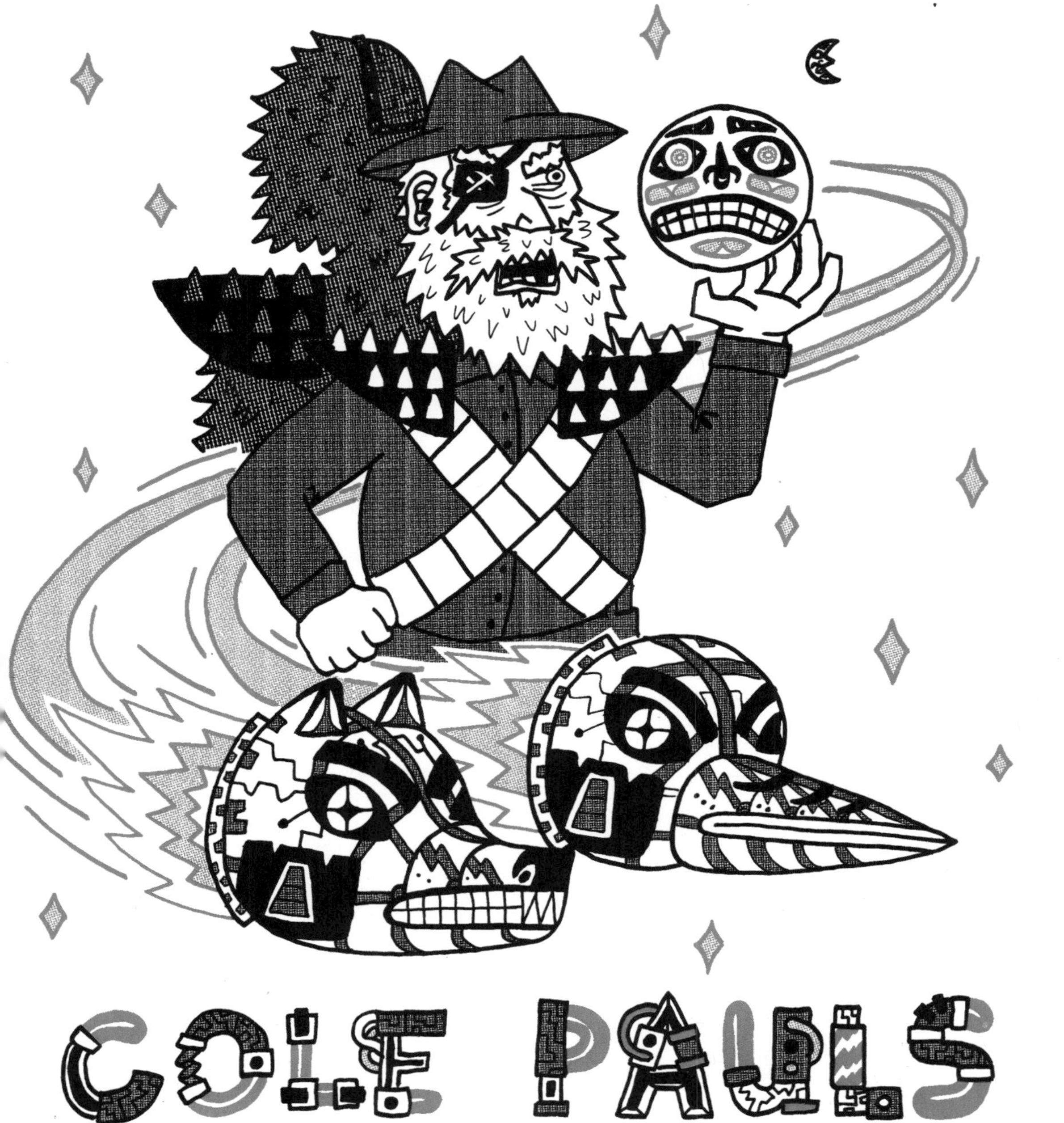

COLE PAULS

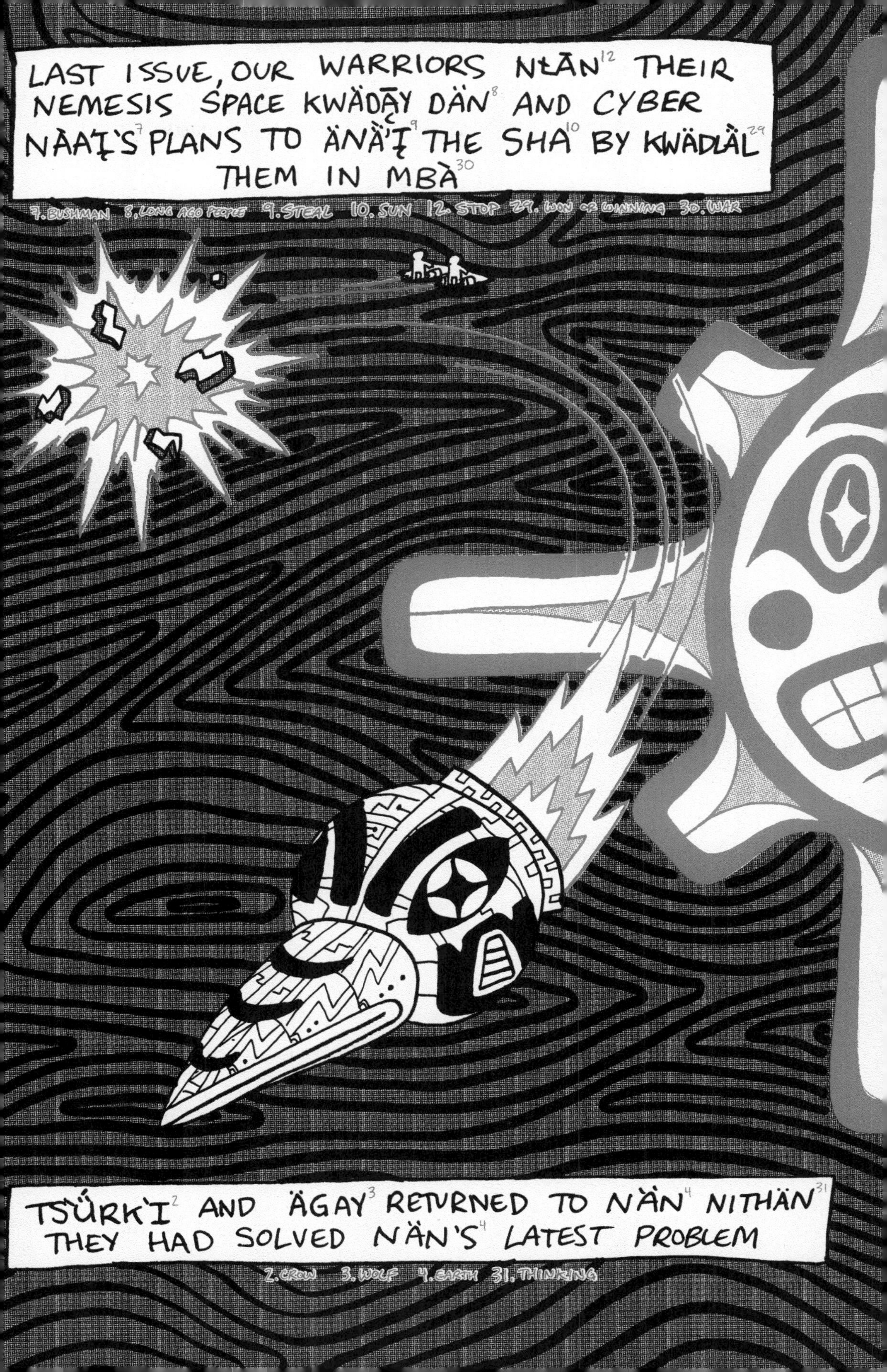
LAST ISSUE, OUR WARRIORS NŁĀN[12] THEIR NEMESIS SPACE KWÄDĄY DÄN[8] AND CYBER NÀĄĮ'S[7] PLANS TO ÄNÄ'Į[9] THE SHA[10] BY KWÄDLÀL[29] THEM IN MBÀ[30]
7. BUSHMAN 8. LONG AGO PEOPLE 9. STEAL 10. SUN 12. STOP 29. WON OR WINNING 30. WAR
TSÜRK'I[2] AND ÄGAY[3] RETURNED TO NÄN[4] NITHÄN[31] THEY HAD SOLVED NÄN'S[4] LATEST PROBLEM
2. CROW 3. WOLF 4. EARTH 31. THINKING

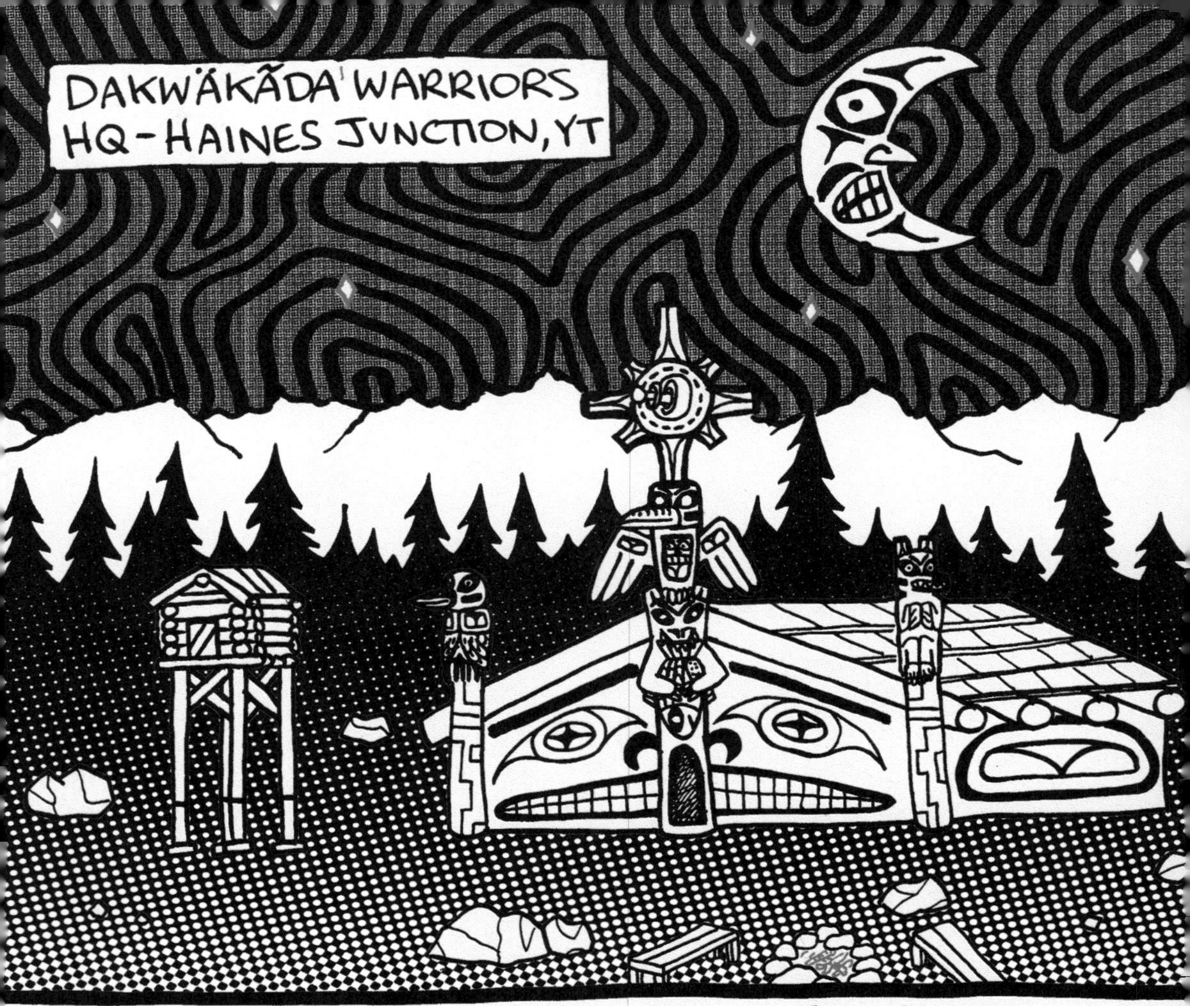
DAKWÄKÃDA[1] WARRIORS
HQ - HAINES JUNCTION, YT

1. HIGH CACHE PLACE 14. PEOPLE 31. THINK 32. BUILD 33. SHIP 34. SAFE

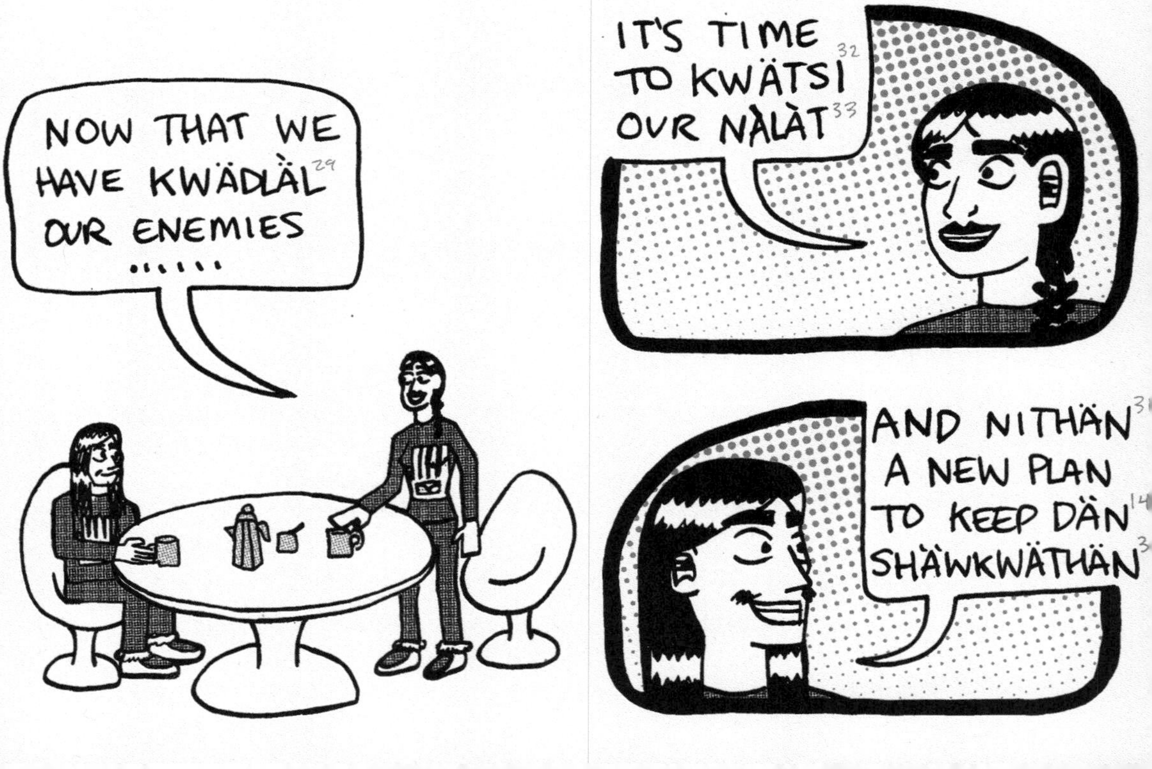
NOW THAT WE HAVE KWÄDLÄ̀L[29] OUR ENEMIES ......
IT'S TIME TO KWÄTSI[32] OUR NÀLÀT[33]
AND NITHÄN[3] A NEW PLAN TO KEEP DÄN[14] SHÄWKWÄTHÄN[3]

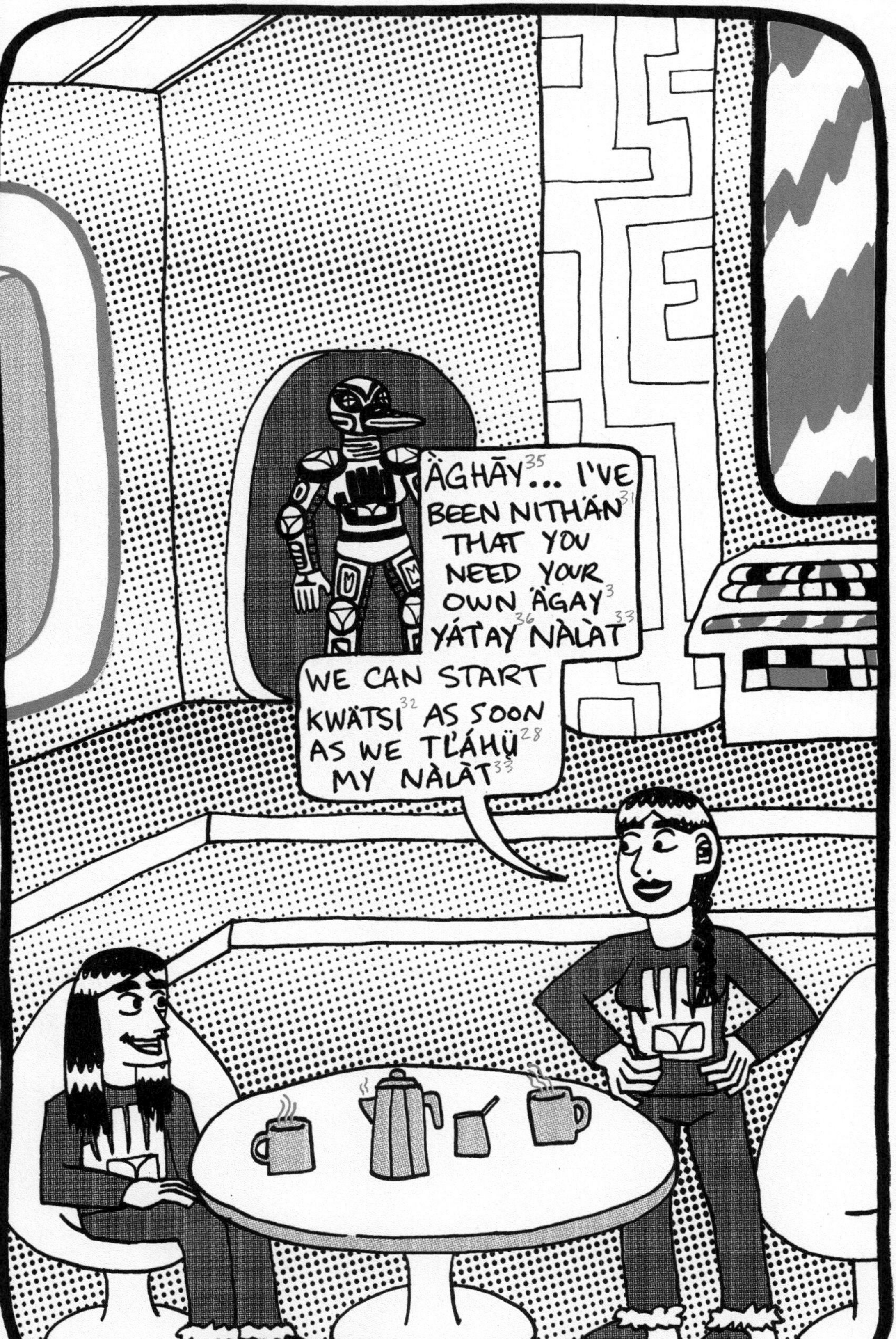
ÀGHĀY[35]... I'VE BEEN NITHÁN[31] THAT YOU NEED YOUR OWN ÀGAY[3] YÁT'AY[36] NÀLÀT[33]
WE CAN START KWÄTSI[32] AS SOON AS WE TL'ÁHŲ̈[28] MY NÀLÀT[33]

3. WOLF 28. FINISH 31. THINKING 32. BUILD 33. SHIP 35. YES 36. SPACE

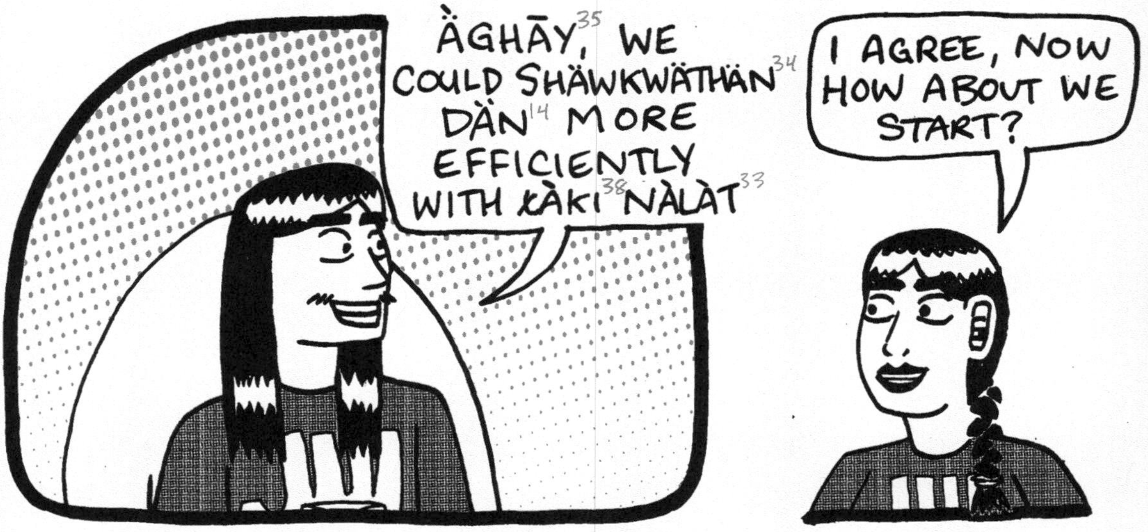
ȀGHĀY[35], WE COULD SHÄWKWÄTHÄN[34] DÄN[14] MORE EFFICIENTLY WITH ŁÀKI[38] NÀLÀT[33]
I AGREE, NOW HOW ABOUT WE START?

14. PEOPLE 28. FINISHED 32. BUILD 33. SHIP 34. SAFE 35. YES 37. LATER 38. TWO

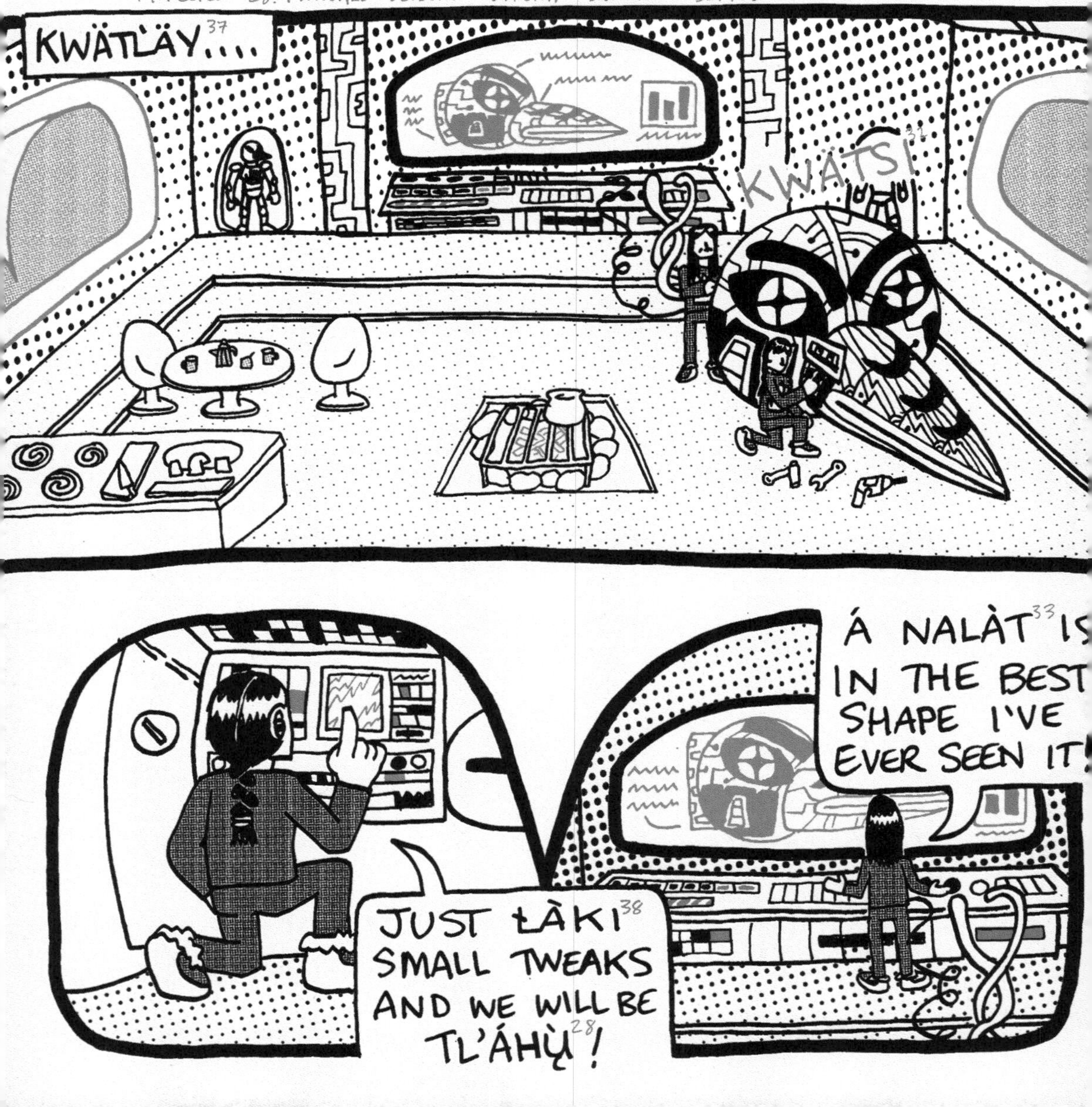
KWÄTLÄY[37]....
KWÄTSI[32]
Á NALÀT[33] IS IN THE BEST SHAPE I'VE EVER SEEN IT!
JUST ŁÀKI[38] SMALL TWEAKS AND WE WILL BE TL'ÁHŲ̀[28]!

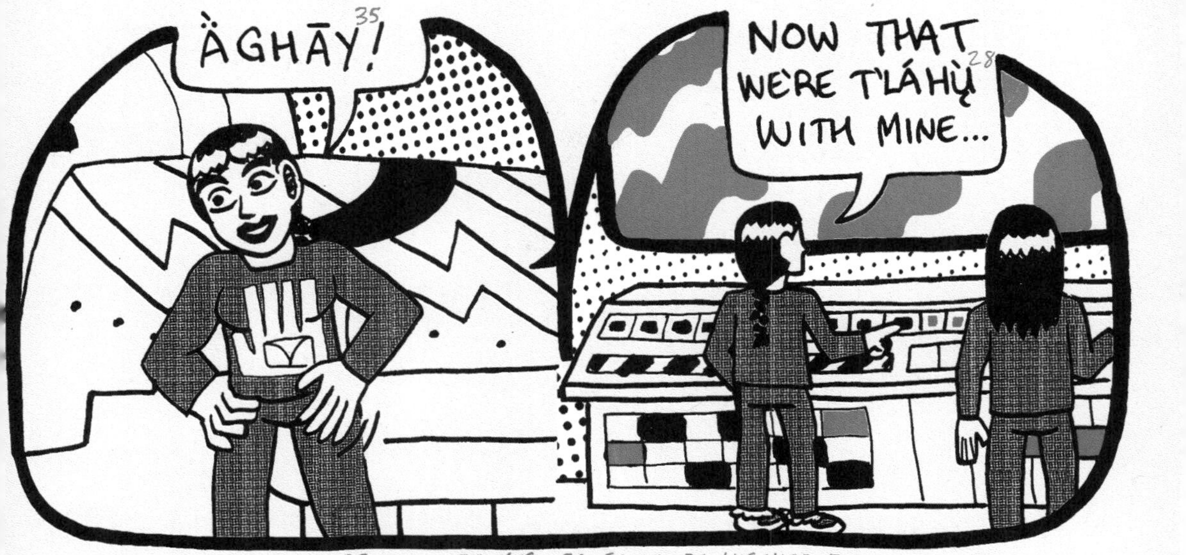
ÀGHĀY![35]
NOW THAT WE'RE T'LÁHṲ[28] WITH MINE...

3. WOLF 28. FINISHED 33. SHIP 35. YES 36. SPACE 39. HIS/HER EAR 40. HIS/HER EYE
41. HIS/HER NOSE 42. HIS/HER TEETH 43. DOOR

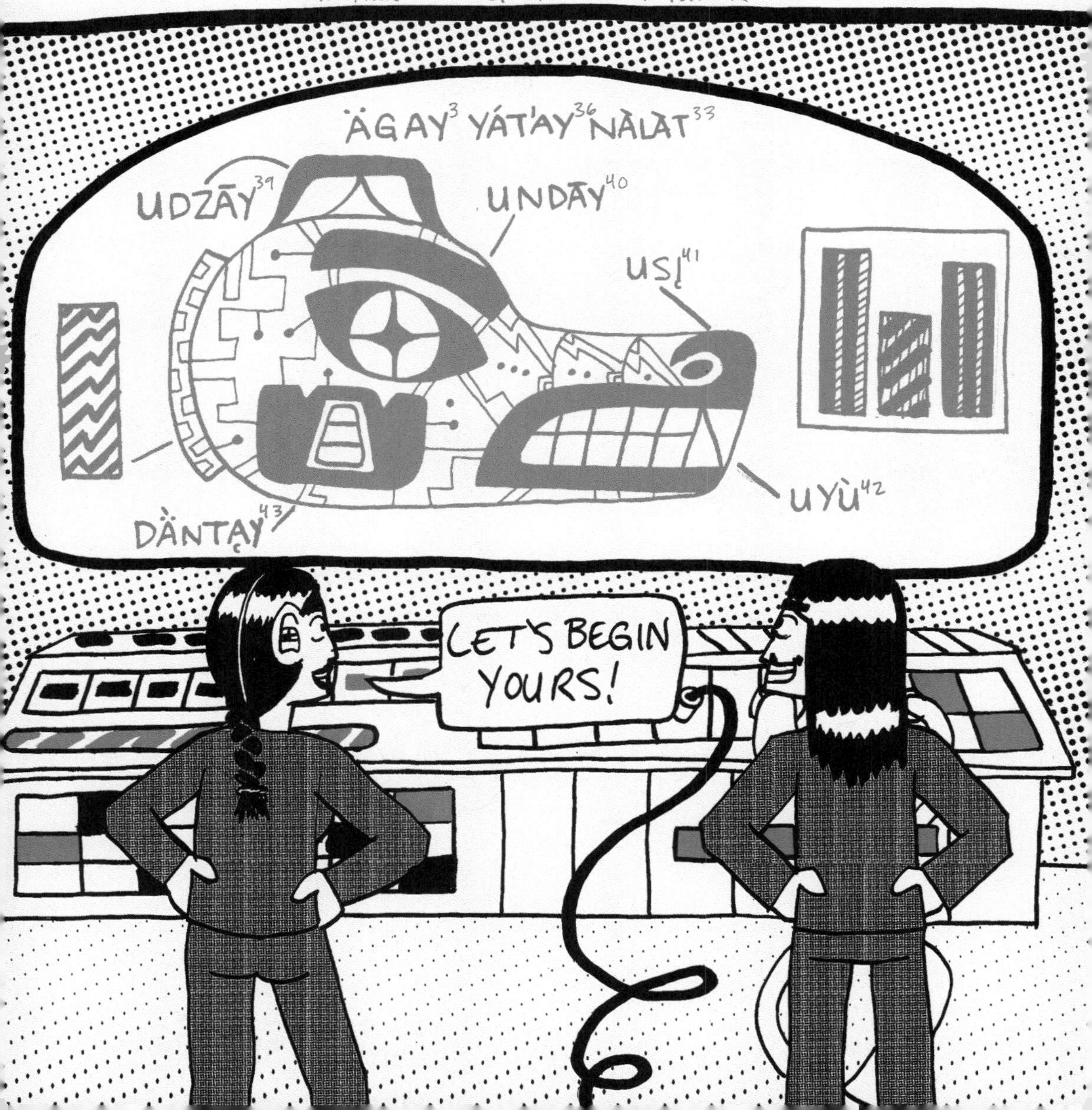
ÄGAY[3] YÁT'AY[36] NÀLÀT[33]
UDZĀY[39]
UNDĀY[40]
USĮ[41]
DÀNTĄY[43]
UYÙ[42]
LET'S BEGIN YOURS!

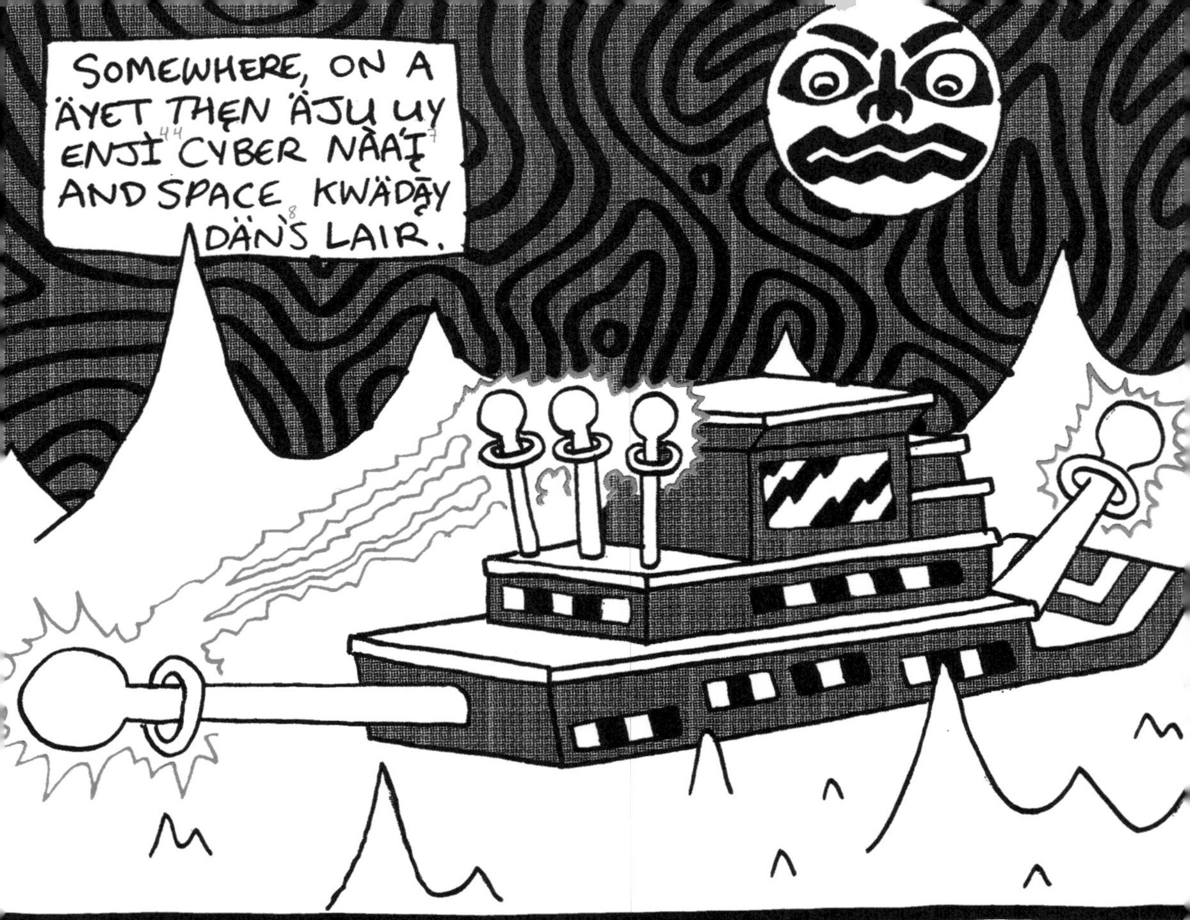
SOMEWHERE, ON A ÄYET THẸN ÄJU UY ENJI[44] CYBER NÄAĮ[7] AND SPACE KWÄDĄY[8] DÄN'S LAIR.

1. HIGH CACHE PLACE 7. BUSHMAN 8. LONG AGO PEOPLE 44. UNKNOWN STAR 45. OUR SHIP IS BROKEN 46. BOOM

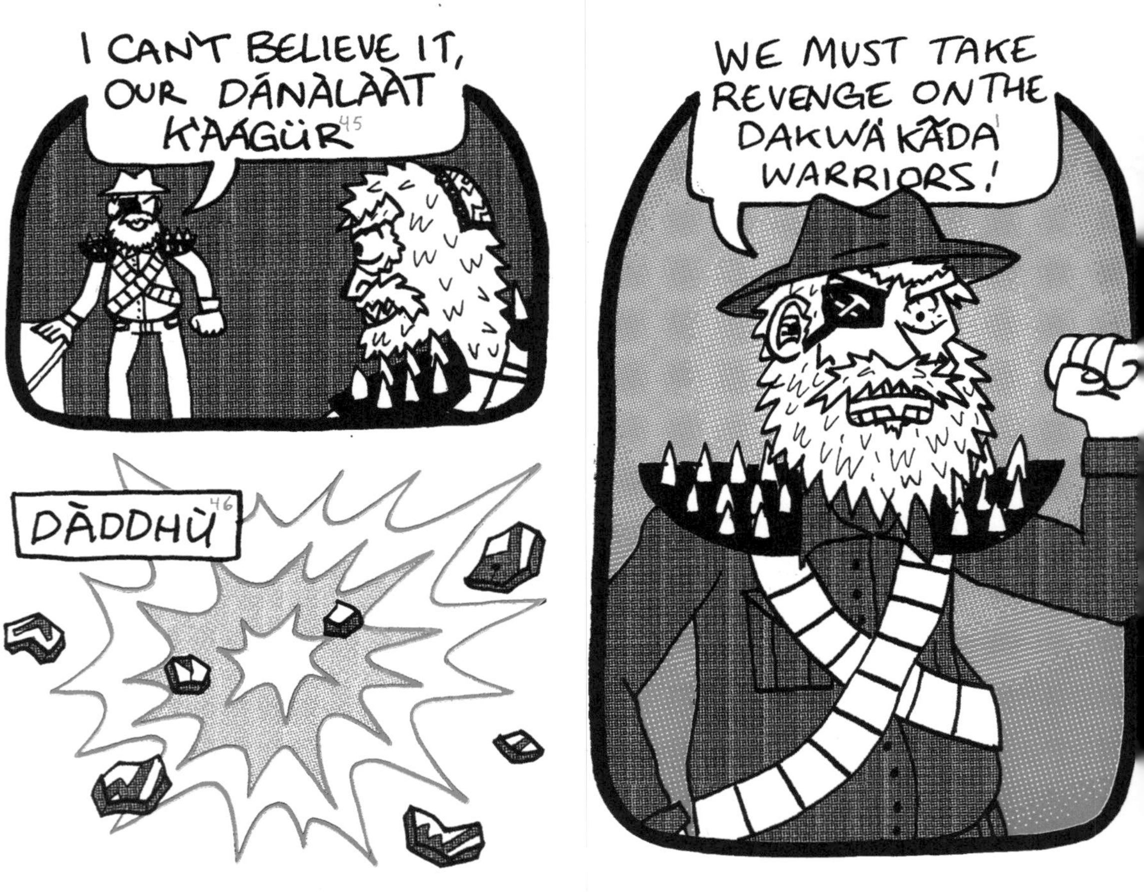
I CAN'T BELIEVE IT, OUR DÁNÁLÄAT K'ÄAGÜR[45]
WE MUST TAKE REVENGE ON THE DAKWÄKÄDA[1] WARRIORS!
DÀDDHÙ[46]

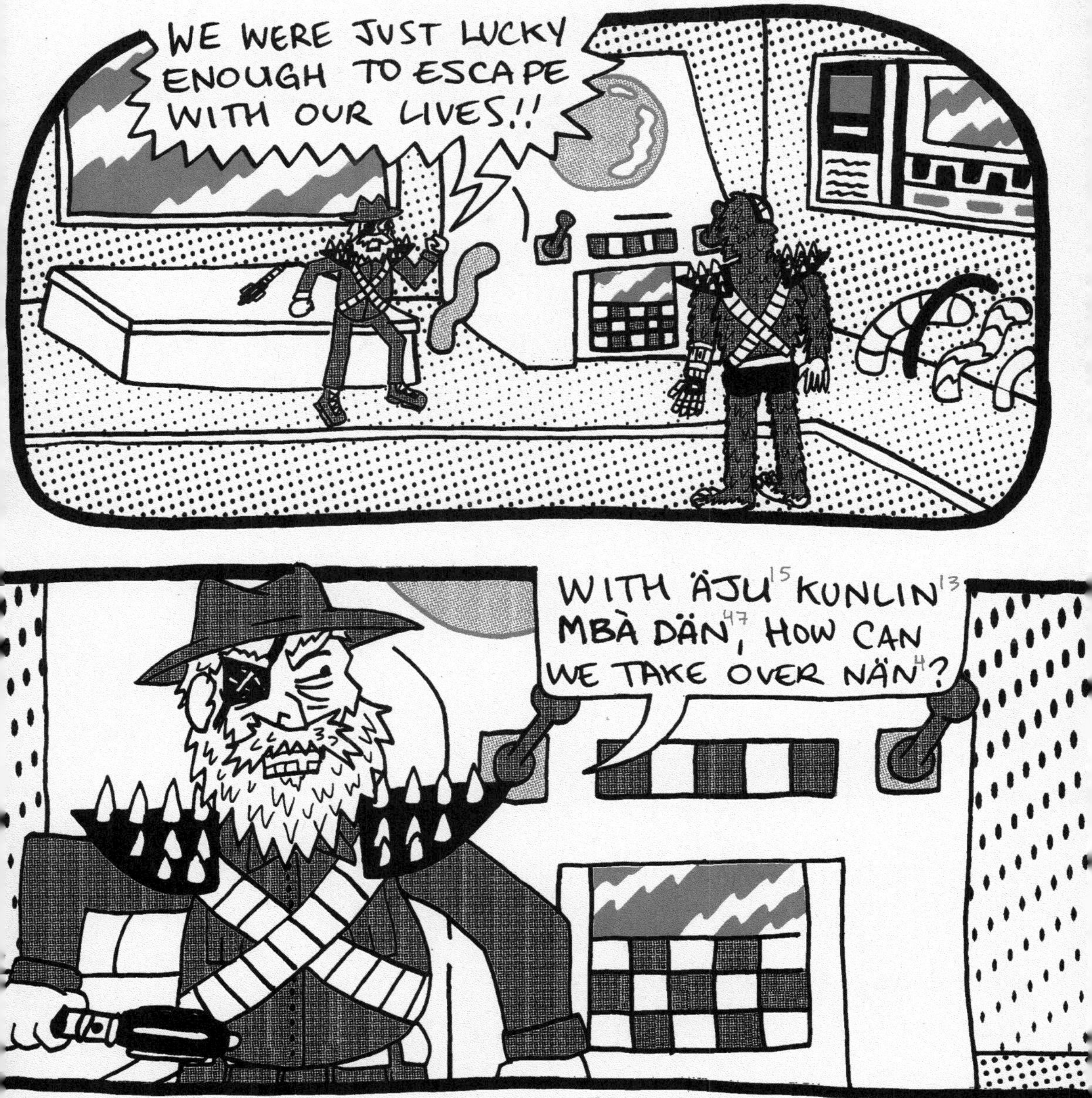
WE WERE JUST LUCKY ENOUGH TO ESCAPE WITH OUR LIVES!!
WITH ÄJU[15] KUNLIN[13] MBÀ DÄN[47], HOW CAN WE TAKE OVER NÄN[4]?

4. EARTH 13. MAMMOTH 15. NO 47. ARMY

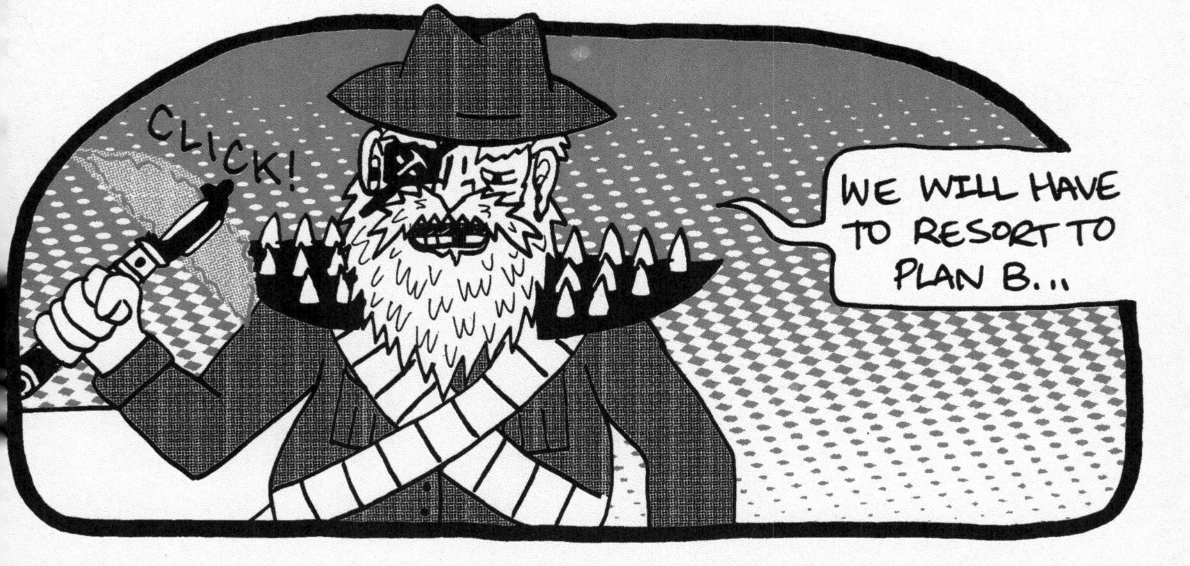
CLICK!
WE WILL HAVE TO RESORT TO PLAN B...

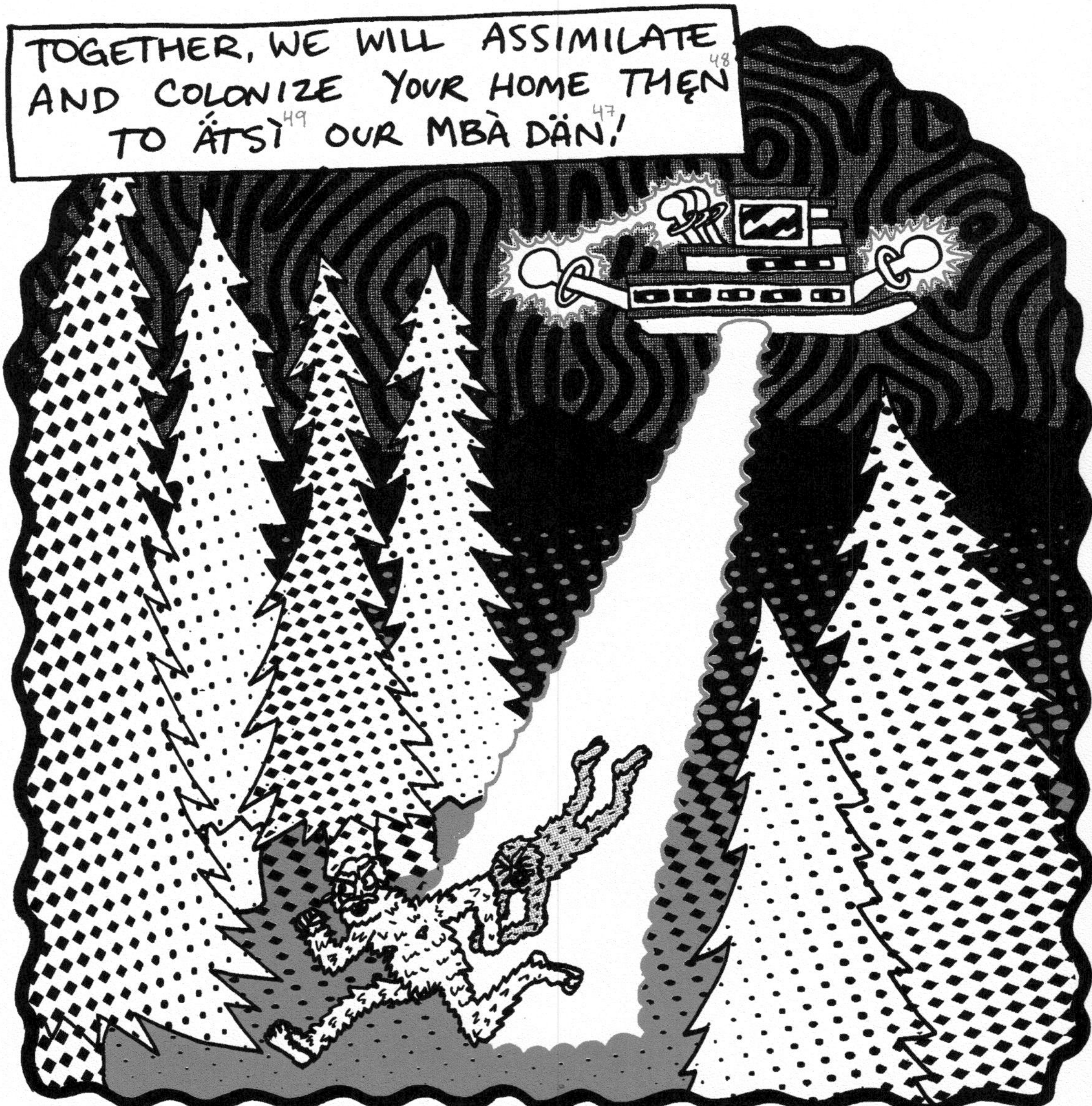
TOGETHER, WE WILL ASSIMILATE AND COLONIZE YOUR HOME THĘN[48] TO ÁTSÌ[49] OUR MBÀ DÄN[47]!

9. STEAL 47. ARMY 48. STAR/PLANET 49. HE/SHE MAKES

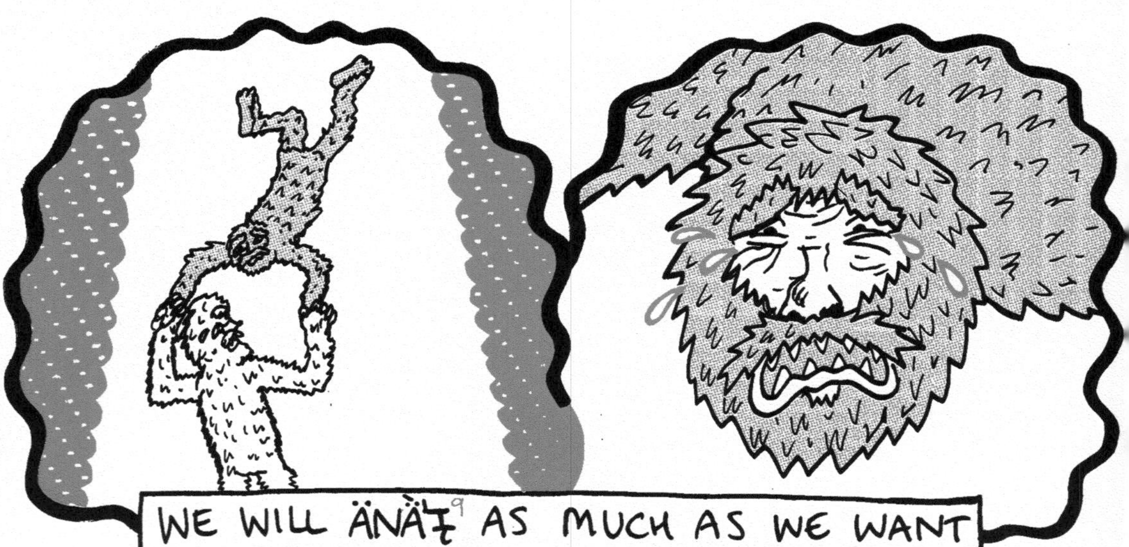
WE WILL ÄNÄƵ[9] AS MUCH AS WE WANT

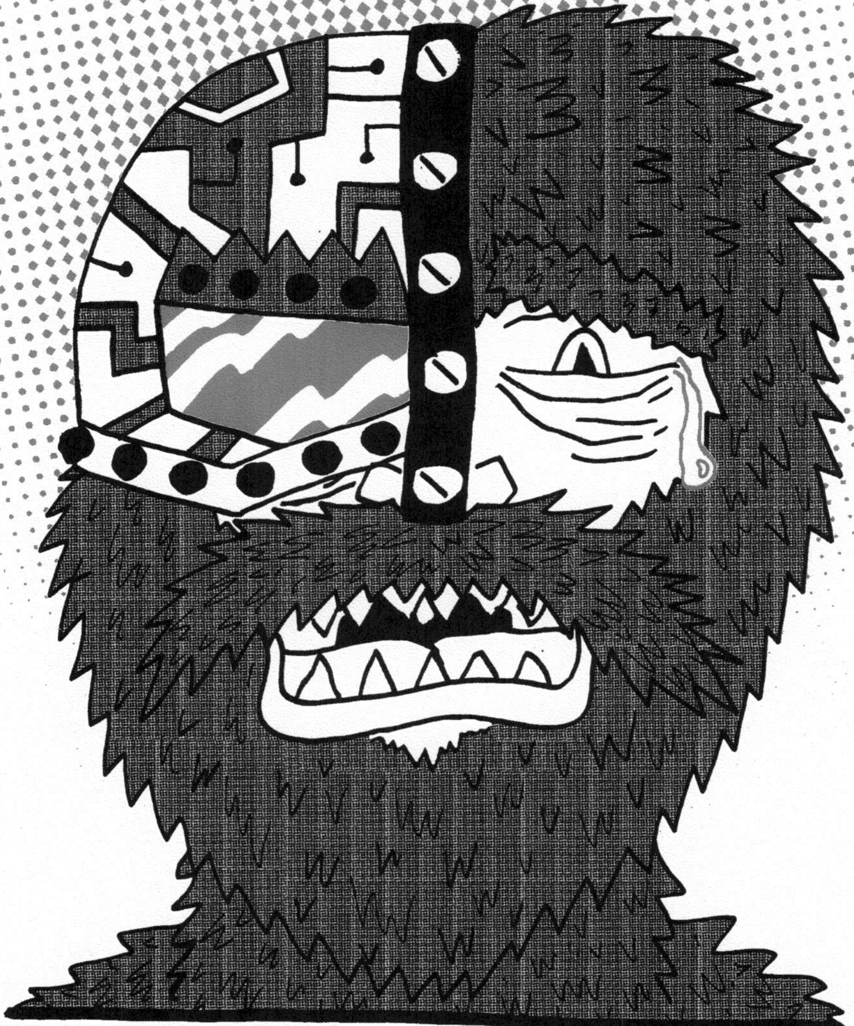

50. DON'T CRY 51. STAB OR POKE

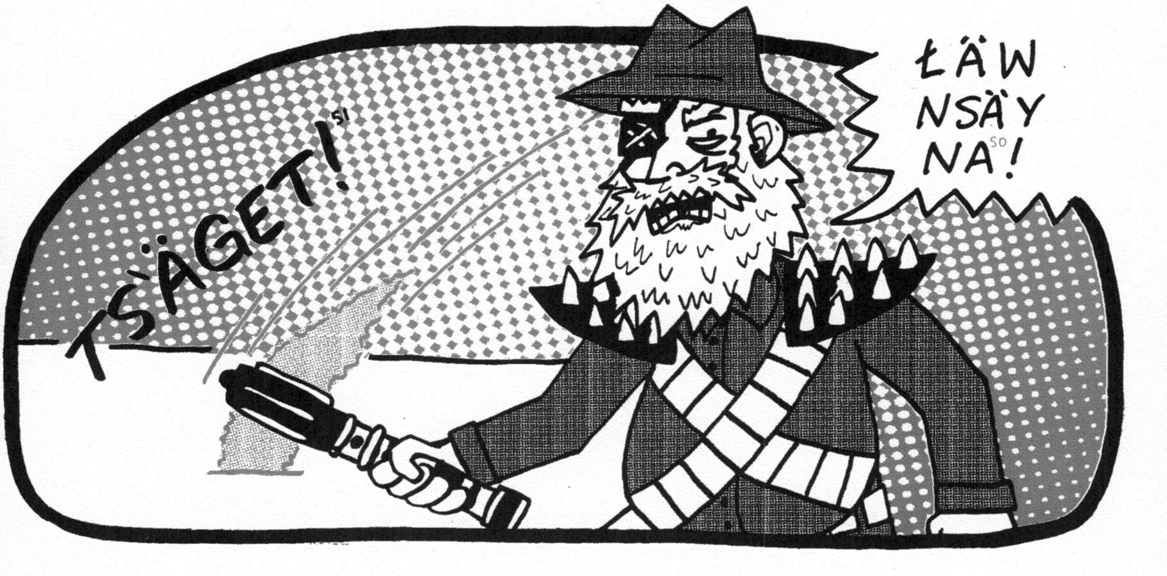
TSÄGET![51]
ŁÄW NSÄY NA![50]

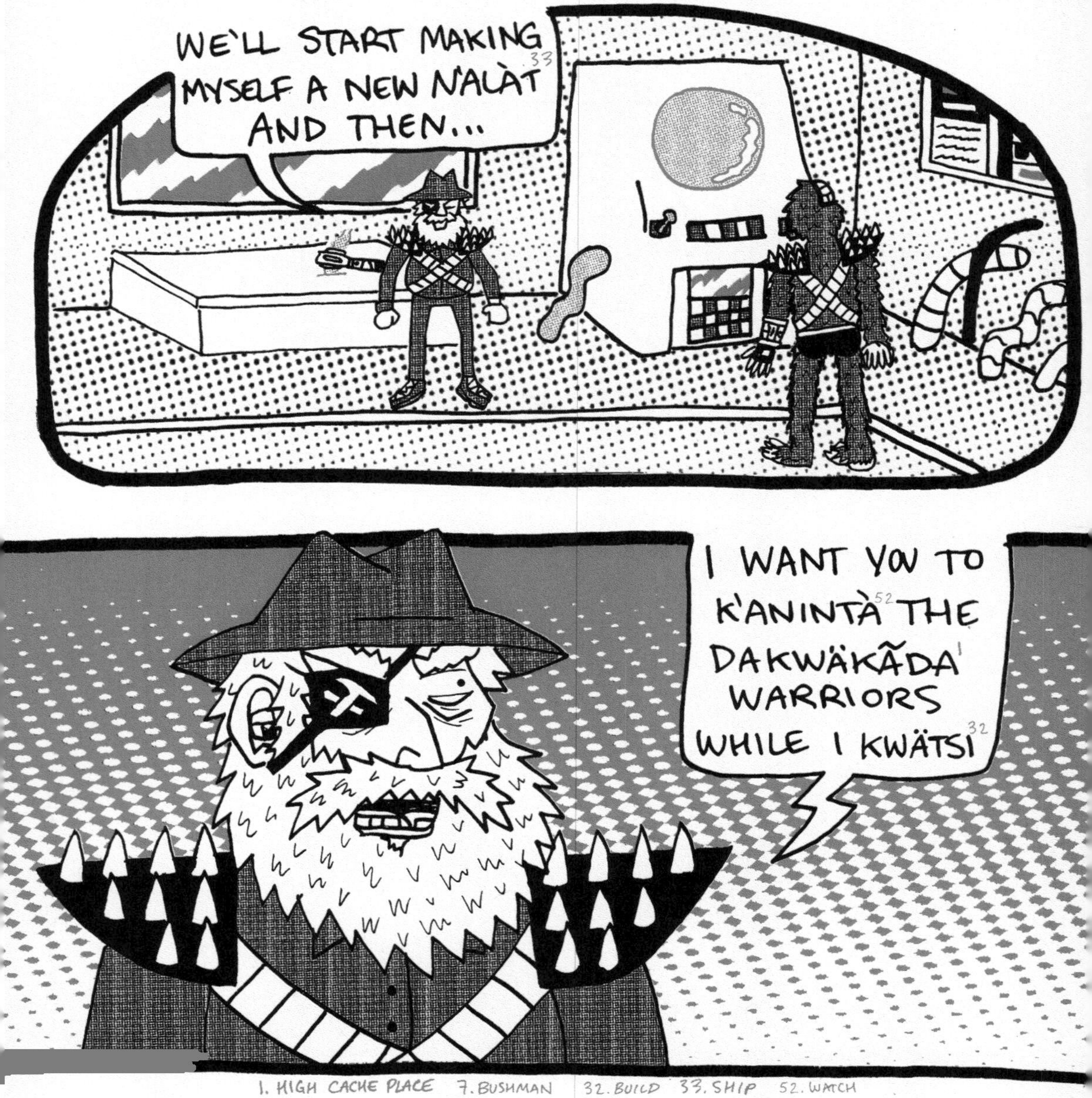
WE'LL START MAKING MYSELF A NEW N'ÀLÀT[33] AND THEN...
I WANT YOU TO K'ANINTÀ[52] THE DAKWÄKÃDA[1] WARRIORS WHILE I KWÄTSI[32]

1. HIGH CACHE PLACE 7. BUSHMAN 32. BUILD 33. SHIP 52. WATCH

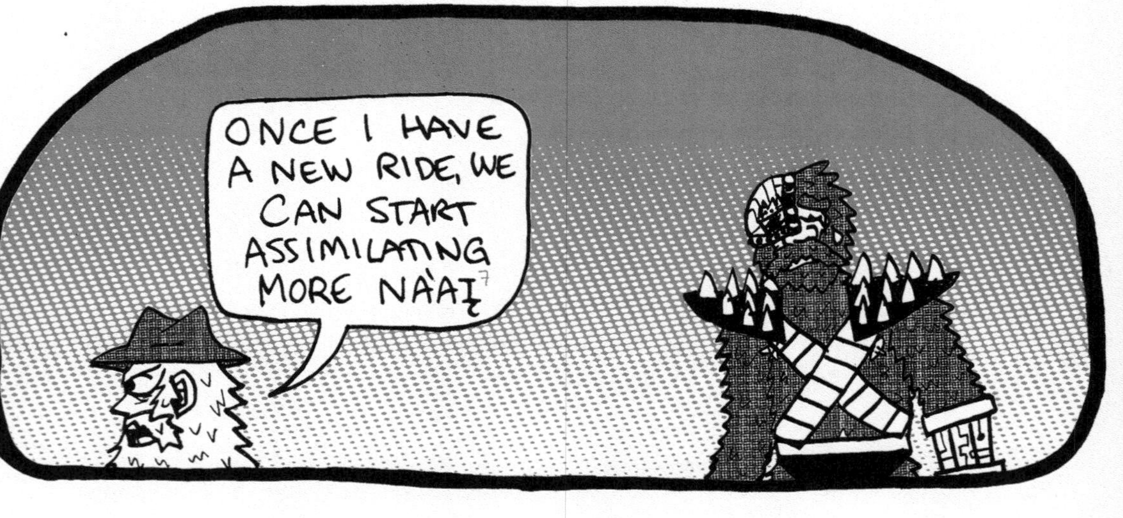
ONCE I HAVE A NEW RIDE, WE CAN START ASSIMILATING MORE NÀ'AĮ[7]

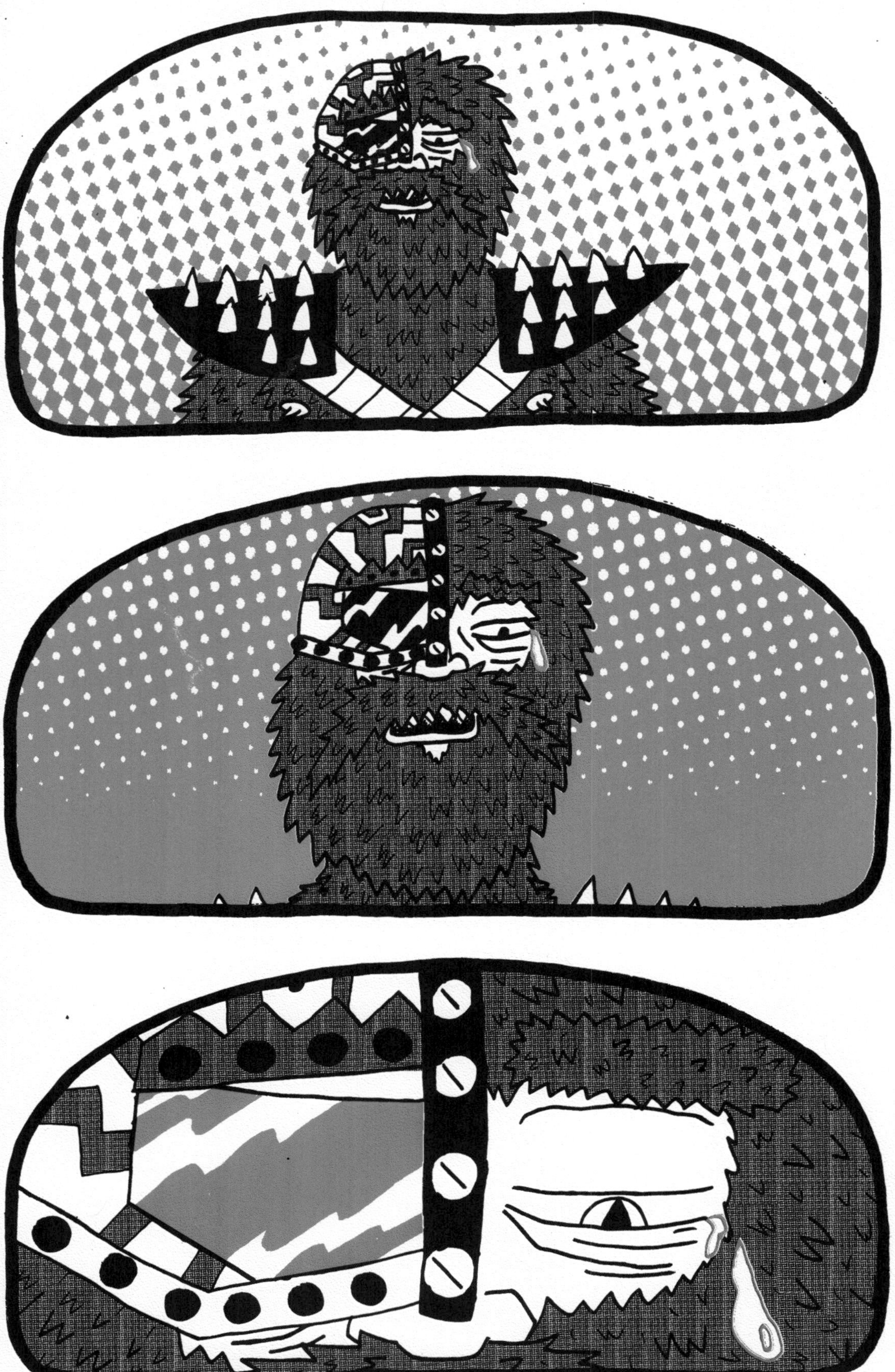

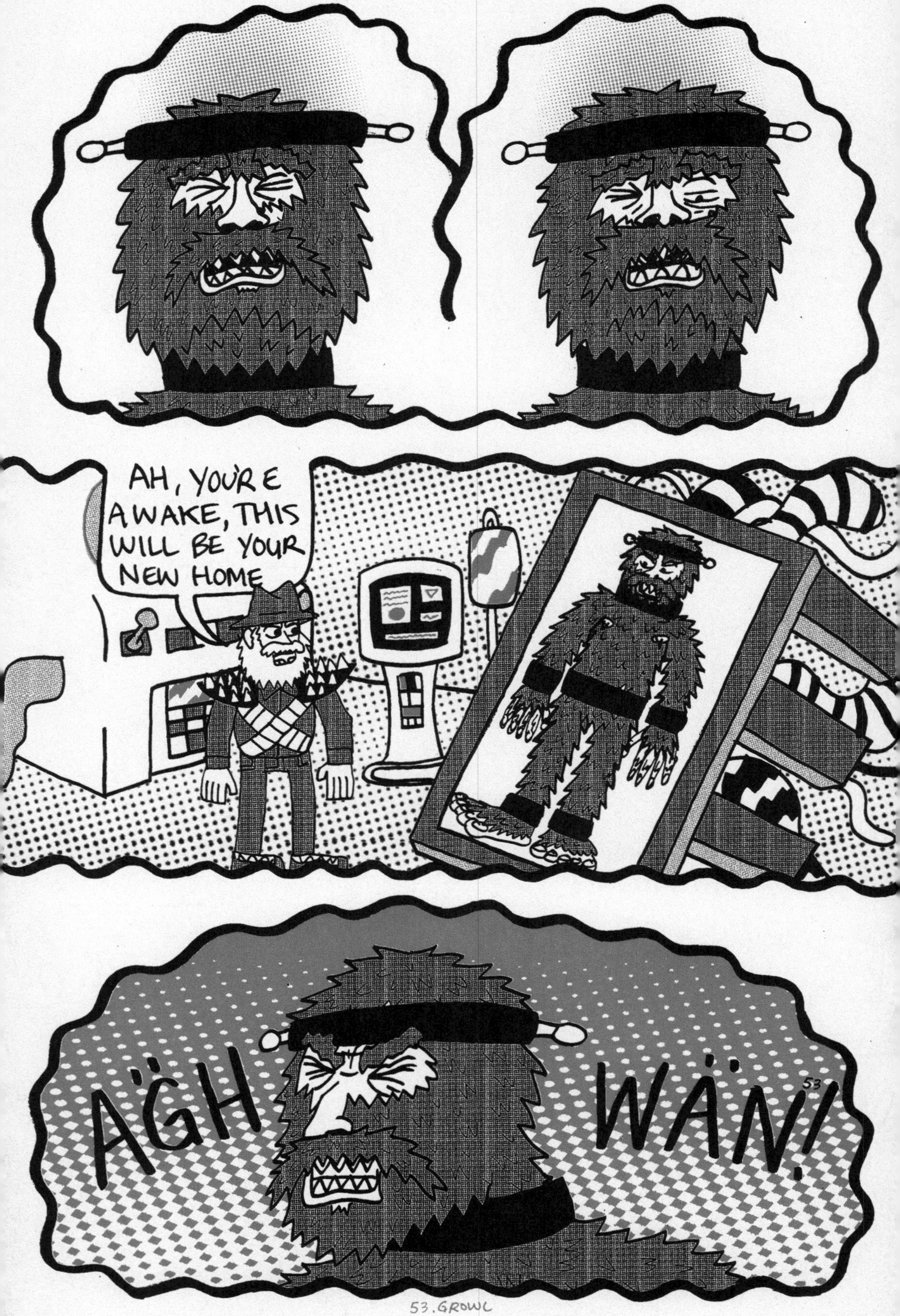
AH, YOU'RE AWAKE, THIS WILL BE YOUR NEW HOME
ÄGH
WÄN!
53

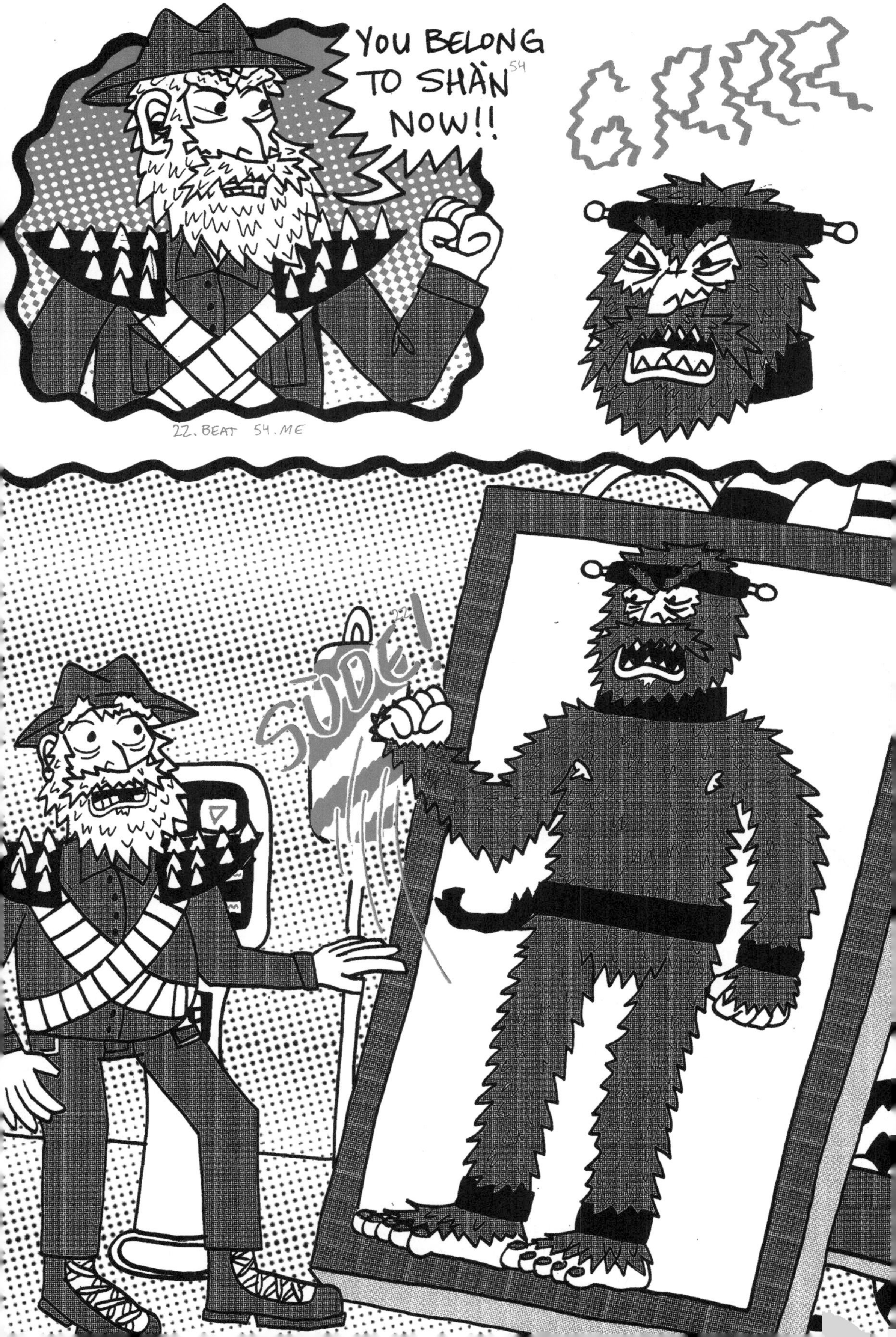
YOU BELONG TO SHÀN NOW!!
54
GRRR
22. BEAT 54. ME
22
SUDE!

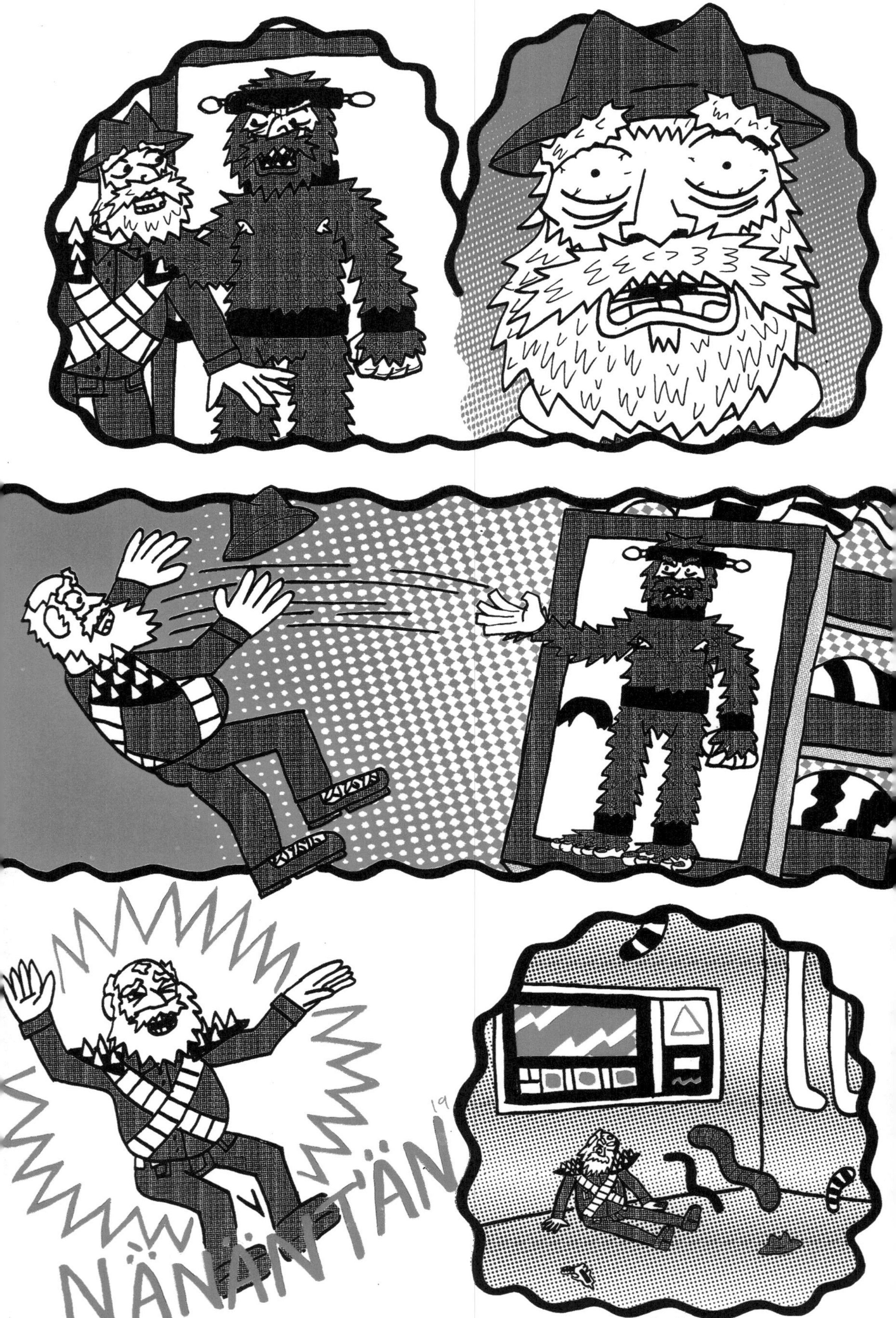
NÄNÄNTÄN[19]

19. HIT

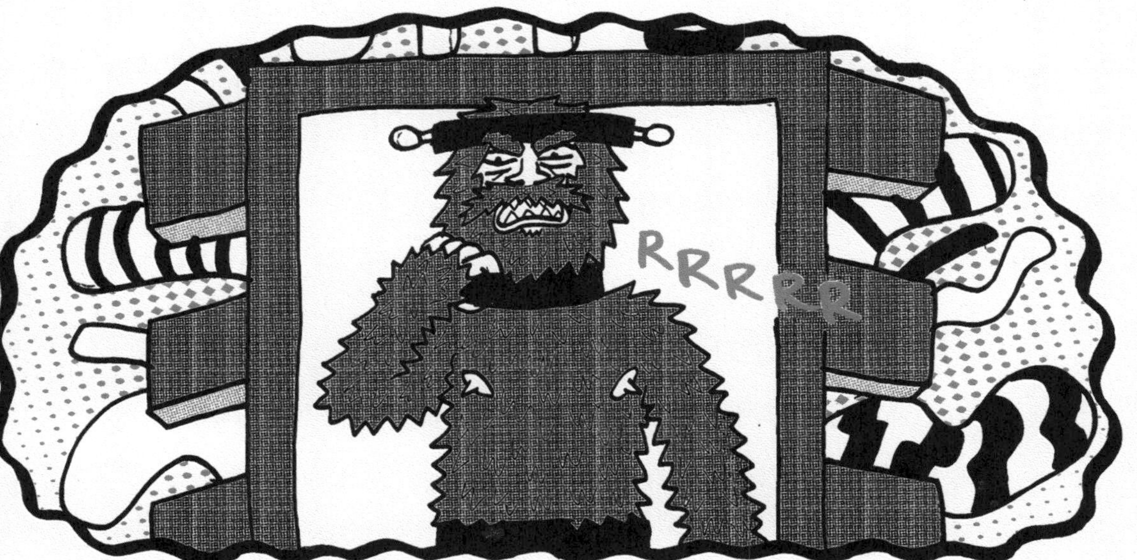
RRRRRR

53.GROWL

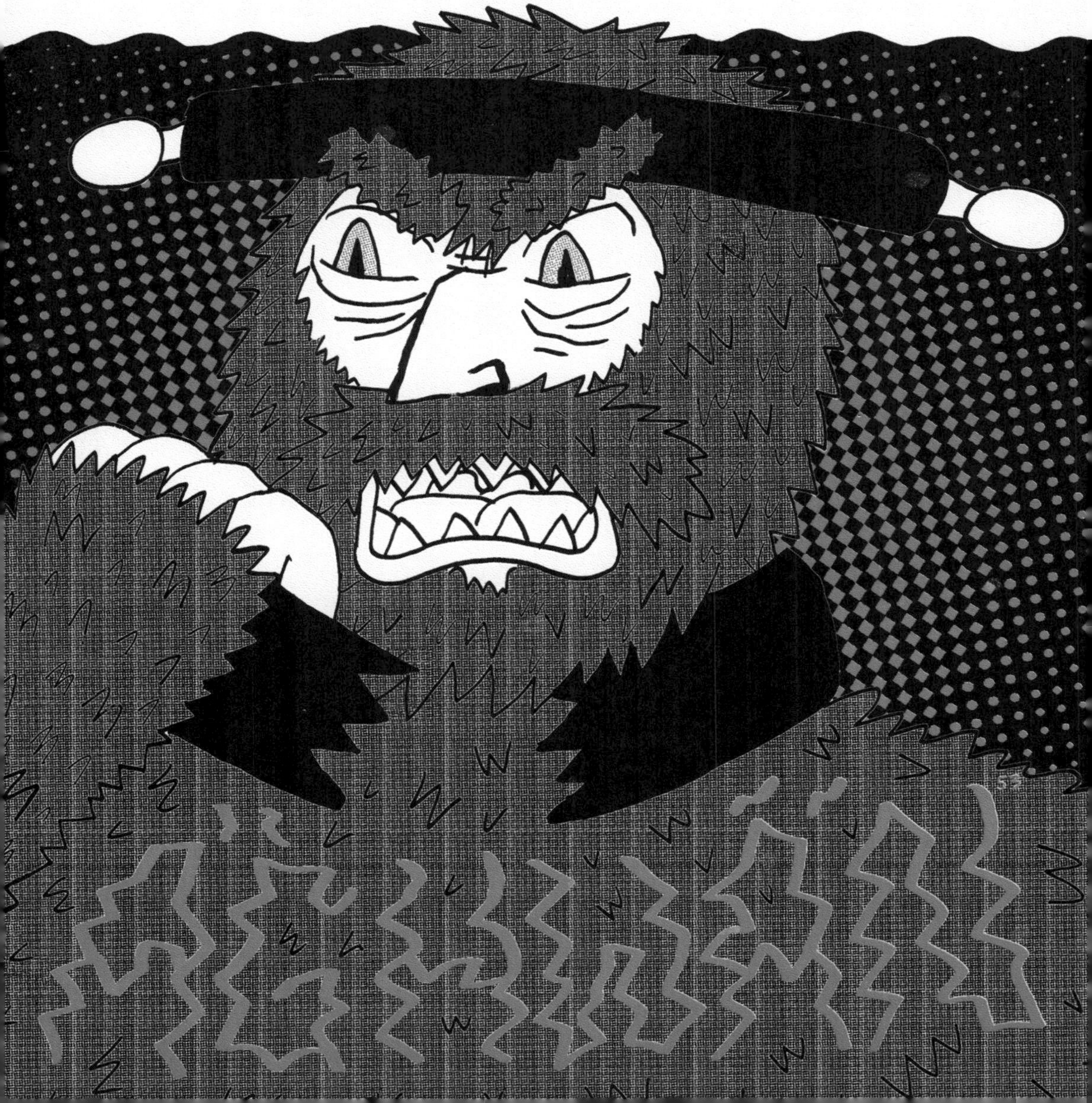

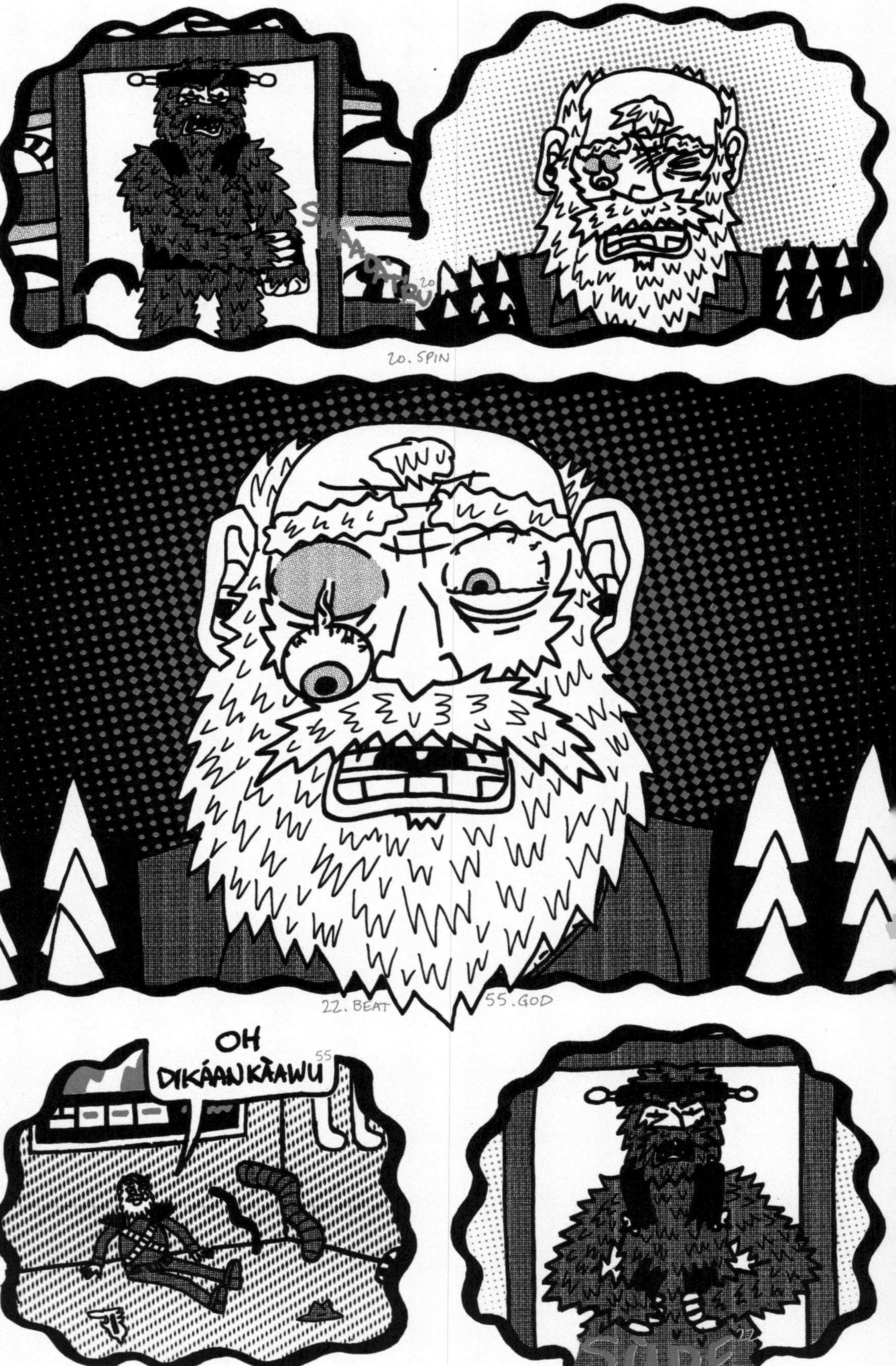
SHAADATRU 20
20. SPIN
22. BEAT
55. GOD
OH DIKÁANKÂAWU 55
SÙDE 22

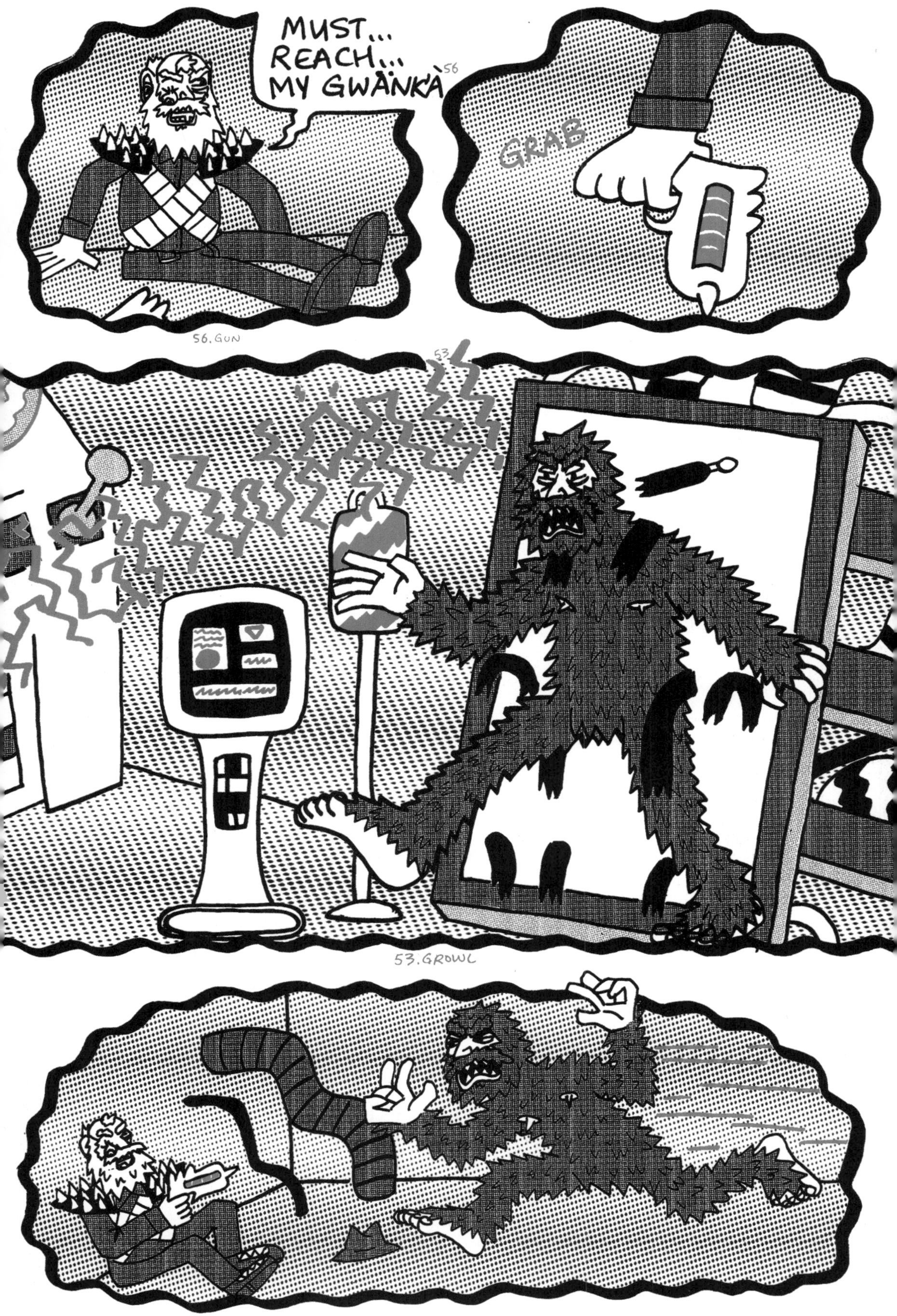
MUST... REACH... MY GWÄNKÀ[56]
GRAB
56. GUN
[53]
53. GROWL

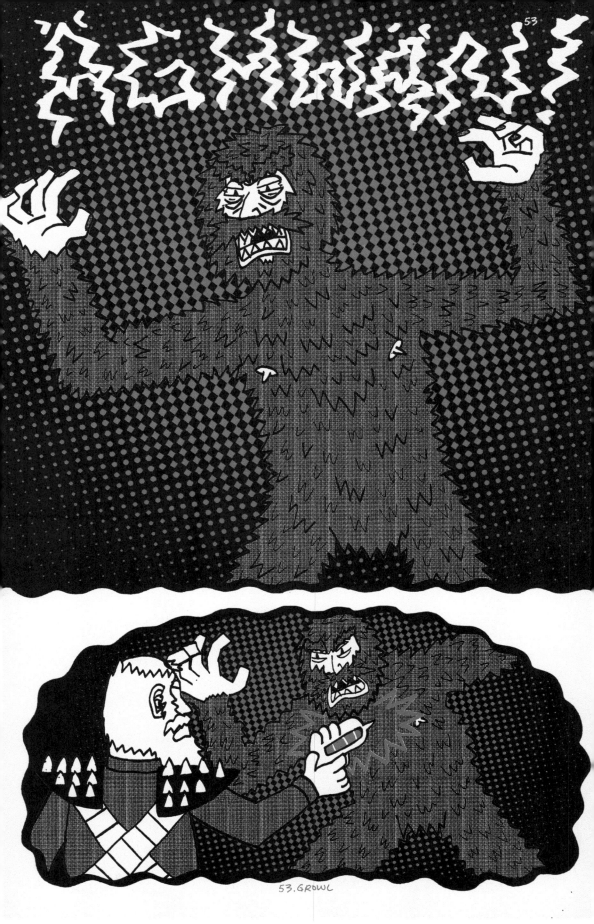

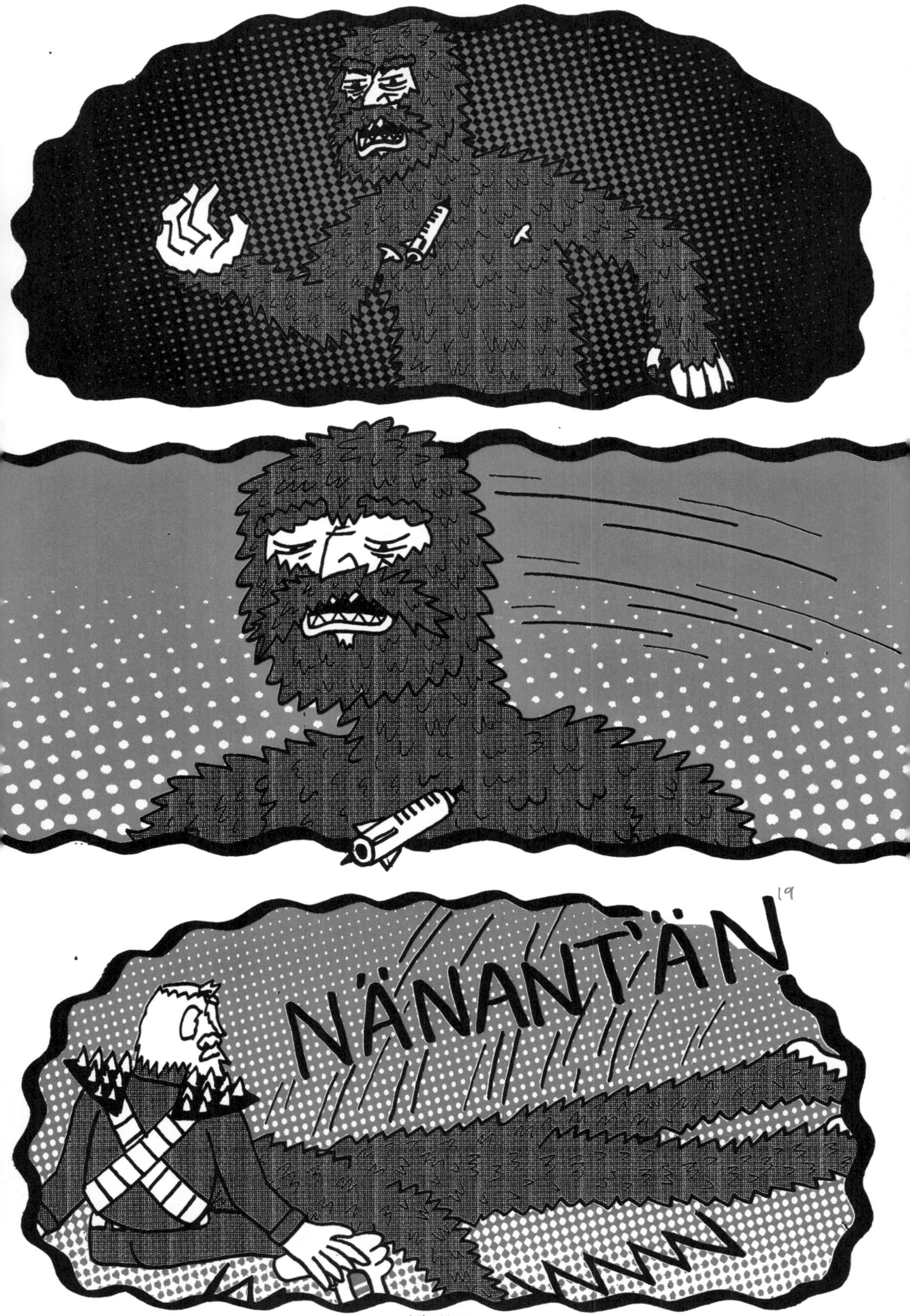
NÄNANT'ÄN
19

19. HIT

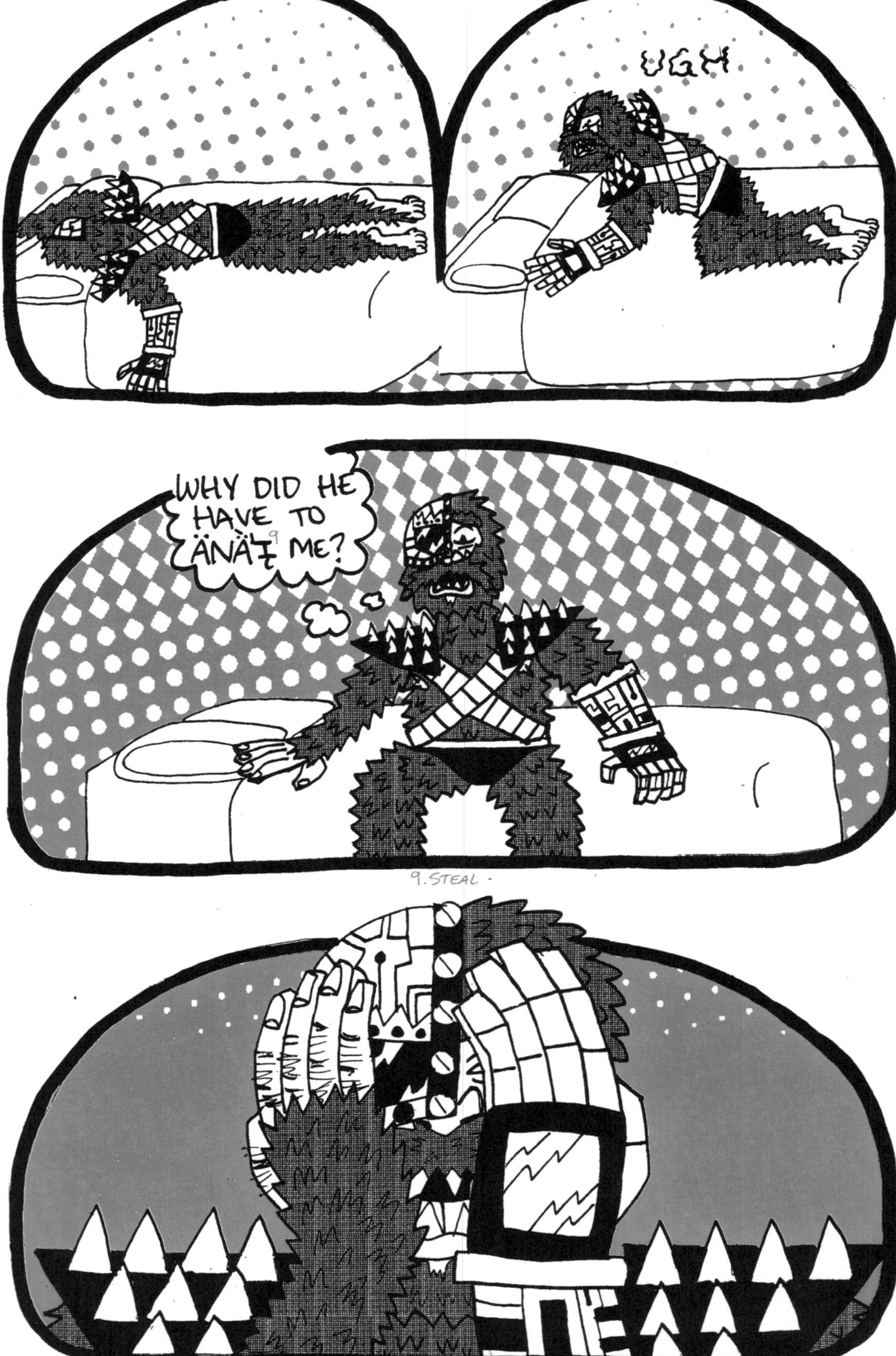
UGH
WHY DID HE HAVE TO ÄNÄZ[9] ME?
9. STEAL -

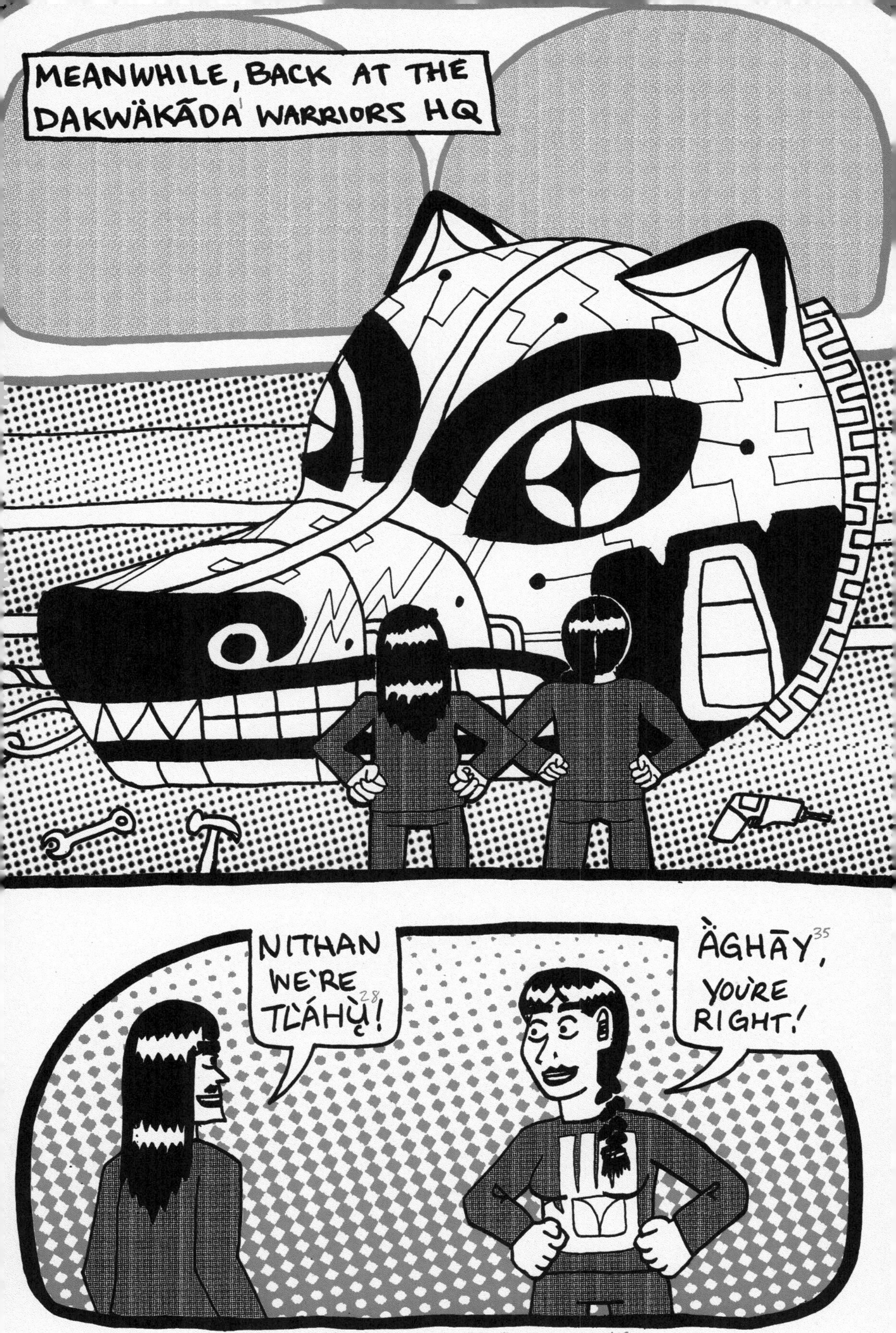
MEANWHILE, BACK AT THE DAKWÄKĀDA[1] WARRIORS HQ
NITHAN WE'RE TŁ'ÁHŲ̀[28]!
ÀGHĀY[35], YOU'RE RIGHT!

1. HIGH CACHE PLACE 31. THINK 28. FINISHED 35. YES

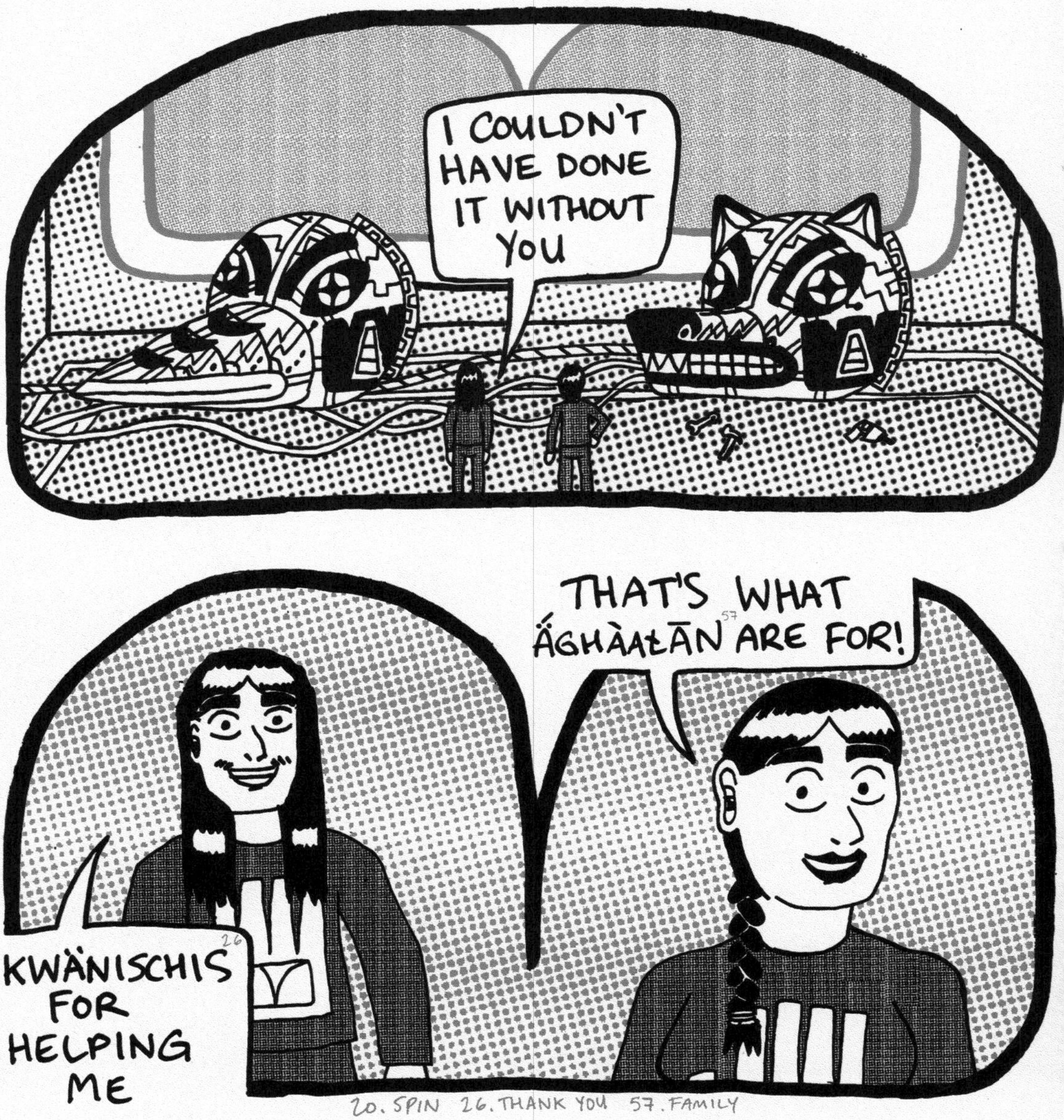

I COULDN'T HAVE DONE IT WITHOUT YOU
KWÄNISCHIS[26] FOR HELPING ME
THAT'S WHAT ÁGHÀAŁĀN[57] ARE FOR!

20. SPIN 26. THANK YOU 57. FAMILY

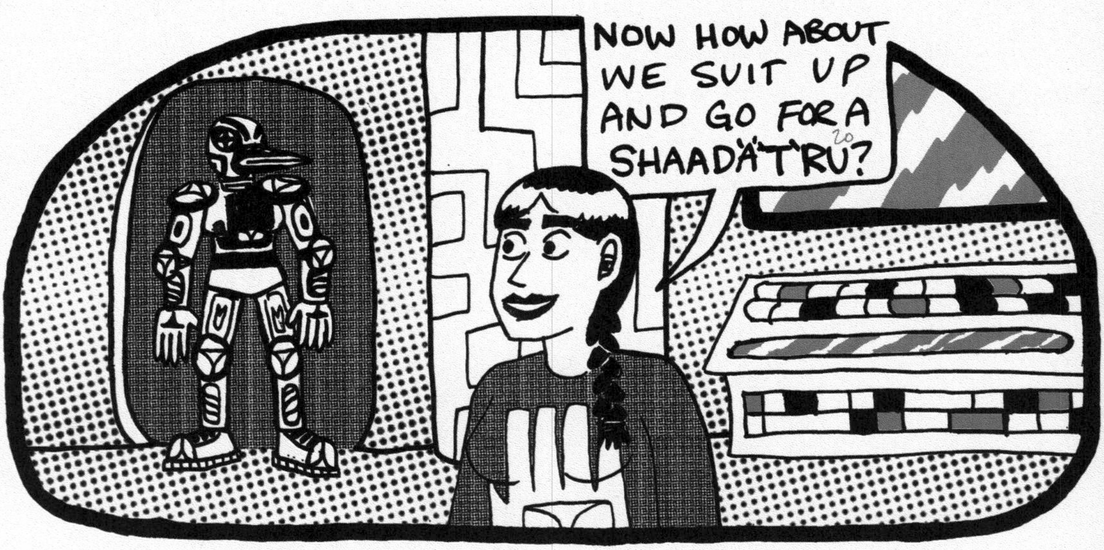

NOW HOW ABOUT WE SUIT UP AND GO FOR A SHAADÄT'RU[20]?

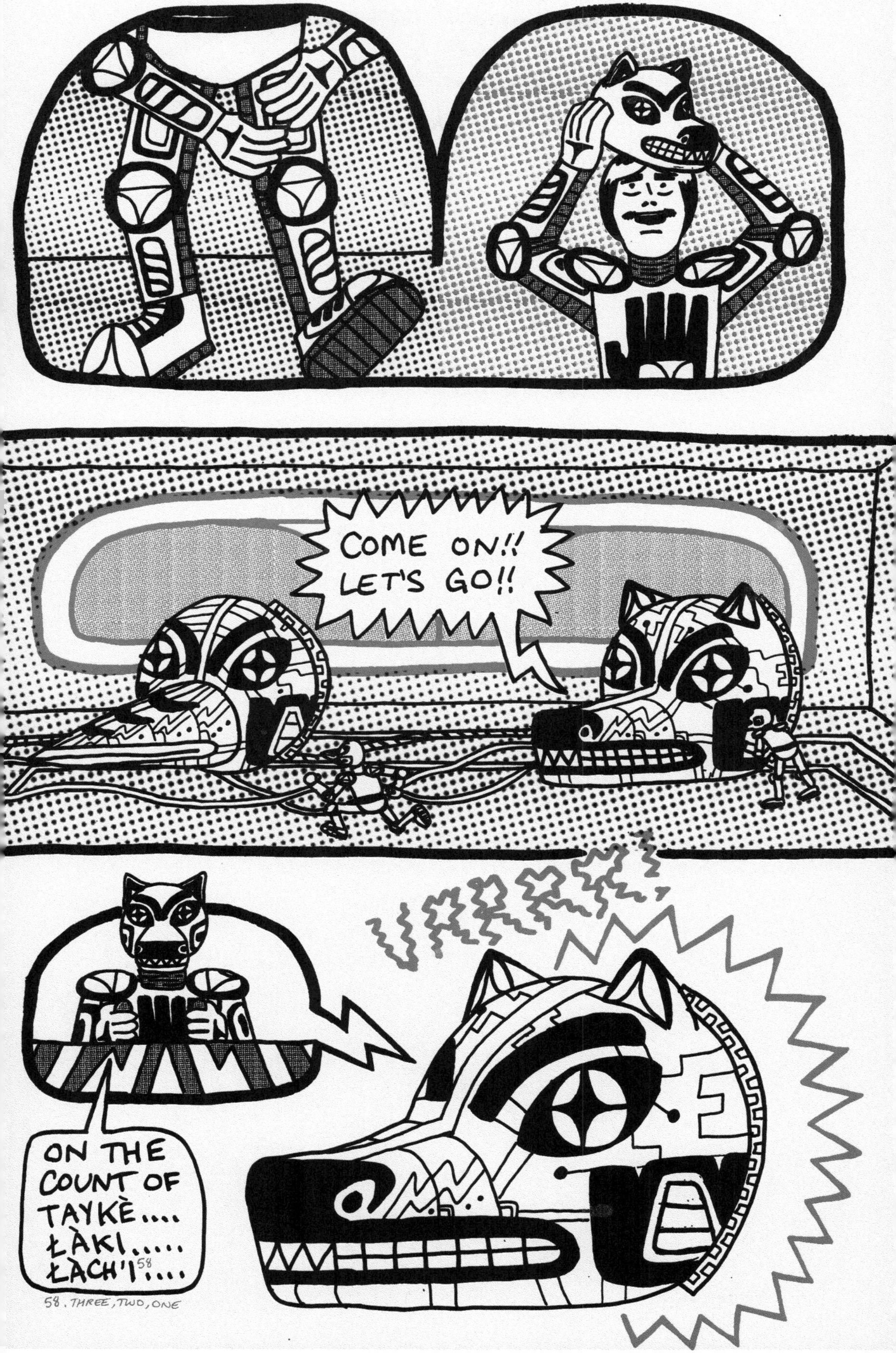
COME ON!! LET'S GO!!
ON THE COUNT OF TAYKÈ.... ŁÀKI..... ŁACH'I[58]....

58. THREE, TWO, ONE

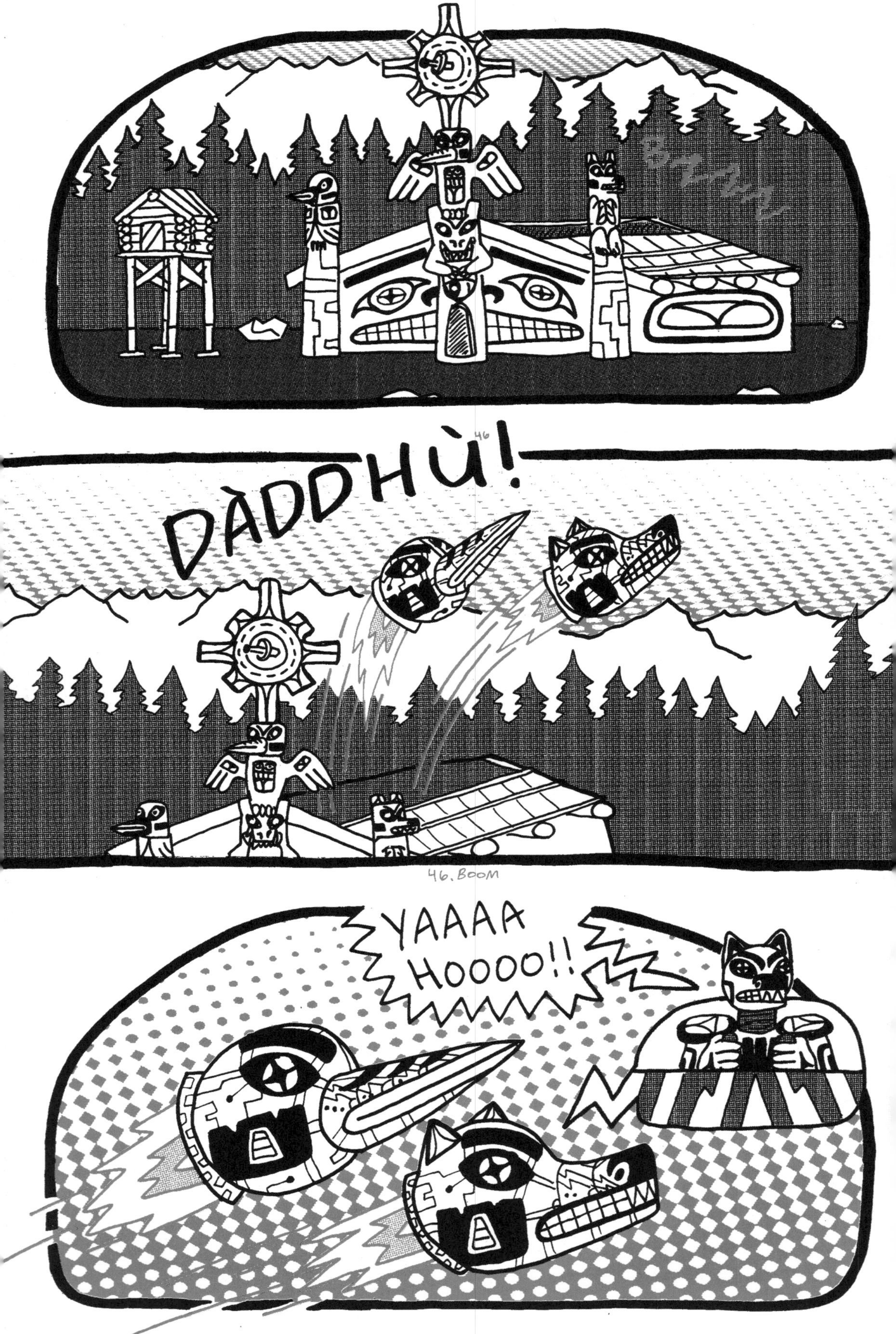
BZZZZ
DÀDDHÙ!
YAAAA HOOOO!!

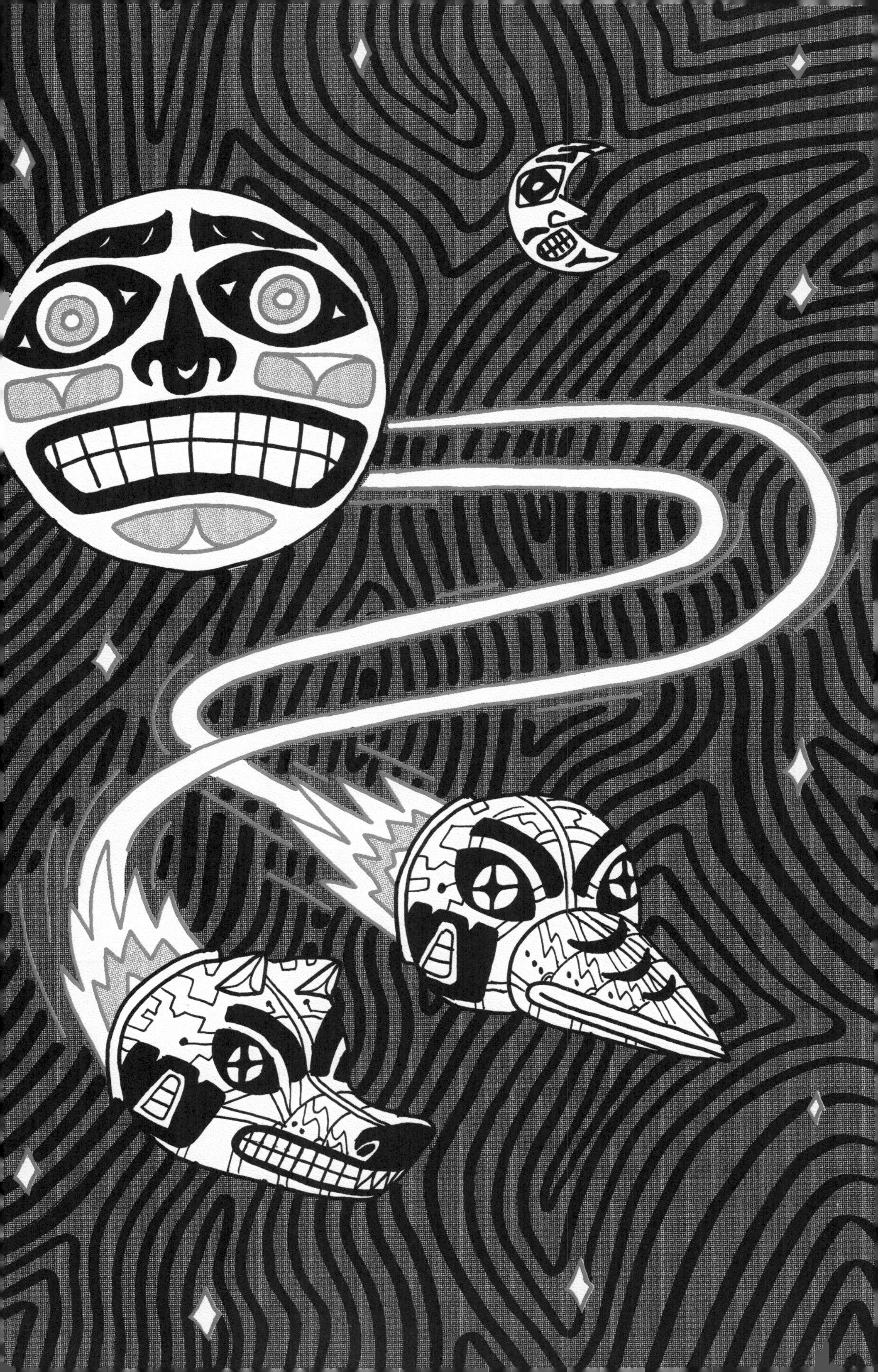

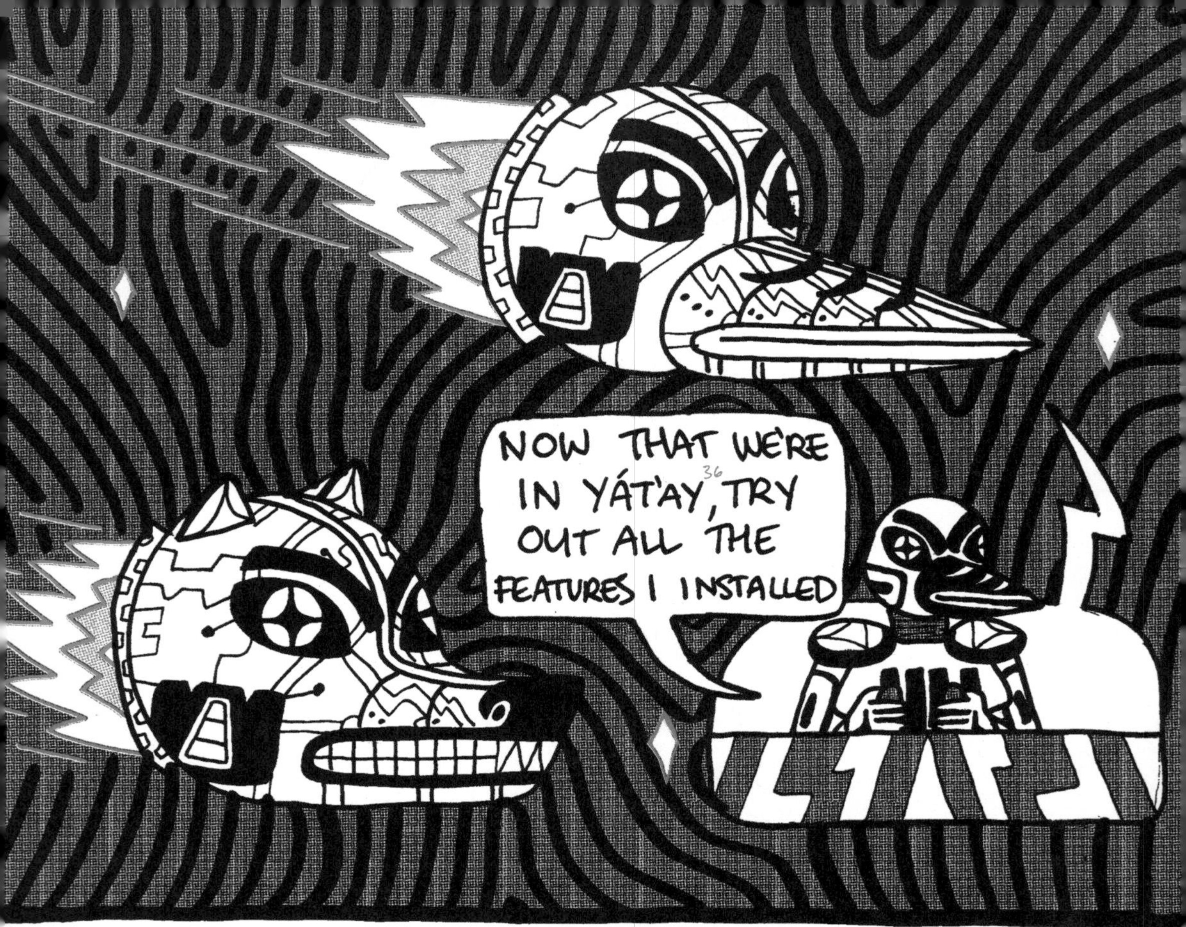
NOW THAT WE'RE IN YÁT'AY, TRY OUT ALL THE FEATURES I INSTALLED

36. SPACE

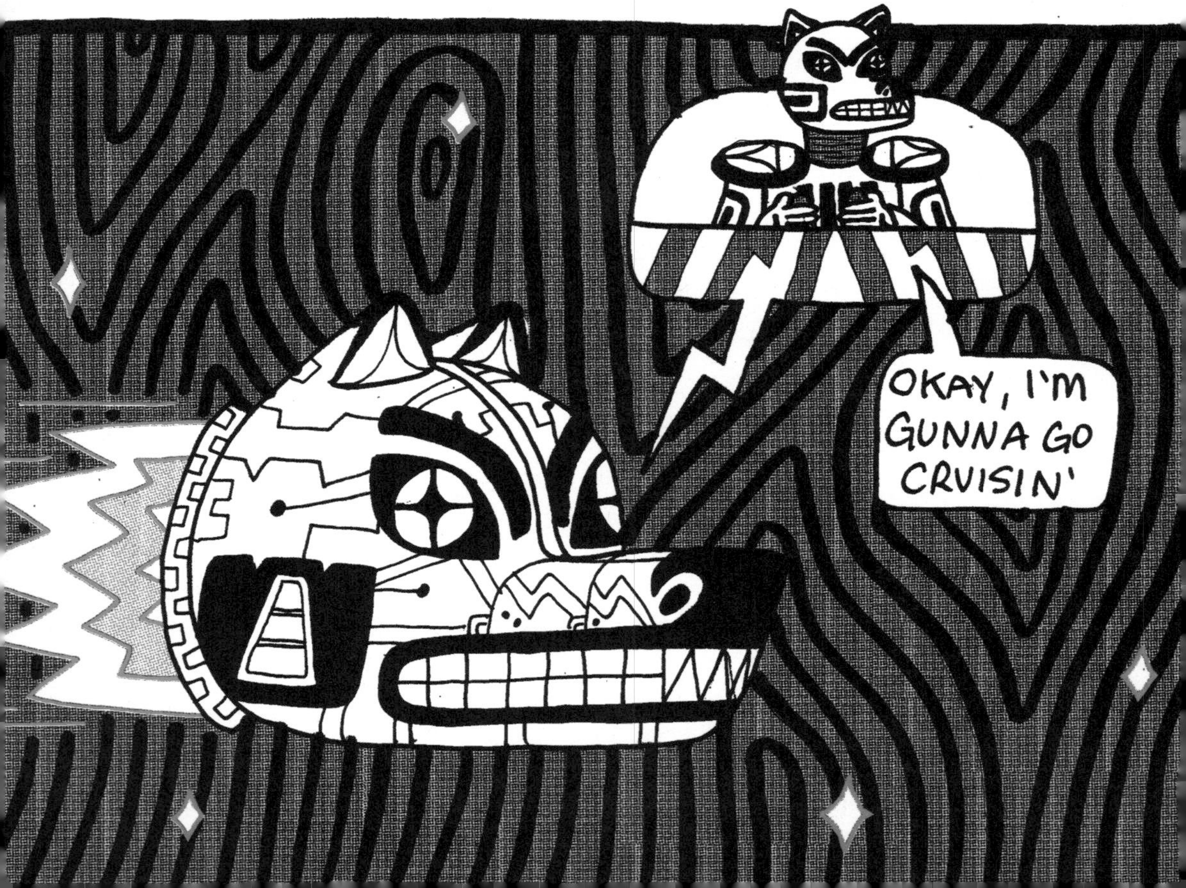
OKAY, I'M GUNNA GO CRUISIN'

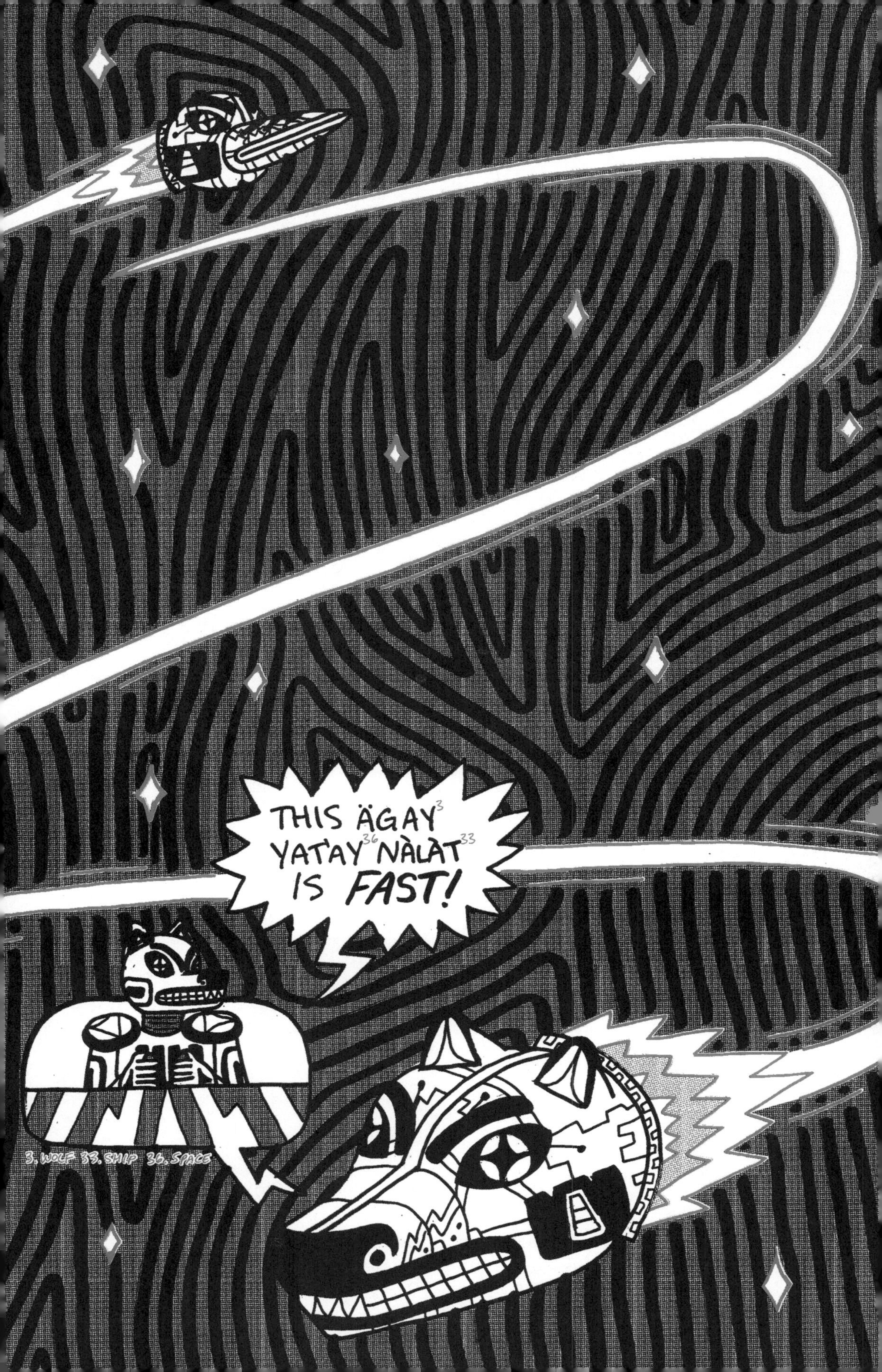
THIS ÄGAY[3] YAT'AY[36] NÀLÀT[33] IS *FAST!*
3. WOLF 33. SHIP 36. SPACE

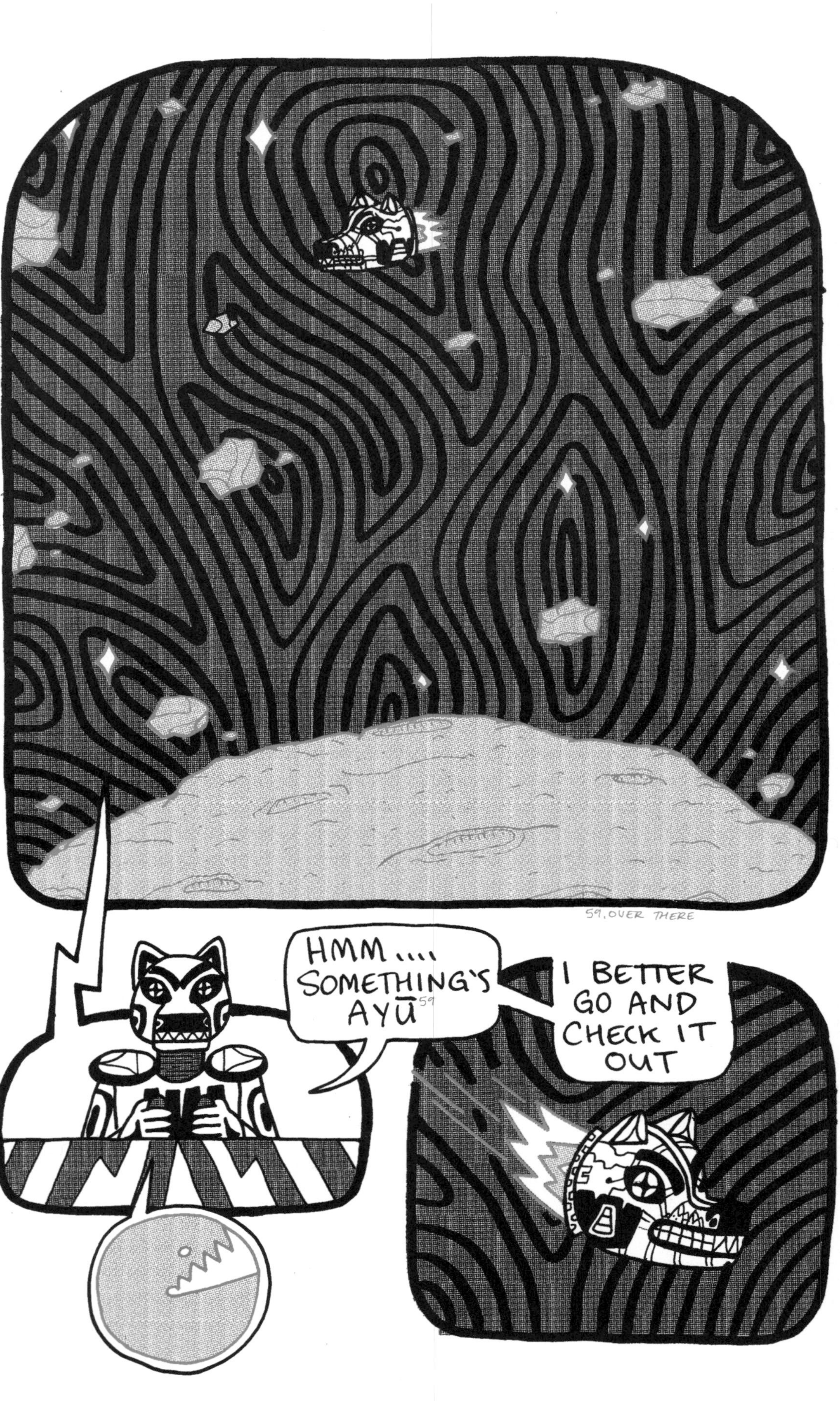
HMM.... SOMETHING'S AYŪ[59]
I BETTER GO AND CHECK IT OUT

59. OVER THERE

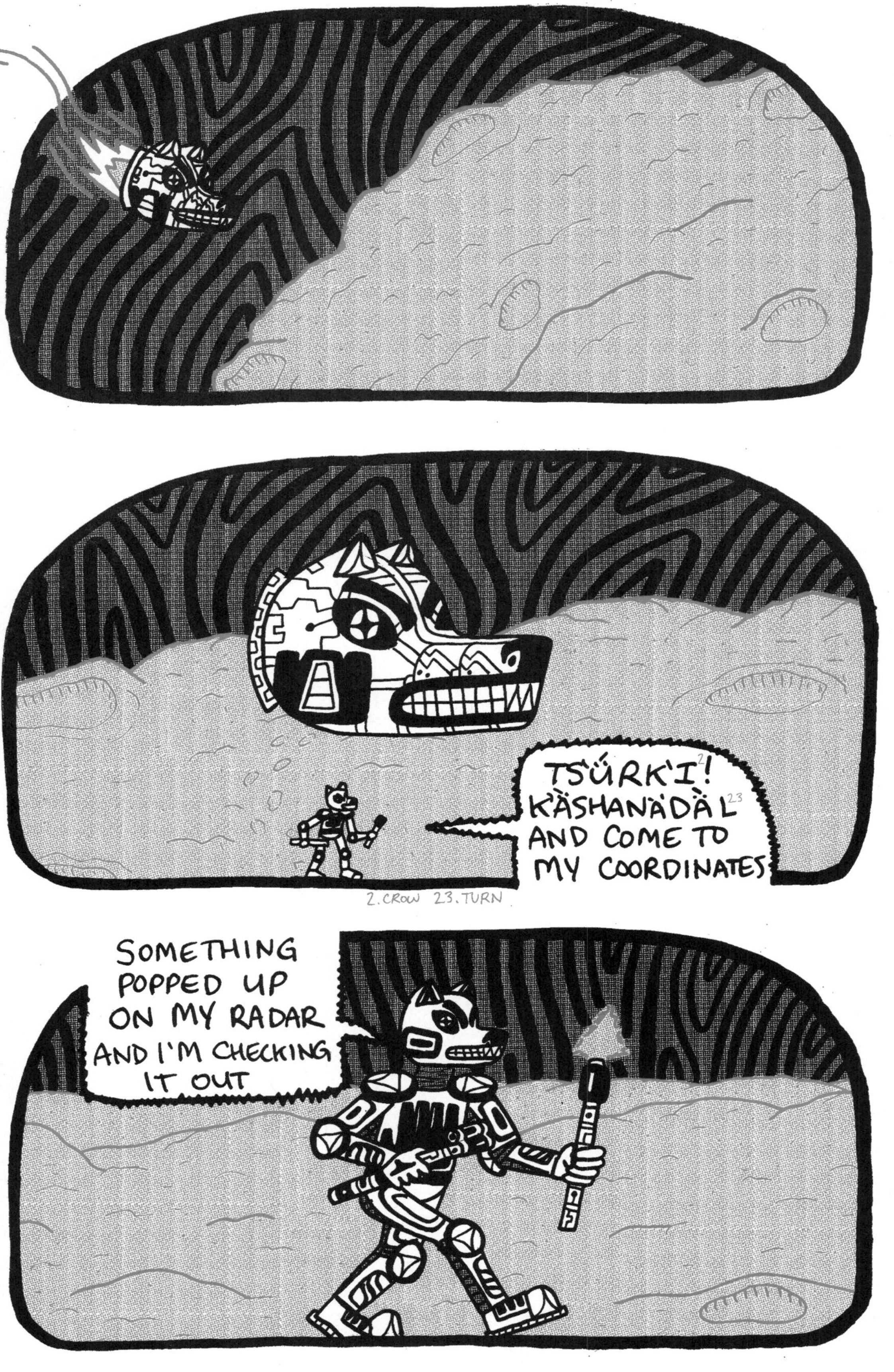
TŠŰRK'I[2]!
K'Ä̀SHANÄDÄ̀L[23]
AND COME TO MY COORDINATES
2. CROW 23. TURN
SOMETHING POPPED UP ON MY RADAR AND I'M CHECKING IT OUT

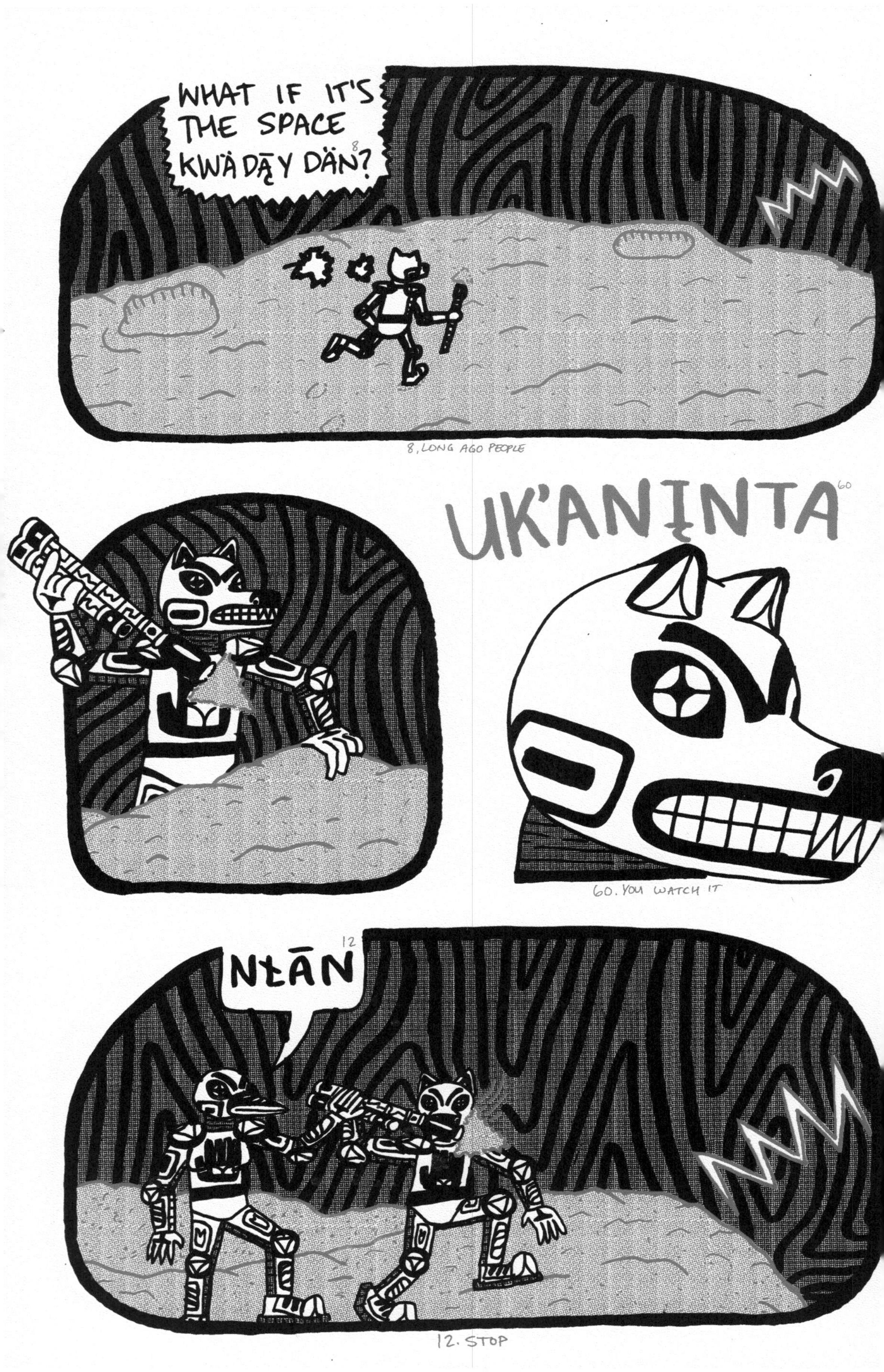
WHAT IF IT'S THE SPACE KWÄDĄY DÄN?[8]
8. LONG AGO PEOPLE
UK'ANĮNTA[60]
60. YOU WATCH IT
NŁĀN[12]
12. STOP

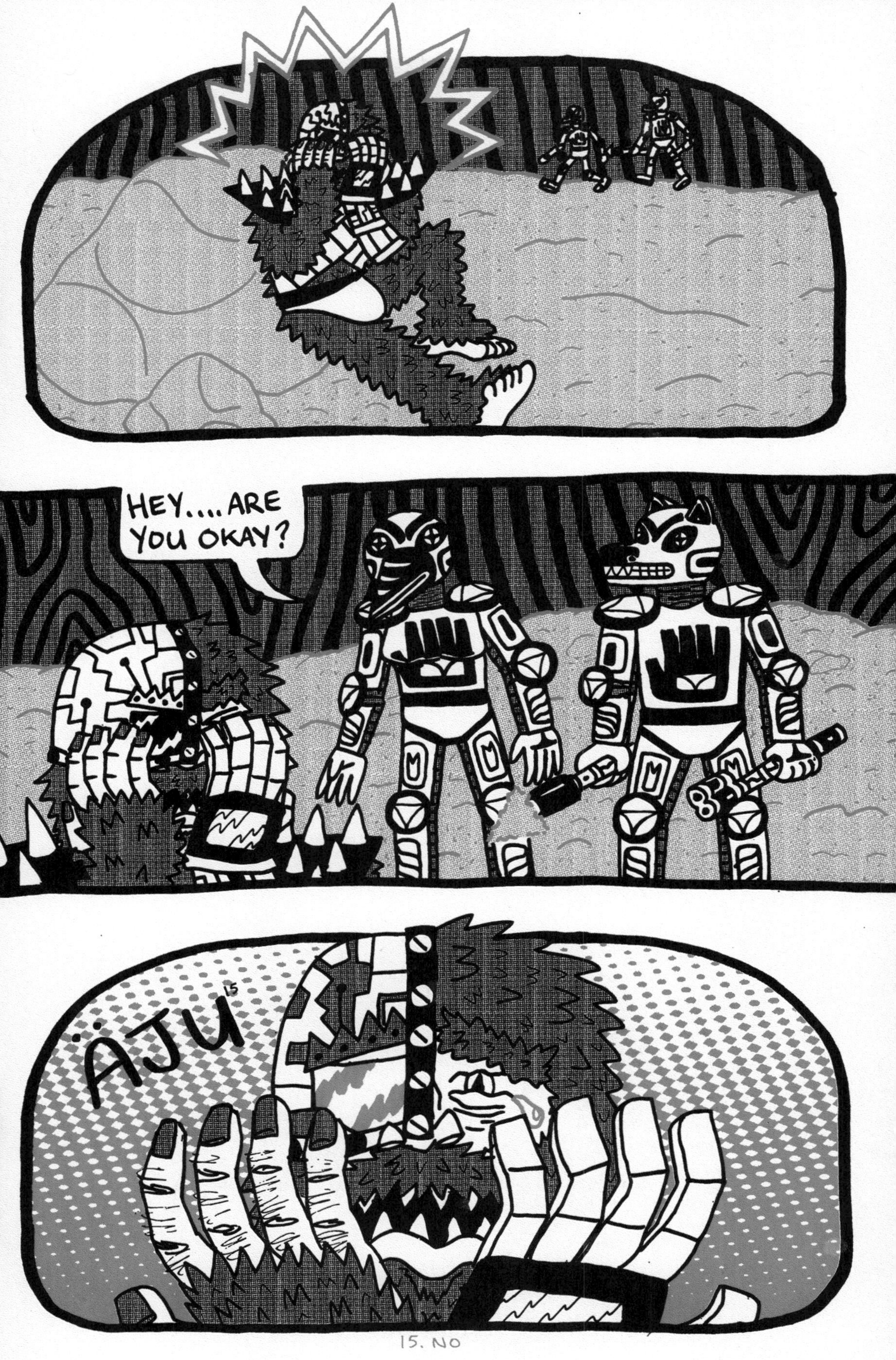
HEY.... ARE YOU OKAY?
ÄJU[15]

15. NO

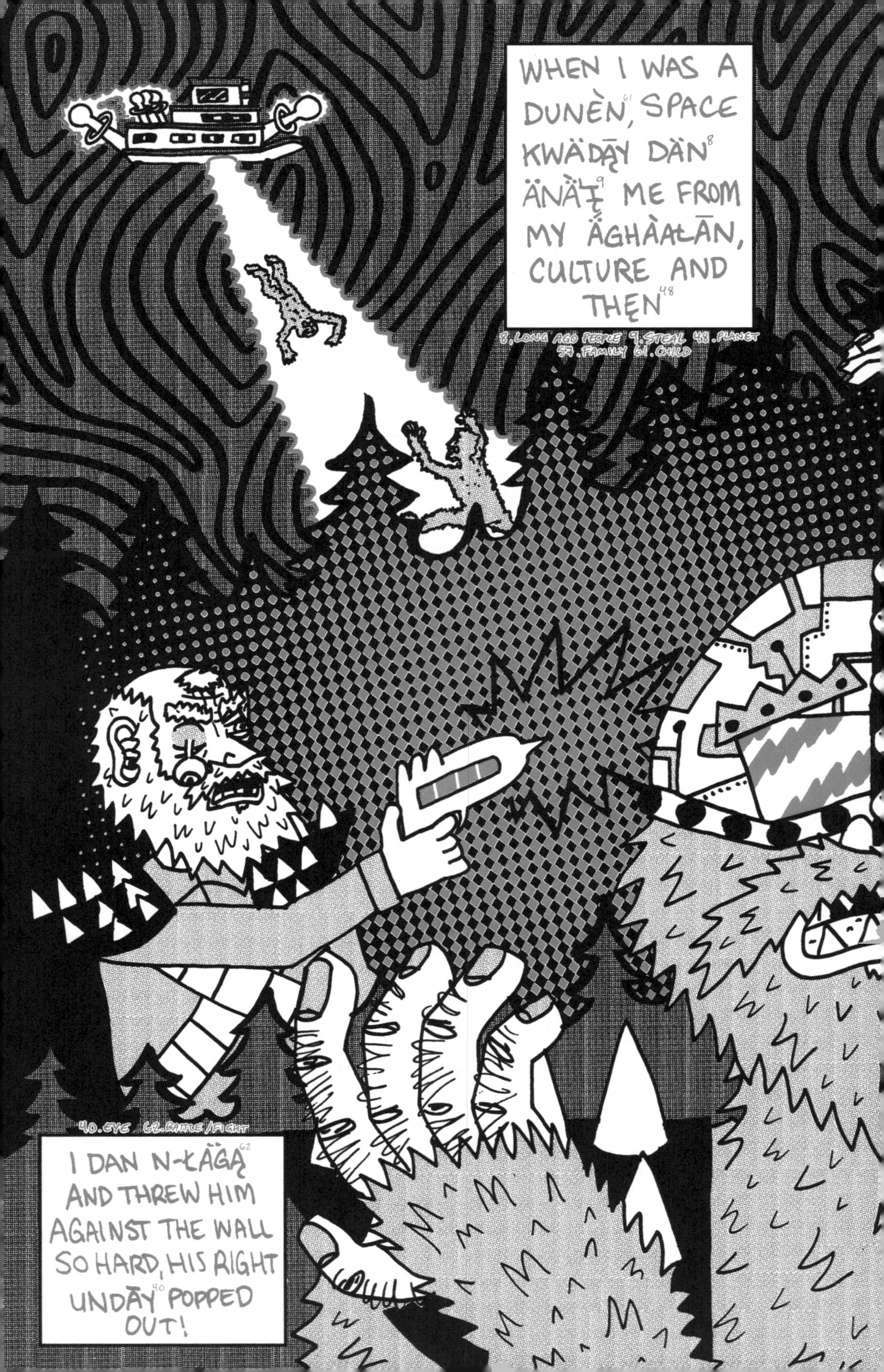
WHEN I WAS A DUNÈN,[61] SPACE KWÄDĄY DÄN[8] ÄNÄ̀Ł[9] ME FROM MY ĀGHÀAŁĀN, CULTURE AND THẸN[48]
8. LONG AGO PEOPLE 9. STEAL 48. PLANET
57. FAMILY 61. CHILD
40. EYE 62. BATTLE/FIGHT
I DAN N-ŁÄGĄ[62] AND THREW HIM AGAINST THE WALL SO HARD, HIS RIGHT UNDĀY[40] POPPED OUT!

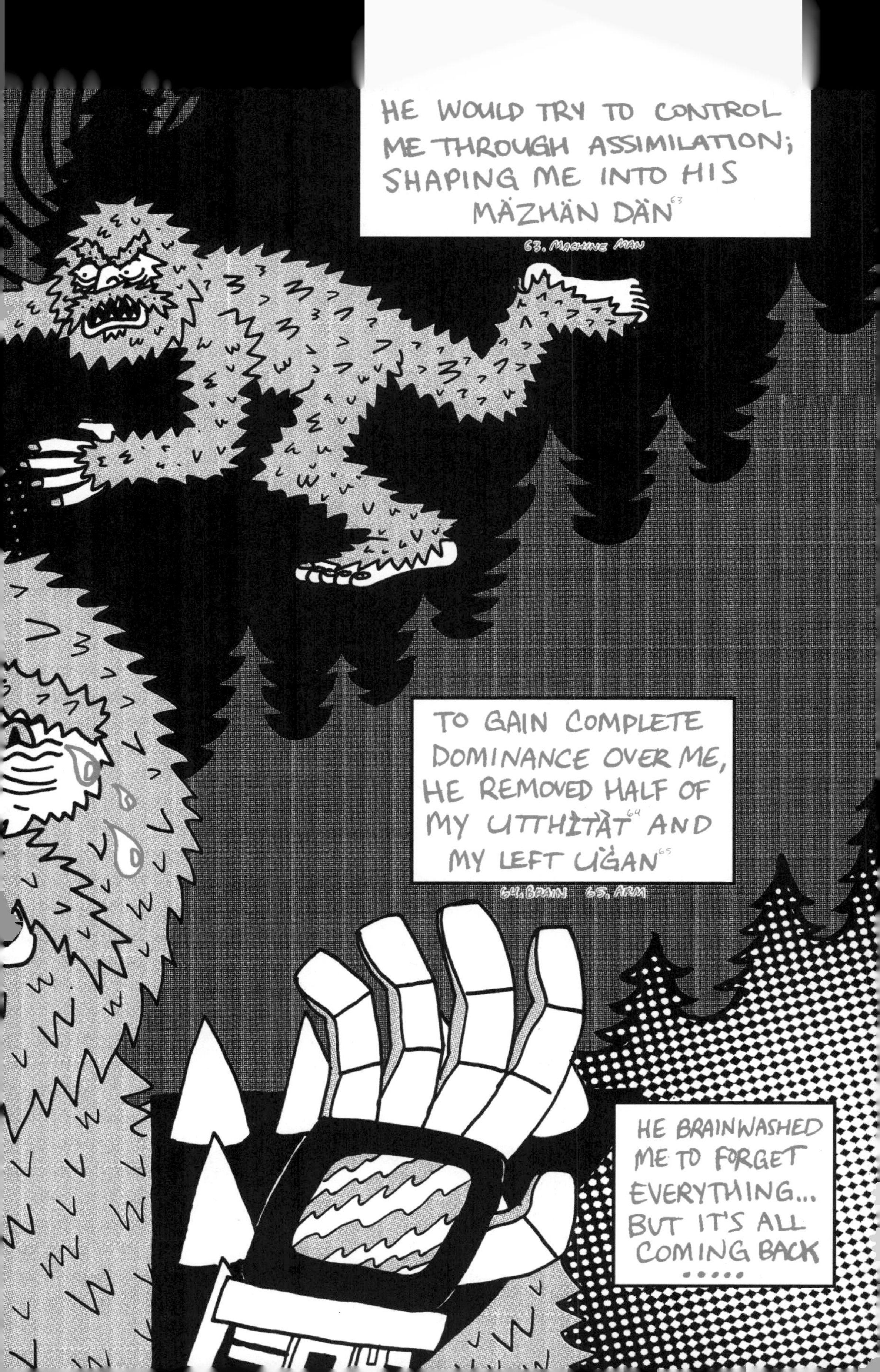
HE WOULD TRY TO CONTROL ME THROUGH ASSIMILATION; SHAPING ME INTO HIS MÄZHÄN DÄN[63]
63. MACHINE MAN
TO GAIN COMPLETE DOMINANCE OVER ME, HE REMOVED HALF OF MY UTTHITÄT[64] AND MY LEFT UGAN[65]
64. BRAIN 65. ARM
HE BRAINWASHED ME TO FORGET EVERYTHING... BUT IT'S ALL COMING BACK .....

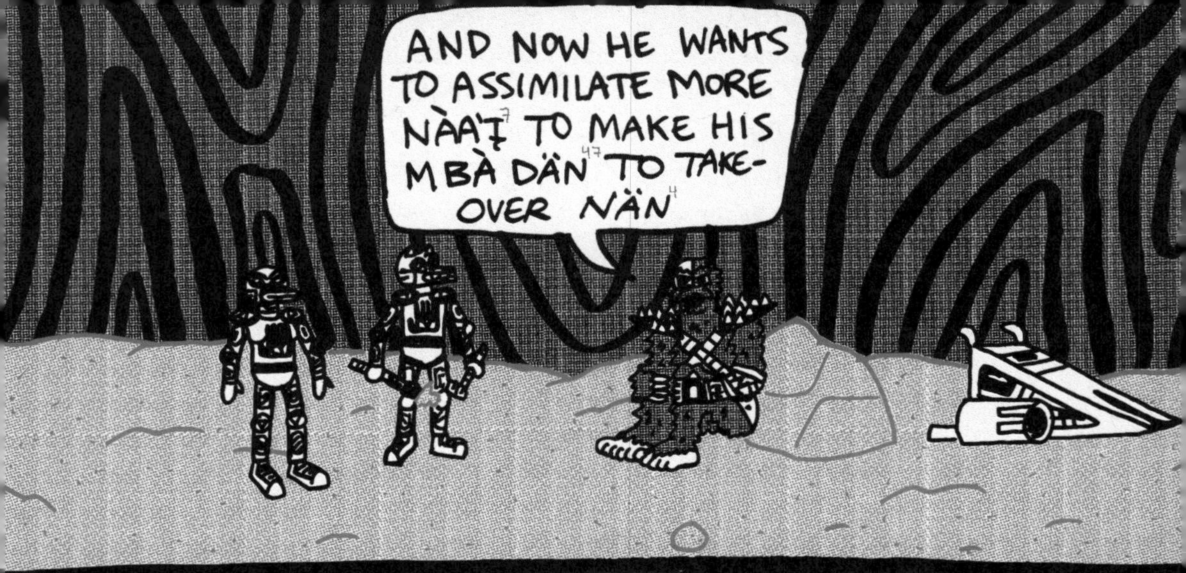
AND NOW HE WANTS TO ASSIMILATE MORE NÀA'Į[7] TO MAKE HIS MBÀ DÄN[47] TO TAKE-OVER NÄN[4]

4. EARTH 7. BUSHMAN 47. ARMY

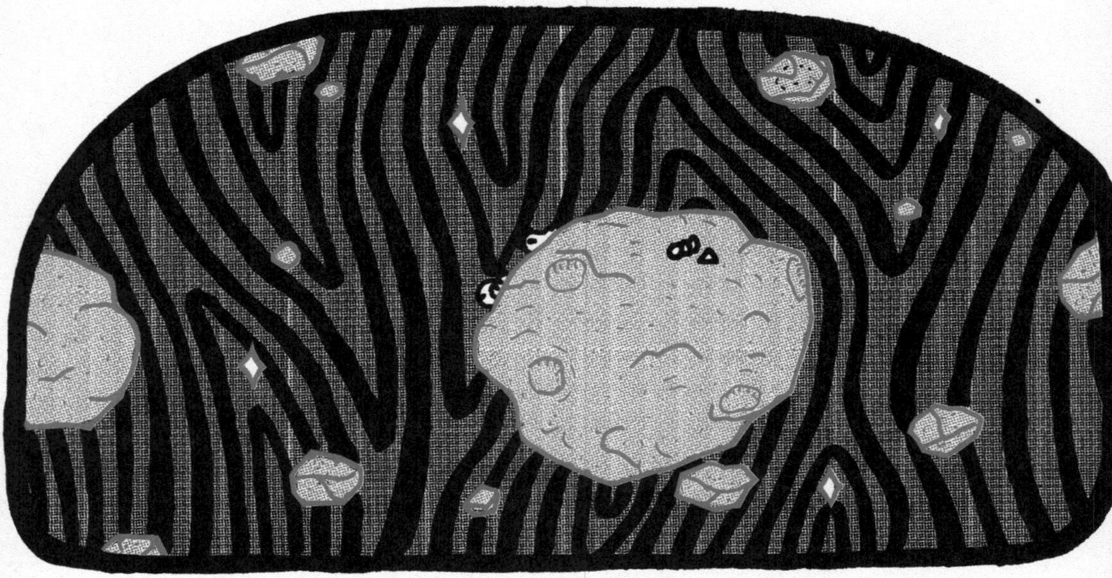

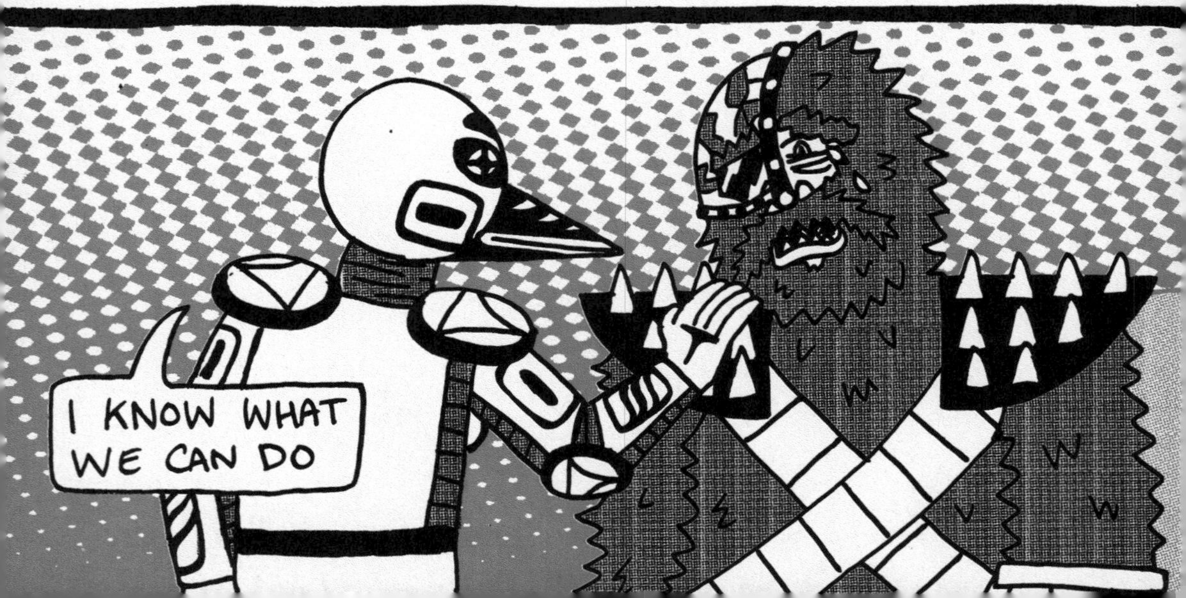
I KNOW WHAT WE CAN DO

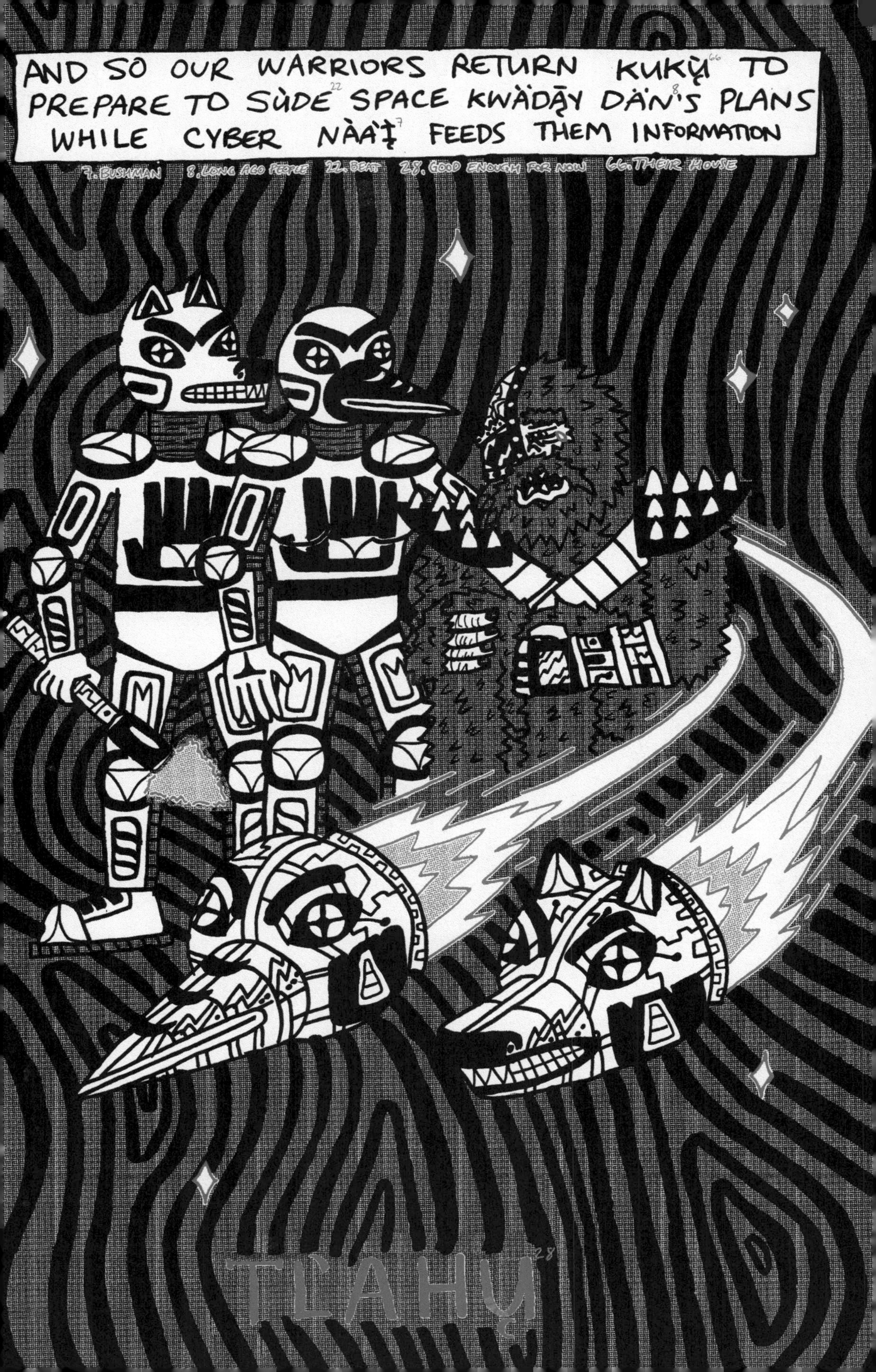
AND SO OUR WARRIORS RETURN KUKŲ̀[66] TO PREPARE TO SÙDE[22] SPACE KWÄDĄ̄Y DÄN[8]'S PLANS WHILE CYBER NÀÀ'Į̄[7] FEEDS THEM INFORMATION
7. BUSHMAN 8. LONG AGO PEOPLE 22. BEAT 28. GOOD ENOUGH FOR NOW 66. THEIR HOUSE
TL'AHŲ[28]

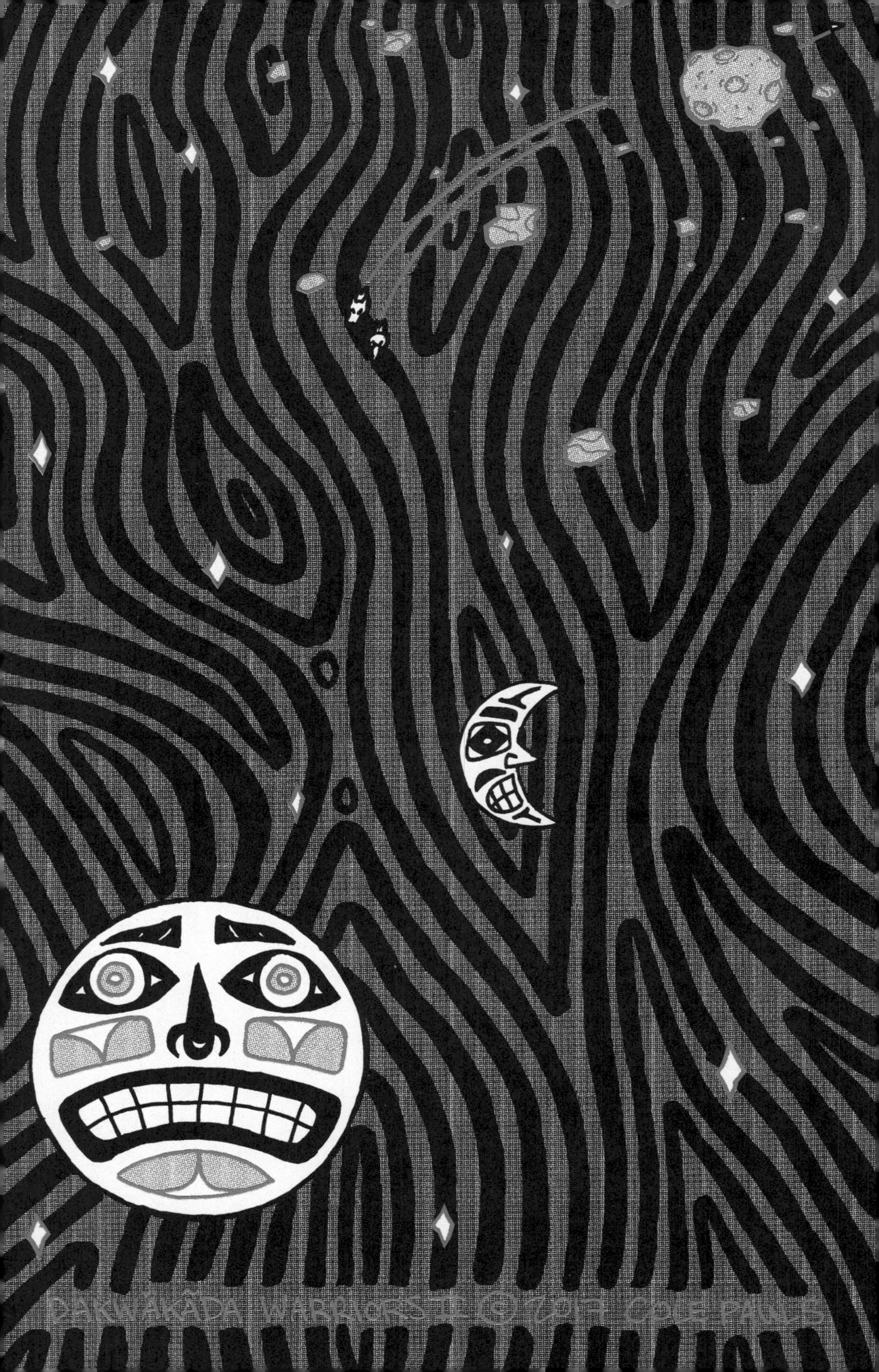
DAKWÄKÃDA WARRIORS II © 2019 COLE PAWLS

DAKWÄKÃDA WARRIORS III

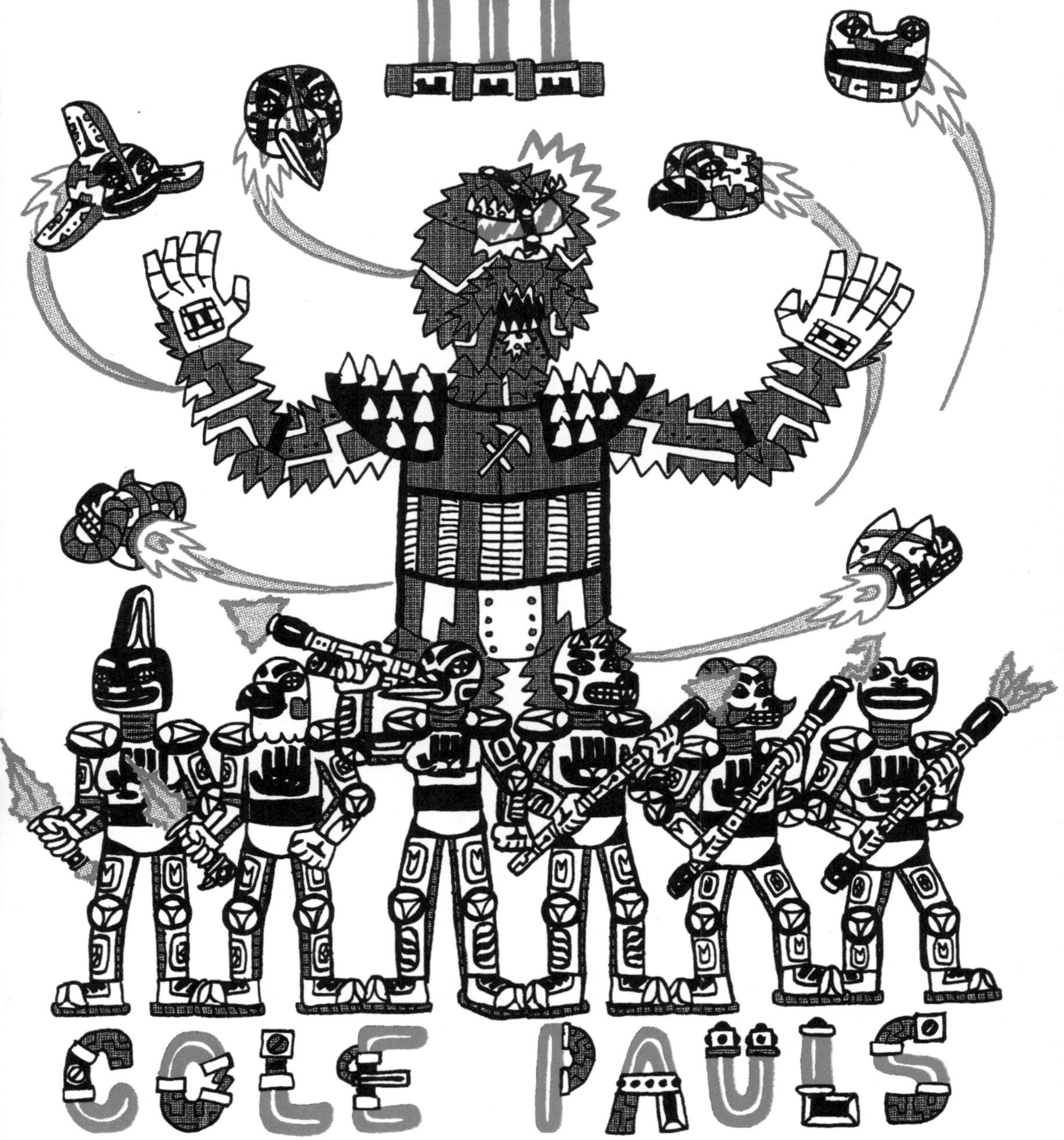

COLE PAULS

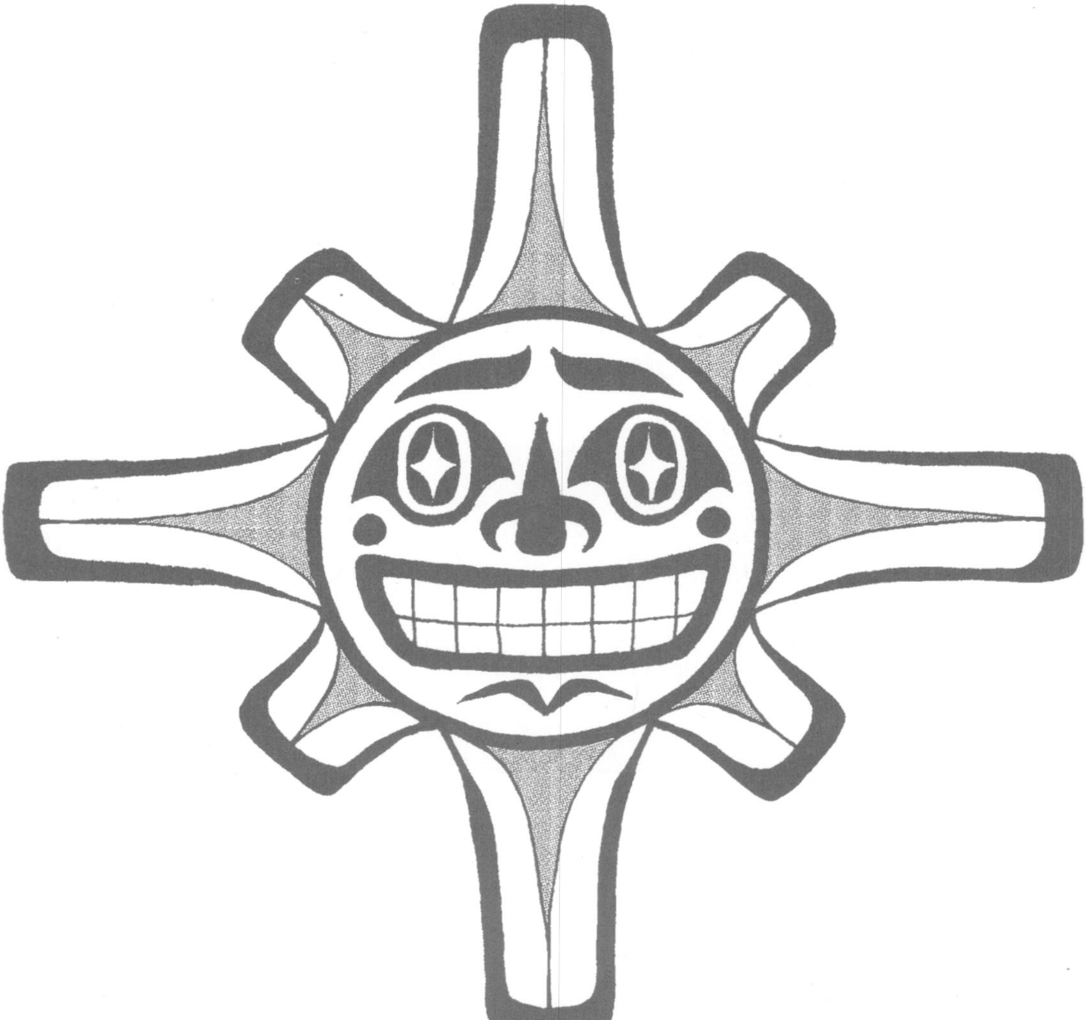

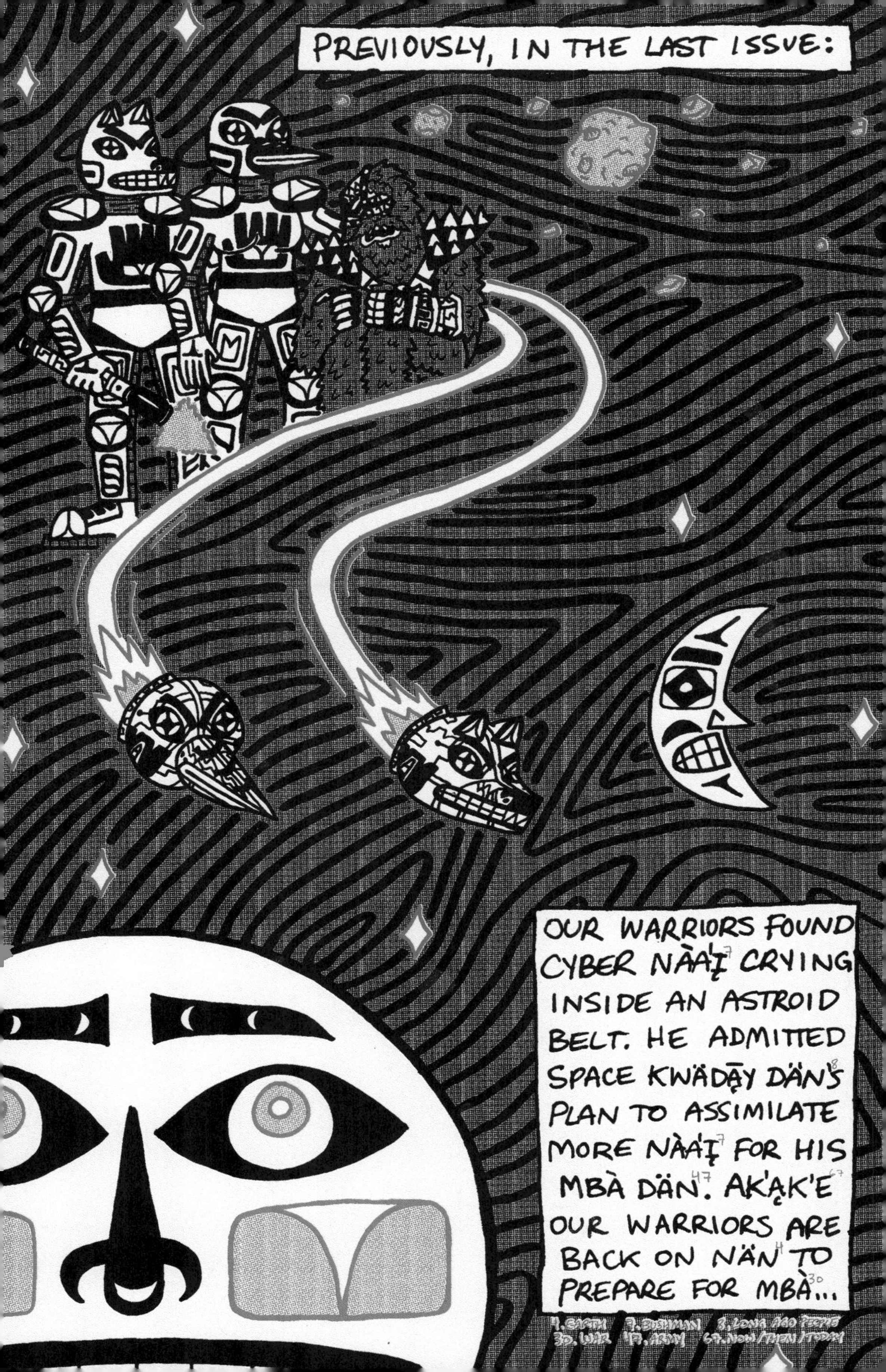
PREVIOUSLY, IN THE LAST ISSUE:
OUR WARRIORS FOUND CYBER NÀĄ̀Į[7] CRYING INSIDE AN ASTROID BELT. HE ADMITTED SPACE KWÄDĄ̈Y DÄN'S[8] PLAN TO ASSIMILATE MORE NÀĄ̀Į[7] FOR HIS MBÀ DÄN[47]. AKĄ̀K'E[67] OUR WARRIORS ARE BACK ON NÄN[4] TO PREPARE FOR MBÀ[30]...
4. EARTH 7. BUSHMAN 8. LONG AGO PEOPLE
30. WAR 47. ARMY 67. NOW/THEN/TODAY

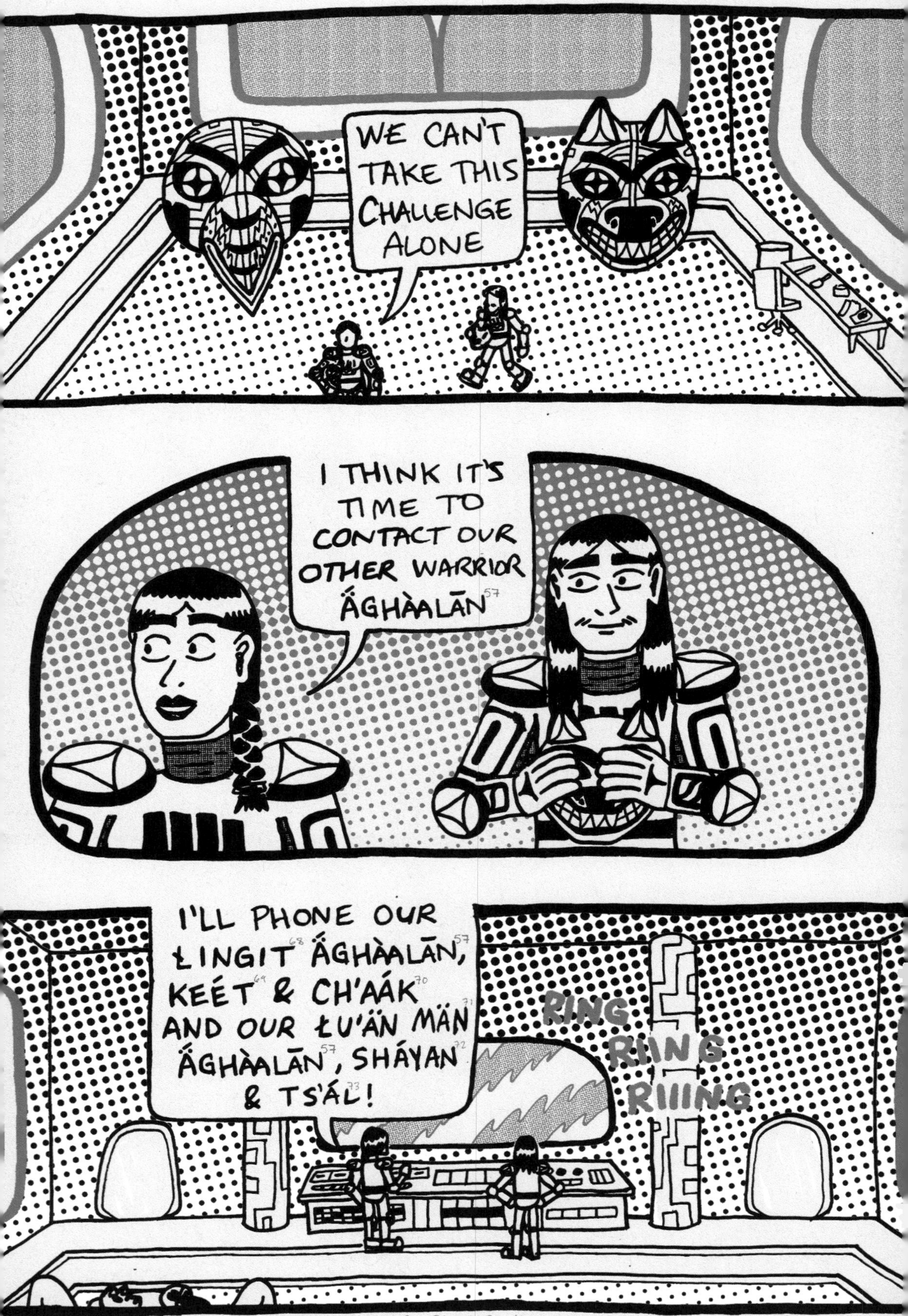
WE CAN'T TAKE THIS CHALLENGE ALONE
I THINK IT'S TIME TO CONTACT OUR OTHER WARRIOR ÁGHÀALĀN[57]
I'LL PHONE OUR ŁINGIT[68] ÁGHÀALĀN[57], KEÉT[69] & CH'AÁK[70] AND OUR ŁU'ÄN MÄN[71] ÁGHÀALĀN[57], SHÁYAN[72] & TS'ÁL[73]!
RING
RIING
RIIING

57. FAMILY 68. TLINGIT 69. KILLER WHALE 70. EAGLE 71. KLUANE LAKE/FISH LAKE 72. RAM 73. FROG

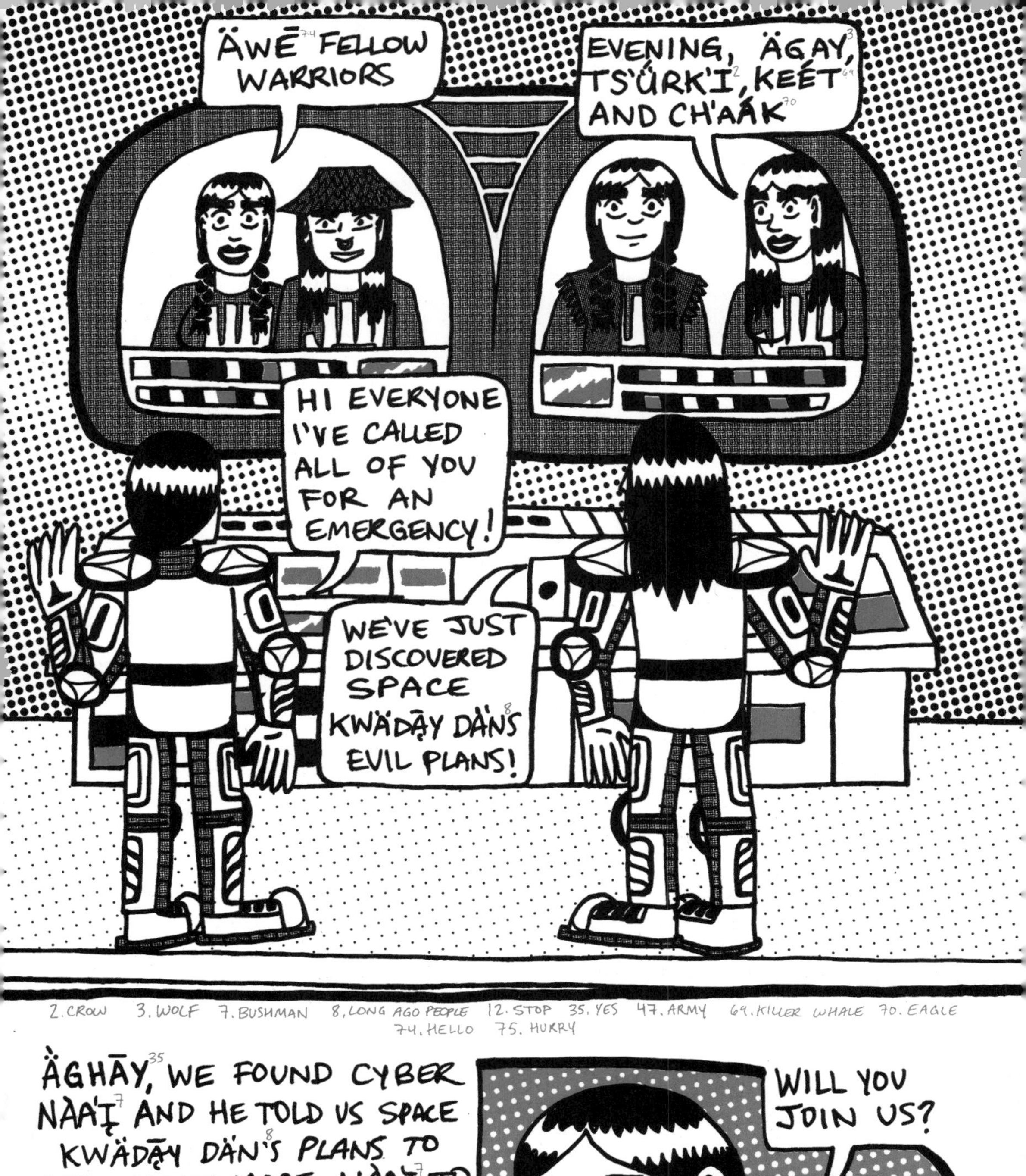
ÄWĒ[74] FELLOW WARRIORS
EVENING, ÄGAY,[3] TS'ÜRK'I,[2] KEÉT[69] AND CH'AÁK[70]
HI EVERYONE I'VE CALLED ALL OF YOU FOR AN EMERGENCY!
WE'VE JUST DISCOVERED SPACE KWÄDĄY DÄN'S[8] EVIL PLANS!

2. CROW 3. WOLF 7. BUSHMAN 8. LONG AGO PEOPLE 12. STOP 35. YES 47. ARMY 69. KILLER WHALE 70. EAGLE 74. HELLO 75. HURRY

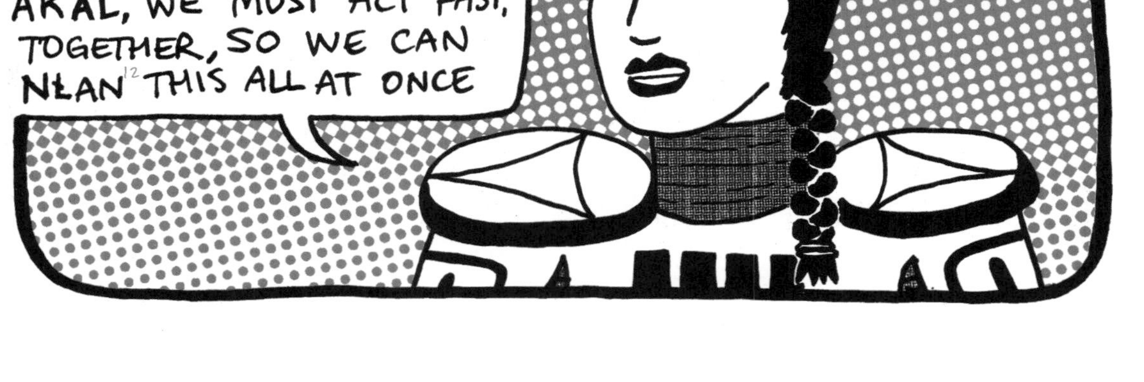
ÀGHĀY,[35] WE FOUND CYBER NÀAĮ[7] AND HE TOLD US SPACE KWÄDĄY DÄN'S[8] PLANS TO ASSIMILATE MORE NÀAĮ[7] TO CREATE HIS MBÀ DÄN![47] ÄK'ÄL,[75] WE MUST ACT FAST, TOGETHER, SO WE CAN NŁAN[12] THIS ALL AT ONCE
WILL YOU JOIN US?

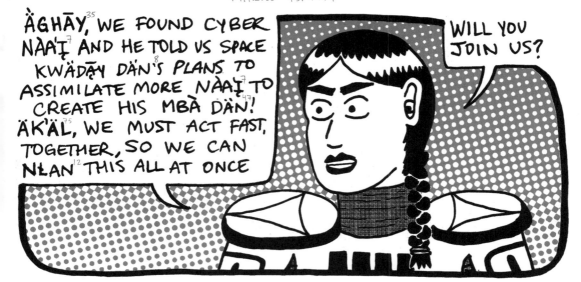

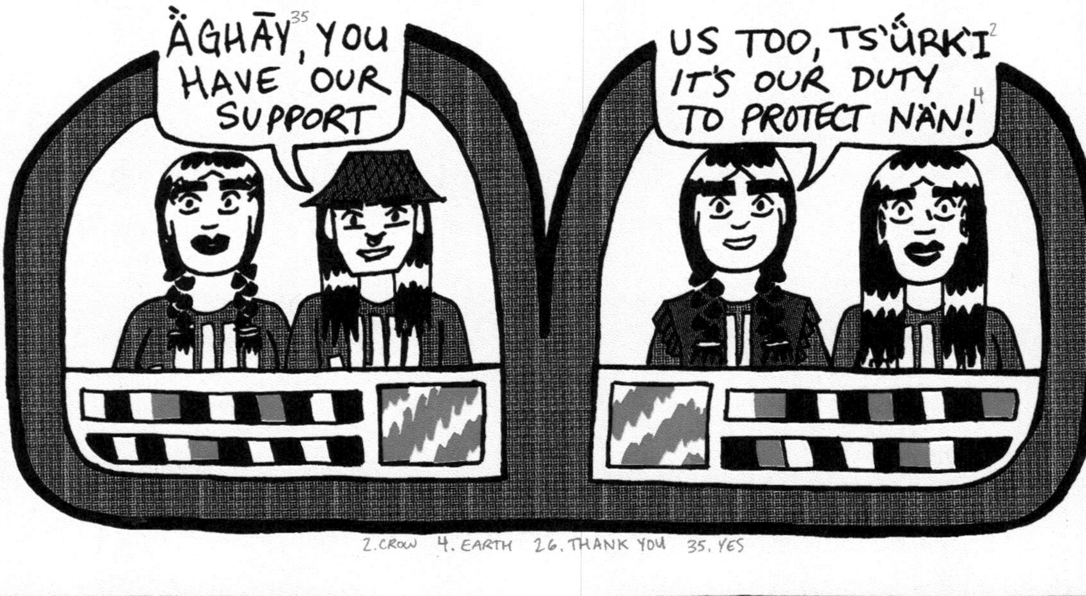
Ä̀GHĀY[35], YOU HAVE OUR SUPPORT
US TOO, TS'ǗRK'I[2] IT'S OUR DUTY TO PROTECT NÄN[4]!

2. CROW 4. EARTH 26. THANK YOU 35. YES

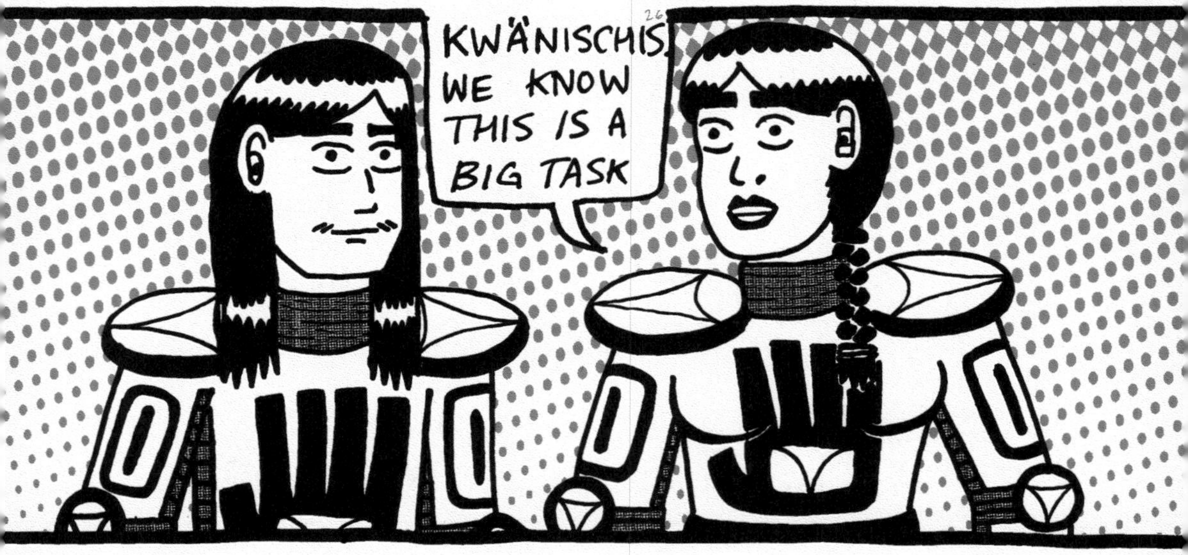
KWÄNISCHIS[26] WE KNOW THIS IS A BIG TASK

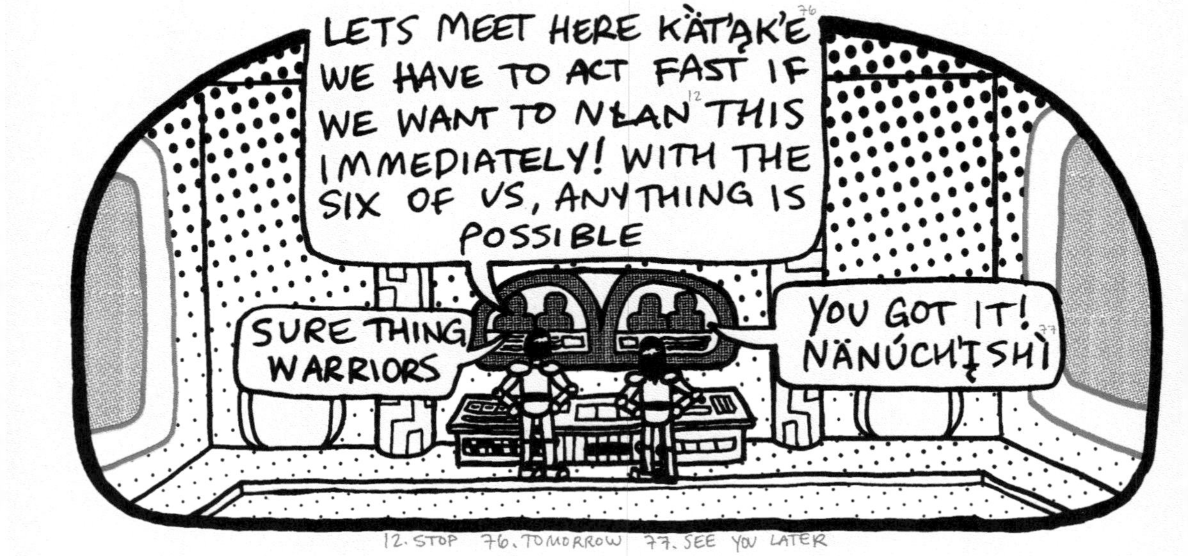
LETS MEET HERE KÄ̀T'ĄK'E[76] WE HAVE TO ACT FAST IF WE WANT TO NŁAN[12] THIS IMMEDIATELY! WITH THE SIX OF US, ANYTHING IS POSSIBLE
SURE THING WARRIORS
YOU GOT IT! NÄNÚCH'ĮSHÌ[77]

12. STOP 76. TOMORROW 77. SEE YOU LATER

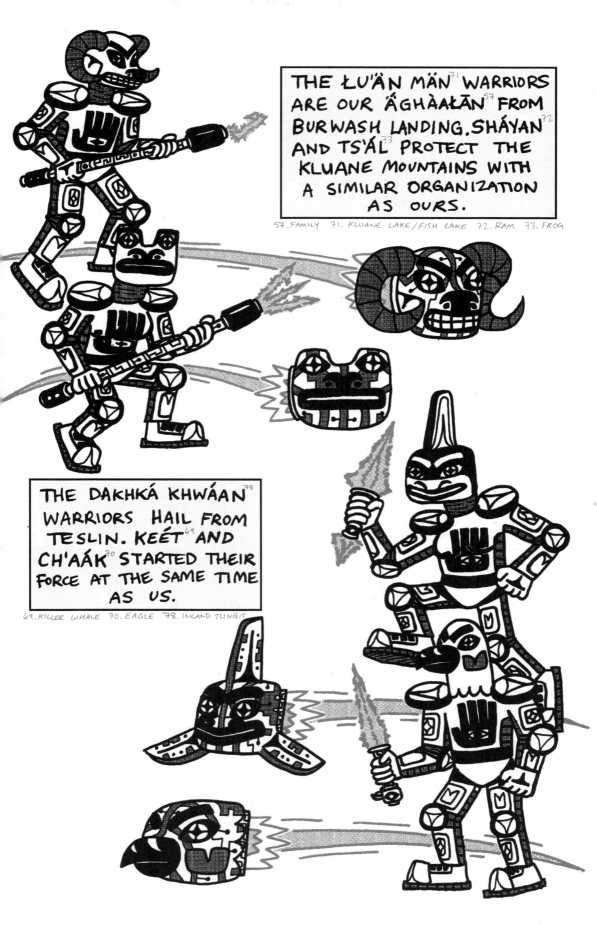

THE ŁU'ÄN MÄN[71] WARRIORS ARE OUR ÁGHÀAŁÄN[57] FROM BURWASH LANDING. SHÁYAN[72] AND TS'ÁL[73] PROTECT THE KLUANE MOUNTAINS WITH A SIMILAR ORGANIZATION AS OURS.

57. FAMILY   71. KLUANE LAKE/FISH LAKE   72. RAM   73. FROG

THE DAKHKÁ KHWÁAN[78] WARRIORS HAIL FROM TESLIN. KEÉT[69] AND CH'AÁK[70] STARTED THEIR FORCE AT THE SAME TIME AS US.

69. KILLER WHALE   70. EAGLE   78. INLAND TLINGIT

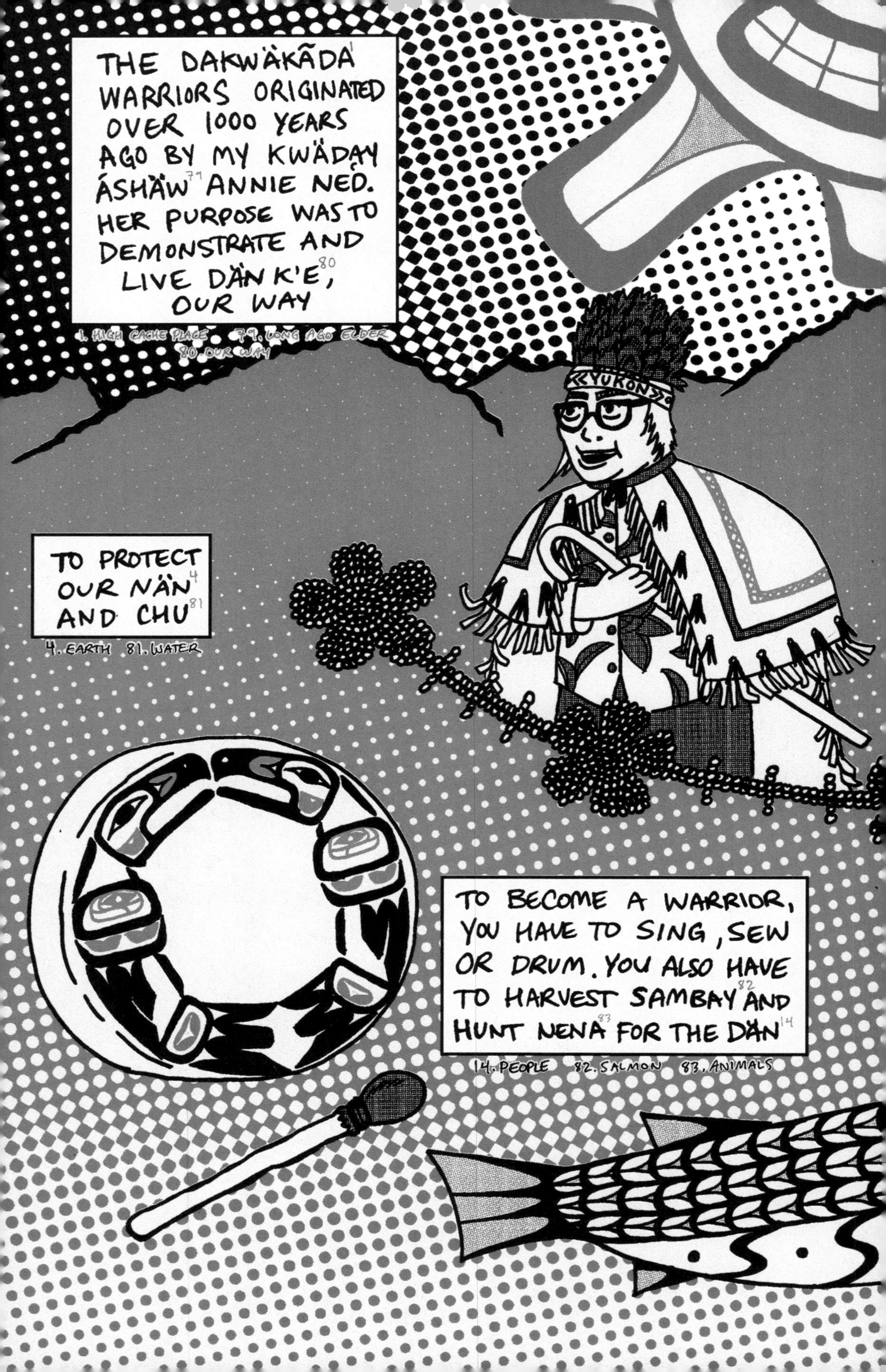
THE DAKWÄKÃDA[1] WARRIORS ORIGINATED OVER 1000 YEARS AGO BY MY KWÄDĄY ÁSHÄW[79] ANNIE NED. HER PURPOSE WAS TO DEMONSTRATE AND LIVE DÄN K'E,[80] OUR WAY
1. HIGH CACHE PLACE 79. LONG AGO ELDER 80. OUR WAY
YUKON
TO PROTECT OUR NÄN[4] AND CHU[81]
4. EARTH 81. WATER
TO BECOME A WARRIOR, YOU HAVE TO SING, SEW OR DRUM. YOU ALSO HAVE TO HARVEST SAMBAY[82] AND HUNT NENA[83] FOR THE DÄN[14]
14. PEOPLE 82. SALMON 83. ANIMALS

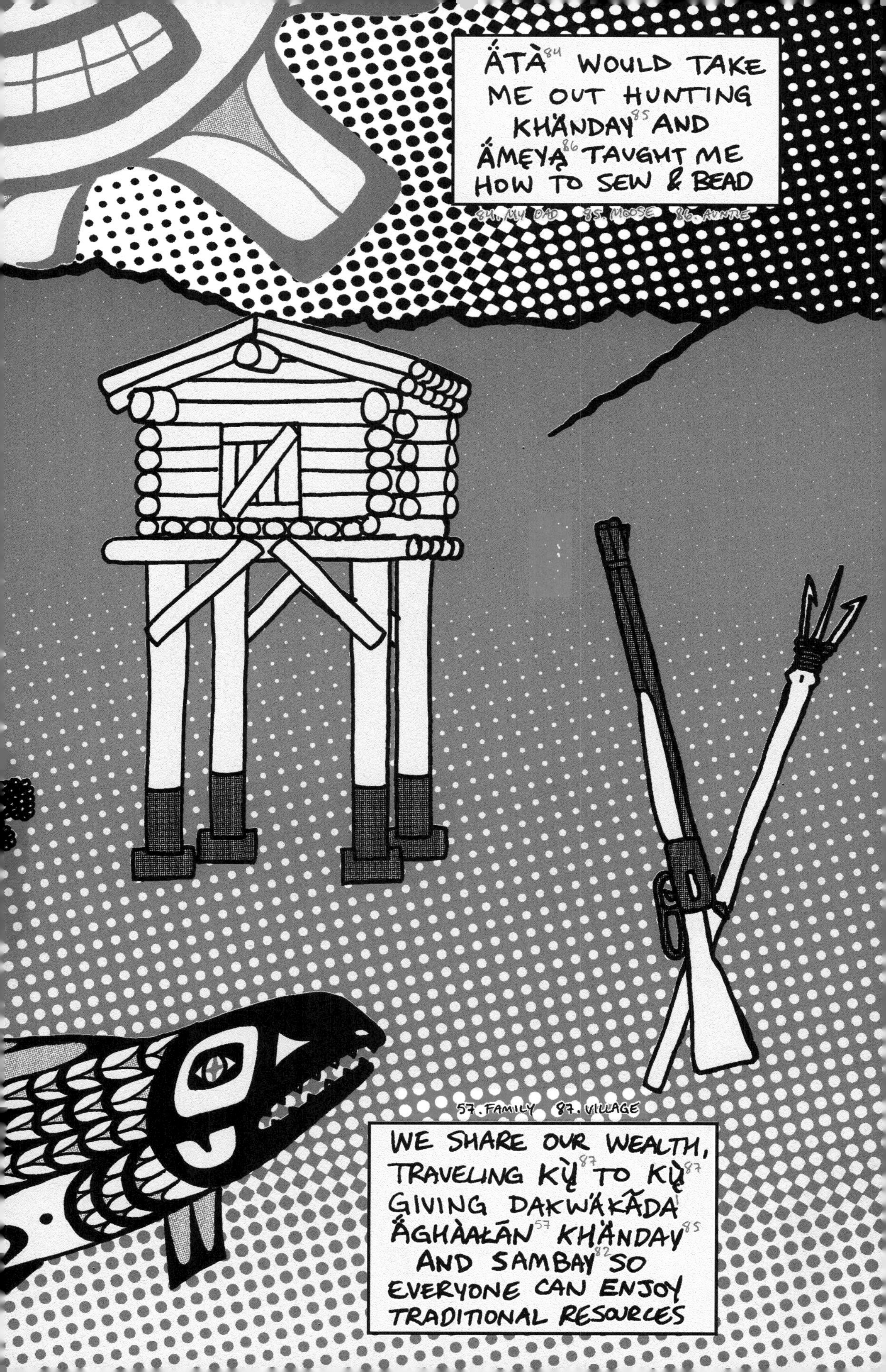
ẮTÀ[84] WOULD TAKE ME OUT HUNTING KHÄNDAY[85] AND ẮMĘYĄ[86] TAUGHT ME HOW TO SEW & BEAD
84. MY DAD 85. MOOSE 86. AUNTIE
57. FAMILY 87. VILLAGE
WE SHARE OUR WEALTH, TRAVELING KŲ̀[87] TO KŲ̀[87] GIVING DAKWÁKĀDA[1] ẮGHÀAŁĀN[57] KHÄNDAY[85] AND SAMBAY[82] SO EVERYONE CAN ENJOY TRADITIONAL RESOURCES

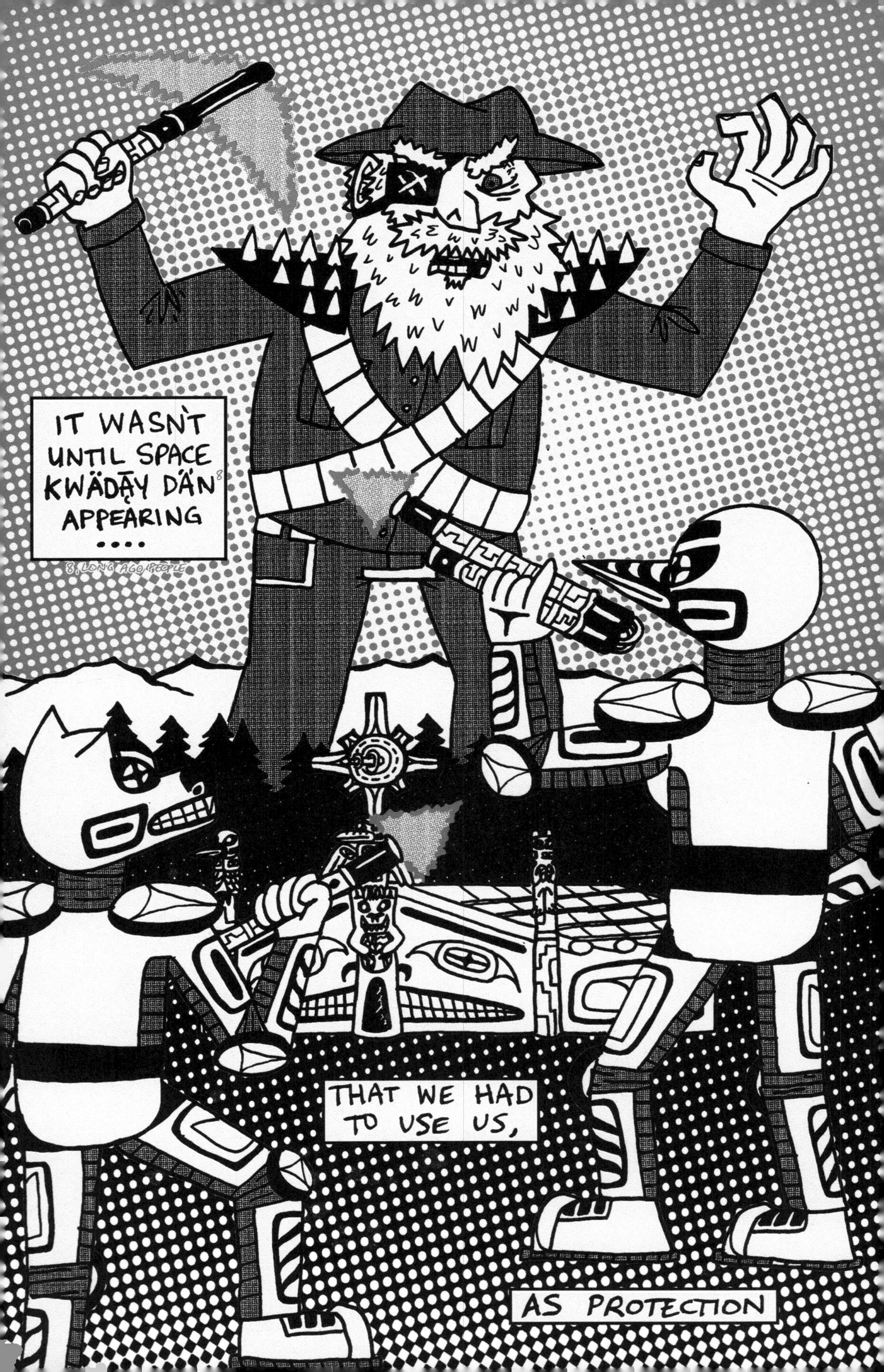
IT WASN'T UNTIL SPACE KWÄDĄY DÄN[8] APPEARING ....
8. LONG AGO PEOPLE
THAT WE HAD TO USE US,
AS PROTECTION

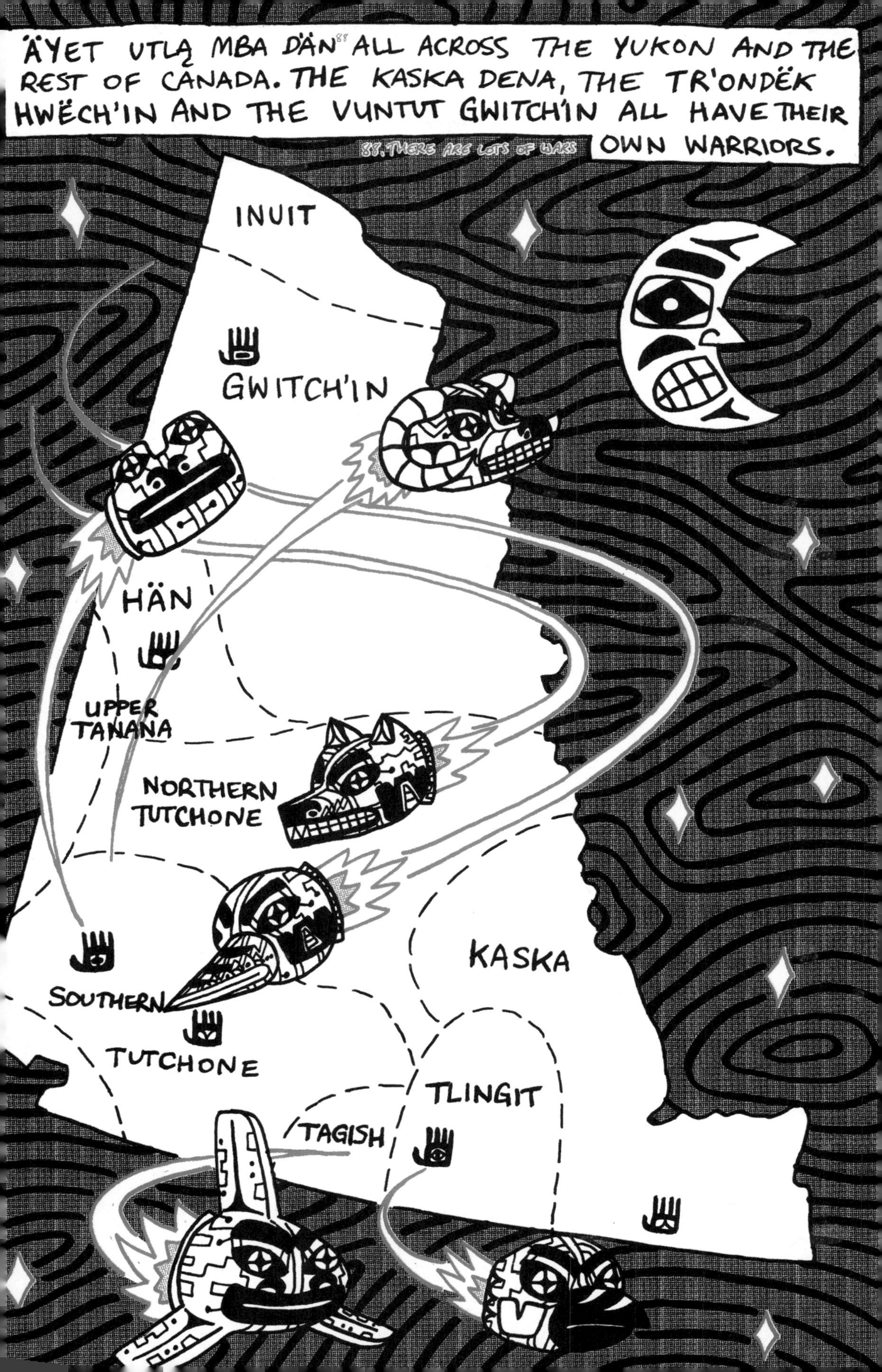
ÄYET UTLĄ MBA DÄN[88] ALL ACROSS THE YUKON AND THE REST OF CANADA. THE KASKA DENA, THE TR'ONDËK HWËCH'IN AND THE VUNTUT GWITCH'IN ALL HAVE THEIR OWN WARRIORS.
88. THERE ARE LOTS OF WARS
INUIT
GWITCH'IN
HÄN
UPPER TANANA
NORTHERN TUTCHONE
KASKA
SOUTHERN TUTCHONE
TLINGIT
TAGISH

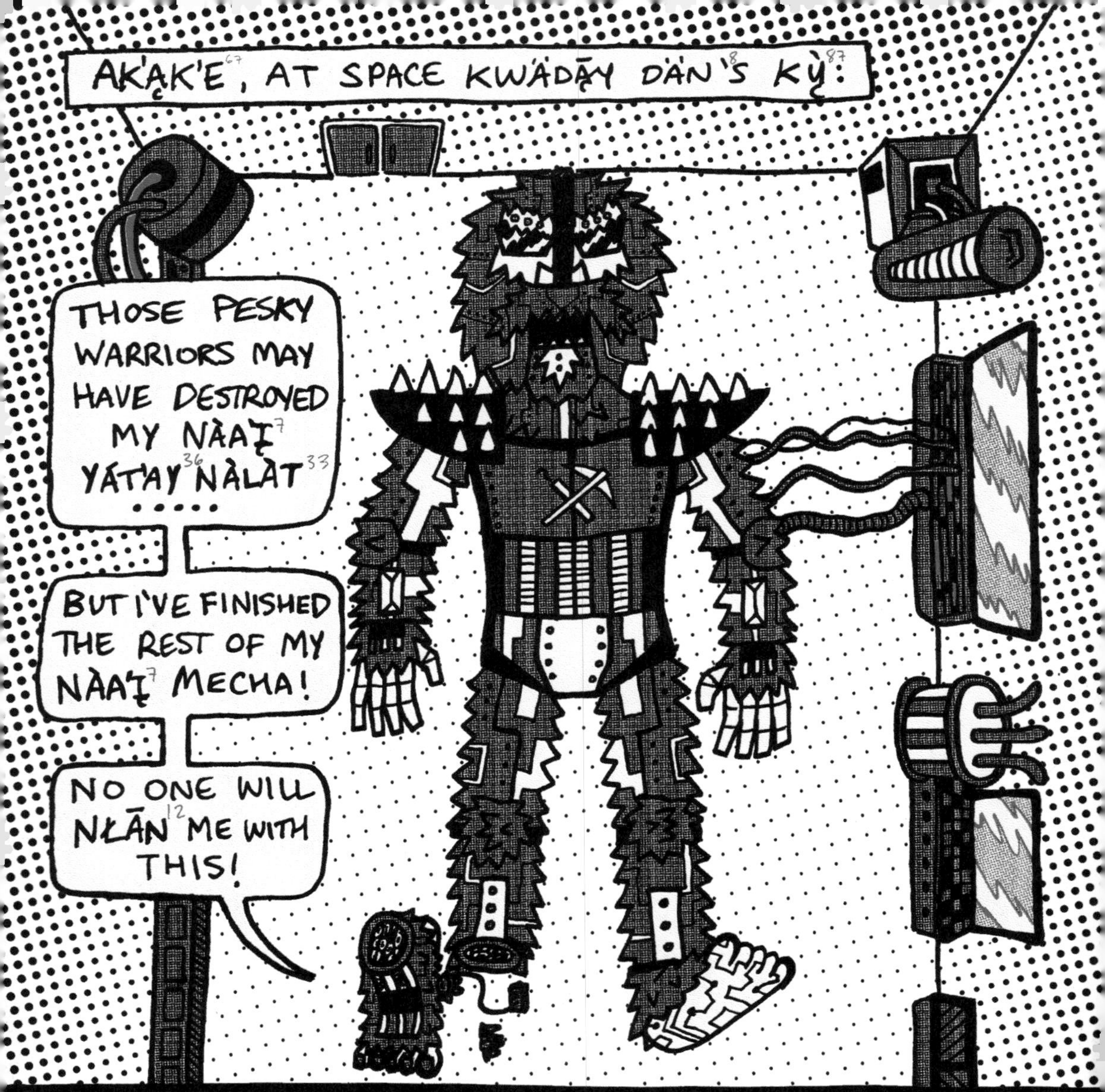
AK'ĄK'E[67], AT SPACE KWÄDĄ̄Y[8] DÄN'S KỲ̨[87]:
THOSE PESKY WARRIORS MAY HAVE DESTROYED MY NÀAĮ[7] YÁT'AY[36] NÁLAT[33].....
BUT I'VE FINISHED THE REST OF MY NÀAĮ[7] MECHA!
NO ONE WILL NŁÄN[12] ME WITH THIS!

7. BUSHMAN 8. LONG AGO PEOPLE 12. STOP 33. SHIP 36. SPACE 47. ARMY 67. NOW/THEN/TODAY 87. HOUSE 89. HEAD

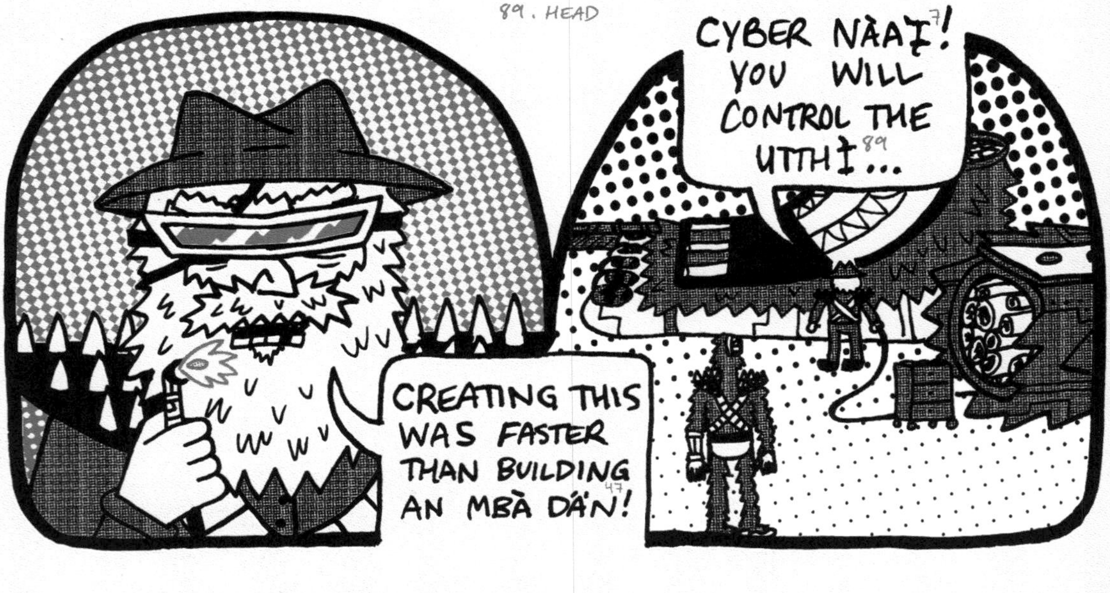
CREATING THIS WAS FASTER THAN BUILDING AN MBÀ DÄN[47]!
CYBER NÀAĮ[7]! YOU WILL CONTROL THE UTTHĮ[89]...

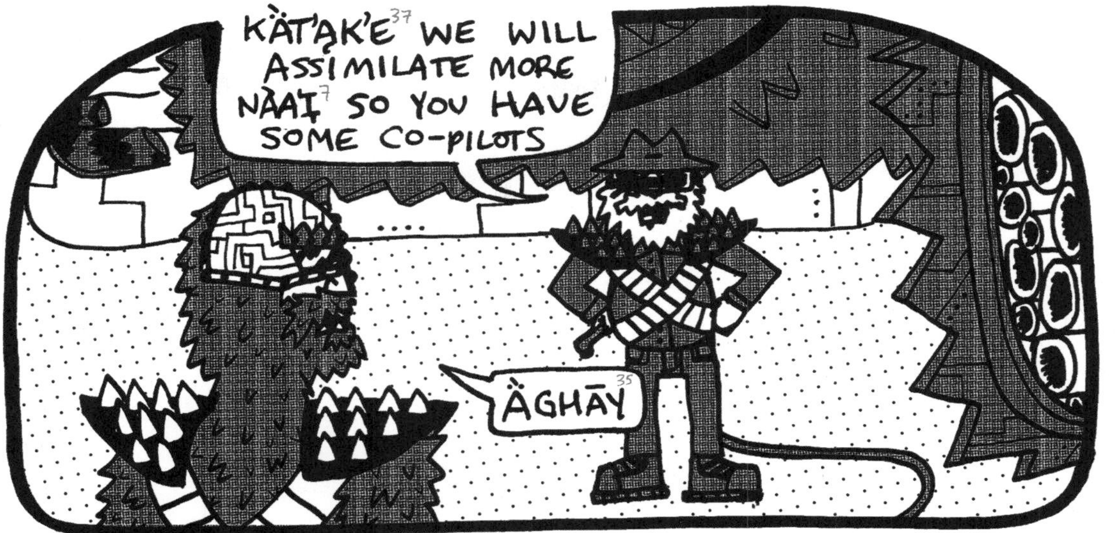
KÀTĄK'E[37] WE WILL ASSIMILATE MORE NÀAĮ[7] SO YOU HAVE SOME CO-PILOTS
....
ÀGHĀY[35]

1. HIGH CACHE PLACE 7. BUSHMAN 35. YES 37. LATER 87. HOUSE 90. EVERYONE

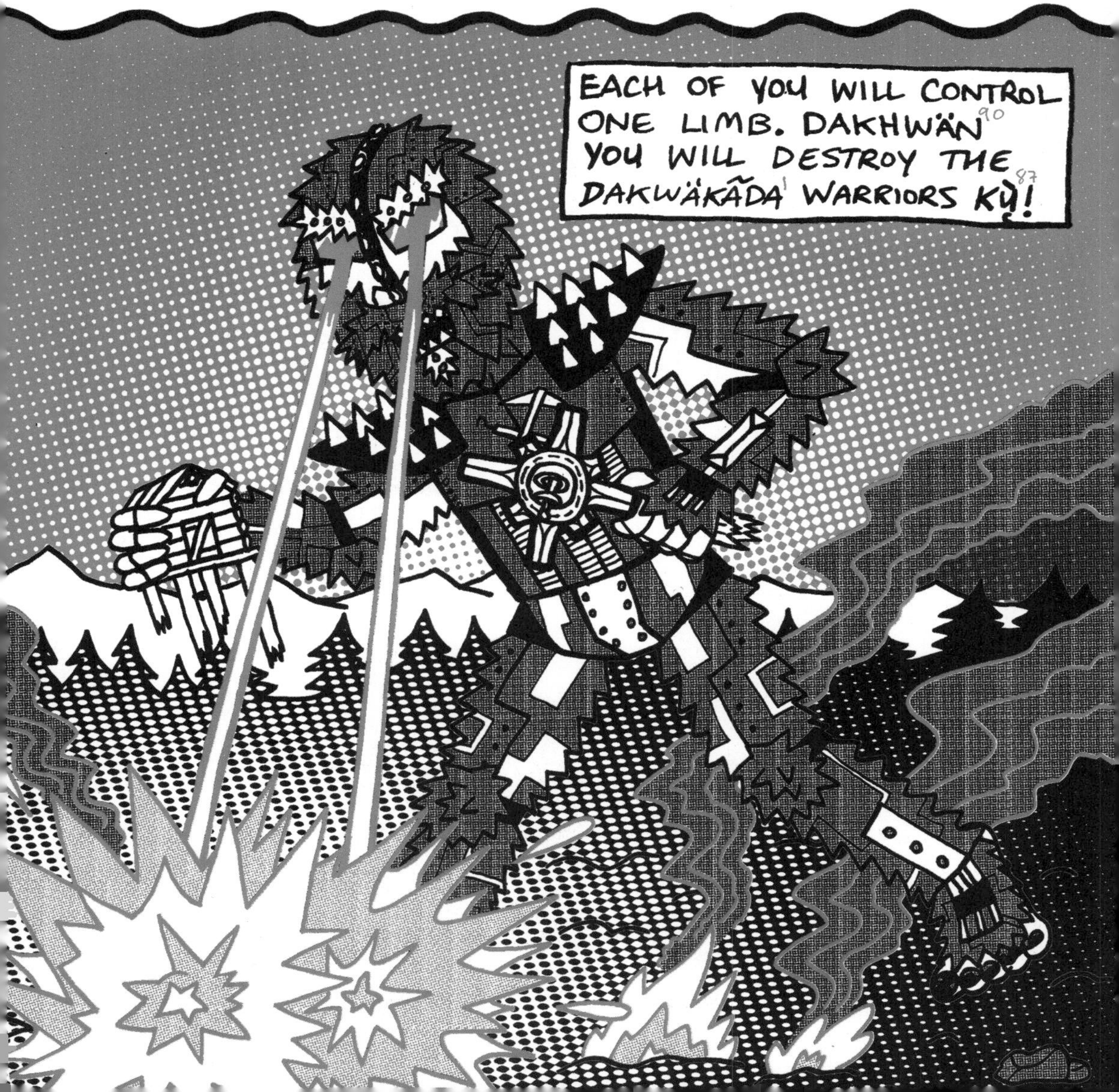
EACH OF YOU WILL CONTROL ONE LIMB. DAKHWÄN[90] YOU WILL DESTROY THE DAKWÄKÃDA[1] WARRIORS KŲ[87]!

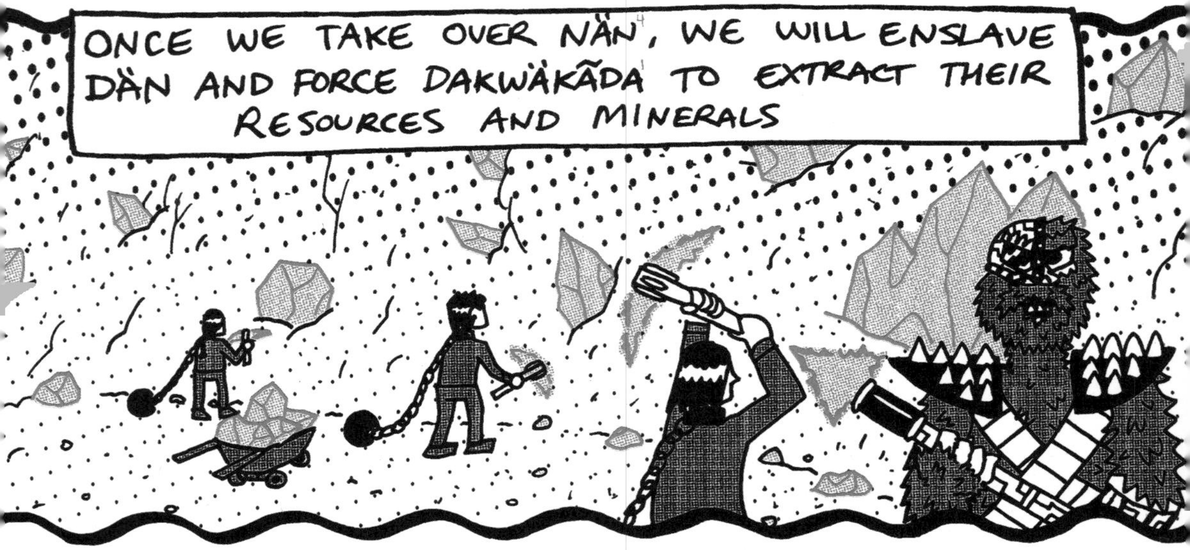
ONCE WE TAKE OVER NÄN[4], WE WILL ENSLAVE DÄN AND FORCE DAKWÄKÃDA[1] TO EXTRACT THEIR RESOURCES AND MINERALS

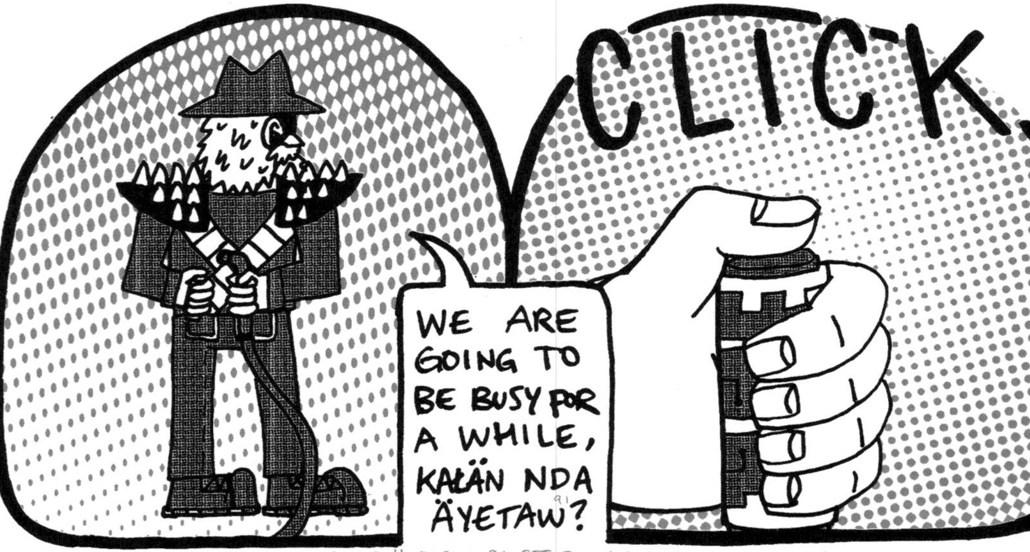
CLICK
WE ARE GOING TO BE BUSY FOR A WHILE, KAŁÄN NDA ÄYETAW[91]?

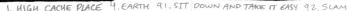

1. HIGH CACHE PLACE 4. EARTH 91. SIT DOWN AND TAKE IT EASY 92. SLAM

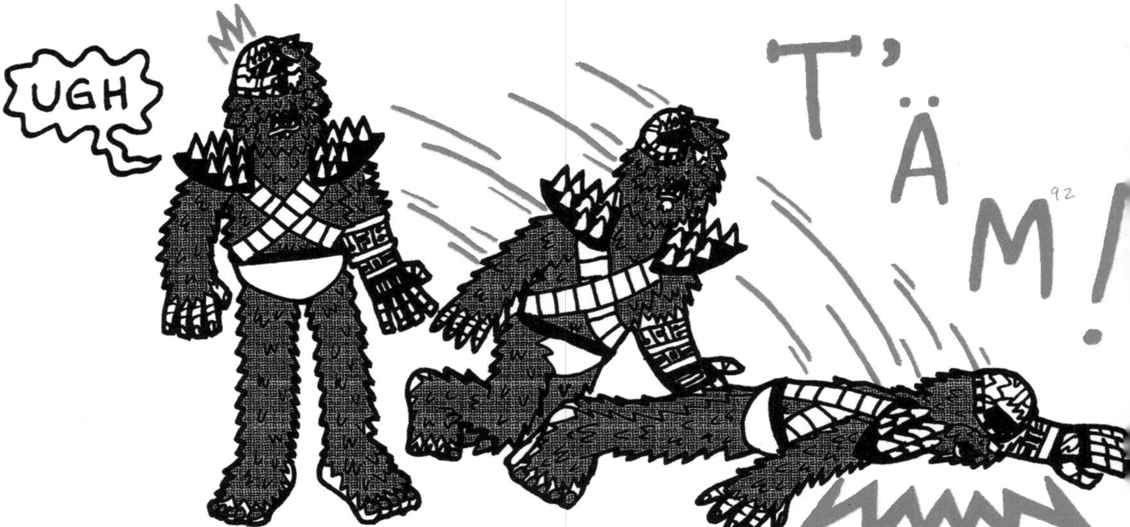
UGH
T'ÄM[92]!

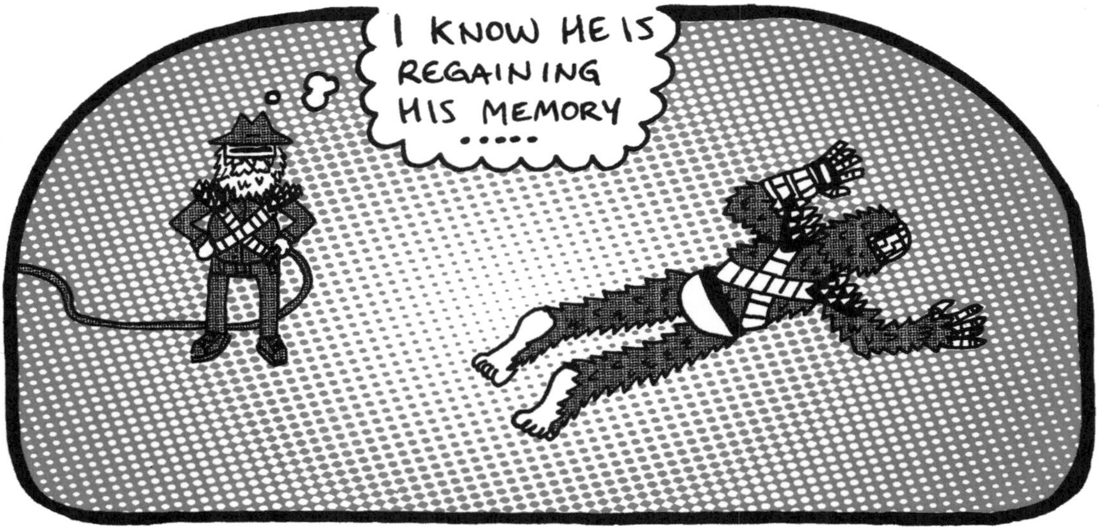
I KNOW HE IS REGAINING HIS MEMORY .....

54.ME

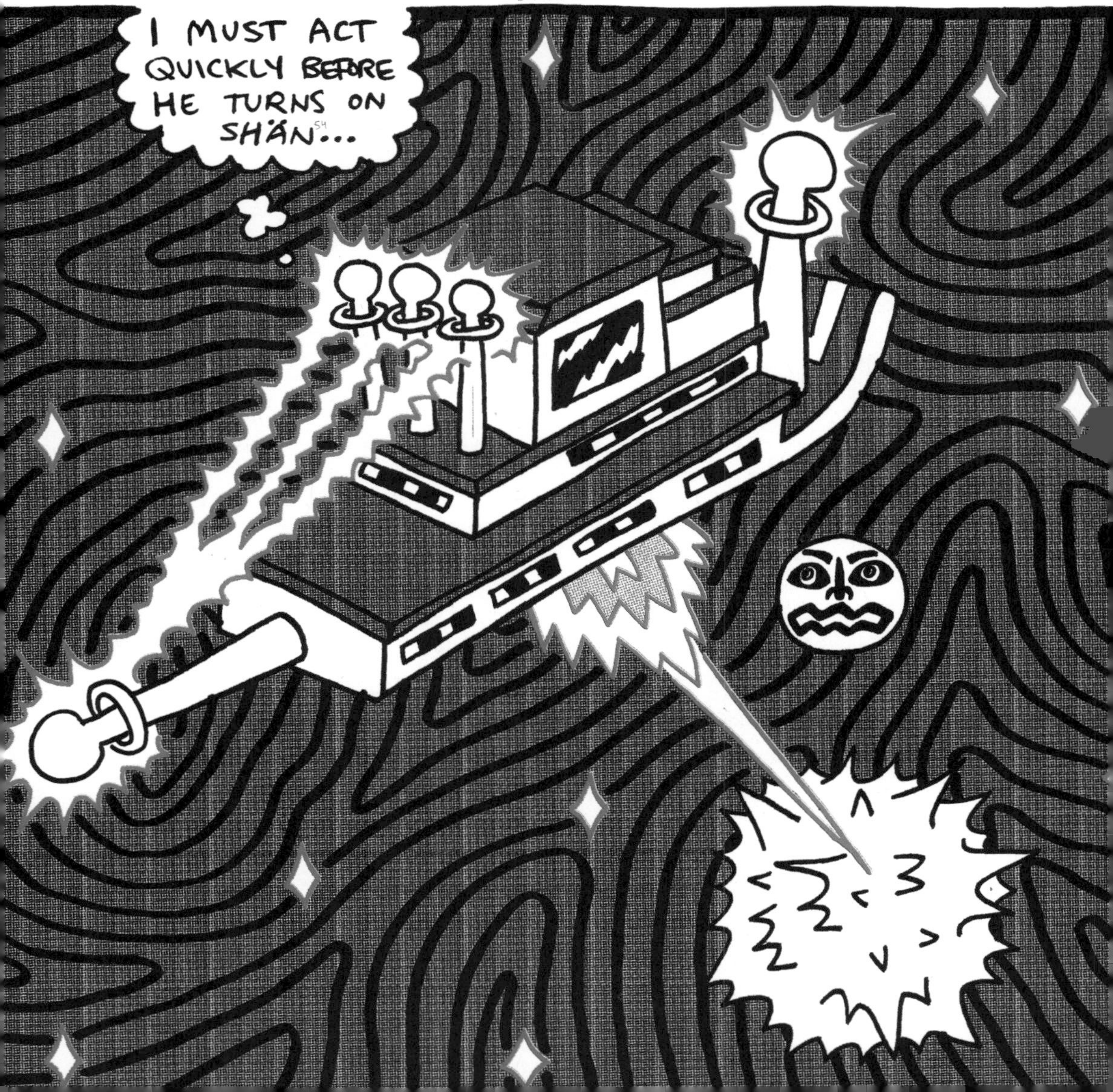
I MUST ACT QUICKLY BEFORE HE TURNS ON SHÄN[54]...

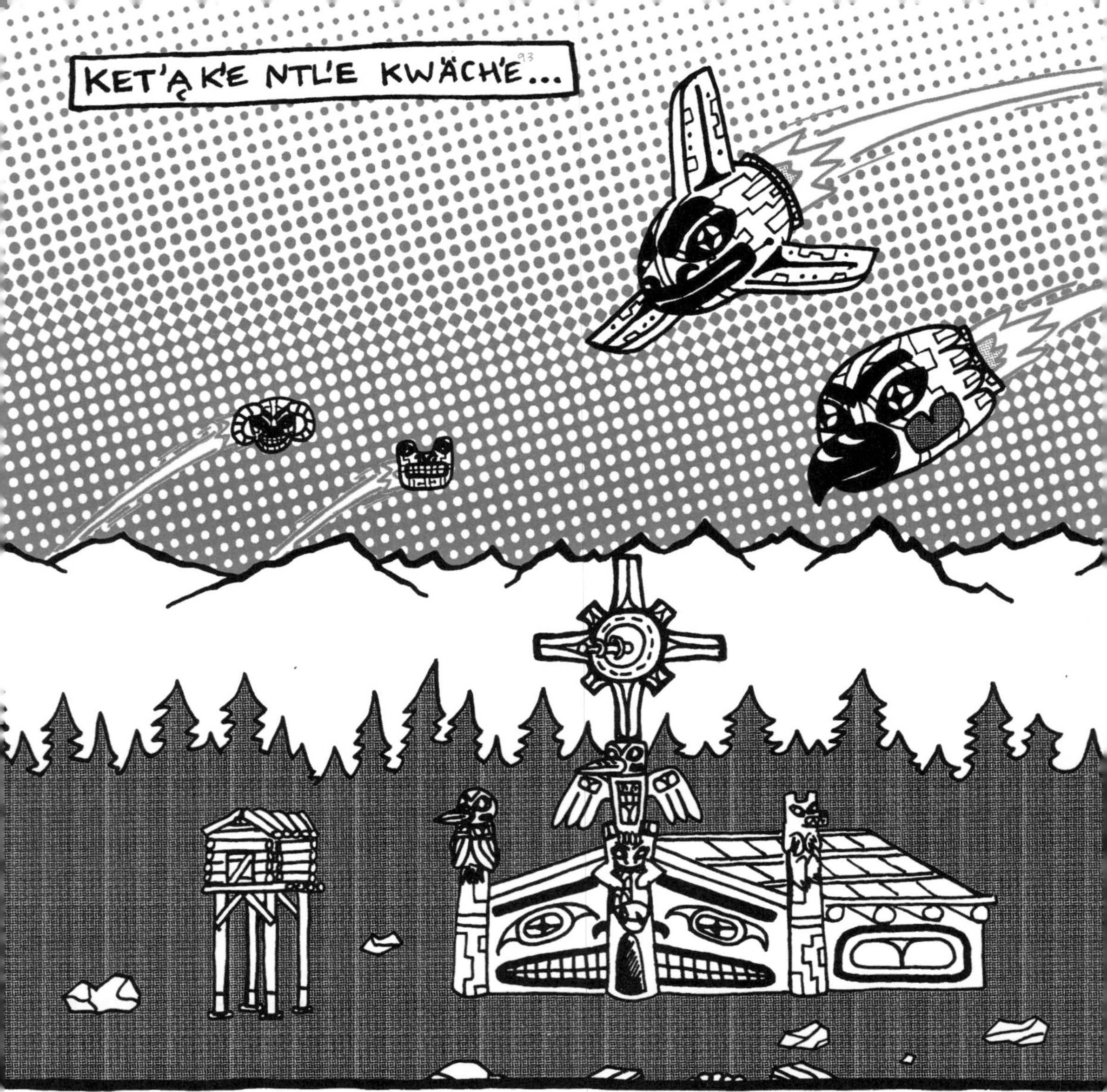
KET'Ą̨K'E NTL'E KWÄCH'E...[93]

2. CROW 71. KLUANE LAKE/FISH LAKE 78. INLAND TLINGIT 93. TOMORROW MORNING

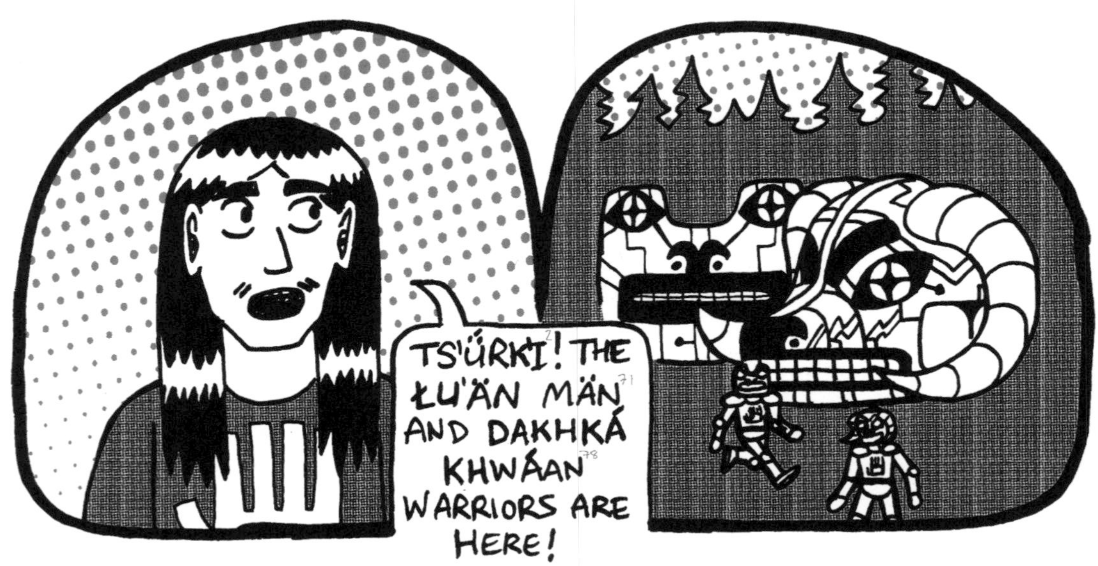
TS'ǗRKI[2]! THE ŁU'ÄN MÄN[71] AND DAKHKÁ KHWÁAN[78] WARRIORS ARE HERE!

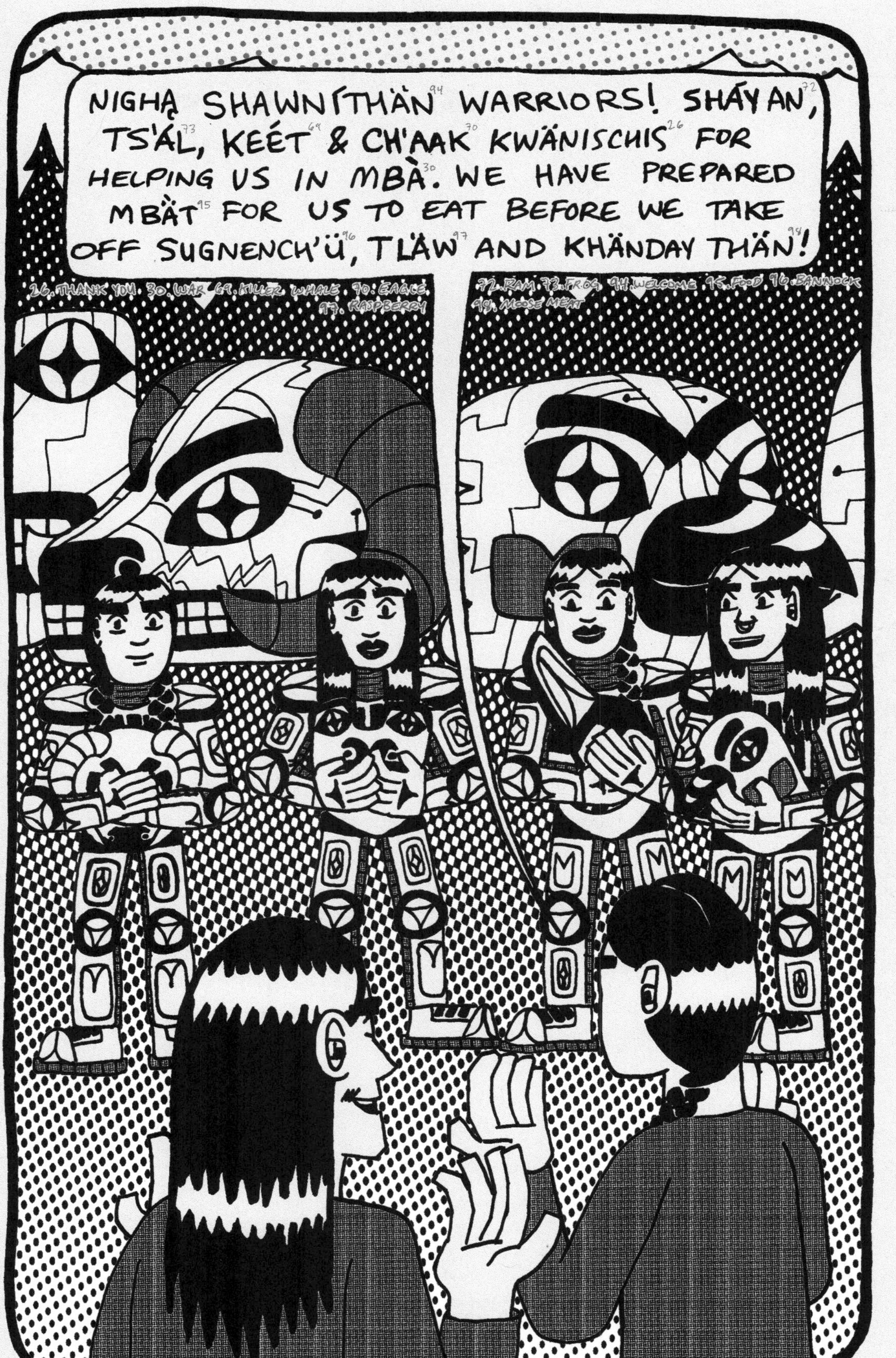
NIGHĄ SHAWNÍTHÄN[94] WARRIORS! SHÁYAN[72], TS'ÁL[73], KEÉT[69] & CH'AAK[70] KWÄNISCHIS[26] FOR HELPING US IN MBÀ[30]. WE HAVE PREPARED MBÄT[95] FOR US TO EAT BEFORE WE TAKE OFF SUGNENCH'Ü[96], TLÄW[97] AND KHÄNDAY THÄN[98]!
26. THANK YOU 30. WAR 69. KILLER WHALE 70. EAGLE 97. RASPBERRY
72. RAM 73. FROG 94. WELCOME 95. FOOD 96. BANNOCK 98. MOOSE MEAT

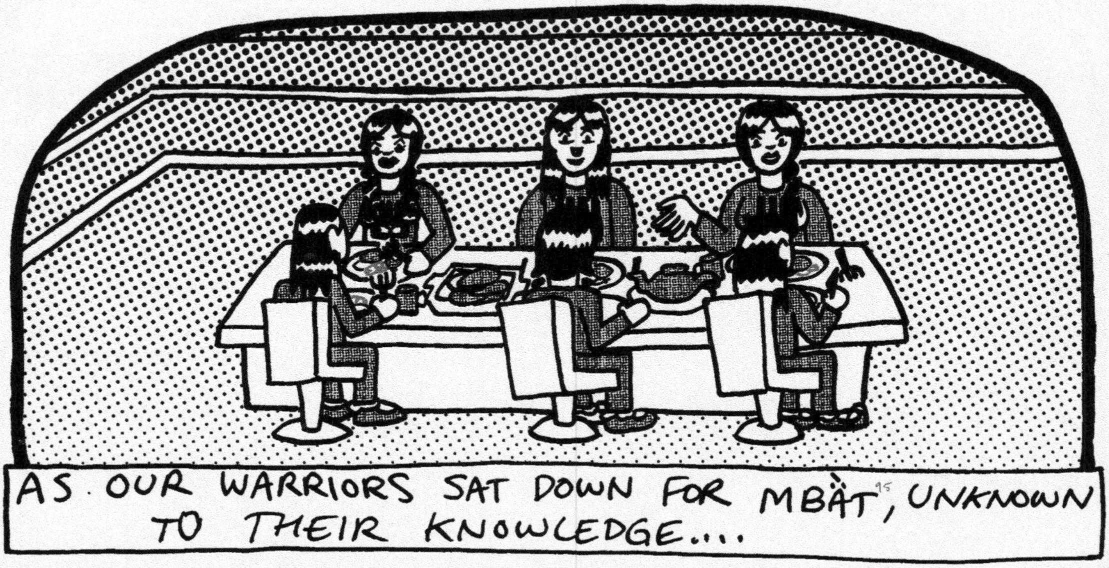
AS OUR WARRIORS SAT DOWN FOR MBÄ̀T[95], UNKNOWN TO THEIR KNOWLEDGE....

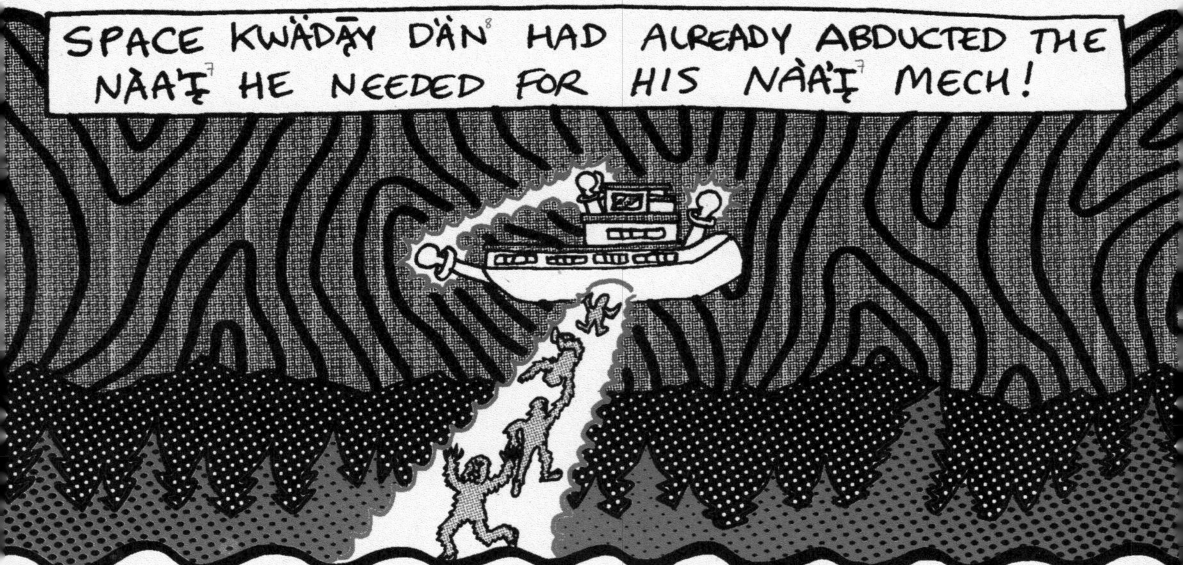
SPACE KWÄDĄ̄Y DÄN[8] HAD ALREADY ABDUCTED THE NÀÁĮ[7] HE NEEDED FOR HIS NÀÁĮ[7] MECH!

7. BUSHMAN 8. LONG AGO PEOPLE 30. WAR 95. FOOD 98. MOOSE MEAT

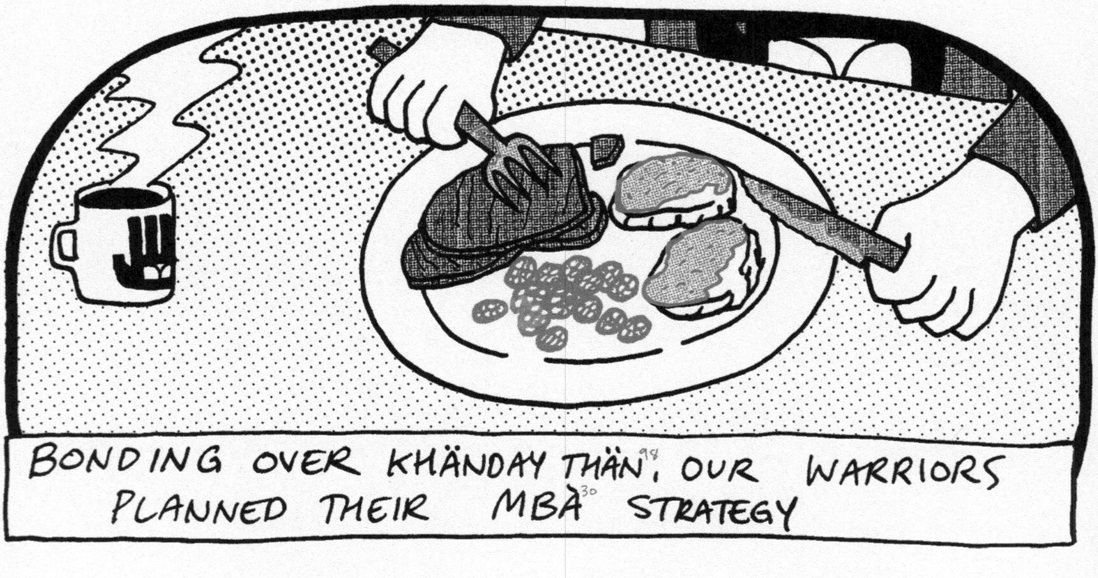
BONDING OVER KHÄNDAY THÄN[98], OUR WARRIORS PLANNED THEIR MBÀ[30] STRATEGY

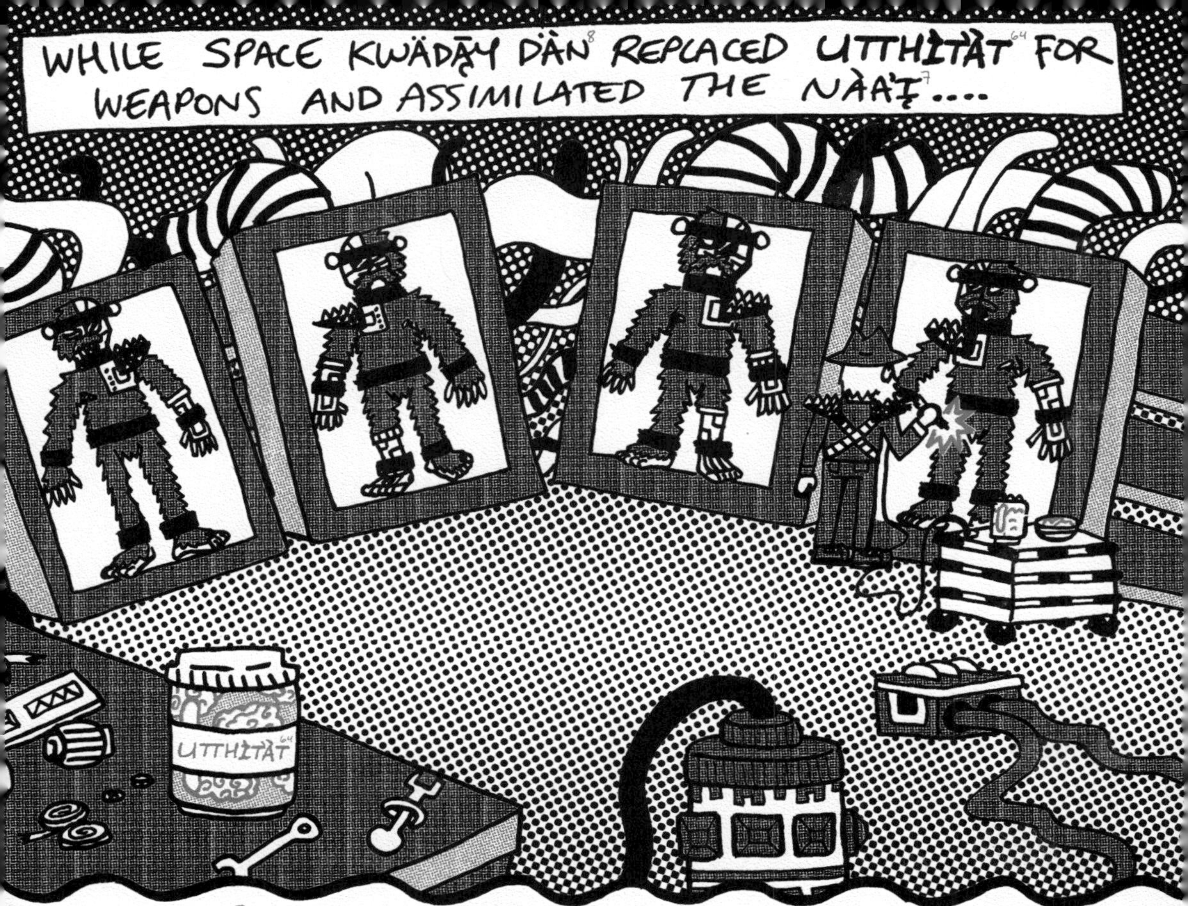
WHILE SPACE KWÄDĄ̄Y DÄN[8] REPLACED UTTHÌTÄT[64] FOR WEAPONS AND ASSIMILATED THE NÀ'ĄĮ[7]....
UTTHÌTÄT[64]

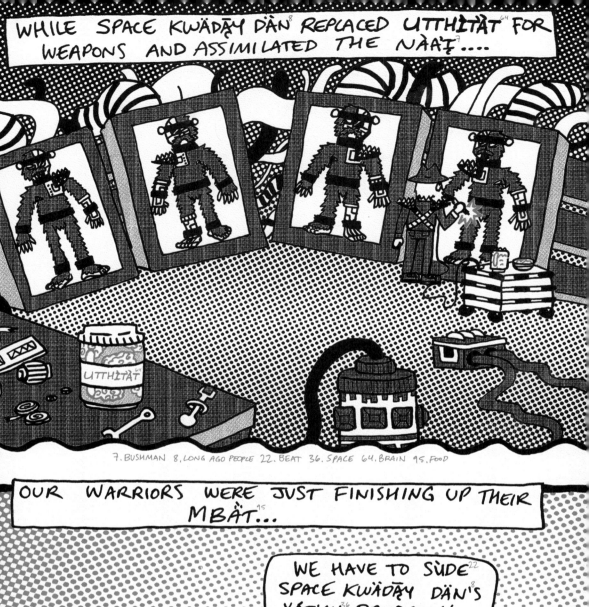

7. BUSHMAN 8. LONG AGO PEOPLE 22. BEAT 36. SPACE 64. BRAIN 95. FOOD

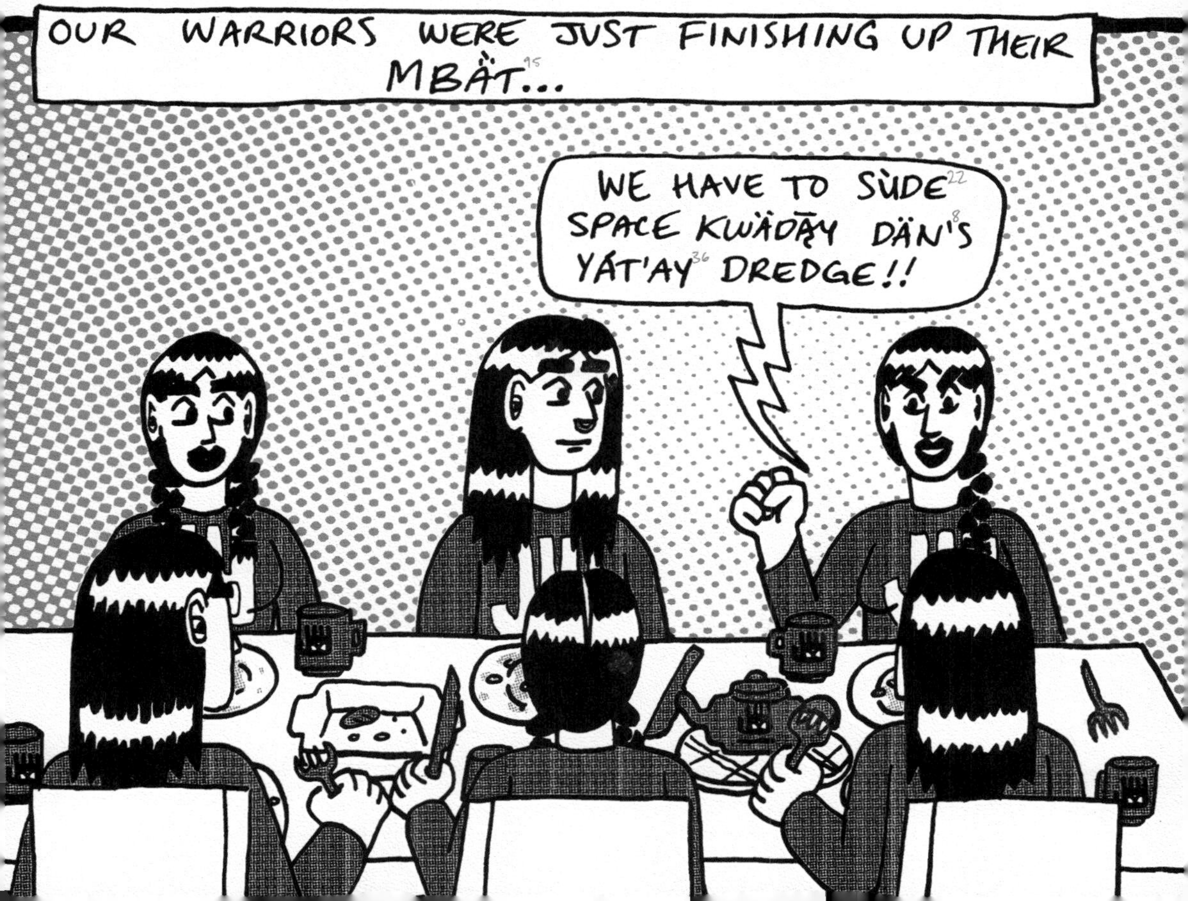
OUR WARRIORS WERE JUST FINISHING UP THEIR MBÄT[95]...
WE HAVE TO SÙDE[22] SPACE KWÄDĄ̄Y DÄN'S[8] YÁT'AY[36] DREDGE!!

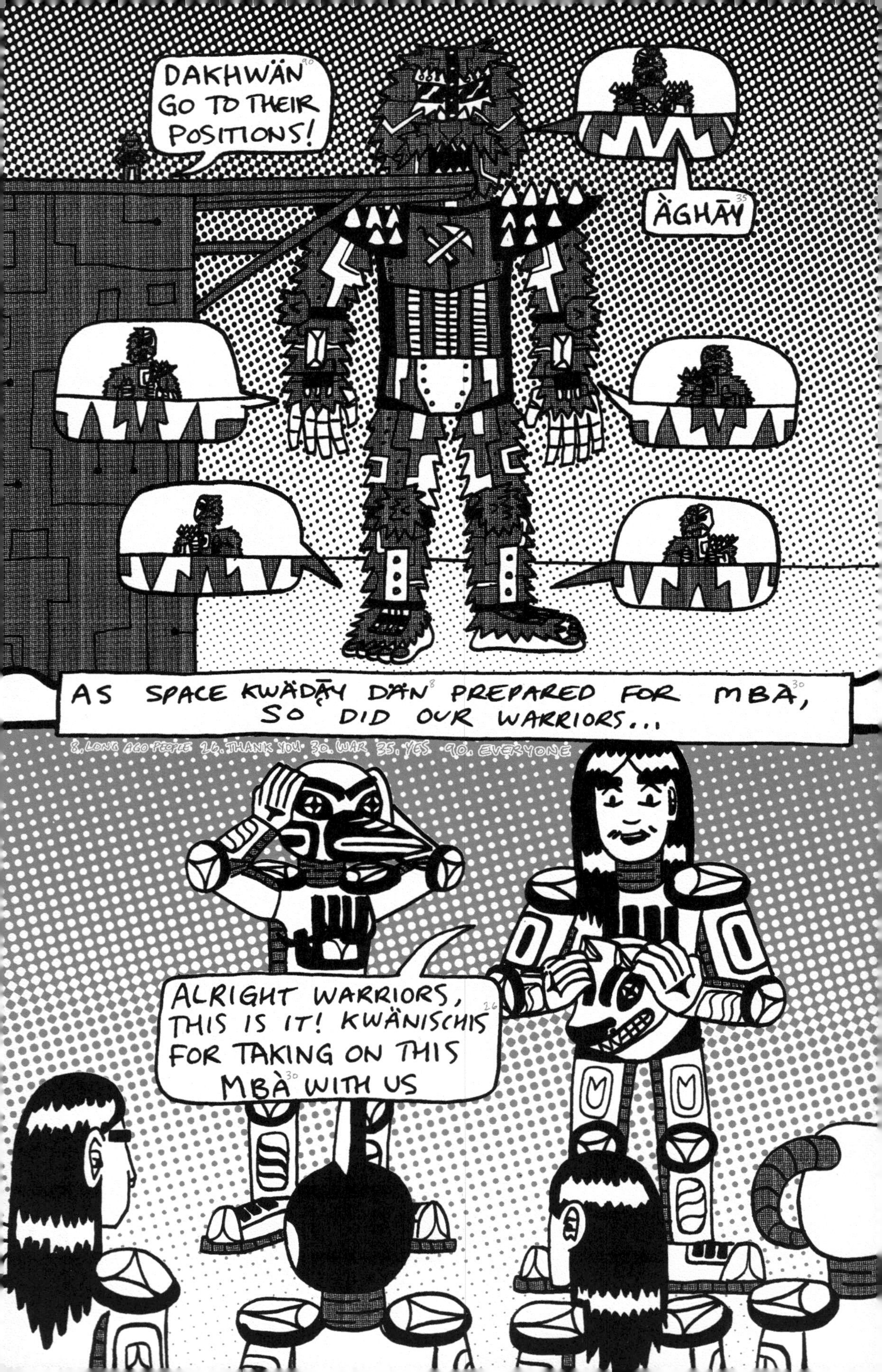
DAKHWÄN[90] GO TO THEIR POSITIONS!
ÀGHĀY[35]
AS SPACE KWÄDĄY DÄN[8] PREPARED FOR MBÀ[30], SO DID OUR WARRIORS...
8. LONG AGO PEOPLE 26. THANK YOU 30. WAR 35. YES 90. EVERYONE
ALRIGHT WARRIORS, THIS IS IT! KWÄNISCHIS[26] FOR TAKING ON THIS MBÀ[30] WITH US

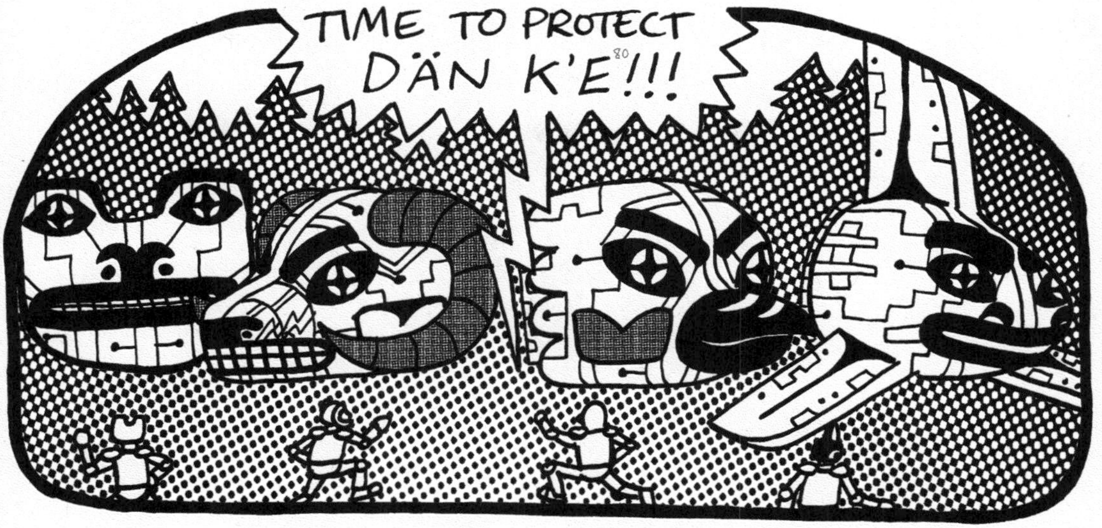
TIME TO PROTECT DÄN K'E[80]!!!

16. SHOOT 80. OUR WAY

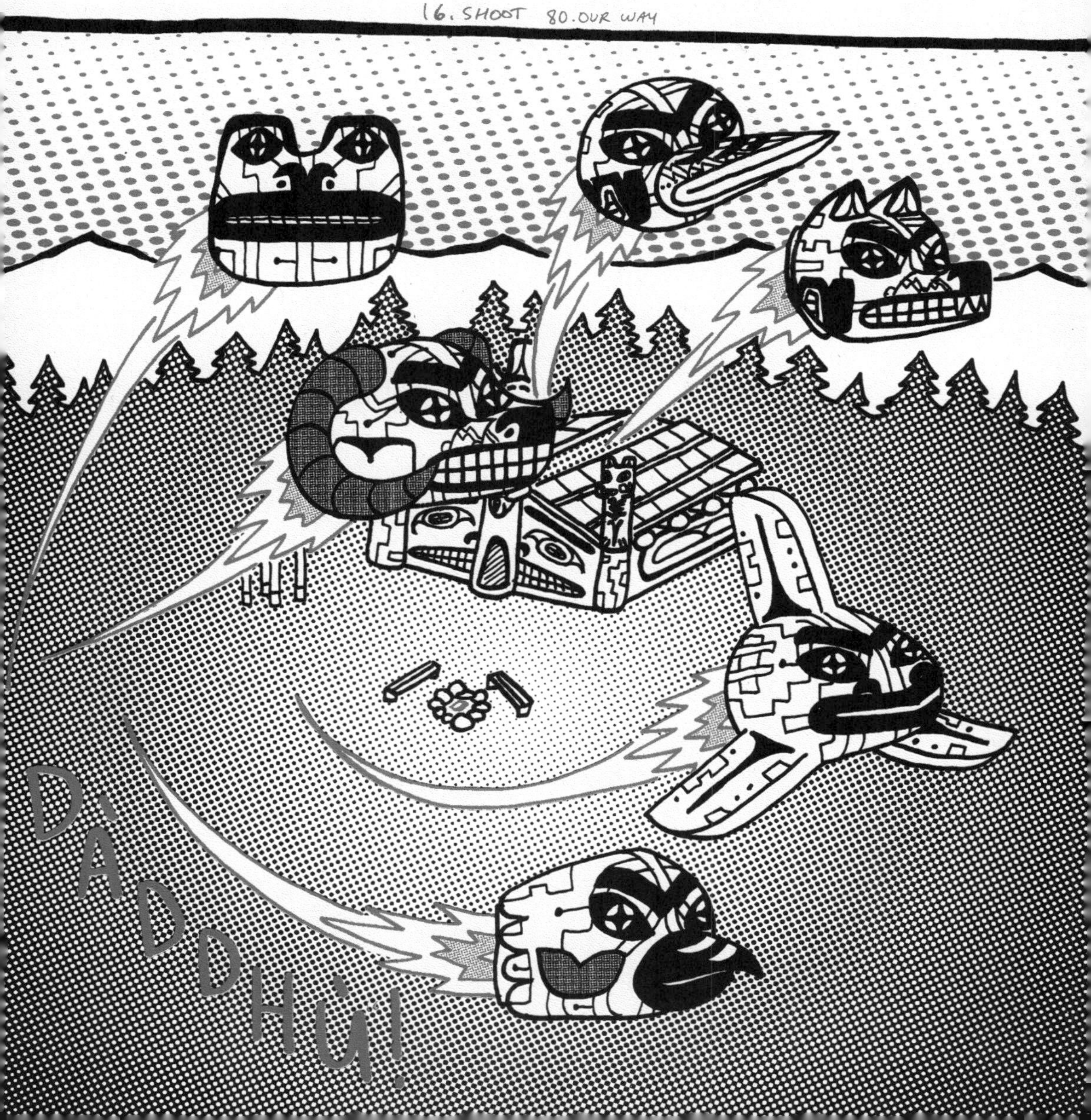
DÀDDHÙ[16]!

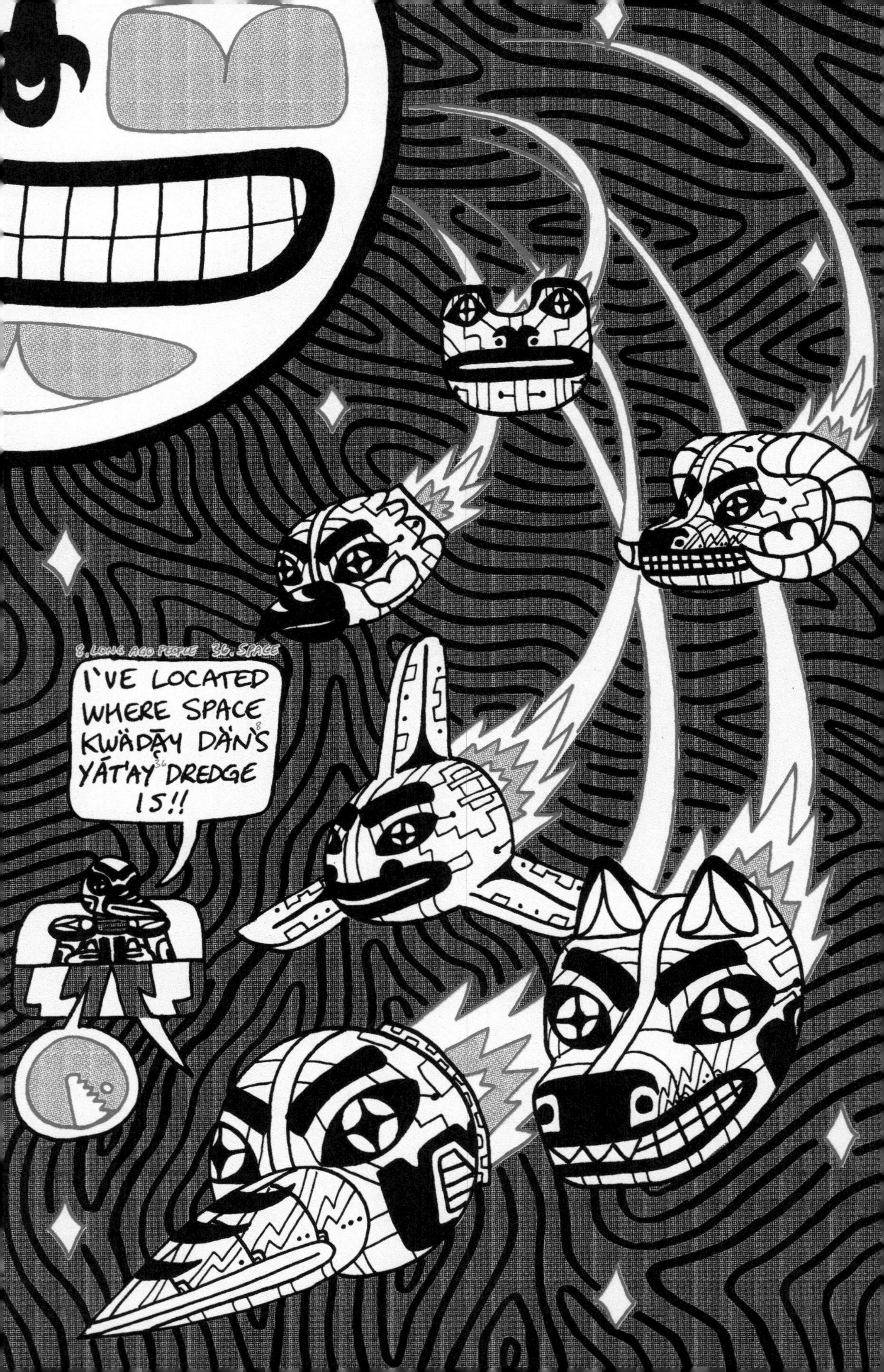
8. LONG AGO PEOPLE 36. SPACE
I'VE LOCATED WHERE SPACE KWÄDĀY DÄN'S[8] YĀT'AY[36] DREDGE IS!!

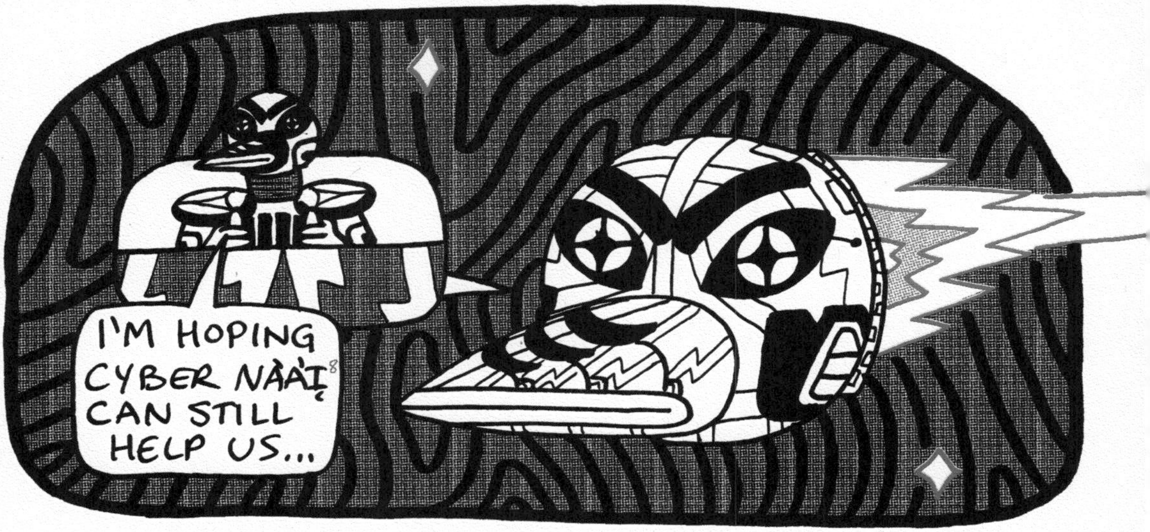
I'M HOPING CYBER NÀÀĮ[8] CAN STILL HELP US...

4. EARTH 8. LONG AGO PEOPLE 10. SUN 11. MOON 59. OVER THERE

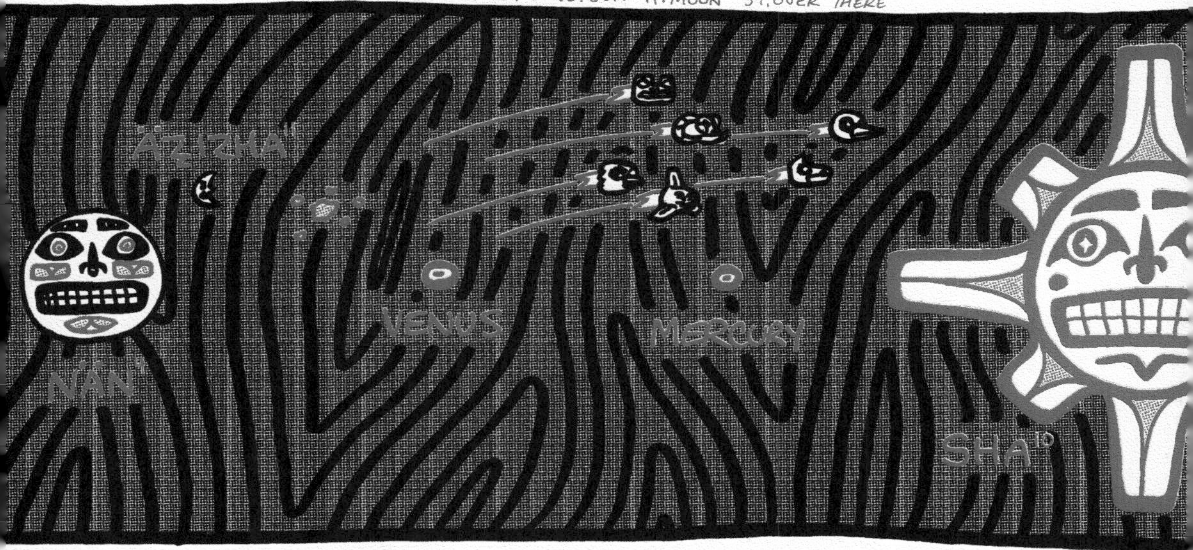
ÄZIZHA'[11]
NÄN'[4]
VENUS
MERCURY
SHA[10]

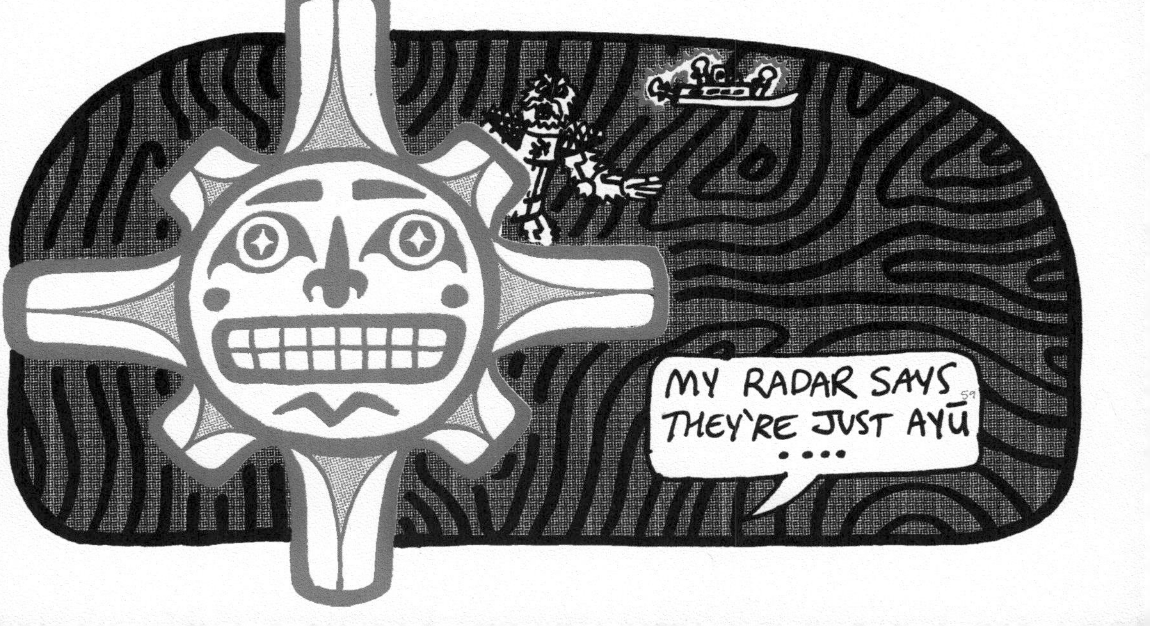
MY RADAR SAYS THEY'RE JUST AYŪ[59] ....

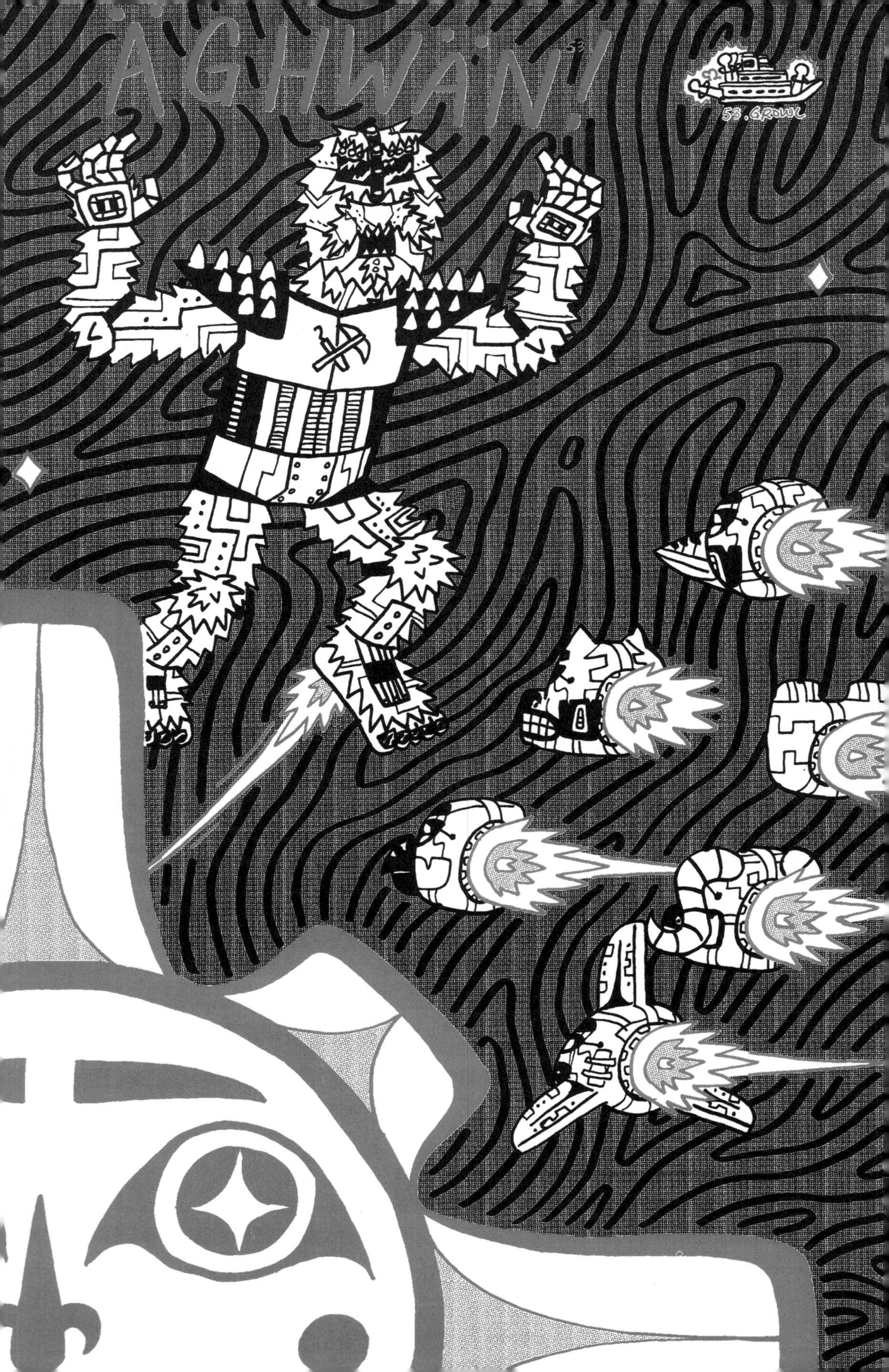
ÄGHWÄN!
53
53. GROWL

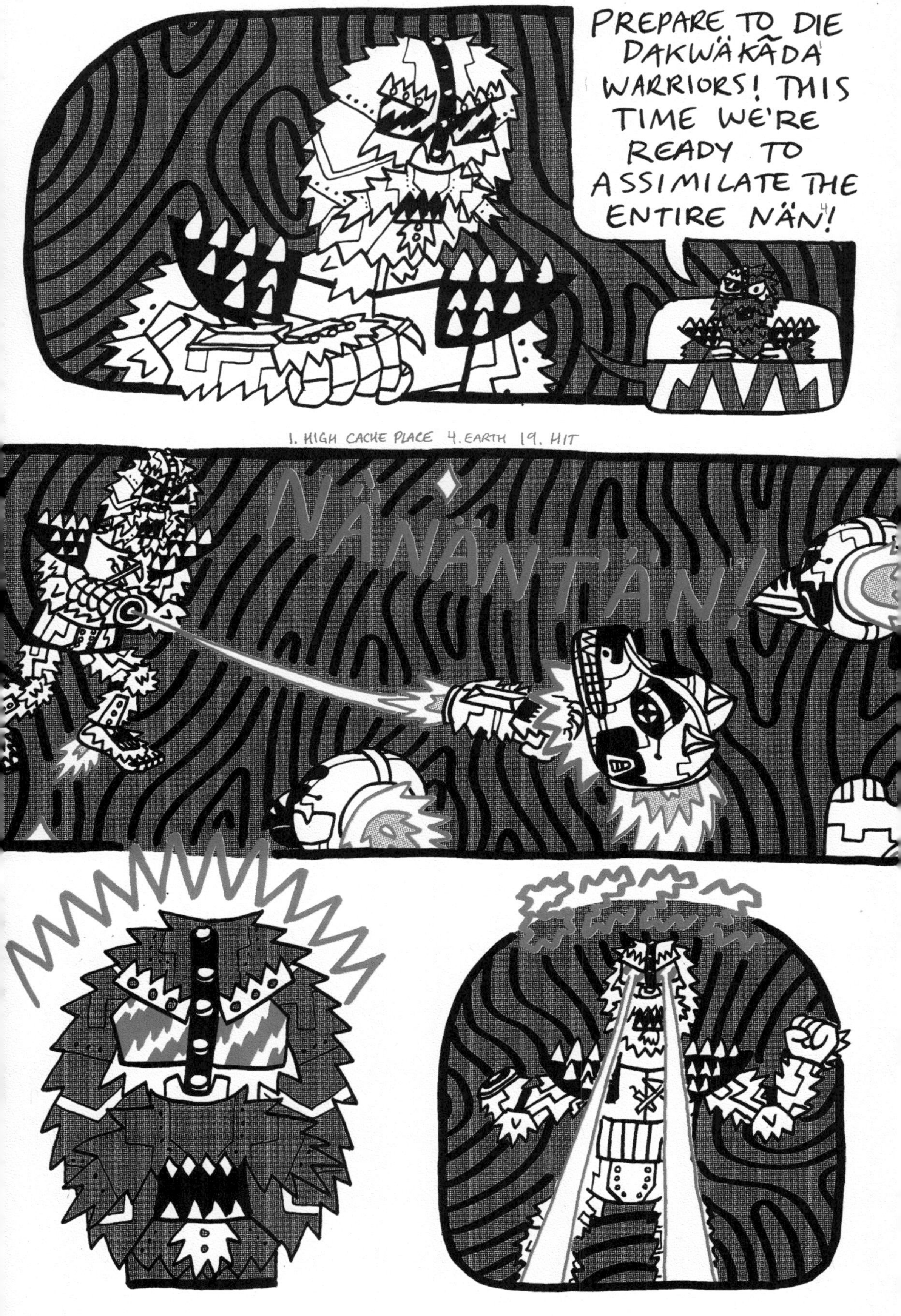
PREPARE TO DIE DAKWÄKÃDA[1] WARRIORS! THIS TIME WE'RE READY TO ASSIMILATE THE ENTIRE NÄN[4]!
1. HIGH CACHE PLACE 4. EARTH 19. HIT
NÅNÄNTÄN![19]

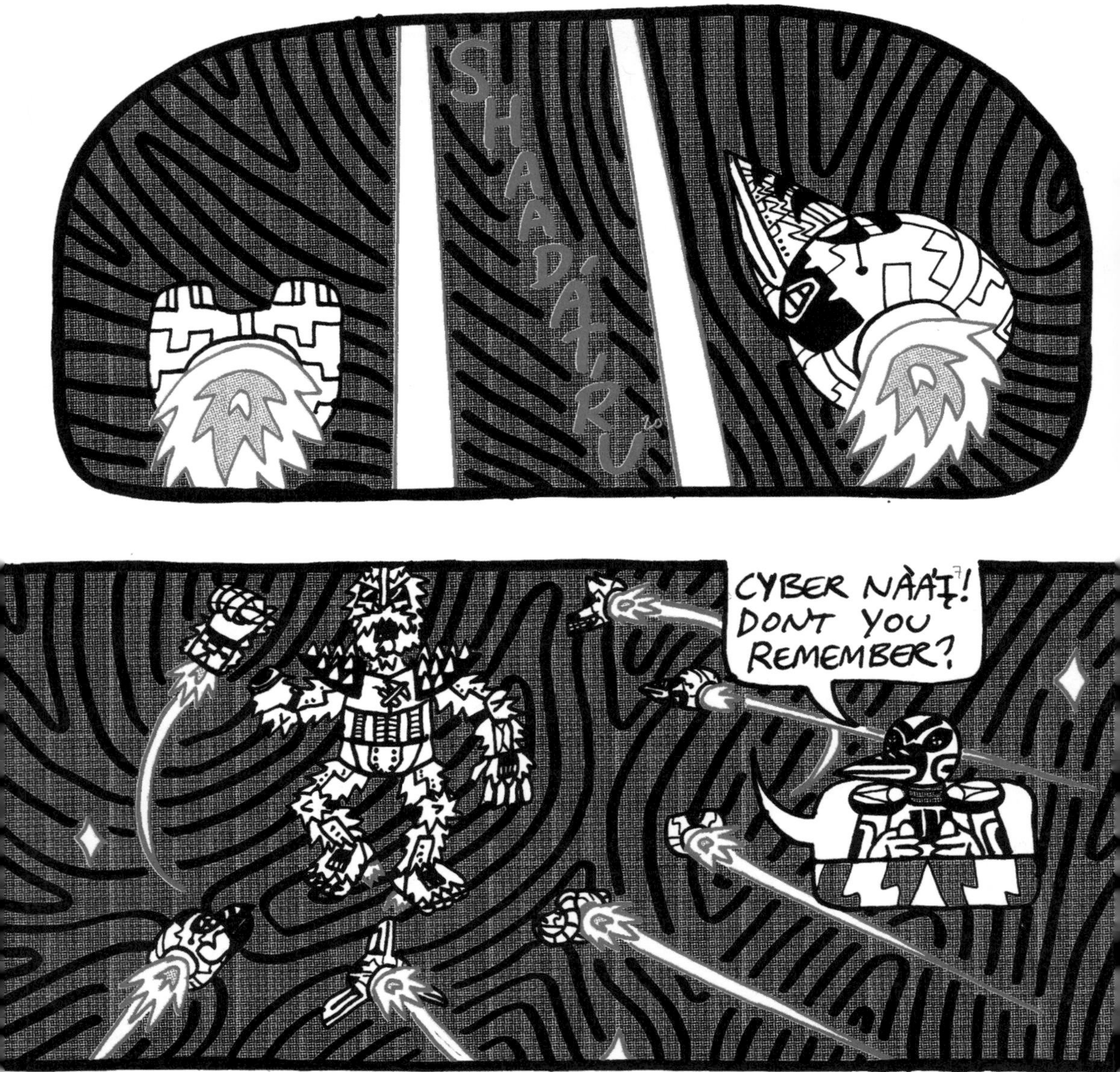

SHAAD́ÁT́RU[20]
CYBER NÀÁĮ[7]! DONT YOU REMEMBER?

7. BUSHMAN 8, LONG AGO PEOPLE 15. NO 20. SPIN 90. EVERYONE

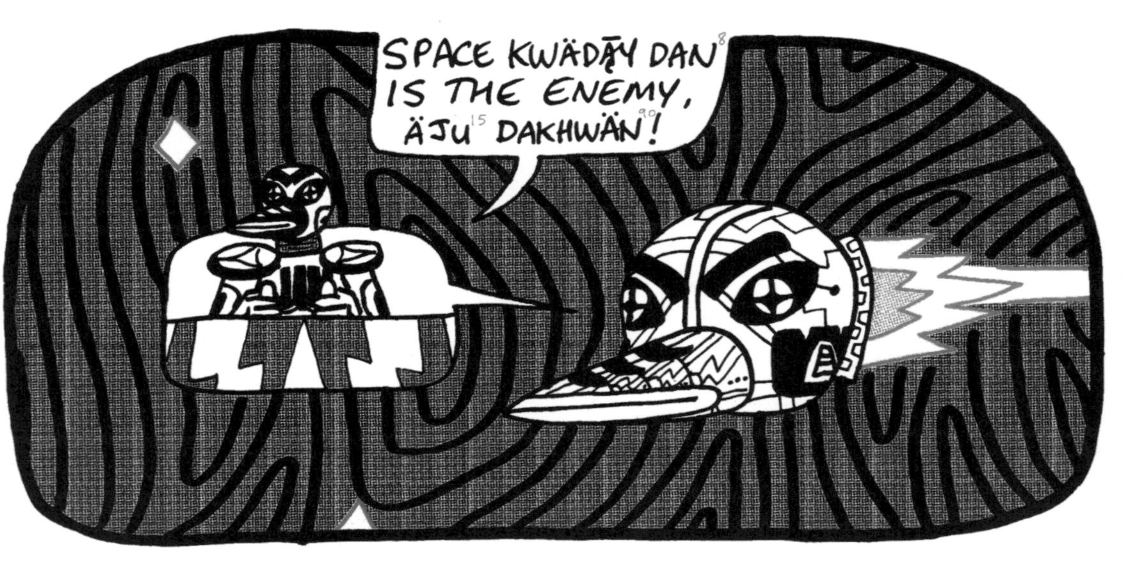

SPACE KWÄDĄ̄Y DAN[8] IS THE ENEMY, ÄJU[15] DAKHWÄN[90]!

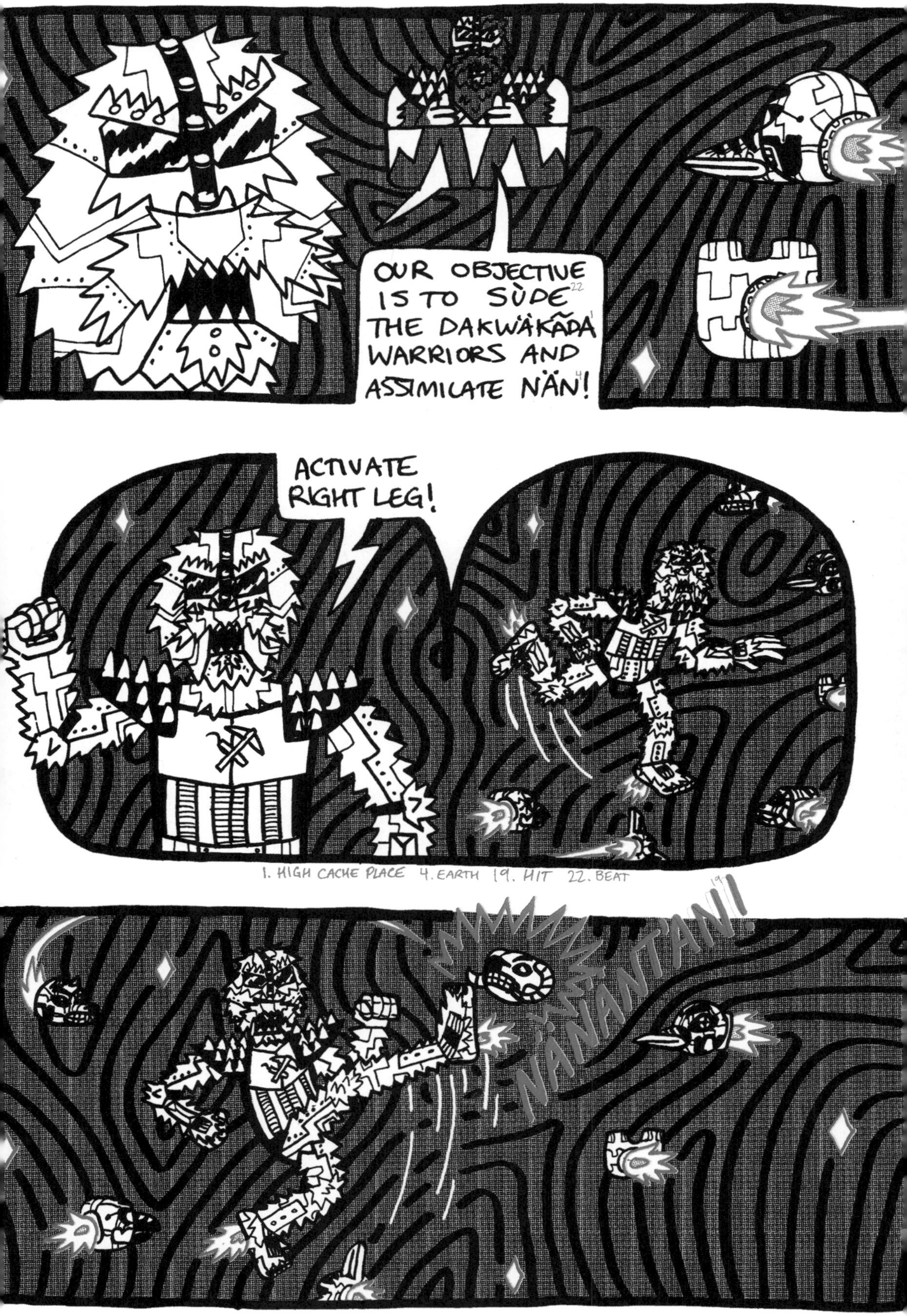
OUR OBJECTIVE IS TO SÙDE[22] THE DAKWÀKÃDA[1] WARRIORS AND ASSIMILATE NÄN[4]!
ACTIVATE RIGHT LEG!
1. HIGH CACHE PLACE 4. EARTH 19. HIT 22. BEAT
NÀNÀNT'ÀN![19]

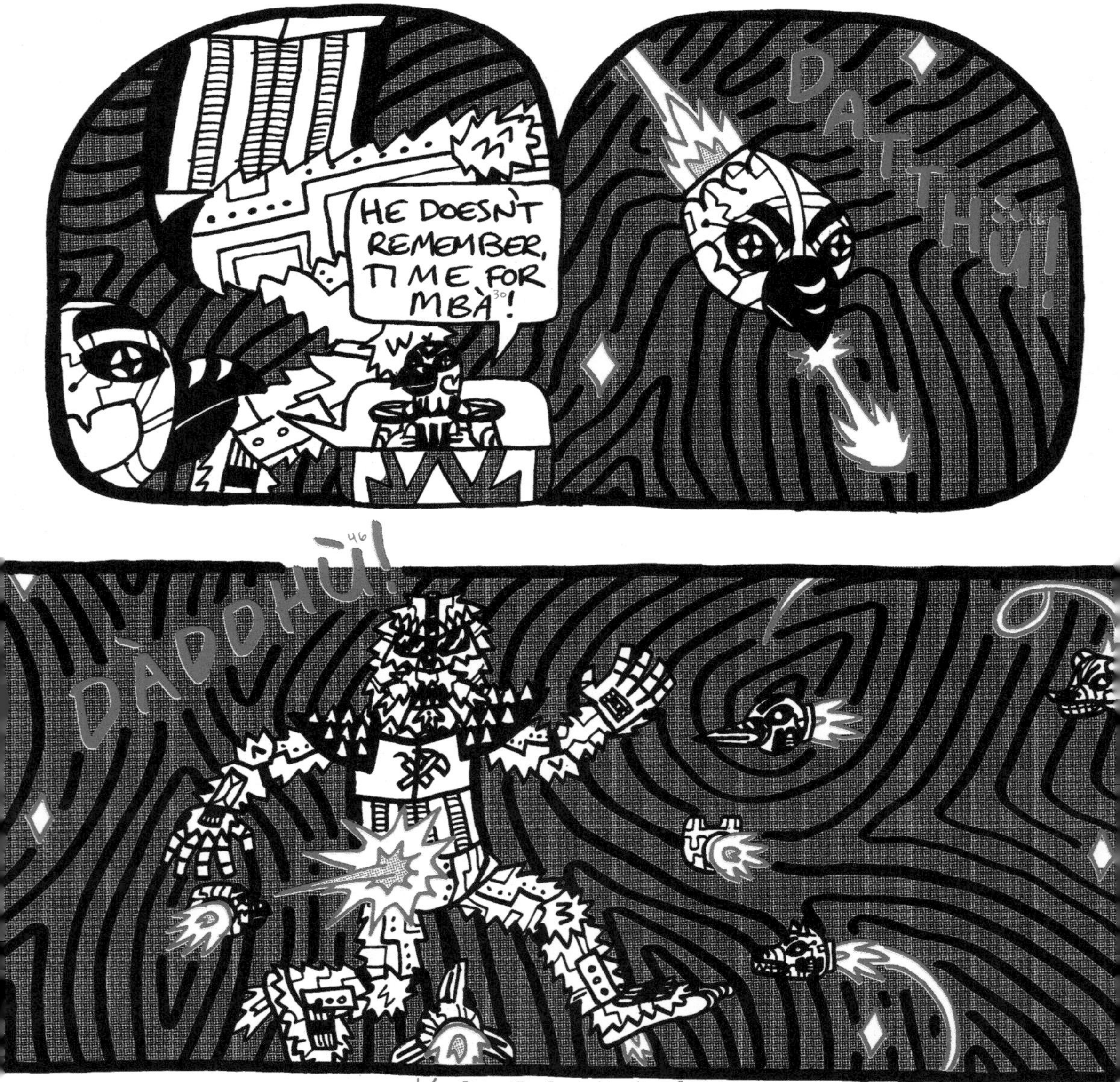
HE DOESN'T REMEMBER, TIME FOR MBÀ[30]!
DATTHÙ[16]!
DÀDDHÙ[46]!

16. SHOOT 30. WAR 46. BOOM

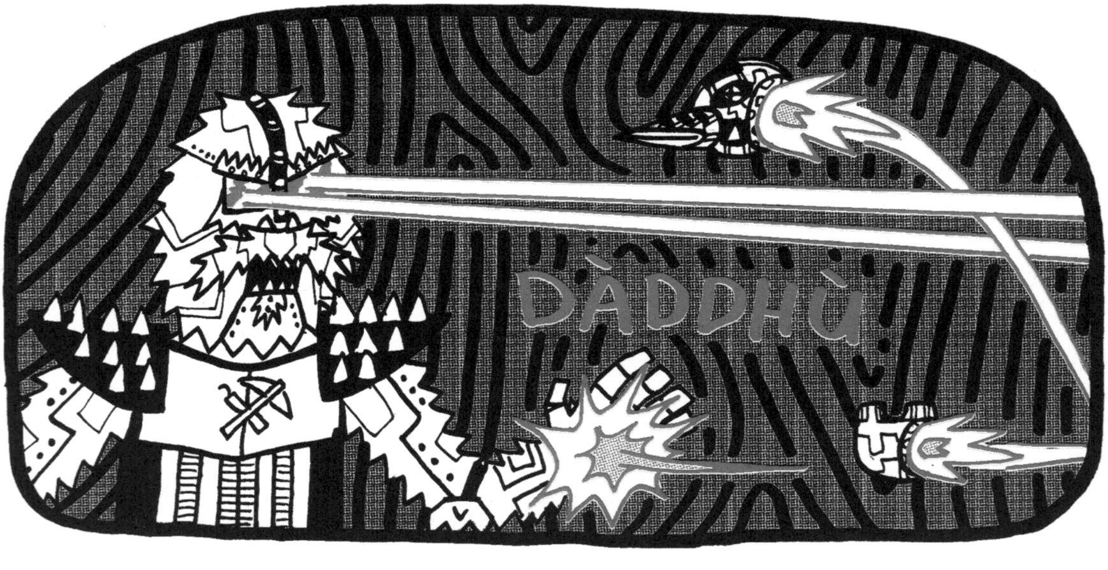
DÀDDHÙ!

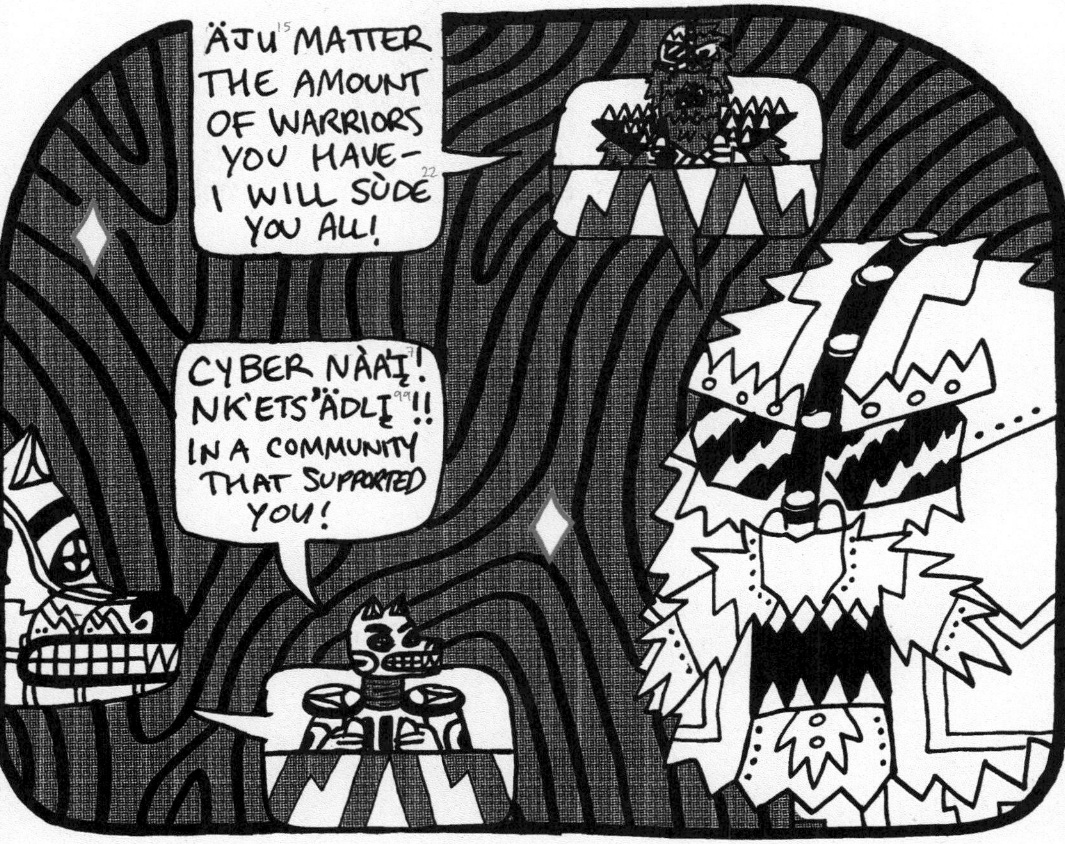
ÄJU[15] MATTER THE AMOUNT OF WARRIORS YOU HAVE- I WILL SÙDE[22] YOU ALL!
CYBER NÀAĮ[7]! NK'ETS'ÄDLĮ[99]!! IN A COMMUNITY THAT SUPPORTED YOU!

7. BUSHMAN 15. NO 22. BEAT 99. YOU ARE LOVED

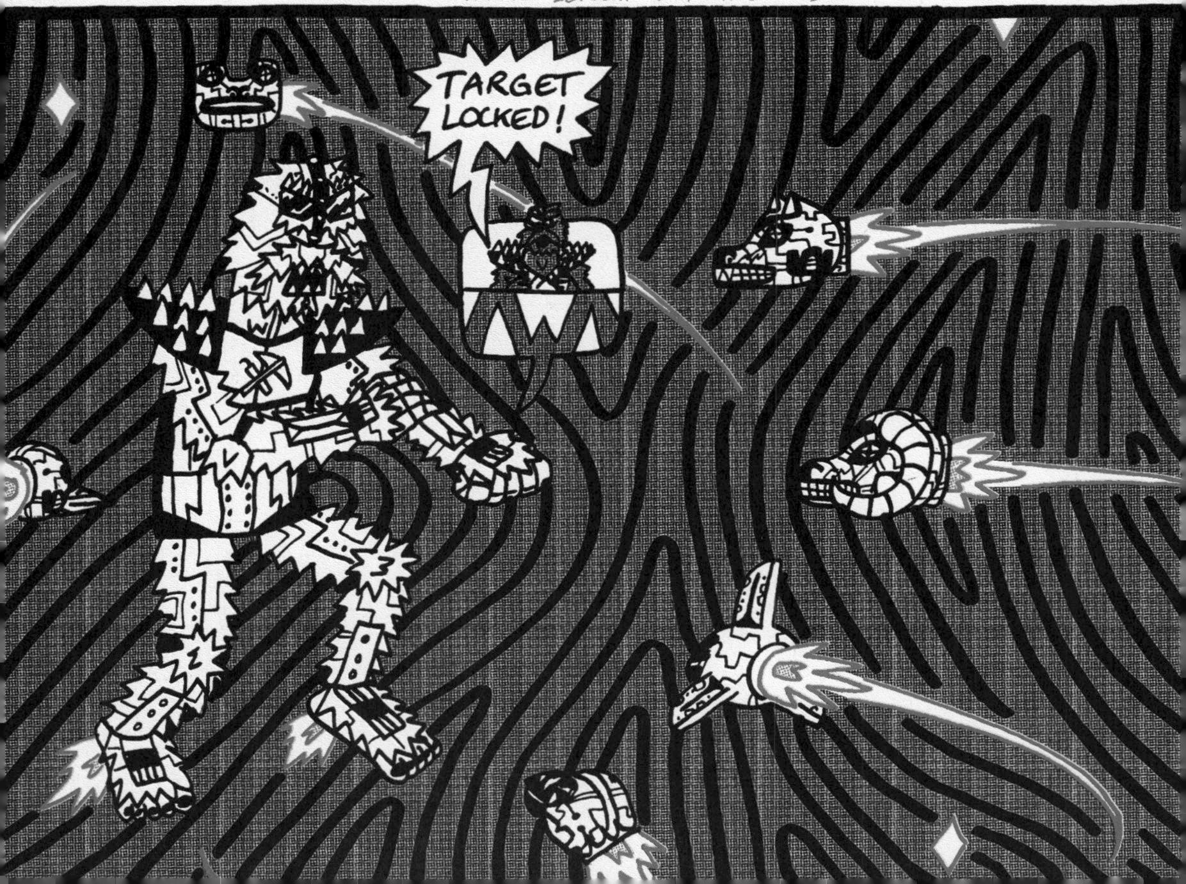
TARGET LOCKED!

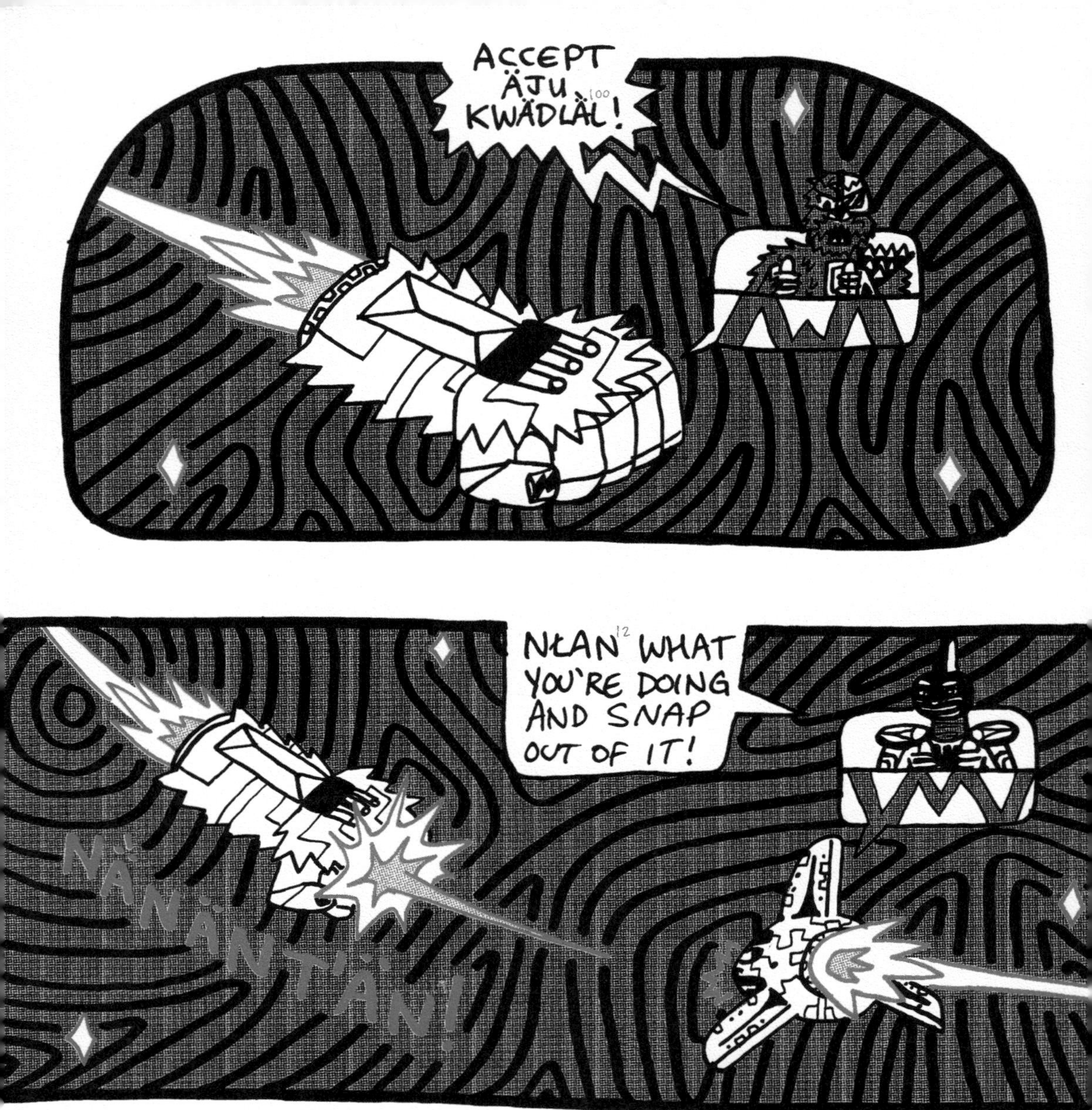
ACCEPT ÄJU KWÄDLÄL![100]
NŁAN[12] WHAT YOU'RE DOING AND SNAP OUT OF IT!
NÄNÄNT'ÄN!

8, LONG AGO PEOPLE 12. STOP 19. HIT 22. BEAT 100. DEFEAT

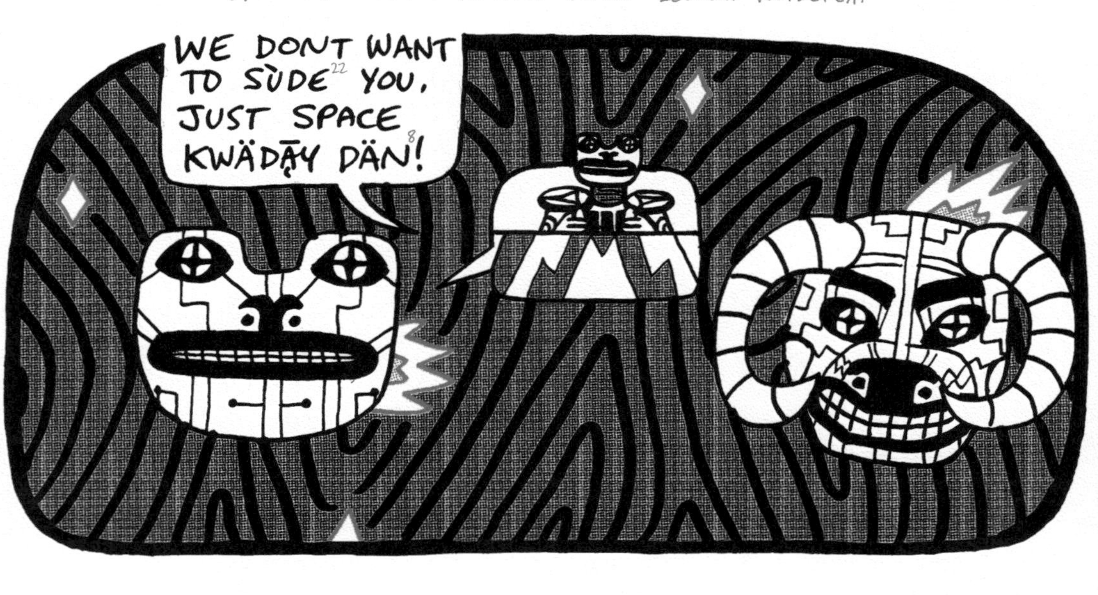
WE DONT WANT TO SÙDE[22] YOU, JUST SPACE[8] KWÄDĄY DÄN!

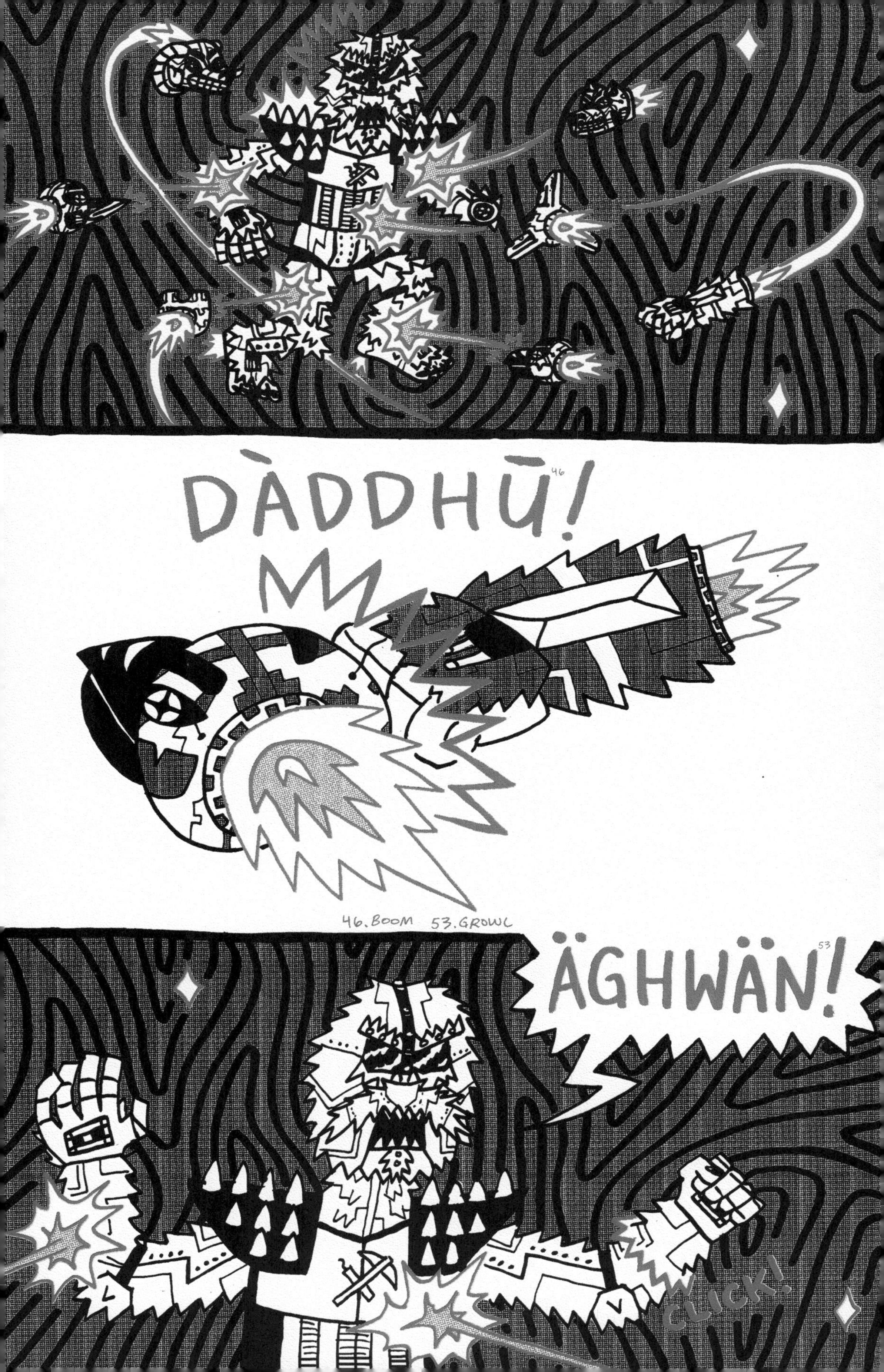
DÀDDHŪ![46]
46. BOOM 53. GROWL
ÄGHWÄN![53]
CLICK!

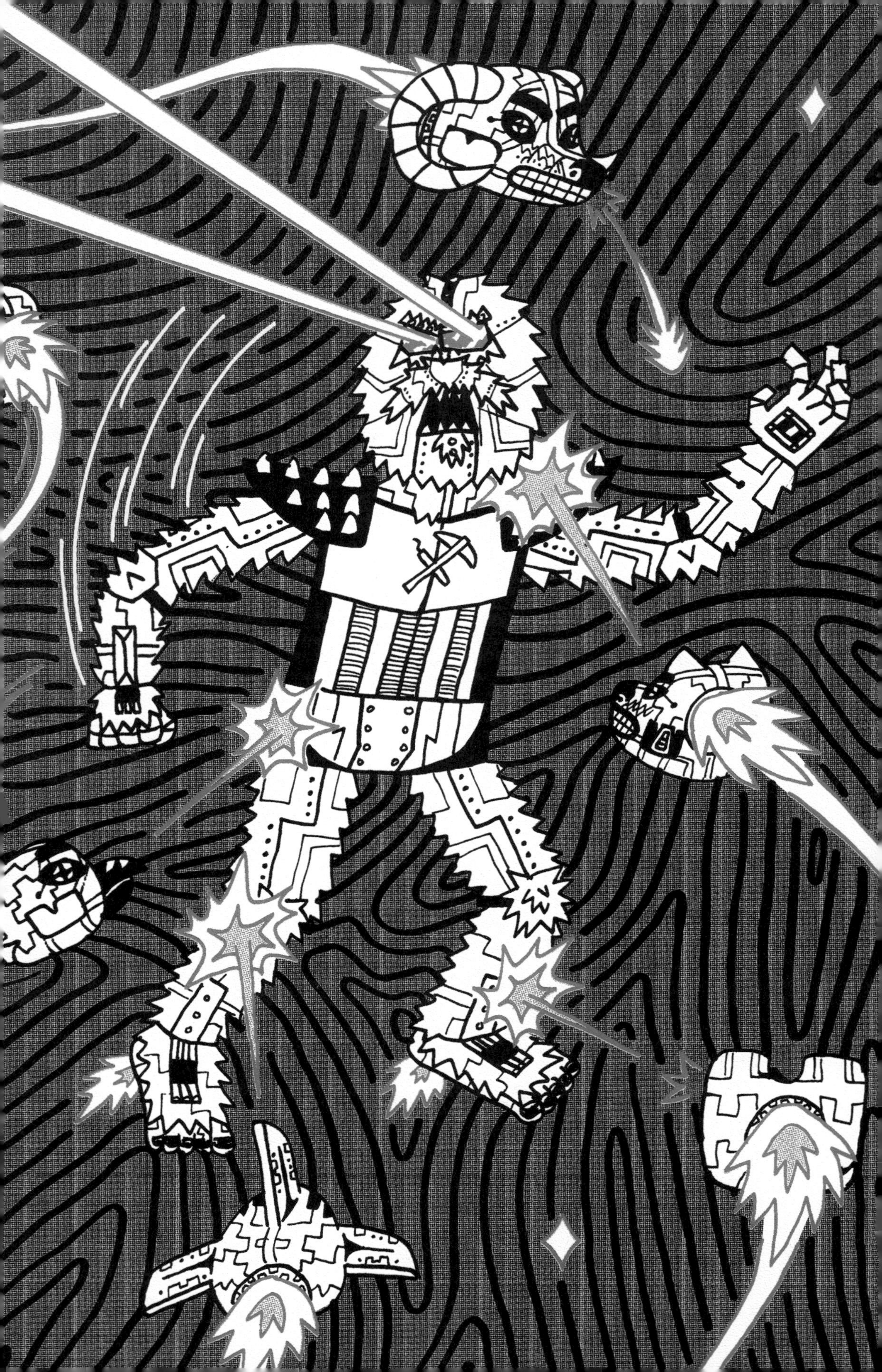

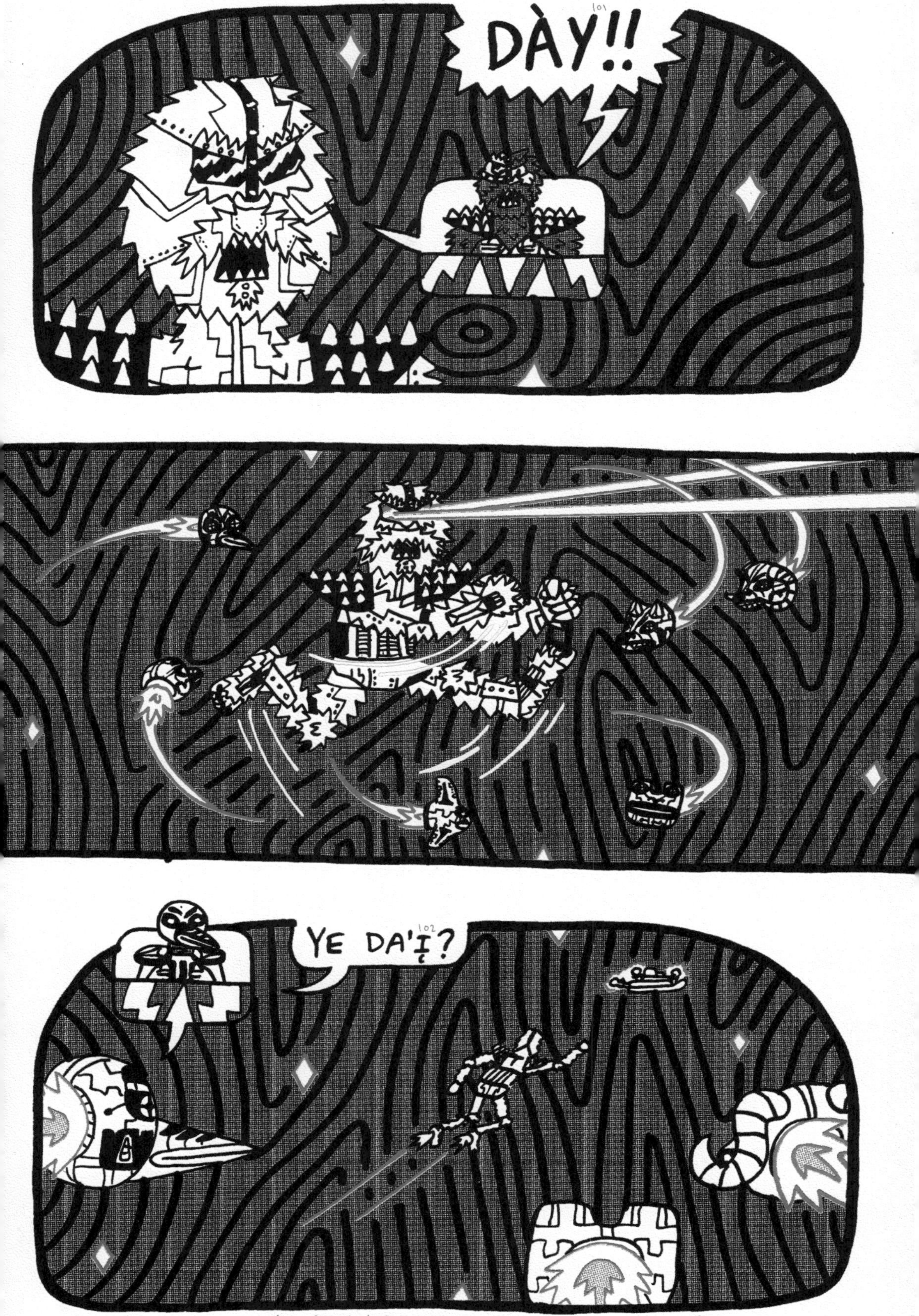
DÀY!![101]
YE DA'Ị?[102]

101. MOVE 102. WHAT ARE YOU DOING?

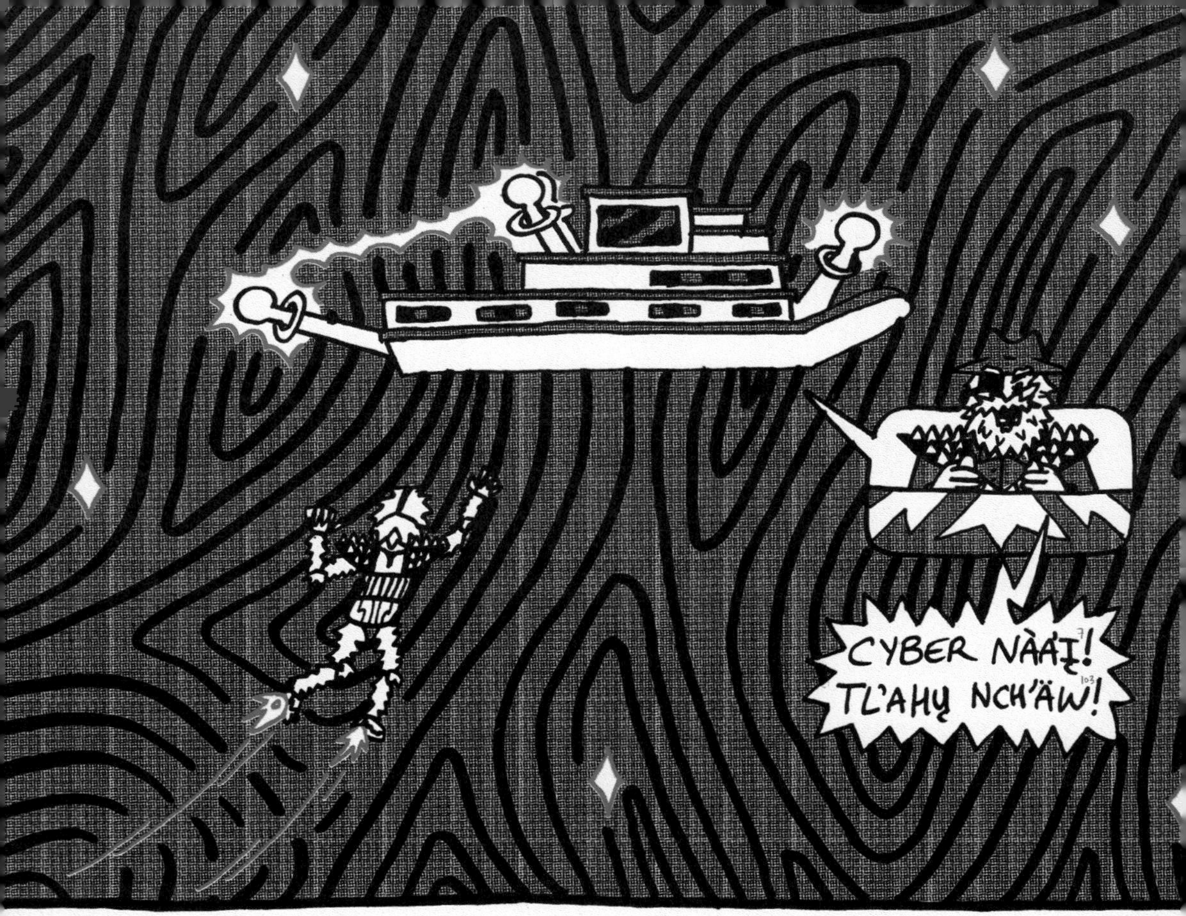
CYBER NÀÁĮ[7]!
TL'AHỤ NCH'ÄW[103]!

7. BUSHMAN 8. LONG AGO PEOPLE 15. NO 103. ENOUGH OF YOU

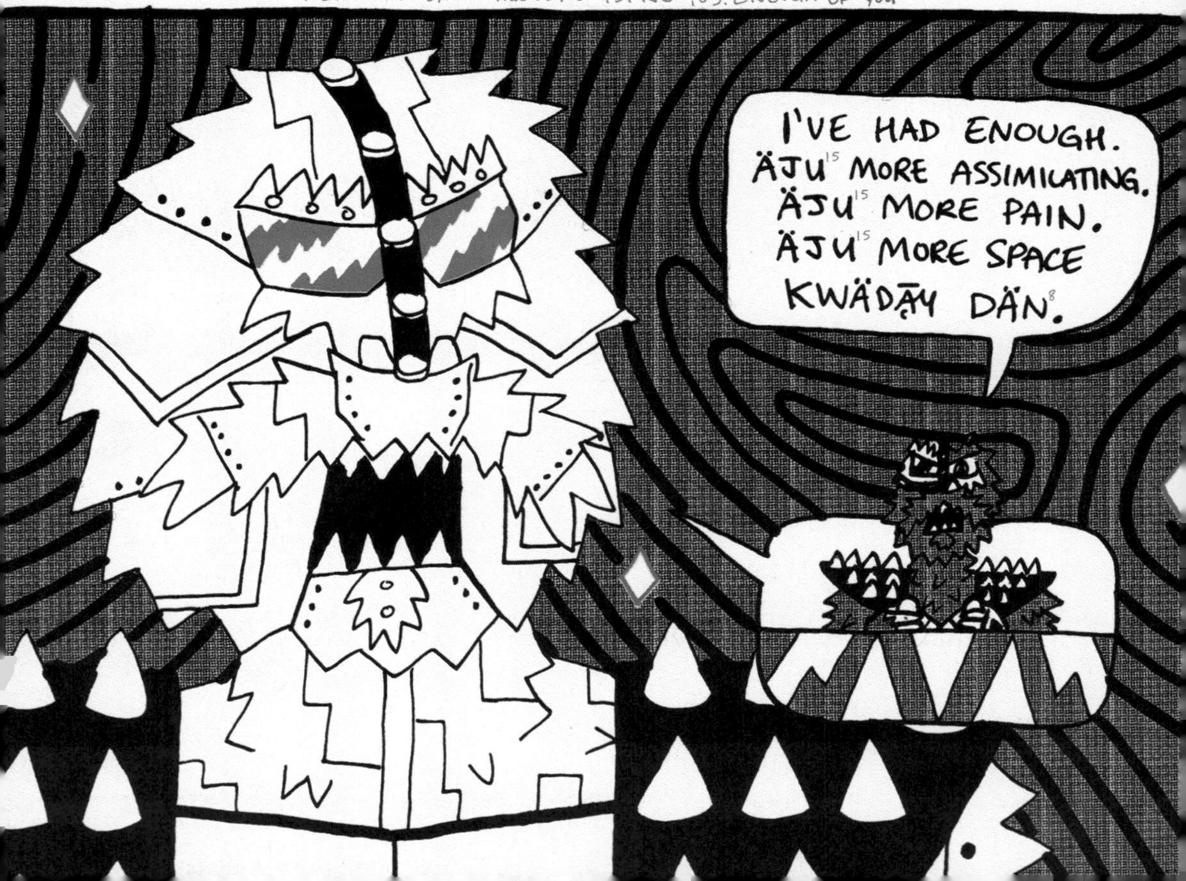
I'VE HAD ENOUGH. ÄJU[15] MORE ASSIMILATING. ÄJU[15] MORE PAIN. ÄJU[15] MORE SPACE KWÄDĄY DÄN[8].

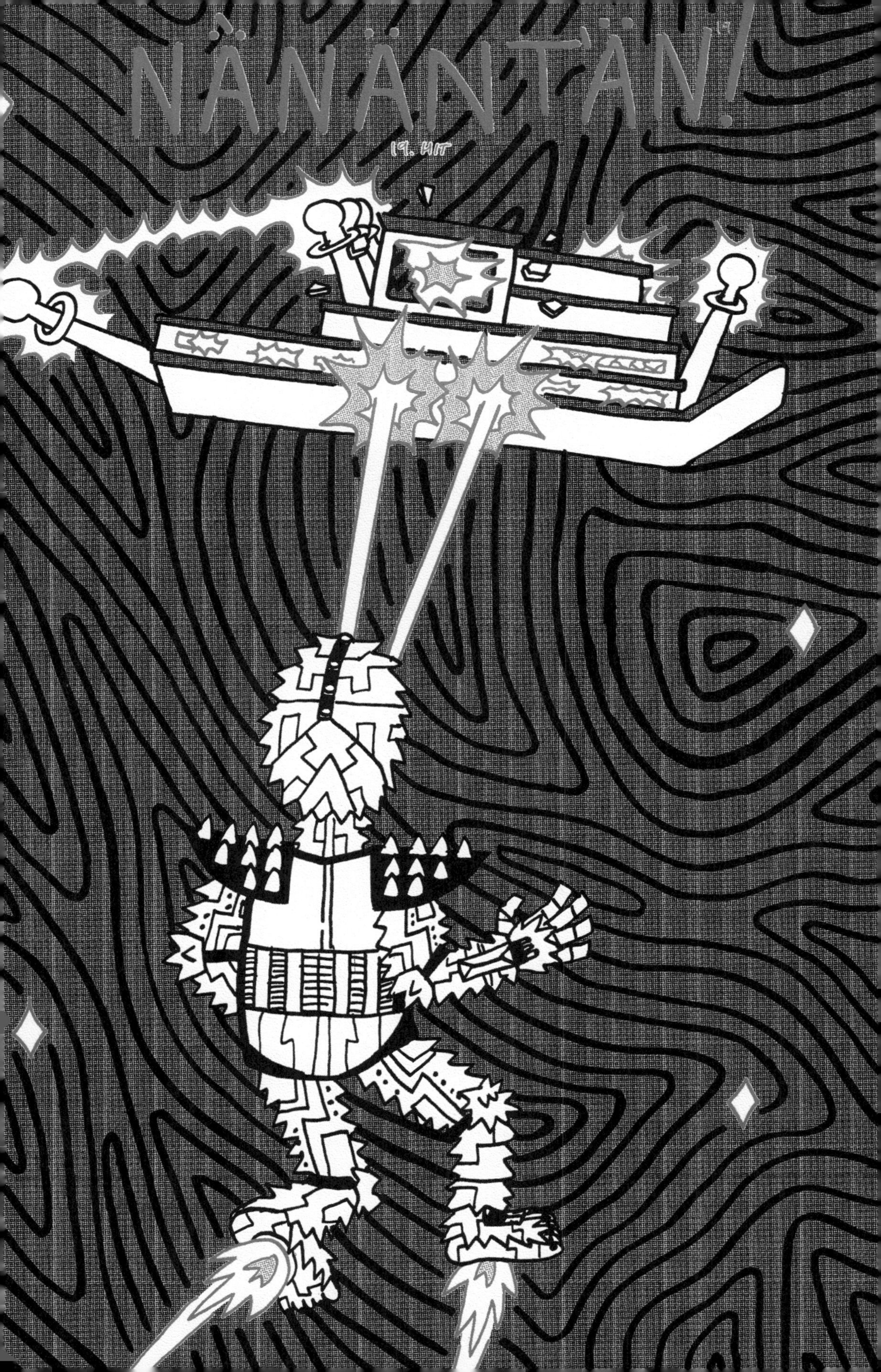
NÄNÄNTÄN!
19. HIT

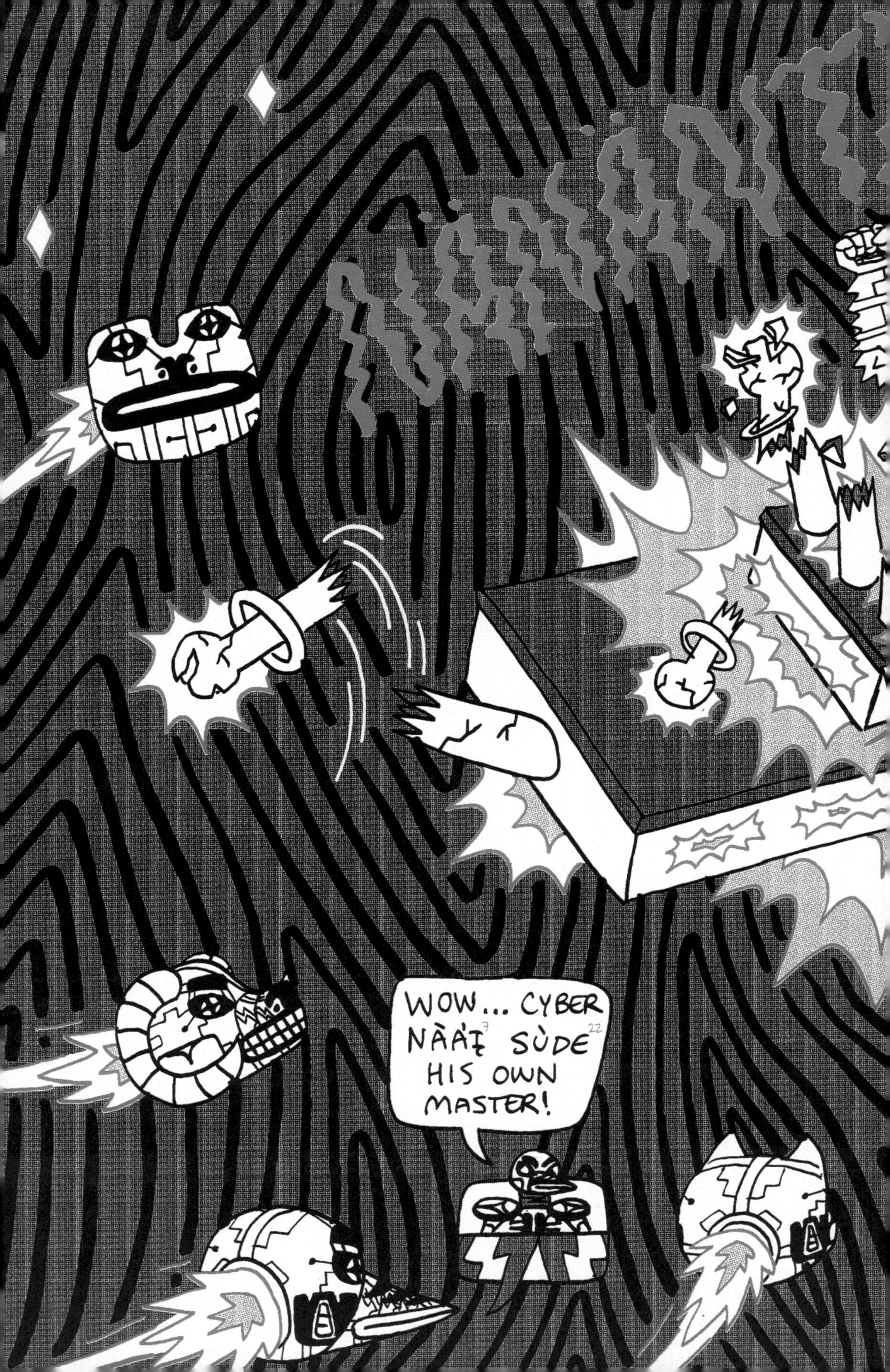
WOW... CYBER NÀÁĮ[7] SÙDE[22] HIS OWN MASTER!

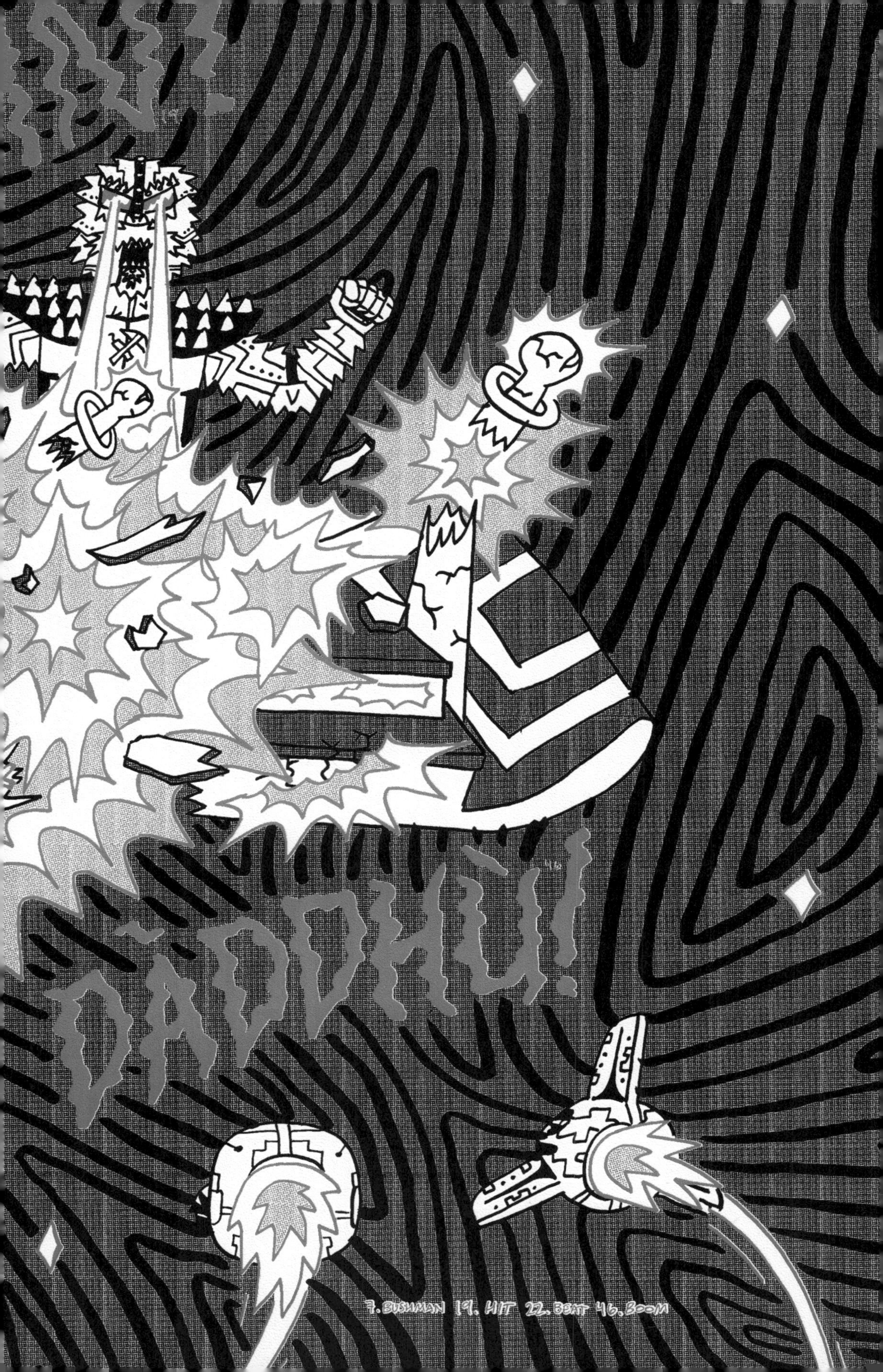
DĂDDHÙ![46]
7. BUSHMAN 19. HIT 22. BEAT 46. BOOM

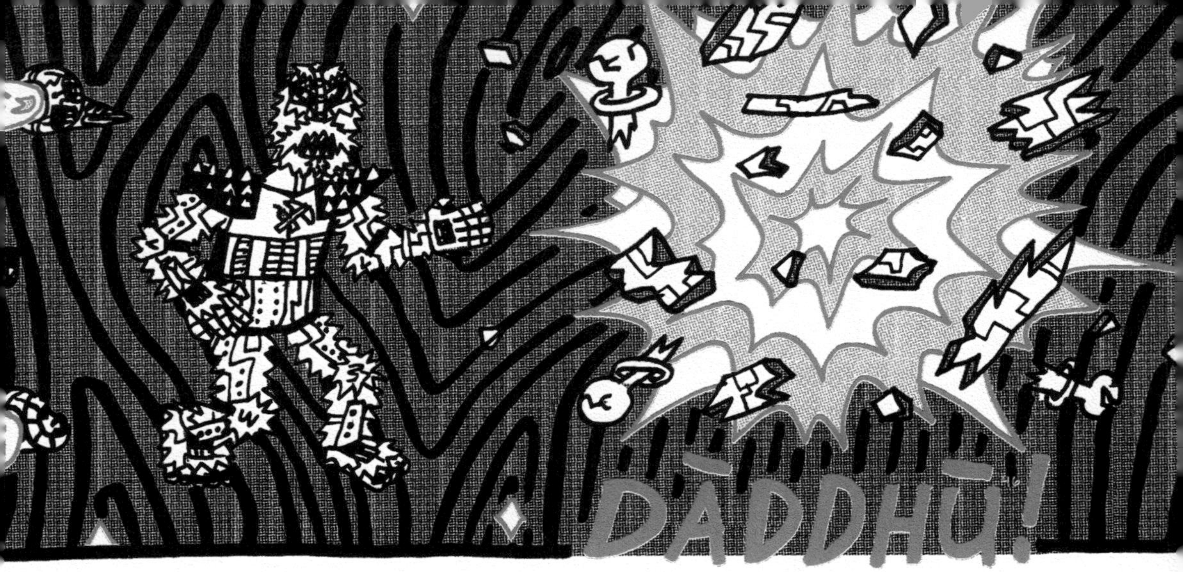
DADDHŪ![46]

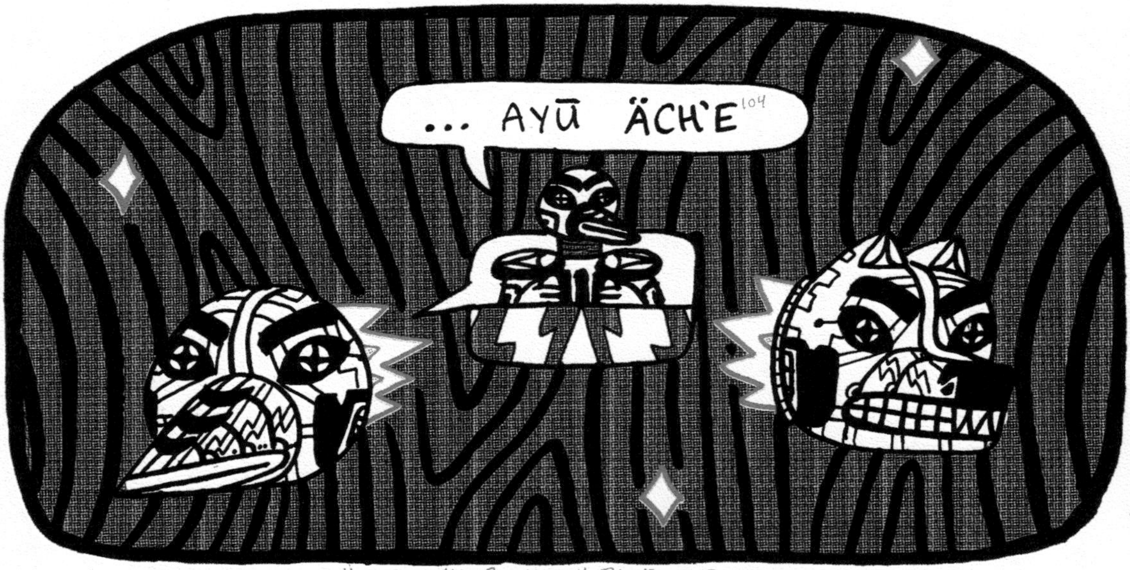
... AYŪ ÄCH'E[104]

4. EARTH 46. BOOM 104. THAT'S IT THERE

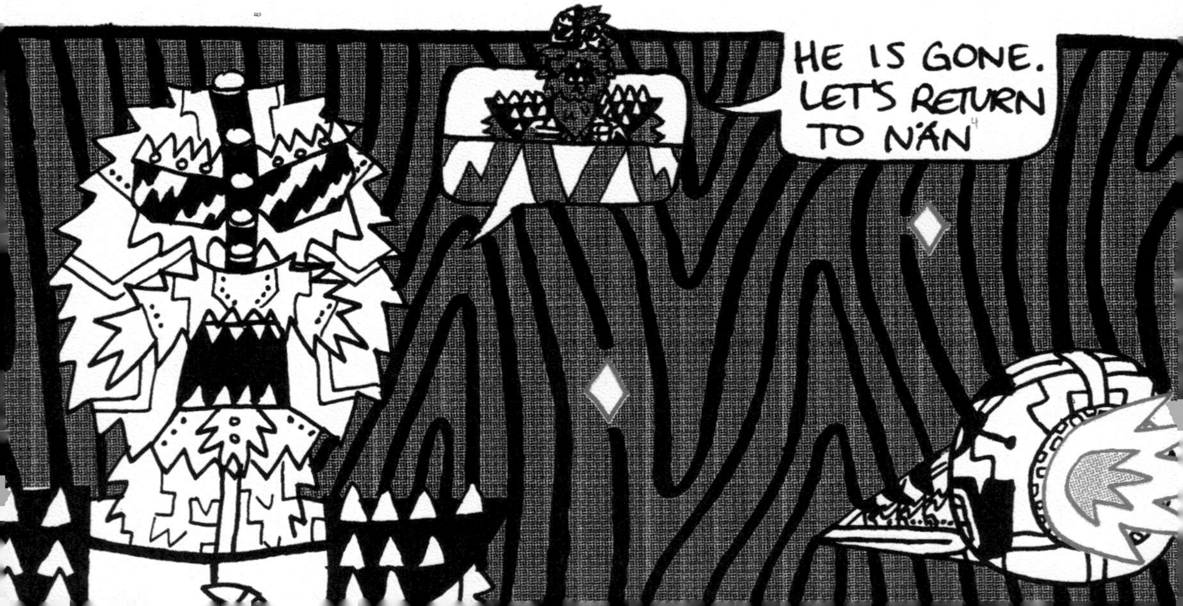
HE IS GONE. LET'S RETURN TO N'ÁN[4]

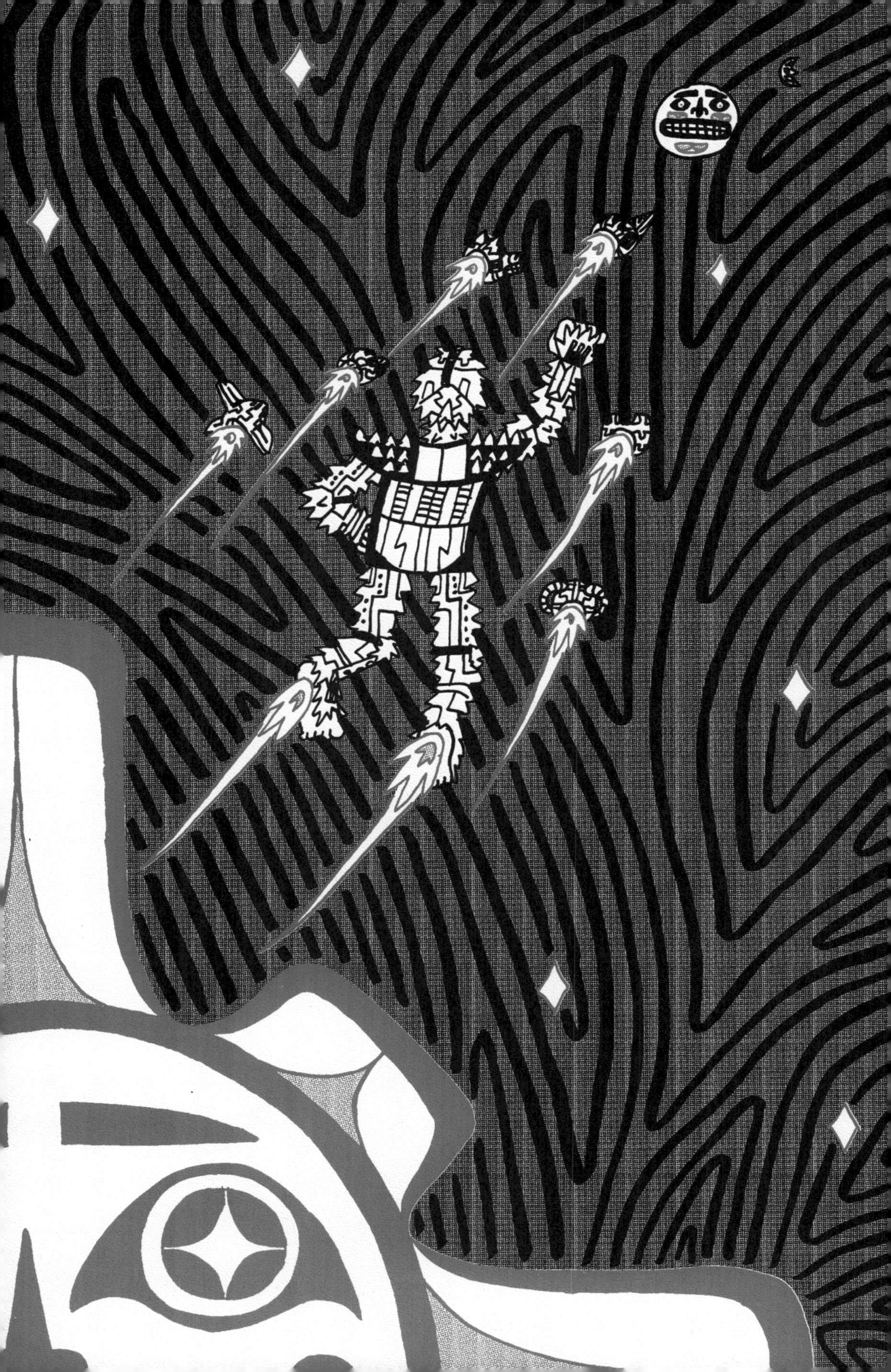

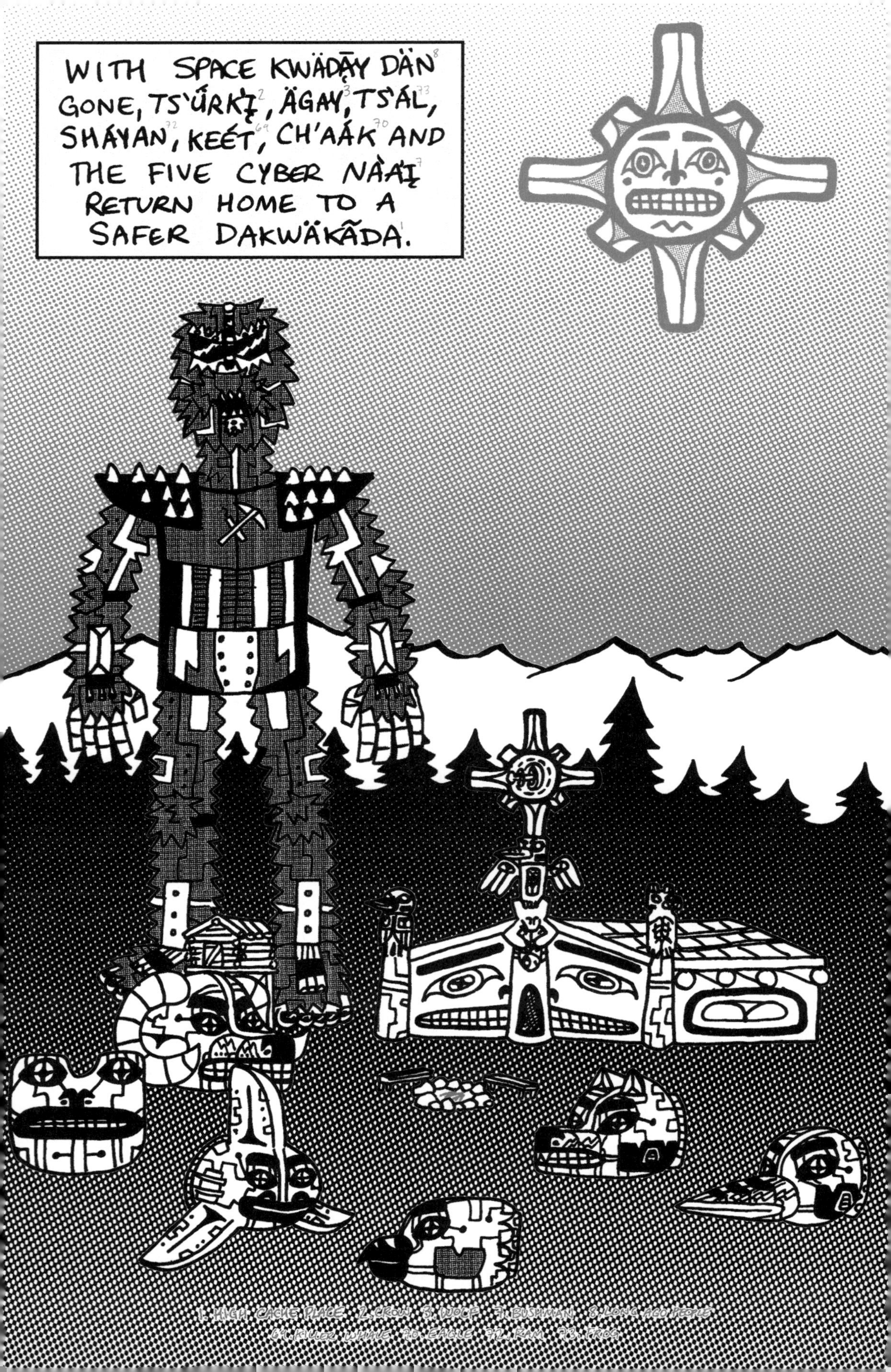
WITH SPACE KWÄDĄ̄Y DÄN[8] GONE, TS'ŰRKĮ[2], ÄGAY[3], TS'ÁL[73], SHÁYAN[72], KEÉT[69], CH'AÁK[70] AND THE FIVE CYBER NÀÀĮ[7] RETURN HOME TO A SAFER DAKWÄKÃDA[1].
1. HIGH CACHE PLACE 2. CROW 3. WOLF 7. BUSHMAN 8. LONG AGO PEOPLE
69. KILLER WHALE 70. EAGLE 72. RAM 73. FROG

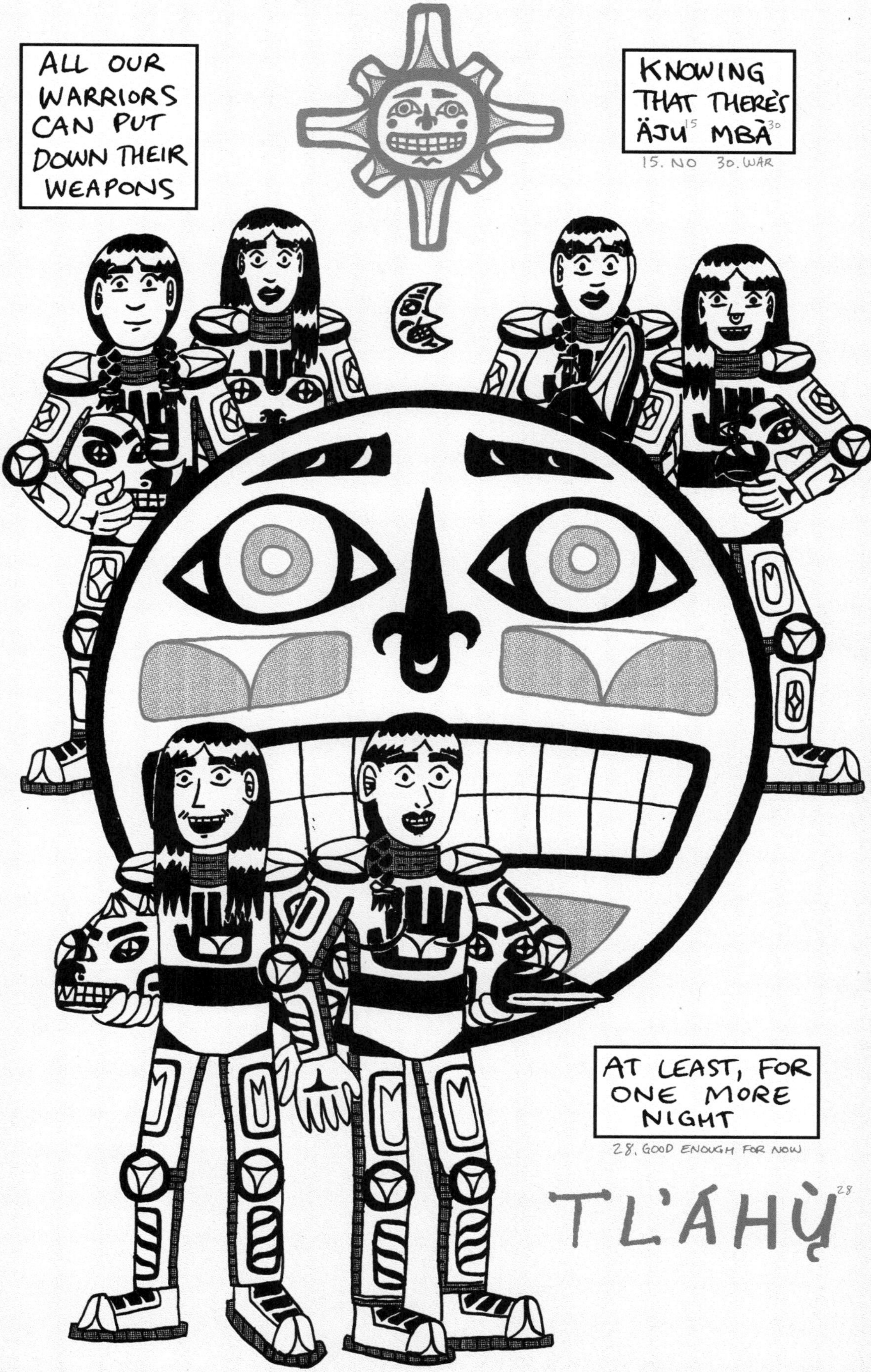
ALL OUR WARRIORS CAN PUT DOWN THEIR WEAPONS
KNOWING THAT THERE'S ÄJU[15] MBÀ[30]
15. NO 30. WAR
AT LEAST, FOR ONE MORE NIGHT
28. GOOD ENOUGH FOR NOW
TL'ÁHỤ̀[28]

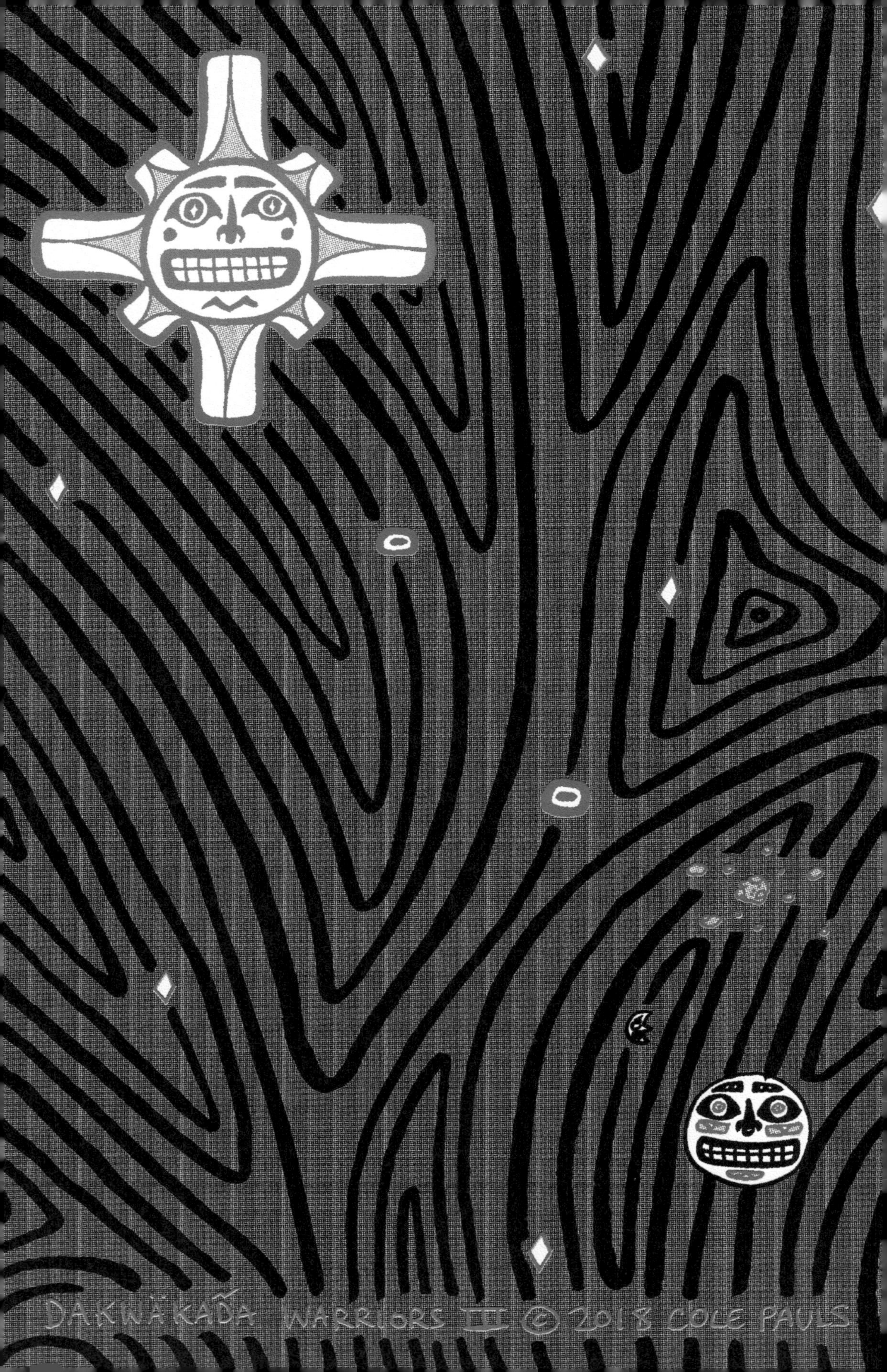
DAKWÄKAΔ̈A WARRIORS III © 2018 COLE PAULS

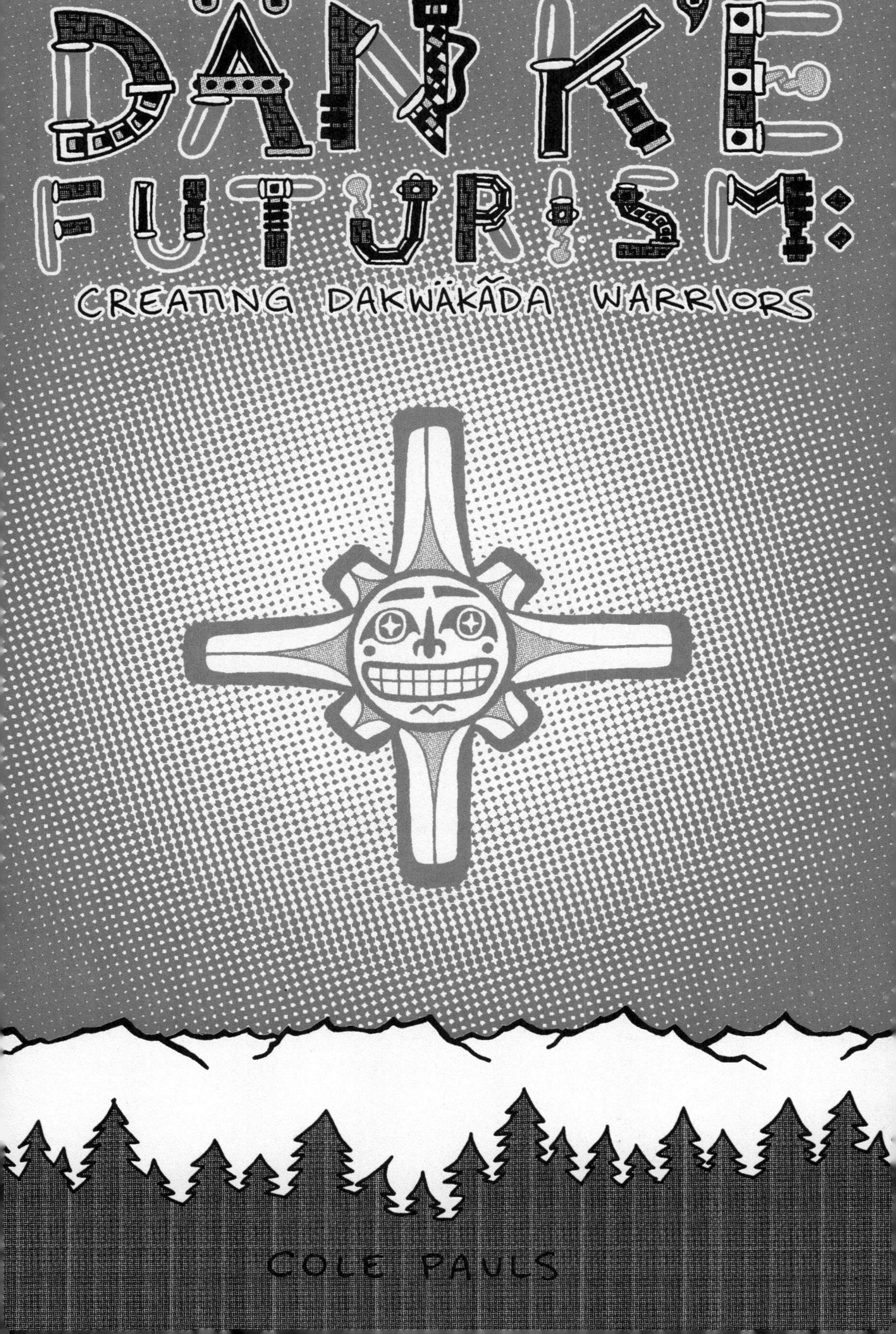
DÄN K'E FUTURISM:
CREATING DAKWÄKÃDA WARRIORS
COLE PAULS

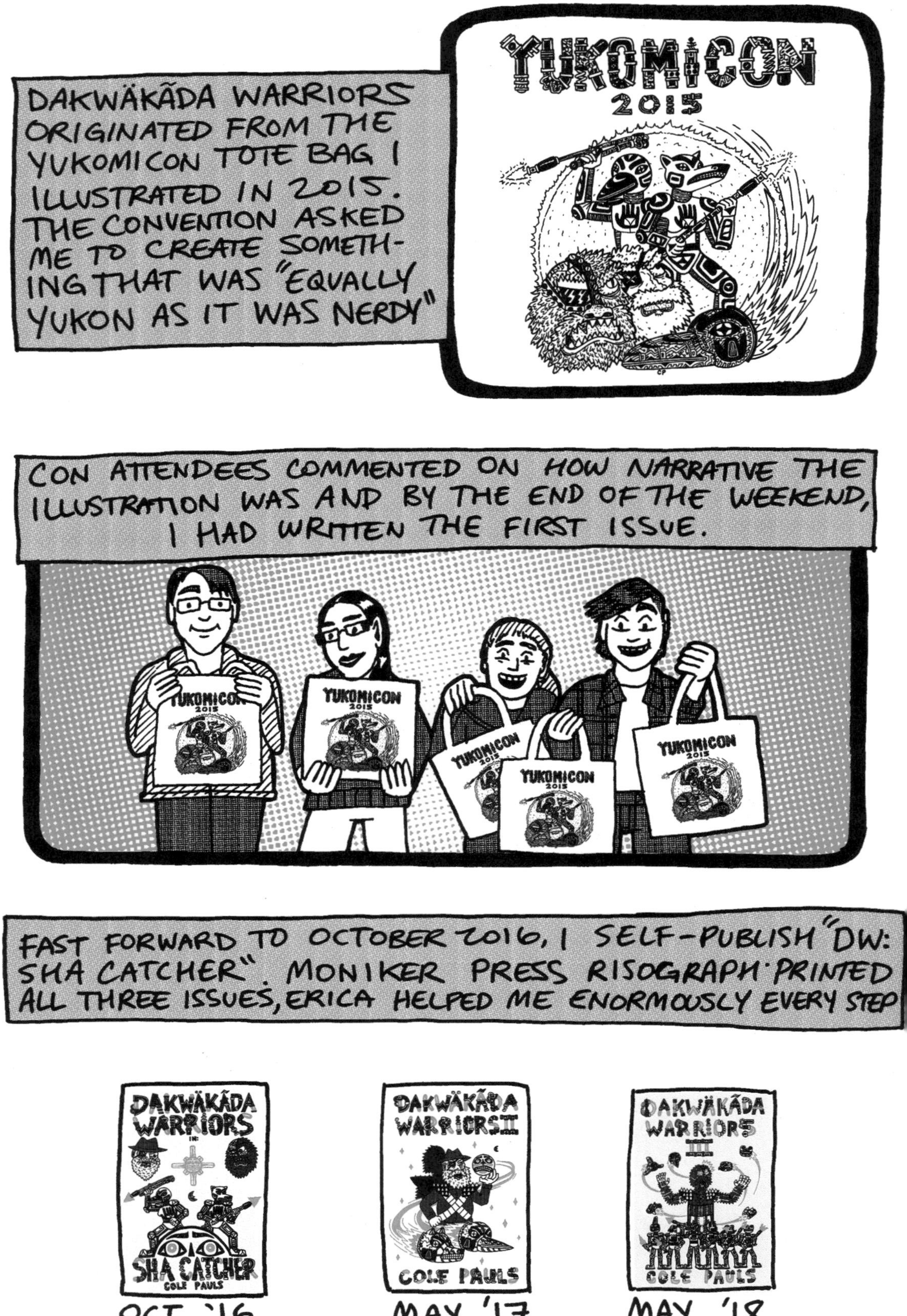
DAKWÄKÃDA WARRIORS ORIGINATED FROM THE YUKOMICON TOTE BAG I ILLUSTRATED IN 2015. THE CONVENTION ASKED ME TO CREATE SOMETHING THAT WAS "EQUALLY YUKON AS IT WAS NERDY"
YUKOMICON 2015
CON ATTENDEES COMMENTED ON HOW NARRATIVE THE ILLUSTRATION WAS AND BY THE END OF THE WEEKEND, I HAD WRITTEN THE FIRST ISSUE.
YUKOMICON 2015
FAST FORWARD TO OCTOBER 2016, I SELF-PUBLISH "DW: SHA CATCHER". MONIKER PRESS RISOGRAPH PRINTED ALL THREE ISSUES, ERICA HELPED ME ENORMOUSLY EVERY STEP
DAKWÄKÃDA WARRIORS IN: SHA CATCHER COLE PAULS
OCT '16
DAKWÄKÃDA WARRIORS II COLE PAULS
MAY '17
DAKWÄKÃDA WARRIORS III COLE PAULS
MAY '18

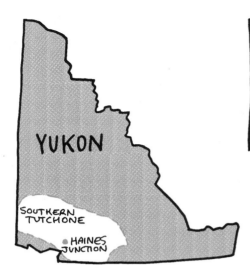

YUKON

SOUTHERN TUTCHONE

HAINES JUNCTION

I WANTED TO MAKE DW A LANGUAGE REVIVAL COMIC SO I ASKED TWO LANGUAGE PRESERVERS FROM MY HOMETOWN—KHÂSHA AND VIVIAN SMITH TO COLLABORATE.

I WOULD TYPE MY SCRIPT FOR THEM AND EMAIL BACK & FORTH WITH WHAT THEY COULD TRANSLATE.

I ALSO WANTED TO CREATE AN IDENTITY FOR ALL SOUTHERN TUTCHONE AND YUKON YOUTH. AS A CHILD I WAS BLOWN AWAY BY CHRIS CALDWELL'S "ALSEK ABC'S" BOOK BECAUSE IT WAS LOCATED IN THE SAME VALLEY MY HOMETOWN IS IN. I WANTED TO RECREATE THAT FEELING WITH THIS COMIC.

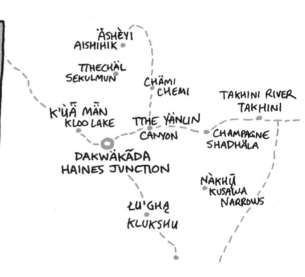

ÄSHÈYI
AISHIHIK

TTHECHÄL
SEKULMUN

CHÄMI
CHEMI

TAKHINI RIVER
TAKHINI

K'ÙÄ MÄN
KLOO LAKE

TTHE YÄNLIN
CANYON

CHAMPAGNE
SHADHÄLA

DAKWÄKÄDA
HAINES JUNCTION

NÀKHÙ
KUSAWA
NARROWS

ŁU'GHĄ
KLUKSHU

THE SOUTHERN TUTCHONE PEOPLE HAVE TWO CLANS, WOLF & CROW, WHICH IS WHY OUR HEROES ARE ÄGAY & TS'ÜRK'I. THE TRADITIONAL COLOURS OF THE SOUTHERN TUTCHONE PEOPLE ARE BLACK, WHITE & RED, WHICH IS WHY THIS BOOK HAS THE SAME COLOUR PALETTE.

TS'ÜRK'I
CROW

ÄGAY
WOLF

THERE ARE TWO SOUTHERN TUTCHONE DIALECTS—CHAMPAGNE (SHADHÄLA K'E) AND AISHIHIK (ÄSHÈY K'E). EACH ARE SPECIFIC TO THE REGION THEY'RE FROM. KHÂSHA SPEAKS BOTH DIALECTS AND VIVIAN SPEAKS THE AISHIHIK DIALECT, THATS WHY BOTH ARE IN THE ORIGINAL ISSUES

"SALMON"

SHADHÄLA K'E
CHAMPAGNE DIALECT
"SAMAY"

ÄSHÈY K'E
AISHIHIK DIALECT
"SAMBAY"

THE DAKWÄKÄDA WARRIORS ARE NAMED AFTER THE TRADITIONAL SONG & DANCE GROUP THE DAKWÄKÄDA DANCERS. FOR 16 YEARS I WAS A MEMBER & BOTH MY PARENTS AND SISTERS ARE CURRENT MEMBERS.

THE LIGHTSABER STYLE WEAPONS DW USE ARE ACTUAL TRADITIONAL HUNTING TOOLS OF THE SOUTHERN TUTCHONE PEOPLE. TS'ÜRK'I WEILDS AN ATLATL, WHICH IS A THROWING SPEAR FOR LONG DISTANCE AND ÄGAY WEILDS AN ARROWHEAD SPEAR, USED FOR CLOSE COMBAT.

ÄT'ATS'ÄTS'ÏK
ATLATL

CHĄL
SPEAR

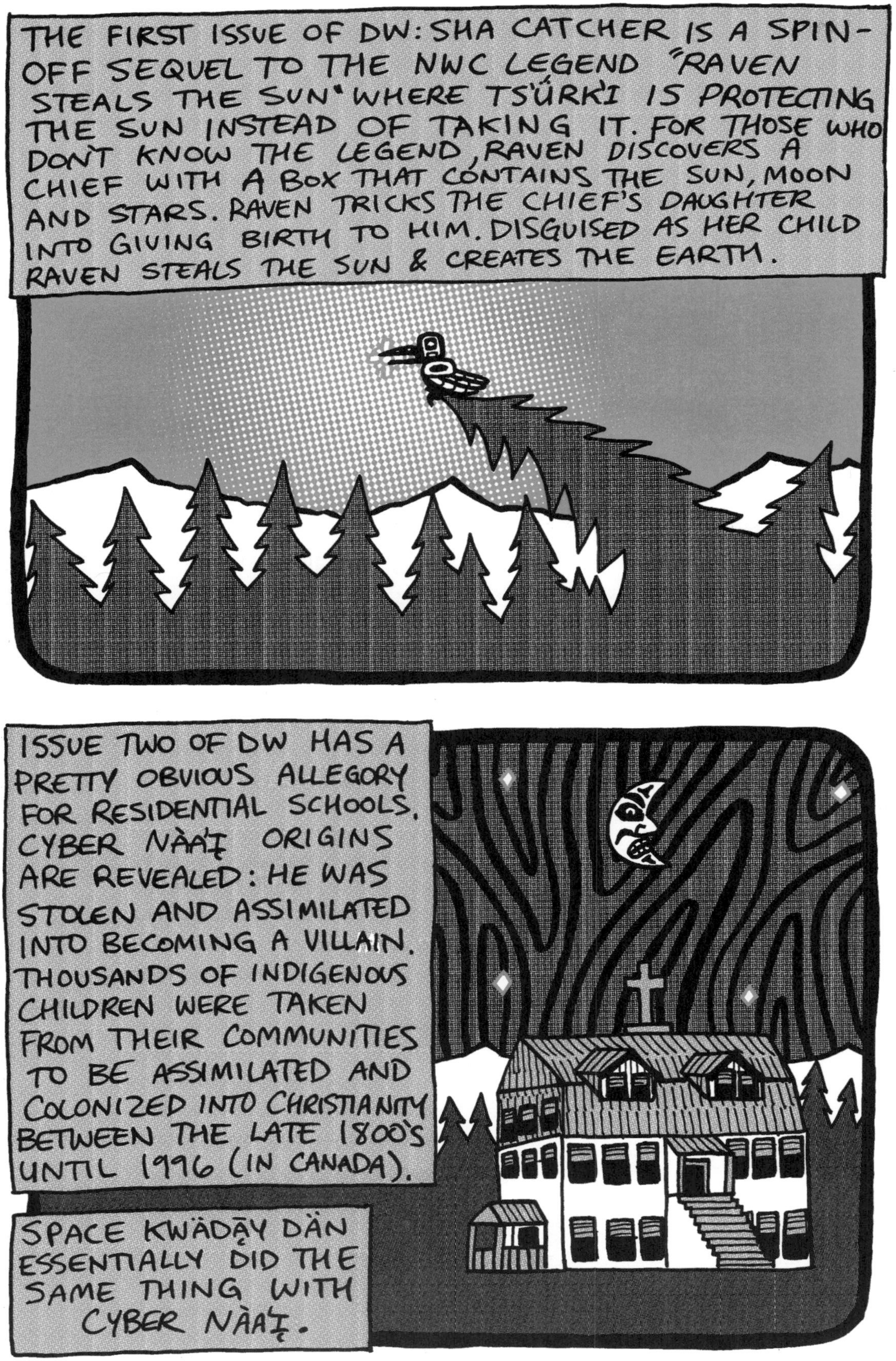
THE FIRST ISSUE OF DW: SHA CATCHER IS A SPIN-OFF SEQUEL TO THE NWC LEGEND "RAVEN STEALS THE SUN" WHERE TS'ǗRK'I IS PROTECTING THE SUN INSTEAD OF TAKING IT. FOR THOSE WHO DON'T KNOW THE LEGEND, RAVEN DISCOVERS A CHIEF WITH A BOX THAT CONTAINS THE SUN, MOON AND STARS. RAVEN TRICKS THE CHIEF'S DAUGHTER INTO GIVING BIRTH TO HIM. DISGUISED AS HER CHILD RAVEN STEALS THE SUN & CREATES THE EARTH.
ISSUE TWO OF DW HAS A PRETTY OBVIOUS ALLEGORY FOR RESIDENTIAL SCHOOLS. CYBER NÀÀ'Į ORIGINS ARE REVEALED: HE WAS STOLEN AND ASSIMILATED INTO BECOMING A VILLAIN. THOUSANDS OF INDIGENOUS CHILDREN WERE TAKEN FROM THEIR COMMUNITIES TO BE ASSIMILATED AND COLONIZED INTO CHRISTIANITY BETWEEN THE LATE 1800'S UNTIL 1996 (IN CANADA).
SPACE KWÄDĄ̈Y DÄN ESSENTIALLY DID THE SAME THING WITH CYBER NÀÀ'Į.

SPACE KWÄDAY DÄN'S YAT'ÄY DREDGE IS BASED OFF OF DREDGE #4 LOCATED IN DAWSON CITY, YT. DREDGES ARE HUGE EXCAVATION MACHINES THAT SCRAPE THE BOTTOM OF CREEKS AND RIVER BEDS, LOOKING FOR VALUABLE MINERALS - LIKE GOLD.

THE THIRD DW ISSUE INTRODUCES NEW WARRIORS, THE DAKHKÁ KHWÁAN & ŁU'ÄN MÄN WARRIORS. THIS WAS INSPIRED BY THE 1973 DOCUMENT "TOGETHER TODAY FOR OUR CHILDREN TOMORROW" THAT YUKON FIRST NATION LEADERS PRESENTED TO CANADA'S PARLIAMENT IN OTTAWA. CHAMPAGNE AND AISHIHIK'S ELIJAH SMITH, HARRY ALLEN AND DAVE JOE WERE LEADERS IN THE YUKON-WIDE LAND CLAIMS NEGOTIATION PROCESS AND ALSO HELPED CREATE THE UMBRELLA FINAL AGREEMENT FOR THE ENTIRE TERRITORY. THE DOCUMENT FINALIZED THE NEW RELATIONSHIP BETWEEN YUKON FIRST NATION AND THE GOVERNMENTS OF CANADA AND THE YUKON.

CHIEF RAY JACKSON OF CHAMPAGNE & AISHIHIK SIGNING THE DOCUMENT

CHIEF CHARLIE ABEL SIGNING ON BEHALF OF OLD CROW FIRST NATION

CHIEF SAM JOHNSTON OF TESLIN FIRST NATION SIGNING THE DOCUMENT

THE DAKHKÁ KHWÁAN WARRIORS ARE NAMED AFTER THE TRADITIONAL SONG & DANCE GROUP, THE DAKHKÁ KHWÁAN DANCERS, BASED IN WHITEHORSE, YT. MY ELDEST SISTER, NIECE, NEPHEW & BROTHER IN LAW ARE ALL CURRENT MEMBERS. THE ŁU'ÄN MÄN WARRIORS ARE NAMED AFTER THE TRADITIONAL NAME OF KLUANE LAKE; ŁU'ÄN MÄN. KLUANE FIRST NATION ALSO SPEAK A DIALECT OF SOUTHERN TUTCHONE AND IS ONE OF DAKWÄKÃDA'S CLOSEST NEIGHBORS.

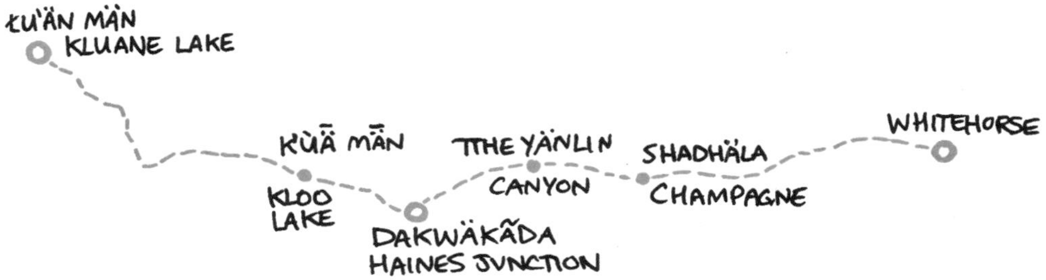
ŁU'ÄN MÄN
KLUANE LAKE
KÙÄ MÄN
KLOO LAKE
DAKWÄKÃDA
HAINES JUNCTION
TTHE YÄNLIN
CANYON
SHADHÄLA
CHAMPAGNE
WHITEHORSE

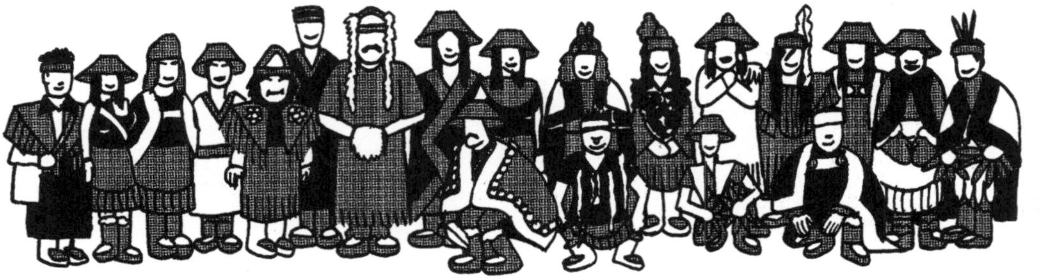

I ALSO INCLUDED OTHER TRADITIONAL TOOLS WITH THESE WARRIORS. THE ŁU'ÄN MÄN WARRIORS HAVE TWO DIFFERENT STYLES OF FISHING GAFF AND THE DAKHKÁ KHWÁAN WARRIORS HAVE DAGGERS

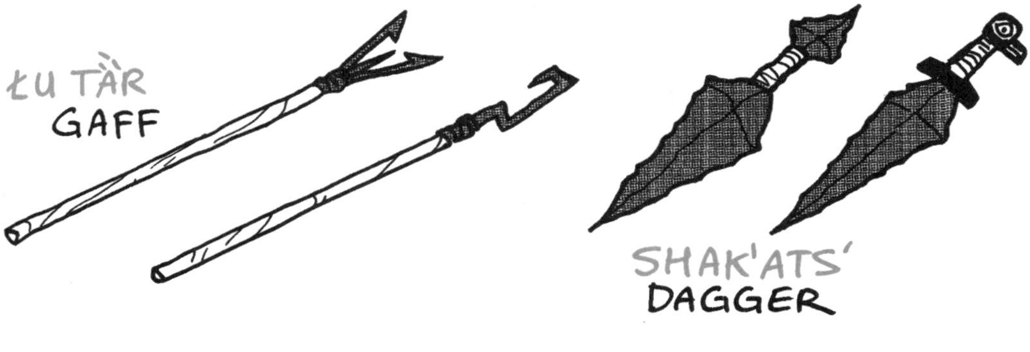
ŁU TÀR
GAFF
SHAK'ATS'
DAGGER

ANNIE NED, THE FOUNDER OF THE DAKWÄKÂDA DANCERS AND A HUGE CULTURAL LEADER IS FEATURED IN THE THIRD ISSUE. I WAS GIVEN PERMISSION TO INCLUDE HER BY MARY-JANE JIM & DIANE STRAND (GRAND-DAUGHTERS) AND CAFN LET ME PICK A REFERENCE PHOTO FROM THEIR ARCHIVES. SHE MADE A HUGE IMPACT SAVING SOUTHERN TUTCHONE CULTURE AND HERITAGE.

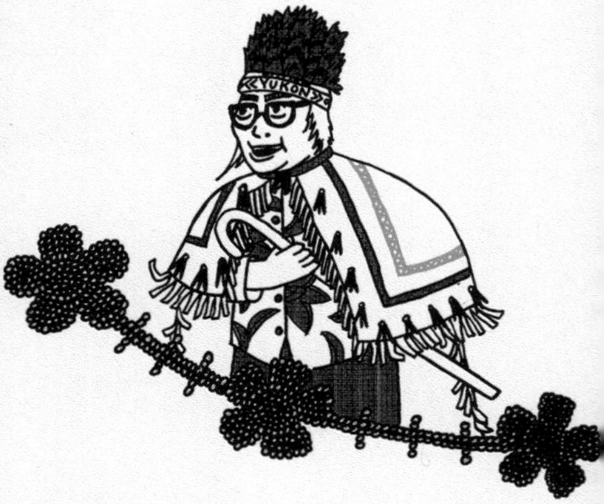
YUKON

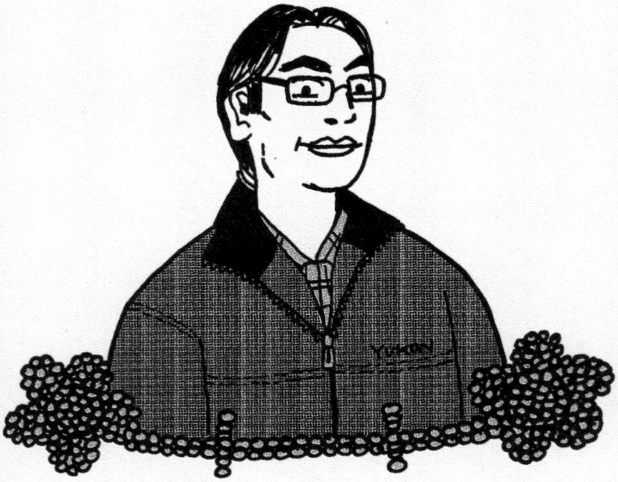
YUKON

VIVIAN SMITH WAS MY SOUTHERN TUTCHONE TEACHER FROM KINDER-GARTEN TO GRADE 12. I HAVE KNOWN HER MY ENTIRE LIFE! SHE SPEAKS THE AISHIHIK DIALECT AND HELPED ME TRANSLATE WORDS INTO SOUTHERN TUTCHONE.

KHÂSHA IS ONE OF THE LANGUAGE TEACHERS FOR CAFN & IS A MEMBER OF THE DAKWÄKÂDA DANCERS. I HAVE ALSO KNOWN HIM ALMOST MY ENTIRE LIFE! HE SPEAKS BOTH DIALECTS AND HELPED ME TRANSLATE WORDS INTO SOUTHERN TUTCHONE. KHÂSHA AND VIVIAN HAVE BEEN SUPPORTIVE SINCE DAY ONE!

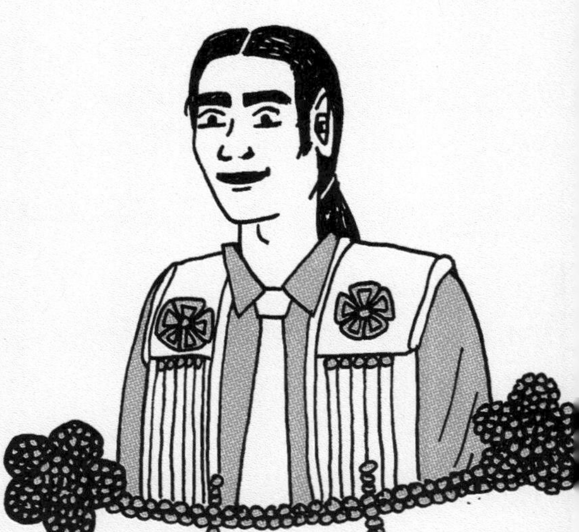

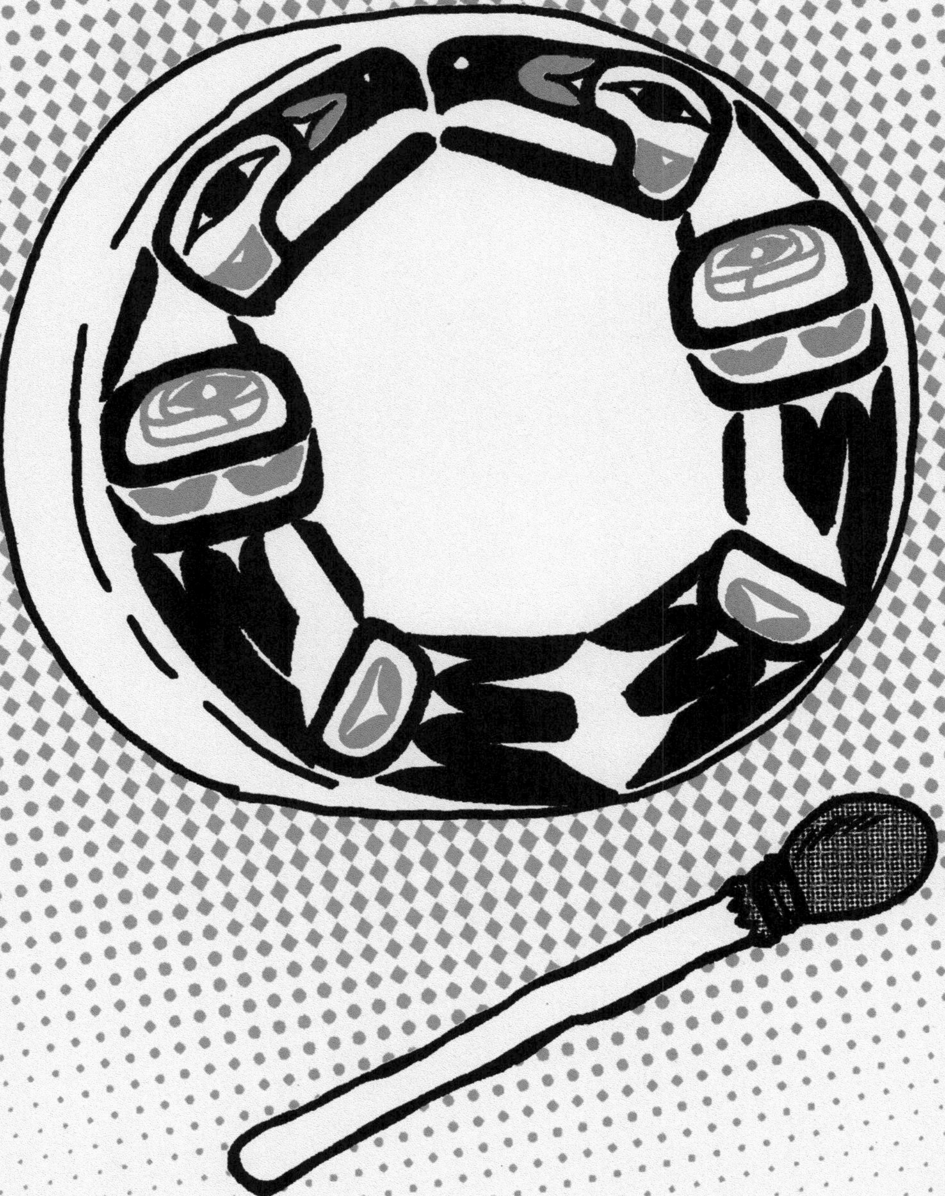

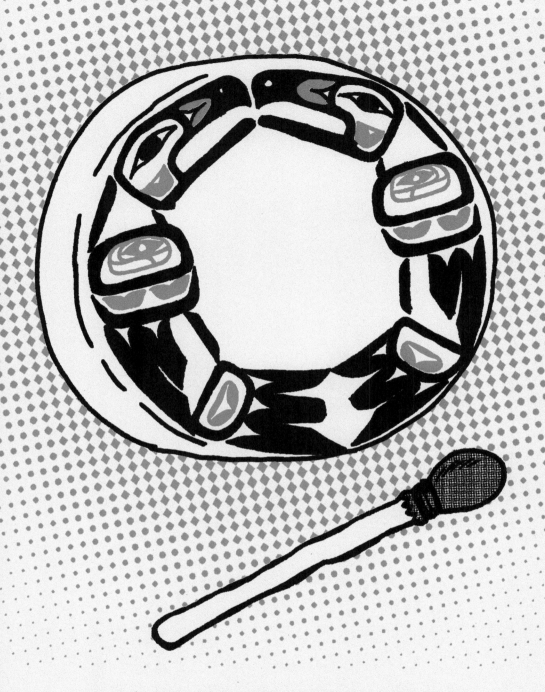

I DEDICATE THIS BOOK TO MY BROTHER, ANDREW MARTIN PAULS- WHO PASSED AWAY BETWEEN ISSUE 2 AND 3. I INCLUDED HIS DRUM ON THE SAME PAGE AS ANNIE NED IN THE THIRD ISSUE. ANDY WAS A MEMBER OF THE DAKWÄKĀDA DANCERS HIS ENTIRE LIFE & ALWAYS PRACTICED OUR CULTURE. I LOVE AND MISS YOU ANDY.

PIN-UPS

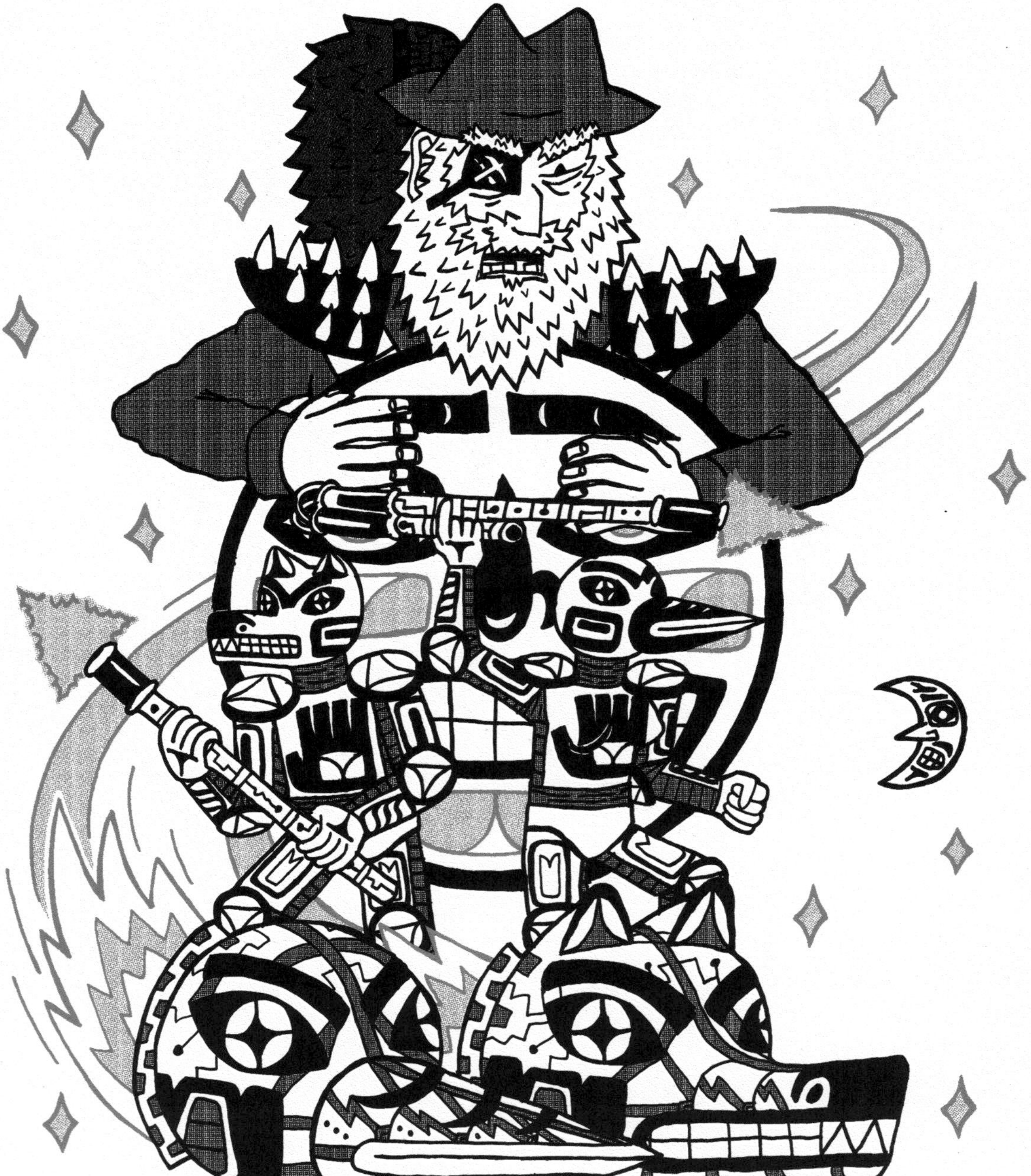

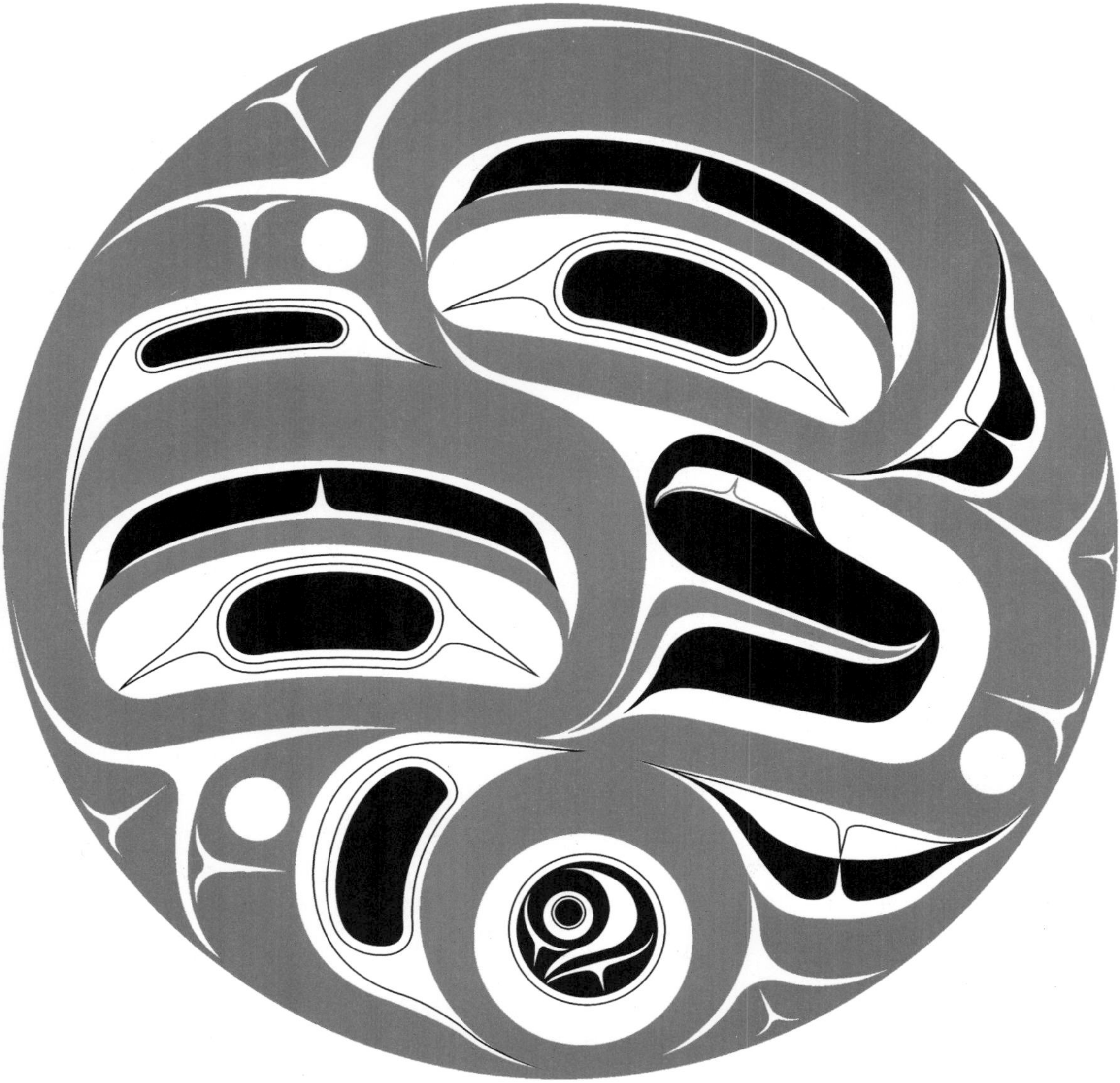

BLAKE SHÁÁ'KOON LEPINE

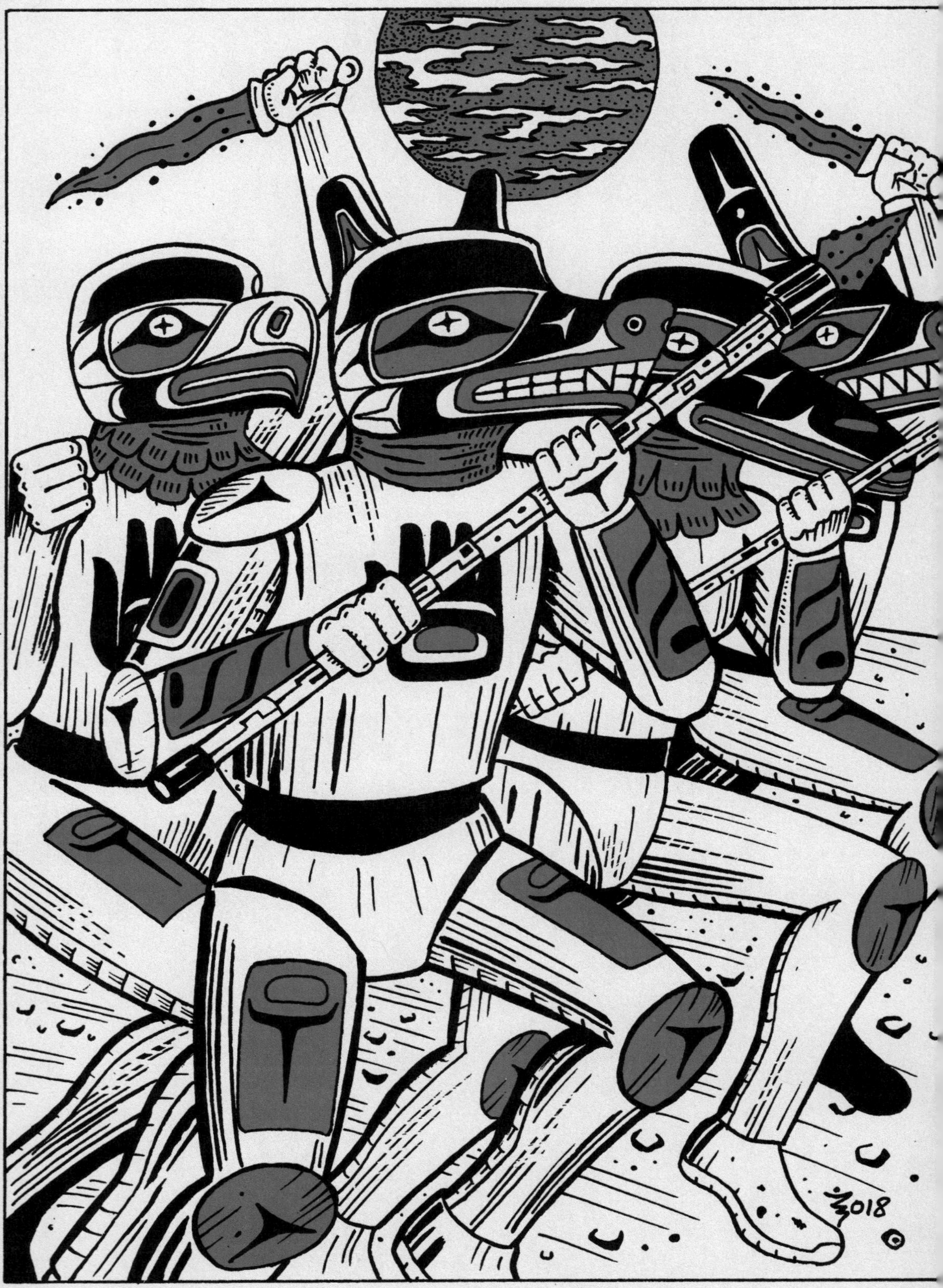
2018 ©

GORD HILL

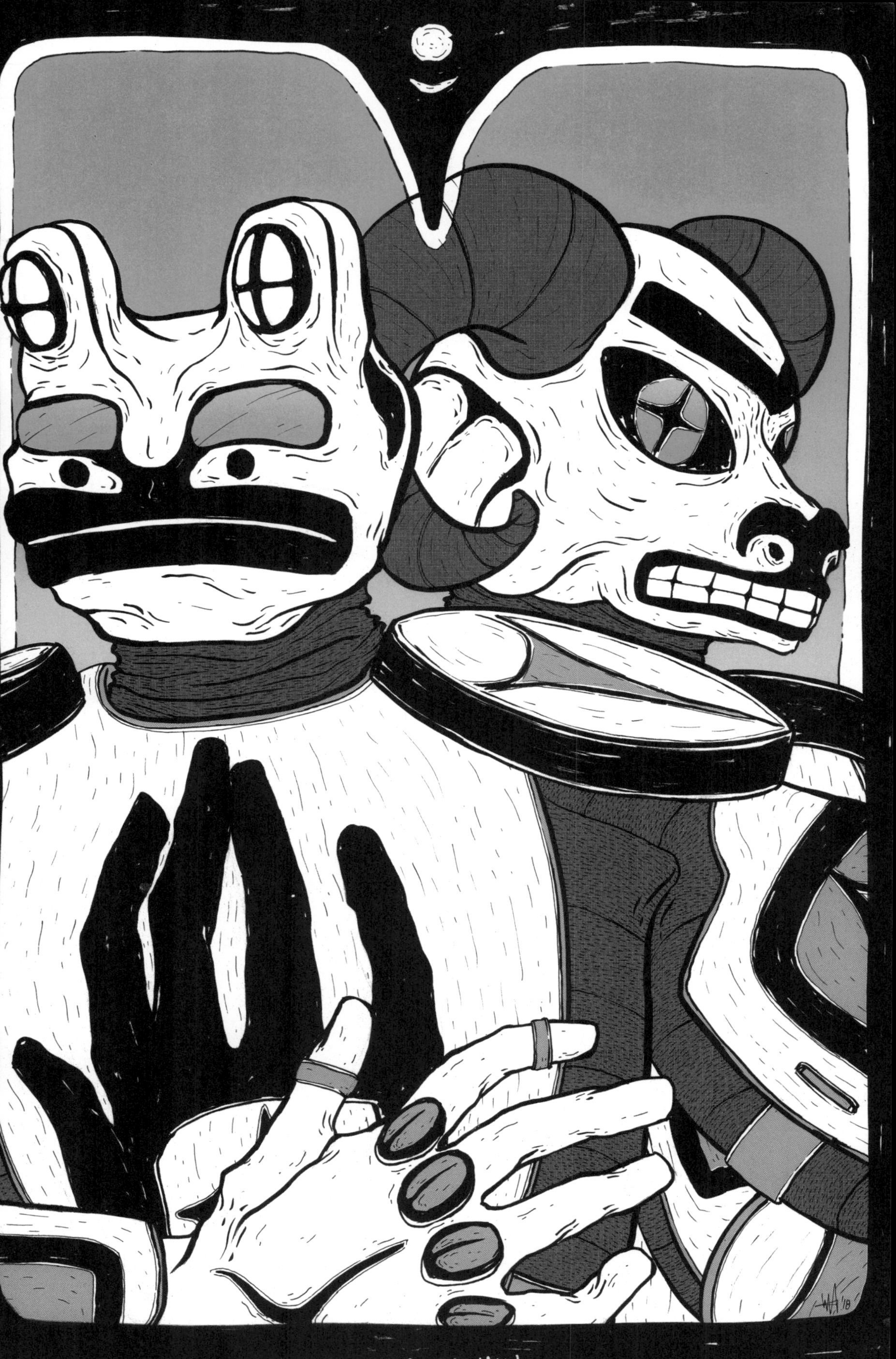

WHESS HARMAN

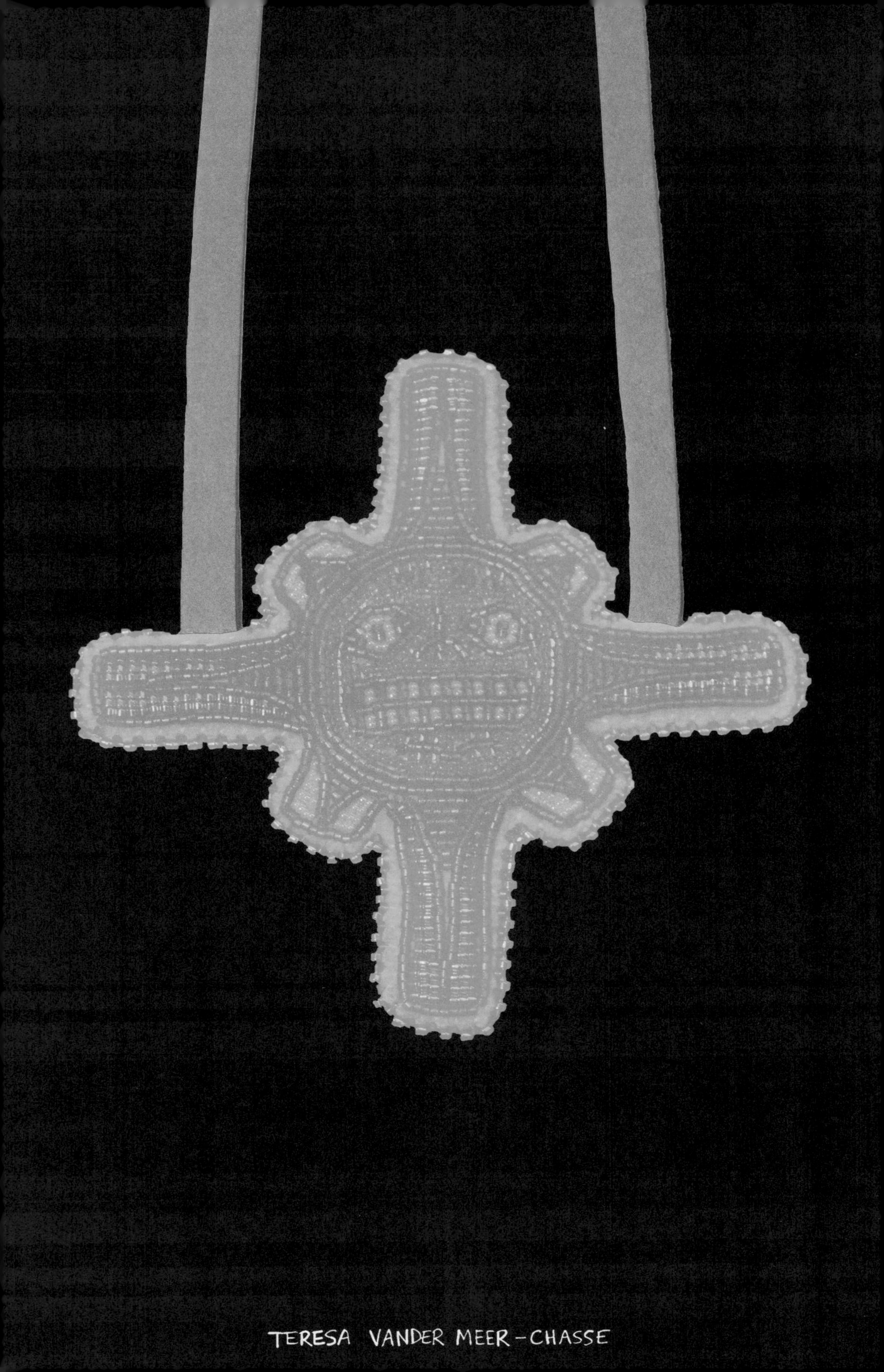

TERESA VANDER MEER-CHASSE

SKETCHES

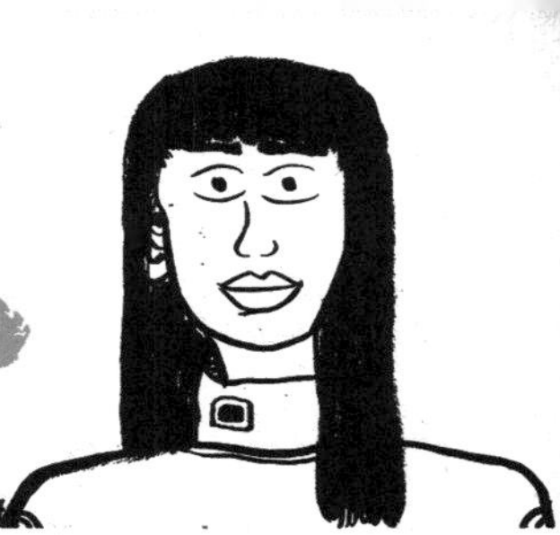
01.31.17

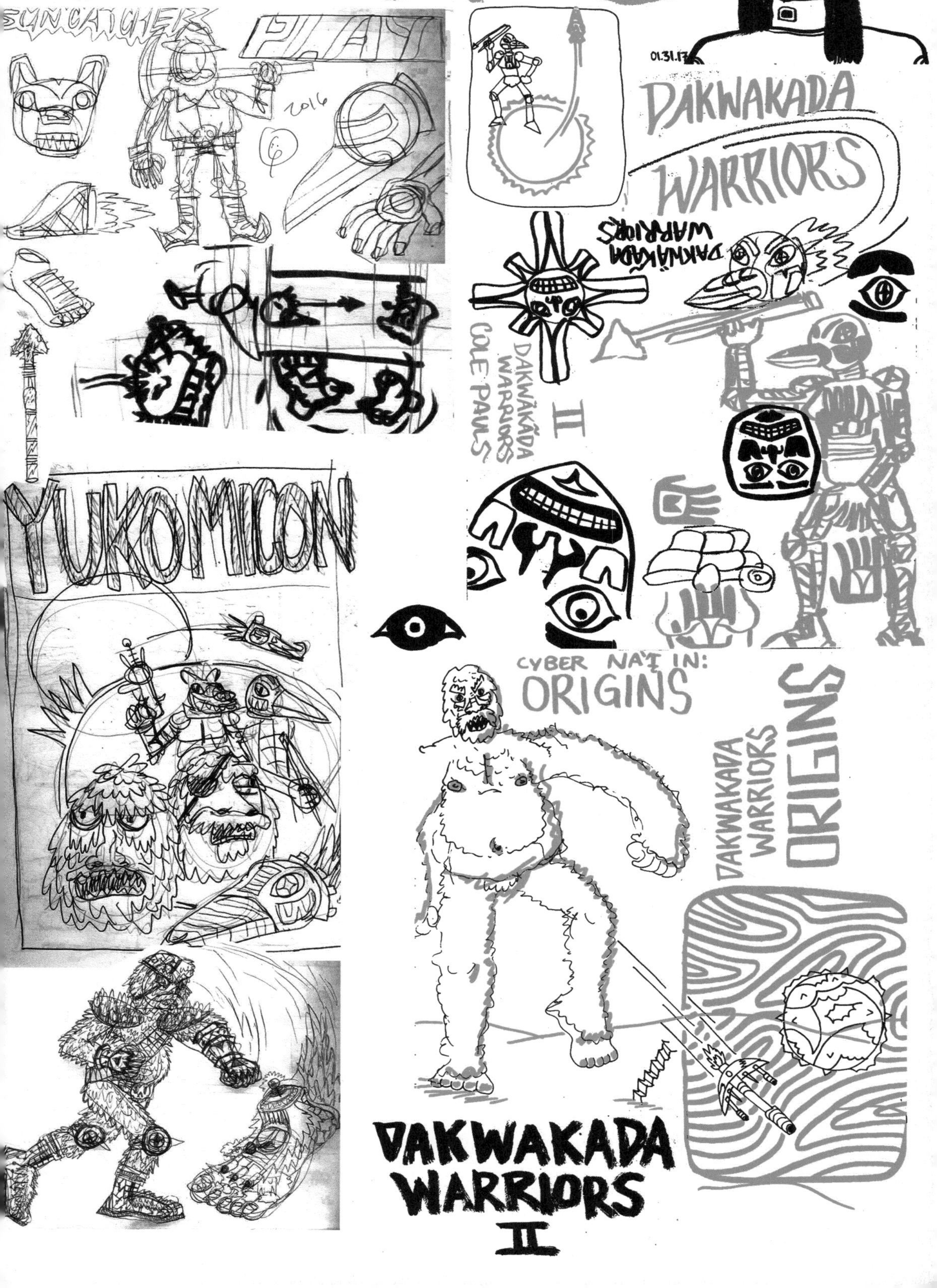
SUNCATCHER
PLAY
2016
DAKWAKADA
WARRIORS
DAKWĀKĀDA WARRIORS II
COLE PAULS
YUKOMICON
CYBER NA'I IN:
ORIGINS
DAKWAKADA
WARRIORS
ORIGINS
DAKWAKADA
WARRIORS
II

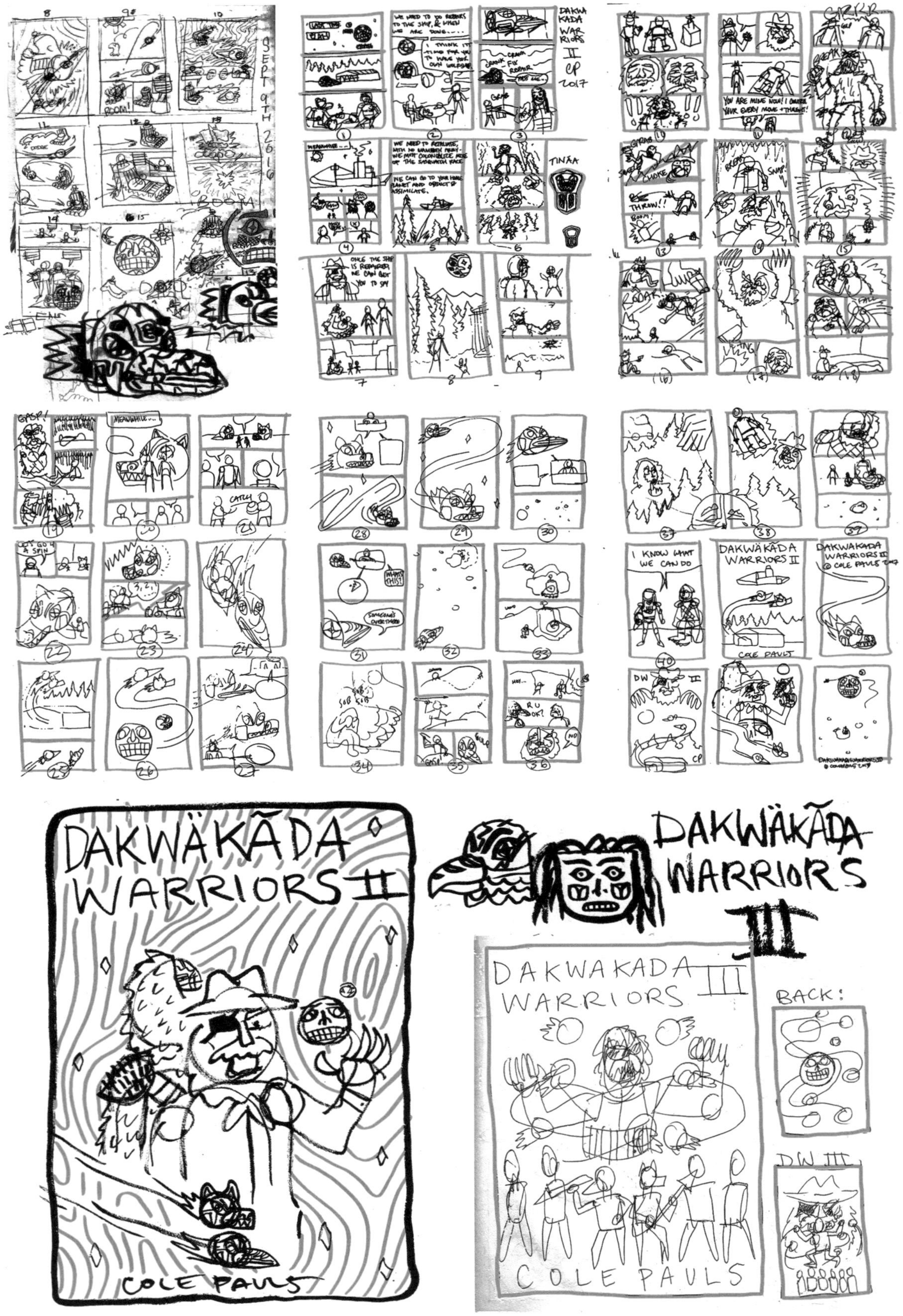

SEPT 9TH 2016
BOOM!
LAST TIME
WE NEED TO DO REPAIRS TO THE SHIP, & WHEN WE ARE DONE...
DAKWAKADA WARRIORS II CP 2017
GRAB
MEANWHILE...
WE CAN GO TO YOUR HOME PLANET AND OBJECT & ASSIMILATE.
TINÄA
YOU ARE MINE NOW! I CONTROL YOUR EVERY MOVE + THOUGHT!
GRAB
CHOKE
THROW!!
BOOM!
BREAK
SNAP
ROAR!
FALL
GASP!
MEANWHILE...
CATCH
LET'S GO 4 A SPIN
WHAT'S THIS?
SOMEONE'S OVERTHERE
SOB SOB
GASP
HEY...
R U OK?
NO
I KNOW WHAT WE CAN DO
DAKWÄKĀDA WARRIORS II
COLE PAULS
DAKWÄKĀDA WARRIORS II
COLE PAULS
DAKWÄKĀDA WARRIORS III
DAKWAKADA WARRIORS III
COLE PAULS
BACK:
DW III

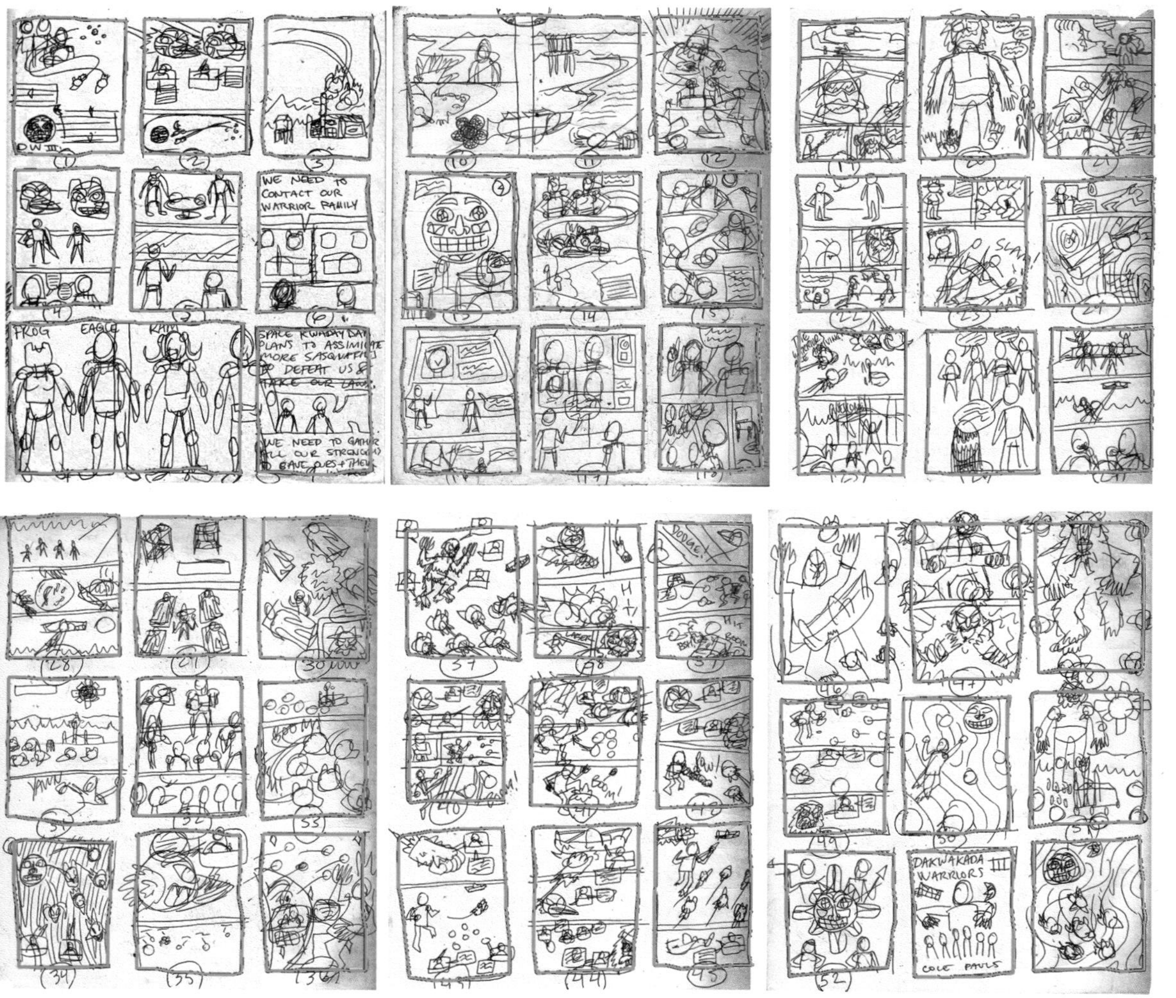
DW III
WE NEED TO CONTACT OUR WARRIOR FAMILY
FROG
EAGLE
RAM
SPACE KWADAY DAN PLANS TO ASSIMILATE MORE SASQUATCHES TO DEFEAT US & TAKE OUR LAND.
DAKWÄKÃDA WARRIORS III
COLE PAULS
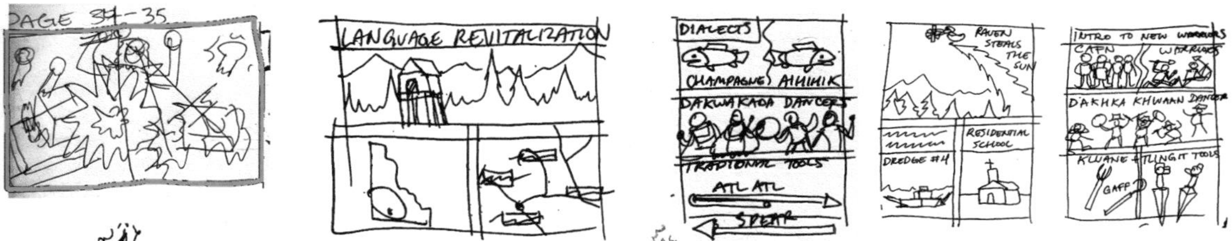
PAGE 34-35
LANGUAGE REVITALIZATION
DIALECTS
CHAMPAGNE/ AISHIHIK
DAKWÄKÃDA DANCERS
TRADITIONAL TOOLS
ATLATL
SPEAR
RAVEN STEALS THE SUN
DREDGE #4
RESIDENTIAL SCHOOL
INTRO TO NEW WARRIORS
CAFN
WARRIORS
DAKHKA KHWAAN DANCERS
KWANE + TLINGIT TOOLS
GAFF
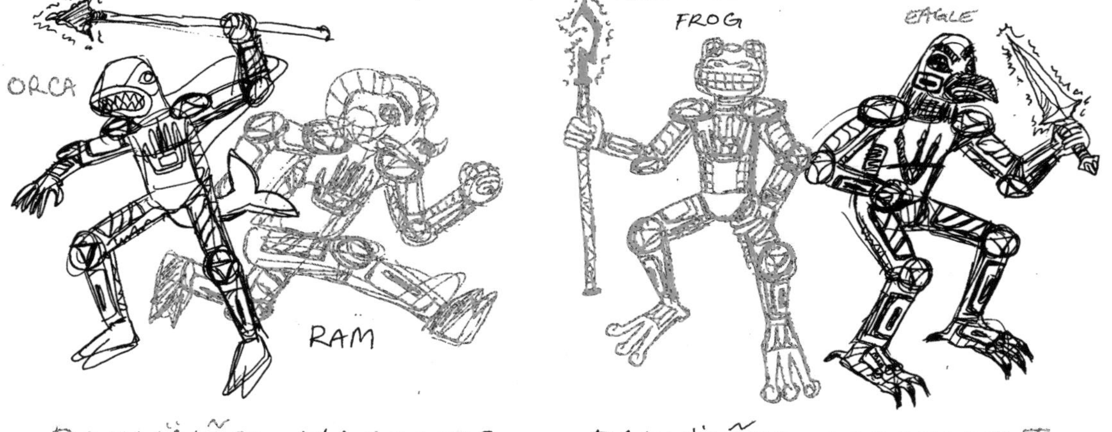
ORCA
RAM
FROG
EAGLE
DAKWÄKÃDA WARRIORS
DAKWÄKÃDA WARRIORS

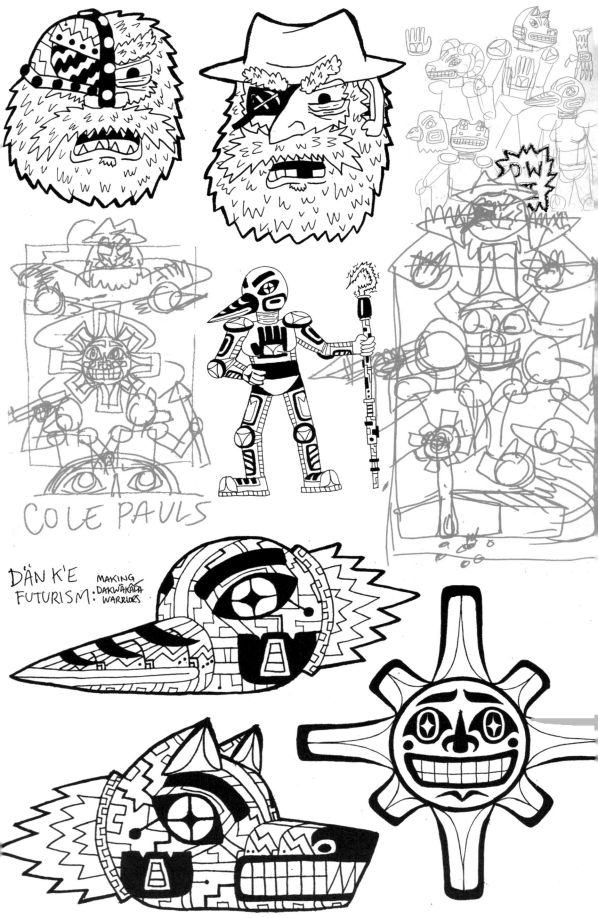

COLE PAULS

DÄN K'E FUTURISM: MAKING DAKWÄKÄDA WARRIORS

LANGUAGE KEY

THERE ARE TWO SOUTHERN TUTCHONE DIALECTS, CHAMPAGNE (SHADHÄLA K'E) AND AISHIHIK (ÄSHÈY KE). THE TWO LANGUAGE PRESERVERS I COLLABORATED WITH, VIVIAN SMITH SPEAKS THE AISHIHIK DIALECT AND KHÂSHA SPEAKS BOTH CHAMPAGNE AND AISHIHIK DIALECTS. THAT'S WHY BOTH DIALECTS ARE USED IN THE ORIGINAL ISSUES. AFTER TALKING TO BOTH OF THEM ABOUT THIS COLLECTION, WE THOUGHT IT WOULD BE WISE TO CHANGE THE COMIC TO JUST BE ONE DIALECT & FOR IT TO BE THE SIMPLIFIED AISHIHIK DIALECT THAT THE YUKON NATIVE LANGUAGE CENTER TEACHES. THIS DECISION WAS MADE SO THERE WOULD BE LESS CONFUSION IN THE FUTURE ABOUT PROPER SPELLING OF THESE WORDS. THE PROBLEM WITH THIS IS, I ENDED UP REWRITING ALMOST ALL OF VIVIAN'S SPELLING & I DON'T WANT TO ERASE THE WORK SHE PUT INTO CREATING THIS WITH ME SO I KEPT HER SPELLING OF DAKWÄKÃDA. THE DAKWÄKÃDA DANCERS ALSO SPELL THEIR NAME THIS WAY, BUT THE YUKON NATIVE LANGUAGE CENTER SPELLS IT LIKE "DAKWÄKÄDA". SO TO HONOR VIVIAN'S WORK I KEPT THE SPELLING. BUT BESIDES THAT, I THINK I CHANGED ABOUT 100 OUT OF 110 WORDS HAHA. KWÄNISCHIS KHÂSHA FOR HELPING ME CORRECT THESE WORDS.

ALL TLINGIT WORDS WERE INCLUDED WITH THE HELP OF MY BROTHER IN LAW BLAKE SHÁÁKOON LEPINE.

1. DAKWÄKÃDA (AISHIHIK) HIGH CACHE PLACE
2. TS'ÙRKI̧ (AISHIHIK) CROW
3. ÄGAY (AISHIHIK) WOLF
4. NÄN (AISHIHIK) EARTH

5. DZENĄ (AISHIHIK) DAY
6. ŃTL'E (AISHIHIK) NIGHT
7. NÀAⱦ (AISHIHIK) BUSHMAN
8. KWÄDⱫ̖Y DÄN (AISHIHIK) LONG AGO PEOPLE
9. ÄNÀ'Ɨ (AISHIHIK) HE STOLE / STEALING
10. SHA (AISHIHIK) SUN
11. ÄⱫIZHA (AISHIHIK) MOON
12. NKAN (AISHIHIK) STOP
13. KUNLIN TÄN (AISHIHIK) FROZEN MAMMOTH
14. DÄN (AISHIHIK) PEOPLE
15. ÄJU (AISHIHIK) NO
16. DATTHÙ (AISHIHIK) SHOT OR SHOOT
17. NJÈDÄO (AISHIHIK) BACKWARDS
18. NÄYÄNɨ'YÙ (AISHIHIK) KICK
19. NÄNÄNT'ÄN (AISHIHIK) HIT
20. SHAADÄT'RU (AISHIHIK) SPIN
21. KWÄNJÈ (AISHIHIK) TALK
22. SÙDE (AISHIHIK) BEAT
23. K'Ä̀SHANÄDÀL (AISHIHIK) TURN
24. ÁKǞNTL'A (AISHIHIK) MY HEEL
25. KWÀLĀN (AISHIHIK) END
26. KWÄNISCHIS (AISHIHIK) THANK YOU
27. NÄDÄGHWAY (AISHIHIK) WE CAN REST
28. TL'ÁHŲ̈ (AISHIHIK) GOOD ENOUGH FOR NOW / FINISH
29. KWÄDLÀL (AISHIHIK) WON OR WINNING
30. MBÀ (AISHIHIK) WAR OR BATTLE
31. NITHÄN (AISHIHIK) THINKING
32. KWÄTSI (AISHIHIK) BUILD
33. NÀLÀT (AISHIHIK) SHIP
34. SHÄWKWÄTHÄN (AISHIHIK) VERY GOOD / SAFE

35. ÀGHĀY (AISHIHIK) YES
36. YÁT'AY (AISHIHIK) SPACE
37. KWÄTLÄY (AISHIHIK) LATER
38. ÀKI (AISHIHIK) TWO
39. UDZĀY (AISHIHIK) HIS/HER EAR
40. UNDĀY (AISHIHIK) HIS/HER EYE
41. USI (AISHIHIK) HIS/HER NOSE
42. UYÙ (AISHIHIK) HIS/HER TEETH
43. DÀNTAY (AISHIHIK) DOOR
44. ÄYET THEN ÄJU UY ENJI (AISHIHIK) UNKNOWN STAR
45. DÁNÀLÀÀT K'ÀÀGÙR (AISHIHIK) OUR SHIP IS BROKEN
46. DÀDDHÙ (AISHIHIK) BOOM
47. MBÀ DÄN (AISHIHIK) ARMY
48. THEN (AISHIHIK) STAR/PLANET
49. ÄTSI (AISHIHIK) HE/SHE MAKES
50. ŁAW NSÄY NA (AISHIHIK) DON'T CRY
51. TS'ÀGET (AISHIHIK) STAB OR POKE
52. K'ANINTÀ (AISHIHIK) WATCH
53. AĞHWÄN (AISHIHIK) GROWL
54. SHÄN (AISHIHIK) ME
55. DIKÁANKÁAWU (AISHIHIK) GOD
56. GWÄNKÀ (AISHIHIK) GUN
57. ÄGHAAŁĀN (AISHIHIK) RELATIONS/FAMILY
58. TAYKE', ŁAKI, ŁÀCH'I (AISHIHIK) THREE, TWO, ONE
59. AYŪ (AISHIHIK) OVER THERE
60. UK'ANINTA (AISHIHIK) YOU WATCH IT
61. DUNÈN (AISHIHIK) CHILD
62. DAN N-LÄGA (AISHIHIK) BATTLE/FIGHT
63. MÄZHÄN DÄN (AISHIHIK) MACHINE MAN
64. UTTHITÀT (AISHIHIK) BRAIN
65. UGÄN (AISHIHIK) ARM
66. KUKÙ (AISHIHIK) THEIR HOUSE
67. AK'AK'E (AISHIHIK) NOW/THEN/TODAY
68. ŁINGIT (TLINGIT) TLINGIT

69. KEÉT (TLINGIT) KILLER WHALE
70. CH'AÁK (TLINGIT) EAGLE
71. ŁU'ÄN MÄN (AISHIHIK) KLUANE LAKE/FISH LAKE
72. SHÁYAN (AISHIHIK) RAM
73. TS'ÁL (AISHIHIK) FROG
74. ÄWĒ (AISHIHIK) HELLO
75. ÄK'ÄL (AISHIHIK) HURRY
76. KÄT'ĄK'E (AISHIHIK) TOMORROW
77. NÄNÚCH'Į SHĮ (AISHIHIK) SEE YOU LATER
78. DAKHKÁ KHWÁAN (TLINGIT) INLAND TLINGIT
79. KWÄDĄM ÄSHÄW (AISHIHIK) LONG AGO ELDER
80. DÄN K'E (AISHIHIK) OUR WAY
81. CHU (AISHIHIK) WATER
82. SAMBAY (AISHIHIK) SALMON
83. NENA (AISHIHIK) ANIMALS
84. ÄTÀ (AISHIHIK) MY DAD
85. KHÄNDAM (AISHIHIK) MOOSE
86. ÅMĘYĄ (AISHIHIK) MOTHER'S SISTER; AUNTIE
87. KỲ (AISHIHIK) HOUSE OR VILLAGE
88. ÄYET UTLĄ MBÀ DÄN (AISHIHIK) THERE ARE LOTS OF WARS
89. UTHĮ (AISHIHIK) HIS/HER/IT'S HEAD
90. DAKHWÄN (AISHIHIK) EVERYONE
91. KAKÄN NDA ÄYETAW (AISHIHIK) SIT DOWN AND TAKE IT EASY
92. T'ÄM (AISHIHIK) SLAM OR SPLASH
93. KET'AK'E NTL'E KWÄCH'E (AISHIHIK) TOMORROW MORNING
94. NIGHĄ SHAWNÍTHÄN (AISHIHIK) WELCOME; I THINK GOOD OF YOU
95. MBÀT (AISHIHIK) FOOD
96. SUGNENCH'Ü (AISHIHIK) BANNOCK
97. TLĀW (AISHIHIK) RASPBERRY
98. KHÄNDAM THÄN (AISHIHIK) MOOSE MEAT
99. NK'ETS'ÄDLĮ (AISHIHIK) YOU ARE LOVED
100. ÄJU KWÄDLÀL (AISHIHIK) DEFEAT

101. DÀY (AISHIHIK) MOVE
102. YE DA'I (AISHIHIK) WHAT ARE YOU DOING?
103. TL'AHU NCHÄW (AISHIHIK) ENOUGH OF YOU
104. AYŨ ÄCH'E (AISHIHIK) THAT'S IT THERE
105. SHADHÄLA K'E (CHAMPAGNE) CHAMPAGNE WAY
106. ÄSHÈY K'E (AISHIHIK) AISHIHIK WAY
107. ÄT'ATS'ÄTSÏk (AISHIHIK) ATLATL
108. CHĄL (AISHIHIK) SPEAR
109. ŁU TÀR (AISHIHIK) GAFF
110. SHAK'ATS' (TLINGIT) DAGGER

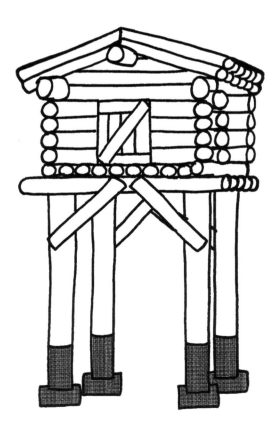

KWÄNISCHIS

MOM & DAD, KHÂSHA, VIVIAN SMITH, KIRSTEN HATFIELD, MY BROTHERS & SISTERS, ALL MY FAMILY, CHAMPAGNE AND AISHIHIK FIRST NATION, BLAKE SHÁA'KOON LEPINE, GORD HILL, WHESS HARMAN, TERESA VANDERMEER-CHASSE, SHEILA GREER, ANNIE NED'S FAMILY, DIANE STRAND, MARY JANE JIM, JOSEPHINE BOYLE, NIGEL BOYLE, BRADLEY JOE, THE DAKWÄKÄDA DANCERS, THE DAKHKÁ KHWÁAN DANCERS, YUKOMICON, SHAWN UNDERHILL, FELIPE MORELLI, ERICA WILK, SEAN KAREMAKER, ANDY BROWN, EVERY YUKONER WHO HELPED ME ALONG THE WAY AND EVERYONE WHO BOUGHT THE ORIGINAL ZINE

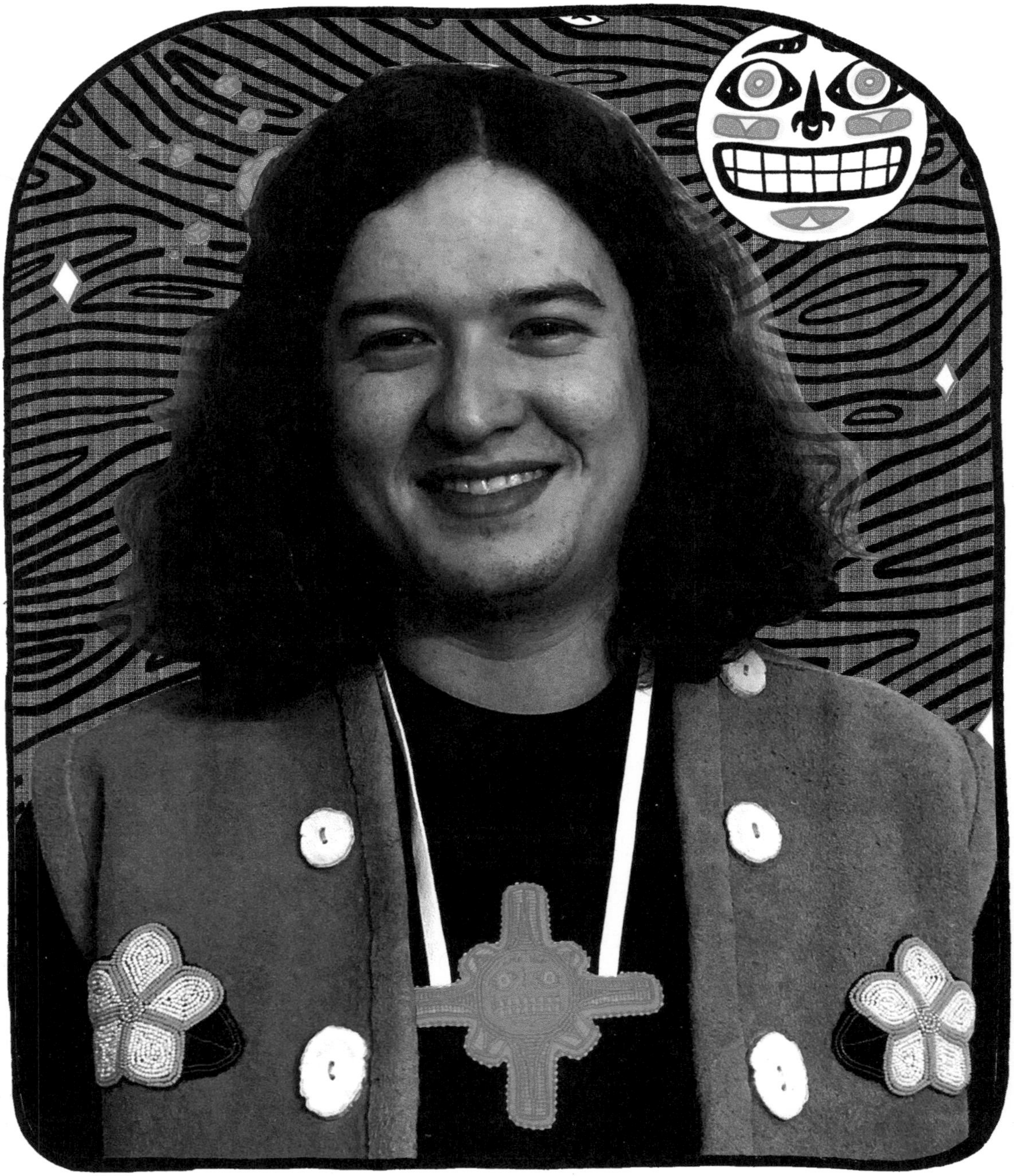

COLE PAULS IS A CHAMPAGNE AND AISHIHIK CITIZEN & TAHLTAN FIRST NATION COMIC ARTIST, ILLUSTRATOR & PRINT MAKER HAILING FROM HAINES JUNCTION, YUKON TERRITORY WITH A BFA IN ILLUSTRATION FROM EMILY CARR UNIVERSITY. PAULS CURRENTLY RESIDES IN VANCOUVER, FOCUSING ON HIS TWO COMIC SERIES, THE FIRST BEING PIZZA PUNKS; A SELF CONTAINED GAG STRIP ABOUT PUNKS EATING PIZZA, THE OTHER BEING DAKWÄKÃDA WARRIORS. IN 2017, PAULS WON BROKEN PENCIL MAGAZINE'S BEST COMIC & BEST ZINE OF THE YEAR FOR DAKWÄKÃDA WARRIORS II.

FIND HIM ON SOCIAL MEDIA AS @TUNDRAWIZARD OR VISIT HIS WEBSITE WWW.TUNDRAWIZARD.COM